MAYHEM AND THE MORTAL

MAYHEM AND THE MORTAL

NEW YORK TIMES BESTSELLING AUTHOR
SHANORA WILLIAMS

RED TOWER
BOOKS™

PENGUIN MICHAEL JOSEPH

UK | USA | Canada | Ireland | Australia
India | New Zealand | South Africa

Penguin Michael Joseph is part of the Penguin Random House group of companies whose addresses can be found at global.penguinrandomhouse.com

Penguin Random House UK,
One Embassy Gardens, 8 Viaduct Gardens, London SW11 7BW

penguin.co.uk

Published by Penguin Michael Joseph, part of the Penguin Random House group of companies, in association with Red Tower Books, part of Entangled Publishing LLC 2026
001

Copyright © Shanora Williams, 2026

The moral right of the author has been asserted

The Red Tower Books name and logo are trademarks of Entangled Publishing LLC and are used here under licence

Penguin Random House values and supports copyright. Copyright fuels creativity, encourages diverse voices, promotes freedom of expression and supports a vibrant culture. Thank you for purchasing an authorized edition of this book and for respecting intellectual property laws by not reproducing, scanning or distributing any part of it by any means without permission. You are supporting authors and enabling Penguin Random House to continue to publish books for everyone. No part of this book may be used or reproduced in any manner for the purpose of training artificial intelligence technologies or systems. In accordance with Article 4(3) of the DSM Directive 2019/790, Penguin Random House expressly reserves this work from the text and data mining exception

Edited by Justine Bylo
Original map illustration by Elizabeth Turner Stokes
Map frame images by n_defender/Shutterstock, pixelsquid, and pingebat/Shutterstock
Interior design by Britt Marczak
Interior image by Tetiana Kletskina/GettyImages
Printed and bound in Great Britain by Clays Ltd, Elcograf S.p.A.

The authorized representative in the EEA is Penguin Random House Ireland, Morrison Chambers, 32 Nassau Street, Dublin D02 YH68

A CIP catalogue record for this book is available from the British Library

HARDBACK ISBN: 978–1–911–75004–8
TRADE PAPERBACK ISBN: 978–1–911–75005–5

Penguin Random House is committed to a sustainable future for our business, our readers and our planet. This book is made from Forest Stewardship Council® certified paper.

MORE FROM SHANORA WILLIAMS

THE TETHER TRILOGY

Vicious Bonds
Wicked Ties
Lethal Souls

THE ATLANTA RAVENS SERIES

Beautiful Broken Love
Sweet Little Hearts

For every reader who has wanted more melanin woven into stories with magic.

Mayhem and the Mortal is a fast-paced romantic fantasy about a fierce young woman who teams up with a lethal sorcerer to save her cursed sister—and ends up on a quest full of magic, monsters, and deadly secrets. However, the story includes elements that might not be suitable for all readers. Violence, death, blood, decapitation, dismemberment, physical injuries, explicit consensual sex, animal attacks, animal death, and cursing are shown in the novel. Death of family members is discussed. Readers who may be sensitive to these elements, please take note.

The Teachings of Orvena
Goddess of Life & Light

I say to you, my creations: be wise, be kind, be brave. You are in this world because of me, and I have dedicated so much of myself to you. Faith in me will provide you everlasting peace.

As you live your days, remember this:

Wisdom is necessary for evolution.
Kindness is needed for peace and hope.
Nobility is imperative whilst dwelling in Thelanor.
And the bravest in heart is the source of true prosperity.

Chapter 1

While I'm kneading dough, I feel an intense surge of heat bloom on my chest.

Gasping, I reach up instantly to unclasp my necklace, then drop it like it's alive on the flour-coated counter. I stare at the pearl pendant attached to the gold chain—the pearl that's now burning hot.

Something is wrong with Analla.

Infused with magic and bonded to my sister, the pendant tells me what words cannot. When it's warm, that means she's dealing with nuisances, survivable troubles.

When it's *hot*—

My throat tightens and my pulse roars in my ears as realization sinks in. If it's hot, that means she's in actual danger.

I was already worried because she hadn't come home last night—or the previous two nights, for that matter. She never stays at work for that long, not without letting me know first.

So, yes, it is possible that she's in danger. And if she is, there's only one place she could be: Seferin's keep.

Living just along the outskirts of Meriva Empire, Seferin is the most corrupt sorcerer in the entire kingdom.

I immediately wipe the sticky dough from my fingers, shove the necklace into one of my trouser pockets, and grab my satchel. I don't tell the other baker where I'm going, despite her calling after me as I storm out of the bakery.

I don't even stop to think.

I just leave.

By the time I reach the edge of the forest, the sun is starting to sink behind the tree line, and a cold sense of dread crawls up my spine with every step. Words Analla has said before repeat in my head.

Never come to his keep.

Warnings be damned. I need to know if she's okay. What if this is a false alarm? What if the pendant's magic is fading, like I was warned it might?

A possibility, yes, but I need to be sure.

The hike takes nearly an hour. My feet ache and my lungs burn, but I don't slow down until I see the familiar shape of Seferin's keep, three stories of black brick crowned by a dome roof rising between the treetops.

The Shadow Nest.

He uses this place as a private, exclusive club, one that's by invite only. It's the sorcerer's coverup for corruption, his last shred of mortality. His way of leading people to believe he's merely one of us...just with a *darker* side.

I've only been here once when I assisted Analla with carrying supplies. It was her first week of work as a nightmaiden. I saw things that day that made my skin crawl, things I still can't put into words. She made me swear to never return...yet here I am.

I crouch behind a tree and scan the area ahead. With sunlight still lingering in the sky, the sorcerer guards that usually patrol the grounds have lowered their defenses. After all, it's night that belongs to the monsters.

After checking that my surroundings are clear, I dash across the open field and slip around the side of the building. A partially open door reveals a kitchen beyond. I give the door a nudge with the tip of my boot and step inside.

Around a corner, a cook bends over the hearth with his back to me. I take that as my opportunity to sneak through the kitchen and slip into a hallway, but I wind up crashing into someone else.

Shit.

She's tall and abnormally slender, wearing a one-piece leather garment that clings to every sharp angle of her body.

She grabs hold of my arm before I can escape and yanks me toward her. "Who are you?" she demands. "I've never seen you before."

"I'm sorry. I'm just looking for my sister," I say, voice trembling. "She works here. I just want to check on her."

The woman's eyes narrow, and the tension in her features softens as she studies my face.

"Your sister?" she repeats.

I nod, swallowing past the thick lump in my throat. Is she going to drag me to Seferin? Kill me herself?

"Analla…" I start.

"Analla?" Recognition sweeps over her face, and her grip slackens.

My eyes expand. "Yes!" I whisper, nodding eagerly. "Do you know her?"

She releases me at once, her gaze darting down the hall. "You need to leave."

I freeze, even though everything in me tells me to do as she says. "Where is she?"

"Look, I am telling you now that you need to leave. If someone else finds out you're her sister, they'll lock you up like they've done to her."

Lock me up?

My stomach tightens into knots as she starts to turn away. "Hey—wait!" I plead. "If she's here somewhere, can you just take me to her? I don't care what happens. I need to see her. Please."

The woman halts and lowers her head, letting out a long exhale. She then looks down both ways of the lengthy hallway before approaching me again.

"Fine," she grumbles. "I'll show you to it, but you need to keep quiet."

I nod and follow her lead. She takes rapid steps through the hallway before turning a corner and approaching a red door, gesturing to it.

"She's down there, in the dungeon." The woman clenches her jaw briefly, stepping away. "You're on your own from here."

My mouth becomes drier. The woman looks frightened as she backs away.

"Thank you," I tell her, grabbing the doorknob.

"You're lucky I liked Analla." With that, she scurries away.

I face the door and twist the knob, opening it slowly. Darkness yawns below, broken only by floating red orbs that shine on a slick staircase. Another lump forms in my throat. I try swallowing past it as I take the first step down.

I'm consumed by darkness when I finally reach the bottom of the stairs but find only a sliver of relief when I turn the corner and see another row of floating lanterns.

I pick up my pace. The air grows colder with every step, heavier, thick with rot and damp stone.

I gag as a horrid smell hits me.

Oh gods. I should turn back. I don't even know what I'm walking into. And that woman could be lying. I might be stumbling my way into a trap.

But what if Analla is *down here?*

That tiny whisper of a question keeps me going.

Heart pounding, I continue, passing several cells occupied with prisoners who are hardly clinging to life. Other cells are empty but have piles of ash and bones. I gulp when it dawns on me that the ashes are that of the dead.

My anxiety heightens as I pass cell after cell, until I finally see a familiar body lying on the floor in one of them.

"Analla," I whisper.

Her eyes snap open.

Orvena's sake.

She looks awful, her face hollowed, brown skin ashen, and the coils in her hair matted to her head.

She sits up quickly, but not without a wince. "Zaira," she breathes. "What the shadows are you doing here?"

"You never came home and then I felt my pendant get hot." I grip the cold bars, studying her again. "What happened to you? Why are you locked in here?"

Her eyes instantly water as she sinks her teeth into her chapped bottom lip. "It's Seferin," she utters feebly. "He placed a curse on me."

I feel a sudden drop in my stomach. "W-what? Why would he do that?"

She sniffles as she points to a corner inside the cell. "Because I tried to take *that*."

I look where she's pointing and spot an indigo crystal. It seems so out of place here, just like she does.

"You tried to steal it from him?" I ask.

"I didn't think he'd miss it. There were so many of them in his study, and I—I don't know. I thought I could sneak one out and sell it, get a bit more coin because we could use it, you know?" She shakes her head and frowns. "He said I was one of his favorites. I didn't think he'd do something like this to me."

"Analla." I wheeze in disbelief, my eyes burning with unshed tears. "Why would you steal from *Seferin* of all people? You should've known better!"

"Shh! I know!" she whisper-hisses as she steps closer and reaches through the bars to grab my hand. Hers are dry and cold as they wrap around mine.

I look her all over in the sheer, black nightmaiden's dress she's wearing. "I told you not to work here. I told you to quit before you got hurt, Analla."

"I know," she murmurs. "But it's too late to do anything about it so I need you to leave, okay? Get out of here and never come back."

"No," I snap. "I'm getting you out of here." I pull away and study the cell door. There is no lock for a key, nothing to even pick at to at least attempt a breakout.

"The locks are controlled by his magic," she mutters sullenly. "Only he can open the cells."

I groan. Of fucking course.

"I'm not getting out of here, Z, and even if there were a possibility of breaking out, the curse will kill me regardless. It doesn't matter where I am." Her head falls in defeat. Or shame. Possibly both. "He said the curse will kill me within thirty days. He...he said it will be a slow and painful death—that I deserve it for betraying his trust."

My tears finally fall as I choke on a sob. How can this be?

My sister, *cursed*.

I don't even know what to say. How do I save her? I usually know what to do under pressure, but right now, my mind is blank.

Analla swipes at her tears, then reaches through the bars, gesturing for me to come closer. When I'm near enough, she cups my cheek in one hand while smoothing down some of my curly hair with her other. She puts on a brave smile even though her eyes are rimmed with tears.

"I know you'll try to find a way to get me out of this, but there is nothing you can do," she says. "This is my problem, and I'm facing the consequences."

"No." My voice trembles. "We always face them together."

"Not this time, dearest." She stands taller. "I want you to live your life and live it well, do you understand?"

"Analla, I'm not leaving here without you—"

"You have to!" she insists, squeezing my hand. "Leave and never come back. Ever. I mean it, Zaira. *Please*."

A door slams in the distance, and we gasp when we hear keys jingling, followed by heavy footsteps.

"That's the guard," she whispers. "Go now. Get out of here!" She gently shoves me away from her cell.

I don't want to leave.

I want to stay.

To bargain with Seferin.

To sacrifice myself if it means he'll set my sister free. As long as we're together, that's all that matters, right?

As the footsteps grow nearer, I realize I can't truly help her if we're both stuck here. That, even if I do bargain with a mad sorcerer, we'll never truly be free again.

"I'll get you out of here," I tell her. "I'll get someone to break the curse before the month is over. I swear it."

She only shakes her head with a sad smile. "I love you so much, Zaira. So, so much."

I step forward one last time, grabbing her hand, clinging to it.

"Go," she demands softly with thick tears flowing down her cheeks.

Throat clogged with emotion, I run in the opposite direction of the approaching footsteps and don't stop until I've made it out of the keep and the dark forest is swallowing me whole.

I do all this while blinded by tears that don't cease, while carrying an aching heart that feels heavier in my chest with every step. When I've made it a good distance away, I collapse against a tree and weep. It's a long cry—hard, ugly, and desperate.

But eventually, my sadness morphs into something else.

Resolve.

Analla only has thirty days to live. That means I must do everything in my power to get that curse broken.

I'll come up with a plan. I'll seek help. I'll do whatever must be done to save my sister because if I don't, I'll lose the only family I have left.

"Fuck that," I grumble as I push away from the tree and march in the direction of my kingdom.

Seferin isn't getting away with his evil this time.

Chapter 2

The most ridiculous thing about this curse is that every mortal under the Crystal Realm knows to *never* try and fool a Grim sorcerer—especially one who carries around cursed artifacts like pocket change.

But then we have Analla Quinlocke. Forever the one to think her beauty makes her invincible.

I release a gut-deep sigh as I hike the strap of my rucksack higher on my shoulder. It's packed with heavy tomes I've borrowed from The Gilded Archive, which contains some of the best knowledge in all of Thelanor.

Each tome I selected purposely revolves around spells, magic, curses—even forbidden black magic. The last set of books I borrowed didn't offer much guidance, so I swapped them out.

I'm going on day three with hardly any luck finding answers, so tonight calls for a different kind of study session—one that involves a few pints of ale.

As I approach the Tilted Crystal Tavern, Bolivar's brown dog is sniffing around the door.

I light up when I see Crumb.

When the scruffy dog notices me, his tail wags immediately, and he dashes my way. I laugh as I drop my rucksack on the ground with a thud so I can lower to one knee and give him a few scratches behind the ears.

"Hi, Crumb," I coo. "What are you doing out here in the cold?"

He buries his nose into a gap in my coat as he sniffs, eager as ever for what awaits.

"Okay, okay. You caught me." Smiling, I dig into my coat pocket and pull out a napkin with several dog biscuits from the bakery. I make them especially for him when I know I'll be going to the tavern. "Here you go. All yours, my friend." I place them on the ground, certain he'll lap up every single crumb, hence his name.

I stroke the soft fur on his back a few more times, wanting to take comfort in this moment, but with a sigh, I grab my rucksack and enter the warmth of the tavern. Crumb trots in after me.

The tavern is busy with life as always.

Mortals, sorcerers, and beastials alike congregate around sticky wooden tables. As I step deeper inside and pass a group playing cards, the heat from the large hearth warms my cheeks, and I feel my body slowly unthaw.

I spot Bolivar behind the bar pulling pints. He tips his head at me in acknowledgment. I shoot him a wave before finding a table in the corner of the room, placing my rucksack down on the floor, and pulling out my first tome, ready to dig in.

As I make myself comfortable in the booth, Crumb curls up on my feet. I smile. At least I have company for another night of poring over dusty tomes.

"There has to be another way," I mumble as I swirl a finger around the rim of my steel mug.

I study the journal where I've written the names of all the sorcerers I've spoken to about Analla's curse. Five of them...and none can help me.

Well, let me rephrase that.

None have the desire to help me. They're all afraid to go against Seferin.

I lean in, lost in thought, until my elbow slips off the edge of the table. I catch myself with a jolt and sit upright, blinking hard.

My gaze bounces around the tavern to make sure no one witnessed my folly. Crumb has, of course. He's still lying on the floor right next to me, head tilted as he peers up.

Someone else has as well — a beastial with gray reptilian skin and an oversize bald head sitting at an adjacent table. His tongue slithers through his lips as his thick tail thumps against his rickety wooden chair. A ghostly smile appears as he focuses those vertical-slitted snake eyes on me.

I force a smile at him while suppressing a shudder. Reptilian beastials have always unnerved me. They'll literally eat their own children if it means getting ahead.

Thankfully, Bolivar appears, towering over me like the giant he is. I've never really paid much attention to the half-giant tavern owner's height until now...or how attractive Analla may have found him, with his thick beard and black hoop in his ear. Then again, I don't spend many nights alone in the Tilted Crystal drinking away my sorrows.

"I think that's enough for you tonight," Bolivar says, glancing at my empty mug.

Hmm. I guess it wasn't just Crumb or the beastial who noticed my tipsiness.

"I've only had three." I pass him a scowl, pressing my back against the worn leather of the booth. "I'm not drunk, B." I pause. "Drunk *enough*," I clarify.

He raises one dark eyebrow. "Do I even want to know why you're drinking this much, Zaira?"

"Well, when your sister does the dumbest thing in the world and gets herself cursed and locked in a dungeon by Seferin, you need a *lot* of ale to accept it. Even more when you finally think up a plan to save her that could be lethal." I shrug. "Or I can just flat out kill the aforementioned sorcerer myself to make everyone's lives a tad easier."

"You try that and you're dead before you can even get the chance to look at him." Bolivar scratches his chin while giving his head a shake. Swinging his gaze around the dimly lit tavern, he accepts the brief calm and slides into the opposite side of my booth.

Crumb takes that as his opportunity to get up and rest his chin on Bolivar's lap.

"I know you're upset, but you need to keep your voice down about Seferin in here," he says, rubbing the top of his dog's head.

"Why should I?" I counter.

The brown skin between his eyebrows wrinkles as he stares at me as if I've lost all my wits.

I give Bolivar an apologetic look. I know I'm being absurd, but I'm bordering on drunk, which means I'm acting bolder than usual. Plus, I'm frustrated and can't help but speak the truth.

"Seferin has connections all over Meriva." Bolivar gestures to the left. "I'm sure there are people in this place getting coin from him. They hear you talking about him, they'll tell him, and he'll come after you, too. Then you'll end up in his dungeon just like your sister, or worse. He's not a man you want trouble with, Zaira."

"Why didn't you tell *her* that?" My eyes burn with tears, but I bite into my bottom lip to prevent them from falling.

No more tears.

I adjust the frame of my spectacles to hide my watering eyes, then lift my chin. Tears won't save my sister. A plan will, and I have the beginnings of one.

I gesture to my empty mug. "Another, please. I'm on the cusp of a breakthrough to save my sister and, quite possibly, the entire world if I can figure out the logistics."

"And what is this breakthrough?" Bolivar asks, feeding into my sarcasm.

"Well, I told you before that I've spoken to a few sorcerers about Analla's curse. None want to help, but one of them did tell me if I'm desperate enough, to seek one of the prosperity stones in the Temple of Elphar. Apparently, prosperity stones can break any curse. I could get one, sneak into Seferin's keep again, then use the stone to break her curse. All I need is to find someone willing enough to guide and protect me on the journey there."

Bolivar's features turn as hard as a rock. "The Temple of Elphar? In The Shallows?"

I snap my fingers and point at him. "That's the one."

"Have you lost your mind?" His question comes out harsh and sharp. He even stops petting Crumb to give me an incredulous glare. Crumb whines. "Going anywhere near The Shallows is a death wish, Z. No one in their sane mind will go there with you."

I blink at him a few times, unsure what to say. I shouldn't be surprised by his change of mood. I know The Shallows is dangerous, hence the reason I'm trying to think of another plan. I've just never seen him like this. So serious and fearful.

Seferin has a chokehold on everyone, it seems.

Bolivar's eyes and shoulders soften as he regards me. "Look, I'm sorry about Analla. I know she's your sister, but you can't save everyone, Z. You shouldn't have to put your life on the line because of her mistakes. I'll walk you home when my shift is over. Just stay put for now." He shoots a quick glance around the tavern, then whispers, "And for the love of Orvena, stop talking shit about *Seferin*. I don't need both Quinlocke sisters getting killed."

The giant leaves my table with a grunt, but not before scooping up my mug and taking it with him. Crumb trails him, tail wagging.

Damn. I really wanted another.

Behind me, rough laughter and bellowing voices rise up in waves. I glance around the corner of my booth, spotting a group of beastials playing cards. Next to them is a table of mortals and charmers. They have a deck of cards as well.

One of them levitates a plate in the air, grinning like he's performed the greatest spell in all of Thelanor. I suck my teeth. That's all charmers are good for—sideshow tricks.

It's just now that I notice the people tucked away in the alcoves. All wear translucent crystal brooches enclosed by sigil-carved metal. That particular brooch signifies to others exactly what they are. Sorcerers.

Ah. Now I understand why Bolivar wants me to keep my voice down. With my nose buried in the tomes, I hadn't realized there were so many of them here tonight.

"I swear I saw him," a man whispers as he and a mate breeze by with mugs full of ale in their hands. "He was near the canal. Just standing there, looking like he'll kill anyone who crosses him."

"I heard he's already slaughtered three men in Redclaw," the mate says.

I watch the men sit at a table in the far corner, guzzling down ale in between their strange gossip.

There have been a lot of murmurs tonight about a man in black strolling through Meriva. They all seem scared when they speak of this person. One passerby said this man only comes out of hiding when he's looking for blood—that spilling it is what he does best.

I ignored the whispers before, but I've been here for well over three hours now, and whoever this stranger is, he has everyone worked up.

Perhaps I should pack up and leave if such danger is lurking. Then again, what does it matter if my sister is going to die and I might, too, if I try saving her?

Bolivar returns to my table with a plate in hand and a short glass of water. He places both on an empty spot on the wooden tabletop and slides them closer to me. "Figured this would help you sober up. Or cheer you up. Whichever one you need right now."

My mouth salivates at the sight of the sweet gold drizzle clinging to the sliced edge of the honey loaf. I press my fingers to the cakey yellow center. It's still warm. I can't help but smile at the gesture.

"Thank you, Bolivar."

He gives me a nod and takes off for the bar again.

I bite into my loaf and moan as the sweetness of the honey explodes on my tongue.

I love honey loaf. It's so hard to come by now—honey, that is. Whenever Bolivar buys a jar of it, he bakes a loaf and sells it for one gold coin per slice, the same we charge at the bakery when we're lucky enough to get a jar ourselves.

The beastials in the back grow louder, and the charmers and humans join them. I study all of them. All I need is one person to guide me to The Shallows. The *right* person. I'll know it when I see them. That's part of the reason I'm in the tavern tonight, too.

Lots of people, mercenaries especially, always wear their combat gear publicly and carry weapons. And many of them love a warm tavern with lots of ale.

Hardly any of the lot here even carry a sword. And to be frank, they all seem a bit…silly.

None of them will do.

As I bite into my loaf again, trying not to feel defeated, the tavern door swings open, and a cool draft sneaks inside. Despite the fire burning in the hearth a short distance away, the chill wraps around me and sinks under my clothes. I shiver, and that alone feels like a warning.

And then I see him. Dressed exactly like the kind of person I'm looking for.

A man in all black enters wearing buffers, worn boots, and a hooded cowl. A hush follows him into the bar.

A mask conceals the lower portion of his face, a common accessory for soldiers and fighting men who want to hide their expressions during combat. He's wearing a hood, so all I can make out are his downturned eyes. The pommels of two swords stand tall and alert behind his head, and another is sheathed at his waist.

The buffers are the main thing that catch my eye. Most who wear them do so because they're more comfortable than steel armor. Made of thick leather with alvanite rock powder packed into each pad, they provide a firm layer on the body that's tougher to penetrate. He wears only a vest as protection, so he must be able to withstand a strike while wielding a sword at the very least.

The ruckus behind me settles instantly as all eyes turn to the mysterious man. Removing his hood, he reveals hair made of tight, dark curls that rise to a full crown, while the edges are clean, tapered, and as sharp as a blade. He scans the room as he moves forward, the metal on his boots rattling with each heavy, methodical step.

The two men who were gossiping in the corner spring out of their chairs and abandon their ales as he walks in their direction. They scurry to reach the door, dodging a group of occupied tables so they can leave the tavern. The masked man grips the back of one of the now-empty chairs and hauls it back before sinking down on it like a rock.

I blink with my mouth full of honey and bread as I pull my gaze from him to look at everyone else. Most dodge his eyes, while others turn their backs to him entirely. Even Bolivar stands at attention behind the bar and studies the man warily while filling a steel mug with ale.

I've never seen this masked person around before, yet everyone in the tavern is too afraid to even cut a glance at him. This must be him—the man in black everyone's been whispering about. And if he's as lethal as they say, maybe he's just the person I've been looking for.

I wonder if I can pay for his protection…

As this revelation strikes me, I close all the tomes on my table and shove them back into my rucksack. I dig farther into my bag and take out a hefty pouch of coins, and after wiping my mouth with my ivory tunic sleeve, I climb out of my booth.

I inhale, exhale, and then nod. "Okay. Let's do it."

With all the confidence I can muster, I make my way toward the ominous man who, if the rumors are true, just might kill me before I even get the chance to utter a single word.

But what do I have to lose?

Time to make a proposition.

Chapter 3

"Zaira," Bolivar calls in warning.

Ignoring him, I pass the hearth and approach the opposite side of mystery man's table. I drop the pouch in the center of the table, and the coins make an obnoxious clatter. Even though I'm shaking, I look right at him.

He glances at the pouch. Then his eyebrows pull together before he slowly drags his gaze up to meet mine.

"Hi." My voice cracks.

His frown deepens.

Shit. What was I thinking? I mean, this guy is *really* scary up close. I think it's his eyes—amber irises swirling with dark flecks of brown. They're fiercer than I expected, especially with the fire mirrored in them. Or maybe it's the obvious grimace he wears beneath the mask.

On the upside, he has really nice skin. Light brown with bronze undertones and minimal pores. Analla would kill for skin as smooth as his.

"I'm Zaira Quinlocke." I press shaking hands to my chest, introducing myself. "You don't know me, and that's fine, but you look like a guy who gets what he wants, and since you're wearing buffers and carrying those insanely cool swords, I'm assuming you're not afraid of a good fight." The words fall out of my mouth like vomit. I need to shut up, but I can't. Not right now. I have to go all in. "I bet you've seen many of the kingdoms in Thelanor, and as luck would have it, I could use someone like that right now."

His glare is heated.

I swallow again, then pull out the seat across from him so I can sit. Before I can, he straightens his back, and a dagger suddenly materializes in his right hand. He snatched it out of thin air faster than I could blink. Fisting the handle, he slams the hilt down on the table and causes the silverware and my coins to rattle.

I stare at his black, fingerless gloves as he cocks his head ever so slightly, awaiting my next move.

Heart hammering in my chest, I drag in a breath and claim the seat. If I don't push past my fear, I'll regret it. Even if I'm a fool and he decides to kill me on the spot, I'm willing to accept that fate because if Analla dies, then I might as well die, too. But my pendant is still warm, so she has to be alive. I need her and would do *anything* for her. Even chat up a ruthless-looking stranger with murder in his eyes, apparently.

"Look, I'm sure you want to kill me right now for invading your space, so I'm sorry for doing that, but I've heard people talking about you. Men like *you* don't walk around wearing buffers and carrying swords unless you're fulfilling certain…*duties*." I whisper that last part.

His eyes give me a cautionary flash, like he's insisting that I stop talking immediately. He and I both know I don't have to say what those duties are out loud.

Bounty hunting.

Kidnapping.

Stealing.

Murder.

The list goes on.

I'm not quite sure what all he does, or that he's even the right guy in black—I mean, a lot of people wear black—but he at least has to know how to fight and protect, otherwise all this gear he's wearing is for nothing.

"You don't talk much, do you?" A nervous laugh bubbles out of me as my gaze bounces to Bolivar, whose nostrils are flaring. His palms are planted on the countertop like he's anticipating my throat getting slit at any moment. A glance around the pub reveals that all present—from beastials to humans to charmers to sorcerers—expect the same outcome.

Yep. I'm dead.

I shift, putting my back to our audience and lowering my voice so that only the man across from me can hear my words or see my face. "Whatever. Doesn't matter. Look, the point is my sister got mixed up in a bad situation, and now she's cursed. I need to travel to a place outside Meriva to get something that's supposed to help her, but I won't survive if I go alone. Now, I'm not sure what all you can do, but I know if I have someone who can protect me along the way, I might be able to make it. And if that person isn't you, maybe you know someone who might be interested and can point me in their direction. I have to try for her—and I'll give you all the coins I have." I nudge the pouch closer to him. "I'm desperate at this point…so I'm begging you to *please* help me. Or show me to someone who can."

He doesn't even bother looking at the pouch. His gaze burns *through* me instead.

Then, before I can blink again, he lifts his other hand and flicks his wrist. Golden wisps burst from his fingertips, and something tight and warm wraps around me, hauling me out of the seat.

"Fuck off," he grumbles.

Wow. The first two words I hear from him are "fuck off"? How insulting.

I gasp, staring down at my feet as they dangle inches above the wooden floorboards. My body moves, but not of my own accord. It takes a moment for everything to register, but it doesn't stop my heart from racing or prevent the panic from crawling up my throat. I'm floating farther away from him, bound by an invisible force, and unable to free myself.

Oh my Orvena.

On top of being feared, he's a *sorcerer*, too? Even though I hate the way he's magically manhandling me, I now feel even more compelled to get him to help me. Why? Because magic offers twice as much protection… though I'm not entirely sure he uses his with virtue, as Orvena instructed in her teachings.

Doesn't matter. Maybe I've had too many drinks and am not thinking this through, but I still want his help. Magic is good. It's an advantage that I need right now. I just need to reason with him.

That turns out being easier planned than done, though. The masked man isn't returning me to my seat as I expected. Gasps fill the tavern as the patrons watch me struggle against my invisible bonds, and it's only now I realize he's sending me floating toward the *exit*.

Oh crap.

Chapter 4

"**W**ait!" I yell as he guides me closer to the door. I breathe faster, my heart pounding dangerously hard now. My panic has heightened tenfold. I try moving my arms or breaking free, but he has me completely bound. I can't move—can't even wiggle out of his grasp.

Oh gods.

"Just let her go, Thane." Bolivar steps out from behind the counter, squaring his shoulders. "She's already had a rough day."

I look from the giant to the stranger and stop struggling against his magical grip. Bolivar knows him? My panic subsides long enough for me to take a deep breath. I lift my chin, trying to look confident—well, as confident as one can be when dangling helplessly above the ground.

"Yeah, *Thane*." More like *bane* of my existence. "Let me go. Now."

The door flies open, and the handle slams into the stone wall. I peer over my shoulder at the slick cobblestone street and the canal that splits the Commons in two. A screech builds in my throat.

Bane of My Existence doesn't let me go. Not until I'm completely outside and several feet away from the door. His hot grip vanishes as he plops me on the ground, causing me to land square on my ass.

"Ow! What the shadows is wrong with you?!" I yell, just as the door of the tavern swings shut. The smug satisfaction in Thane's eyes is the last thing I see. "Oh no he fucking *didn't*."

I haul myself up, push my spectacles back in place, and storm back to the tavern, shoving the door open.

As if Bolivar was expecting my furious return, he stops me with a solid hand to the chest before I can even get two feet in the door.

"Do not go back over there. Do you hear me, Z?"

I maneuver around him and stomp toward Thane's table regardless of Bolivar's warning. Thane doesn't pay me any mind as he wipes the blade of a dagger on the hem of his cloak with an air of boredom.

"Whoa, Zaira. Come on," Bolivar whisper-hisses as he follows me. "You don't want to get into it with this one, okay? I've seen what he can do, and believe me, that son of a bitch *will* kill you." He catches me by the elbow to stop me again.

"So let him! All I did was ask for help!" I shout, directing my words to the masked jackass, not giving a shit who hears me. At this point, I have nothing to lose. "Everyone around here is so afraid of *Seferin*, but I'm not, and I don't care if he has henchmen or snitches in this place to tell him that! All I want is to get my sister back!"

Thane freezes. Then his eyes dart up to mine. I swear his bright irises absorb the fire as they swell with fury.

There it is. *His attention.* It seems I'm not the only one around here who despises Seferin.

"Orvena's sake, Z," Bolivar grumbles.

"Please. My sister is going to die within the next month if I don't do something," I plead to Thane. "All I need is someone to look after me—to simply escort me on a brief journey. It'll take two weeks, max. If I leave tomorrow, I can make it there and back in time."

"Let her go." Thane's voice has a deep, gravelly timbre. I swallow as those fierce eyes scan every inch of me.

Bolivar huffs and then glares at me. "Zaira, this *isn't* the way."

I pull away from him, matching his stare. "I have to try." Without another word to Bolivar, I turn back toward Thane, this time with more poise. "Can I sit, or are you going to toss me into the fire this time?"

He narrows his eyes briefly before he folds his arms and gives me one simple curt nod.

I sit and blow out a deep breath, rubbing my forehead, as if that action alone will lessen my stress. That's when I feel all eyes on me now. The weight of them is heavy.

I look around, and of course everyone is watching us.

With what might be a low growl, Thane stares everyone down, his body tense like a predator ready to strike. With some exaggerated throat clearing and shuffles, the tavern patrons melt into the background, resuming card games and overly loud conversations about anything except what just happened.

"How do you know Seferin?" Thane asks, cutting straight to the chase.

"I don't know him personally. My sister worked for him, but then she tried to steal from him, and matters…escalated."

He studies me like he's searching for lies. "Start from the beginning."

"My sister stole a crystal from Seferin, and now he's punishing her for it."

"A *crystal*?" he questions with a hint of annoyance.

"Yes. She had the terrible idea to sell it, so she tried to steal it. The only reason I know is because I snuck into his keep when I sensed something was wrong. She's down there…and he's placed a curse on her." I feel eyes on me. I glance toward the bar, and one of the beastials with feathers on her arms jerks her gaze away when I catch her staring.

"Don't worry about them." He takes a thorough look around the tavern. "Even if you scream, they won't hear you."

I sit up, confused and, quite frankly, disturbed by that statement. "Why can't they hear me?"

"Because I don't want them to." He waves a hand, and that's when I notice an almost imperceptible shimmer of gold light surrounding us like a dome.

I gulp. "Oh." I don't know how I feel about this, but something tells me I should be terrified by it. I finger the pendant of my necklace as if the action will provide me a bit of security.

He narrows his eyes at my necklace before leveling his gaze with me. "Continue."

Despite my stomach doing back flips, I do as the man says. "Right. So, um, she's trapped and cursed and will die within the next thirty days if I don't do something."

I expect Thane to say something—to show a bit of sympathy for my woes.

He doesn't.

He seems rather bored, spinning his dagger in lazy circles on the tabletop, watching the blade whirl.

"Anyway, I've asked a few sorcerers for help breaking the curse, and it seems the only way I can break one as powerful as this one is by visiting the Temple of Elphar and collecting a certain stone."

"A prosperity stone." He stops the blade's rotation but doesn't look at me.

"Yes." I nod.

He leans back in his chair, spins the blade again, and gestures for me to continue.

"I've asked around about the temple, and it's too far of a journey for me to make alone." And evidently impossible to reach, but I leave that part out. "I have to go through some pretty rough kingdoms in order to reach my destination."

A moment of silence passes between us.

Yeah. There's no chivalrous offer to help me out or anything. Just indifference as he stares at the slowing blade and gives it another twirl.

"I don't know much about the lands outside of Meriva," I continue, "so I need protection. If I can get one of the stones in time, I can sneak into Seferin's keep, give her the stone, and once it's in her possession, that'll break the curse. After that, I get her out, and we flee."

"What was the name of the crystal she touched?" Thane asks, halting the blade by the handle as if none of the other details matter.

"I—I don't know. It was an indigo color."

The features I can see on Thane's face harden. "A liphanet." He blinks at me before his eyes land on the bag of coins. "If Seferin cursed it *and* she's mortal, it's true. She'll die, and soon. Liphanets are one-time crystals that bond well with mortal curses and never lift until they've absorbed all energy and soul, which usually takes close to a month. There are crystals out there that can be used to get the job done quicker, but he clearly wants her to suffer."

My mouth becomes drier with every word he says. "So she's in a lot of pain?"

"More than likely."

"But not dead yet," I mumble under my breath. Maybe that's why the pearl is still extremely warm. A swirl of nausea hits me, and I close my eyes. I've never been more afraid for Analla than now. "That's not okay. He shouldn't be doing that to her."

"Well, he is. And once the absorption is complete, he'll most likely take her soul and use it…or sell it to the highest bidding sorcerer."

"What would they even do with her soul?"

"Use it for whatever they want."

"Like?"

"Many things."

"Can you please elaborate?" I ask, trying desperately hard not to get frustrated by his vagueness.

He blows out an irritated sigh. "I don't know—they could pour life back into someone who may be dying or is already dead. Most would probably just use it to boost their own magic."

I try not to react externally, but internally my heart is hammering against my rib cage and I've become full-on queasy. I grip the edge of my chair to keep myself steady.

"But one of the prosperity stones in Elphar can save her," I remind him. "It can break any curse."

"A possibility," Thane says, mulling it over. "But not likely to happen. Those stones are hard to obtain. Many have tried making it through The Shallows to reach the Temple of Elphar, and most have died doing so."

"I don't care." I push a deep breath out through my noise, quelling the nausea as best I can. "It's better than doing nothing." Sure, I can say that, but now my whole body is trembling at the sheer idea of it.

I've heard tales about The Shallows. The mere thought of that place is terrifying. So many horror stories circulate about vicious beasts, traps, and other wickedness. There's a reason that land has been abandoned.

I tuck my hands between my thighs so Thane won't see them shake. "Can you even fight?"

He frowns, seeming offended.

"I just mean how skilled are you? For all I know, you're not worth hiring."

His jaw tightens. "There's a reason no one in here has bothered looking me in the eye—no one but you, anyway. But you're naive, foolish, and obviously don't understand the dangers of this world, so I suppose that gives you a pass."

I give him my deepest scowl. "So you are the man in black everyone's been whispering about, then."

He says nothing to that. He doesn't have to. I can sense it. There's danger written all over him.

"So, will you help me get there or not? I just need someone to watch my back. That's it. Everything else, like lodging and eating, I'll take care of myself."

He narrows his gaze just a touch, analyzing me. Then he grabs the pouch with an oversize hand and dumps the coins onto the table. They clatter as they collide.

After counting them, he says, "Double the payment and I'll assist. And make it gold coin only."

"W-what?" My stomach drops. "But I don't have that kind of money." I gesture to the coins. "*This* is all I have right now. It's at least sixty silvers—and look." I pick up one of the gold coins. "Gold. There are five gold coins in there."

He reclines in his seat. "If this is all you have, I can't help you. I'll need more than that if I'm going to risk my life for yours."

"Please," I beg. "This is my sister. I know it's risky but—*please*. You asked me for details—for a reason. You obviously hate Seferin, too."

This time, he doesn't react to Seferin's name. Instead, he raises a hand and gestures for Bolivar to come over. The privacy dome evaporates.

Bolivar migrates our way with pure reluctance. "What do you want?"

Thane picks up a few of the coins on the table—*my* coins—and slides them toward Bolivar. "Ale and broth noodles."

Bolivar's jaw works while collecting the coins. Once he's out of earshot, I focus on Thane again, but he's already staring at me.

"Double the payment and bring it to me in the morning. This tavern. All gold coin. You do that, and I'll get you to Elphar for one of the stones," he assures me. "You don't, then may your sister's soul rest in the Crystal Realm with Orvena."

I shove back in my chair as anger courses through my veins like venom. Heads turn as the legs scrape the floor.

"You're an asshole, *Thane*."

For the first time since he walked into the tavern, he lowers his mask. I have to stop myself from drawing in a sharp breath at the reveal of his unexpectedly chiseled jaw and full, pouty lips. A dark scar along his left cheek juts up to his temple, while another marks the right side of his upper lip all the way to his chin.

Ugh.

Of course he's wickedly handsome. I hate him even more.

"You're the one who approached this asshole expecting him to risk his life." Thane's eyes spark gold, presenting a clear threat to me and only me. "Double the coin and bring it back in the morning or leave me alone."

Bolivar returns with his ale and a bowl of hot rooster broth with noodles. Thane doesn't hesitate to pick up the steel mug. Foam spills over his fingers as he tips the rim toward his mouth. He chugs down a few sips, unbothered by my anger.

He isn't going to change his mind about the coins. Knowing this makes me bite back tears of frustration because I don't have that kind of money and I'm not sure who else to ask. Who else is there to help me?

Clearing my throat, I rake up all my coins and shove them back into the pouch.

My eyes water again as I grab my rucksack and storm away. Snatching my wool coat off one of the racks by the exit, I rush out of the building before I end up slapping that dickheaded sorcerer.

Chapter 5

The crisp autumn wind bites at my skin as I walk the streets of the Commons.

Houses, inns, and boutiques made of stone, white brick, or a neat combination of both line either side of the wide canal. The dark ripples in the water shimmer beneath the crescent moonlight, flowing all the way to the Crystal Palace. A sundial crafted in gold is attached to the face of the fortress, displaying the time.

I grip the collar of my coat as I glimpse the clock tower. It's nearing the tenth hour of night. Merchants closed their shops long ago, and most people are tucked away in their warm homes, carefree and oblivious to nuisances of curses and death.

But to my left, a pawn shop is still open. A single lantern on the counter inside reveals the owner locking some of his items away for the night.

I come to a halt, digging beneath the neckline of my tunic and fingering my pendant—a beautiful pearl embraced in gold ribbons. The pearl has always reminded me of a bird in a gilded cage, protected and loved. I got it from my mother, who got it from her mother as an heirloom.

A gorgeous thing.

Magical.

Sacred.

Special.

It's stayed warm ever since I found out about Analla and hasn't bothered to cool down.

I can sell it. I'm certain I can gather at least three hundred and fifty gold coins for it, possibly more. My throat starts to close in on itself. I shake my head, clutching the pendant as I watch the pawn shop broker mill about with a feather duster in hand.

"No." I march past the shop. I *can't* sell it. It's all I have left of my mother—of Ember Coast. It's the only way I'll know Analla is still alive. It holds so many of my memories, things words can *never* explain.

And pearls are rare now. Ever since Ember Coast broke off from Thelanor, pearls have become harder to find, which has increased their value significantly. Ember Coast was famous for collecting and selling them.

But if you don't sell it, Analla will die.

I stop again, an exasperated breath falling through my lips as my spectacles slip down my nose. A quiver starts in my bottom lip, but I force it to stop, swallowing my emotions and my pride.

Over my shoulder, I notice the pawn shop broker slipping into his coat. Oh my Orvena. This is my only chance. If I don't do it now, I won't have enough time to prepare in the morning.

Damn it. I hate that masked jerk for making me do this. I hate it even more that he might be the only person who's shown even a smidge of interest in joining my side. All others before flat out declined. I'm not sure where else to look and I'll never make it to the temple without someone who can handle a weapon. Even with him, failure is probable, but I have to give it a shot. If he backs out, I'll run back to the shop first thing and get my necklace back.

I twist around and jog toward the shop, gripping the door handle and yanking it open.

The broker raises his head with alarm. "I'm just closing up," he announces. "Can you return tomorrow?"

"I won't have time tomorrow," I respond as I approach the glass counter. Fiddling with my necklace again, I release a shaky breath. "I...um...I have something to sell."

The man raises a bushy brow, studying my empty hands. "Well? Where is it?"

I reach for the back of my neck and unclasp the necklace, then place it on the counter gently. The tiny *clink* on the glass may as well cause a massive crack in my heart.

The broker's eyes widen as he looks from the necklace to me. "This better not be fake."

I shake my head. "It's not."

He picks it up, eyes me warily, and then brings it to his mouth.

I immediately frown and ask, "What the shadows are you doing?"

"Testing if it's real or not."

He slips a protruding canine through the gaps between the gold ribbons so he can scrape the pearl with his tooth. Each scrape makes my heart break even more. I want to snatch it away from his grubby hands and run home. This was a stupid idea anyway. I can find something else at home to sell. Maybe Analla has some jewels or fancy dresses in her room somewhere.

The man pulls the necklace back and licks his teeth. "Huh."

"What?"

"Grit on my teeth." He sets it back on the counter. "Must be real."

"So how much can I get for it?" My voice betrays my sadness.

He studies it once more, eyeballs me, then says, "One hundred coins."

Is he fucking *kidding me*? That necklace is worth *at least* three hundred and fifty coins. "Do better. Three fifty."

He gives me a mock chuckle. "Two fifty."

I scoff. "Three hundred *and sixty*."

"You're being ridiculous," he sputters.

"Listen. That pearl is from Ember Coast and has been infused with magic. The wearer can designate it to whoever they want to trace, and it'll tell them if that person is in trouble. It warms to a certain degree so you're left with no choice but to feel it. There's a whole process and chant a sorcerer can use to activate it, but I'll only share that if it's bought. You won't find a necklace like this *anywhere* else in the Commons—and if you're haggling with me like this, I'm sure you'll be able to sell it to someone a whole lot dumber than I am for double the price I'm asking."

His smile fades, and he taps the counter with a chubby finger, studying the necklace again, contemplating. Sighing, he shifts on his feet and says, "Three hundred and sixty and that's final."

"All in gold coin," I reply.

His face reddens as he opens his mouth to speak, but then he clamps it shut and chuckles dryly. "You're not dumb at all, are you, girl?"

I fold my arms. "I'm not a girl. I'm a woman. And I'm sure you wish I was dumb so you could better rip me off."

He huffs a laugh. "Fine. Three hundred and sixty in all gold coin. *That* is final. Deal?"

I smirk as I stand taller. "Deal."

Chapter 6

First thing the next morning, I walk through the doors of the Tilted Crystal, and luckily, Thane is sitting in the same seat as the night before. Only this time he's removed his cowl and he's wearing a sleeveless gray tunic.

Since he held up his end of the bargain, this alliance is clearly meant to be.

His arms are thick, muscles rippling as he sips from a mug. He directs his gaze across the tavern, surveilling the place as if he's on the lookout for threats, but when his eyes swing in my direction, he sighs and looks away.

Yep, I got the coins, dickhead.

The closer I come to his table, the clearer I can see the corded veins on his biceps and forearms. Sweat clings to his skin, and his curls are flatter and slightly damp, as if he just finished some kind of workout.

Or just hunted someone down and gutted them.

Whatever. I don't care.

I slam the pouch down on his table with a triumphant huff. "I was able to double the coins, and they're all gold. You'll only get half up front. The rest you can collect if we make it back alive." I don't have the other half on me, just in case he changes his mind and robs me instead. The rest are stored in a boot under my bed.

"How do I know you even have the other half?" he asks.

I shrug. "I guess you'll just have to take my word for it."

"So let me get this straight. You're asking me to trust the word of a person I don't even know about the coins I'm owed in order to protect them on a journey where we both will probably die along the way?"

I shift on my feet. "Well…when you put it that way…"

He narrows those amber eyes at me. "They're hidden in a boot under your bed. Clever."

I gasp. "How did you—"

Now I want to run home and hide them somewhere else. How does he know that? Can he read minds with his magic? Yes, that must be it. What else could it be? Unless he has some kind of spying spell or something.

He picks up the pouch and dumps the coins on the table, cutting through my thoughts. The wisps of sunlight streaming through the window behind him cause the money to gleam, highlighting Orvena's profile etched into each one.

Silently, he counts the coins one by one, taking his sweet damn time doing so. Once finished, he slips them all back into the pouch and pushes to a stand. With his rise, I angle my chin upward, trying to appear taller than I am.

Damn. I knew he was tall, but I didn't realize we have such a massive height difference until now. He has to be nearly as tall as Bolivar, and that giant is usually the tallest in any room.

Speaking of, I'm glad Bolivar isn't on duty yet. One of the other barmen is at the counter, his gray eyebrows raised as he studies us. He'll probably snitch on me to Bolivar, but I'll be long gone by then.

Stopping short of Thane's bicep, I twist my lips when his eyes descend to mine. He looks at me, as if he's seeing me for the first time. Like he's trying to make sense of me. I swear I notice his eyes stop at the swell of my chest before dragging down to my hips and legs.

I shift on my feet under his stare as a sudden wave of warmth swims through my veins. That same warmth, however, comes with a hint of agitation. I step back and fold my arms to block his view. So typical of men to stare.

"You sure this is what you want?" he asks, connecting his eyes to mine again. "To go to the Temple of Elphar?"

My heart races a bit, but I nod before my mind can form a rejection. "Yes."

He scans me again before nodding. "Okay. Let's go, then." He snatches up his cowl, vest, swords, and a black rucksack from a nearby table before trudging around me to exit the tavern.

"Wait. Where are we going?" I follow him into the street as a cluster of children giggle and run past. There is hardly a chill in the air today. That's the thing about weather in Meriva Empire. One day you'll need a coat, and the next you can rest on a patch of grass near a lake with the sun beaming on your face even though it's still fall.

"Elphar," Thane says, already weaving his way through the crowd. Well, I'm the one weaving. People are jumping out of his way to create a clear path for him.

"Now?"

He frowns over his shoulder. "Is that a problem?"

"No—well, yes, actually. I thought I'd have a little more time to prepare. I still need to pack, stop by the bakery I work at, and the refugee center. I need to let everyone know I'll be gone for a few days."

Thane comes to a rapid halt, and I slam into his solid back, only to be knocked off center and stumbling sideways. He twists around and catches me by the forearm just as a mule wagon rolls by.

He towers over me, glaring. Without his mask, his scars are much more prominent and twice as intimidating. The one beneath his eye is slightly red and raised around the edges, as if it happened recently.

He releases me. "That should've been handled already."

I brush his hand away. "Yeah, well the bakery just opened, and the refugee center will only take a minute."

"Refugee center?"

I push my specs back into position. "I volunteer there."

"Of *course* you do."

I frown. What's that supposed to mean?

Thane starts to walk away from me.

I scurry behind him to catch up. "All I need is thirty minutes."

He doesn't even turn around but says over his shoulder, "Meet me back at the Tilted Crystal when you're done fucking around."

Uh, no.

I catch him by the upper arm before he can get too far away. He stares at my hand on his rock-hard bicep, then turns his absolutely livid eyes to me.

"I advise you not to do that again," he warns.

Or what? I start to ask. But then I realize only a fool who has a death wish would counter with that question. I jerk my hand away.

"You have a pocket full of coins I paid you that you can easily run off with," I explain, placing a hand on my hip.

He clenches his jaw, his patience clearly waning.

"Just follow me. My home is a short walk away from the bakery. We can stop at my place first, I'll pack, and the next two stops will be a breeze."

"You want me to follow you around like a *dog*?" he asks in a low growl...like a dog.

I blink up at him as his nostrils flare. Then, with a shake of his head, he closes his eyes, inhales, and then exhales, as if to calm himself.

"Wow. Nice breathing technique," I quip when his eyes open again. "I didn't take you for a man of patience."

With a grimace, he tucks his thumb under the strap of his rucksack and grumbles, "Just stop talking and walk."

Chapter 7

"Aren't you going to ask how I got the coins?" I eye Thane as he purposely trails a few steps behind me. We just left my home in the Commons, and I now have my rucksack and satchel in tow. When he doesn't answer, I say, "I sold my necklace."

I spot a fruit stand ahead and dig into my satchel for two silvers, handing them to the merchant and swapping them for pears.

"It was a family heirloom," I go on as I leave the stand. "It had a pearl, which I'm sure you know is worth a *lot* of coin, plus it contained magic. My mother gave it to me as a way for me to look out for my sister. It was all I had left from her, so this journey to Elphar is serious. I'm not *fucking around*, as you stated earlier."

I glance over my shoulder, but Thane isn't looking my way. Is he even listening?

I huff, biting into my pear and speeding up my pace. I don't stop until I reach The Flour Tower. I'm glad to see the owner and my boss, Ellanoch, working behind the counter.

"Zaira!" Ellanoch sings as she slides tea cakes into one of the displays next to the loaves of freshly baked bread. "You're not scheduled to work today, are you?" Thane strides in after me, and Ellanoch's gaze catches on my companion. I watch as her already pale face turns even whiter.

"Orvena's stars," she whispers.

"Don't worry about him," I grumble, approaching the counter.

"Zaira, who *is* that?" she whispers. "Are you in some sort of trouble?"

I understand her alarm. Men like Thane, strolling around with scars on their faces, death glares, and several swords aren't exactly an everyday sight in Meriva. We avoid men like him.

"No—well, yes," I answer. "But it's not exactly *me* who's in trouble, and having him around is not what you think."

She rushes around the counter, giving Thane a once-over before stopping in front of me. Taking hold of my shoulders, she says, "Tell me what's going on."

"It's my sister...and a long story. I'll tell you when I come back...which will be in a few weeks, if I'm lucky."

"*A few weeks?* Why? Where are you going?"

"I have to take a journey to get something important for Analla. I just wanted to let you know so you don't worry about me, and so you can make arrangements to cover my shifts."

"Oh." Ellanoch still looks uneasy. "But I don't understand. Why do you need *him*?"

I take note of her worried gray-green eyes, wanting so badly to tell her everything. But I can't. I can't risk word accidentally getting out and reaching Seferin. I also don't want to cause concern... After all, I have plans to return, and nothing is going to stop me.

I remove one of her hands from my shoulders to enclose it in mine. "I'll tell you everything when I'm back. I promise."

"All right." I can tell she isn't satisfied with that answer, but she lets it go. "Well, at least take a loaf or two with you if you'll be gone for that long."

I smile as she returns to the counter to wrap two loaves of bread in an ivory cloth. I accept them and thank her as we hug.

My impatient companion clears his throat and cocks his head at the door.

Ellanoch frowns at him. "Come back in one piece, you hear me?" Her smile is warm as she rubs my upper arm.

"I will." My eyes sting, but I bat the emerging tears away.

As we leave the bakery, I walk even faster to reach the refugee center. It's going to be even harder leaving all the children I help teach, but I don't want them or the director worrying about my absence.

Saying farewell for now to them all makes me cry.

I was in my ninth year when I came to the refugee center and didn't leave until three years ago, when Analla was able to move us into our own place during her nineteenth year and my seventeenth. We were still in school, but we took up jobs on the side to afford our home in the Commons. I loved the center so much that I returned to volunteer.

When I finally exit the building, still swiping my eyes, I search for Thane, but he isn't in front anymore. My heart plummets as dread seizes me.

"No." I walk to the middle of the street as carriages and wagons rush by. Merchants yell, and people sit on the edge of the canal ahead, fishing or chatting away, but there is no sign of that wicked-looking man anywhere.

Then a whistle splits the air.

I turn around and my jaw drops when I spot Thane sitting on the edge of the roof of the refugee center three stories up. The roof is built at a sharp pitch, an almost vertical angle, and many of the clay shingles are loose and have fallen off. He causes shingles to slide downward as he stands up, and they shatter on the ground in loud clatters. How the shadows did he get up there?

To my shock, Thane jumps off the roof, and I gasp when he lands right in front of me with hardly a sound. He's wearing his cowl and buffers again, his weapons strapped to him like he's prepared for combat. For a second, I have to ask myself if this is the man I *really* want to take a journey with. I mean, who jumps off of dangerously high roofs when they're bored?

"Took you long enough," he says, biting into a pear.

I glare at the fruit.

Wait a minute...

"Hey..." I frown, taking my rucksack off and digging through it, searching for the extra pear I bought. When I can't find it, I ask, exasperated, "Are you serious? I just gave you a bunch of coins! Can't you buy your own damn pear?"

He finishes off the fruit, licking the juice from his fingers. Then he tosses the pear core into the air. It halts, hovering in front of my face. In seconds, it's no longer just a core.

It's been restored to a whole pear and looks exactly like the one I just bought.

How is he this good with his magic? With his skills, he could've joined The Divine or at least become a city guard.

I disregard those thoughts and snatch the pear out of the air. "I don't want your sloppy seconds."

And, for a second, I swear he almost smiles.

We trek silently through the streets of Meriva until we reach the end of the Commons and enter the Scraps.

"What are we doing in the Scraps? Shouldn't we be heading toward the bridge that takes us through the southern half of Ruvain? I looked up the route on a map, and it showed that we have to cross through Ruvain to get to Gadonia, which will lead us to Elphar."

The sheer thought of passing through *Ruvain* is terrifying. No good comes from that kingdom.

"Have to make a stop before we go that way," Thane says.

The deeper we walk into the Scraps and the closer we get to the trees lining the border, the more the atmosphere shifts from busy and uplifted to drab and weary. The canal disappears, leaving only streets riddled with weeds between ruined cobblestones. It smells like pee or fish…or both.

I'm certain the thick black smoke billowing from some of the chimneys is the cause of the phlegmy coughs echoing through the run-down buildings and alleys.

For the first time, I stick close to Thane, who's pulled his mask up. I force a smile at the hollow-cheeked Scrappers sitting on the side of the road. Some have dark streaks on their hands and faces from working the coal and wood factories. But all appear tired, even the children.

Beastials live among them, too. I'd figure more would take their chances in the forests than starve here, but I suppose even beastials aren't all that great at surviving out there alone. Not with the wilder beasts roaming Thelanor.

A young girl with messy pigtails sitting next to a broken barrel catches my attention.

"Just keep your eyes ahead," Thane says in a low voice.

I'm confused by his statement and the urgency in his tone.

I glance at the girl again. She's standing now, smiling sadly at me. I toss her a subtle wave, offering a smile, to which she cracks a full smile and reveals rotting teeth.

My skin immediately prickles with unease. Something about her grin causes my smile to slip away.

And before I know it, she's running swiftly in my direction.

Chapter 8

The girl snarls like an animal as she shoves Thane away with all her might, then grabs hold of me, attempting to drag me away. I gasp as my legs stiffen and my stomach feels weighed down with a thousand rocks.

Her skin that was once pale, nearly translucent, has transitioned to a putrid green. Her dark irises are now rimmed with red, and what should be the whites of her eyes aren't white at all, but a sickly yellow.

What the shadows is wrong with her? How has she changed from an innocent girl to...to...this green thing with *claws*?

She grabs my wrist and manages to press the tips of her claws into it. Any deeper and she'll puncture my skin. I scream and push a hand against her chest, trying to free myself, but it proves near impossible.

Her teeth extend, saliva dripping down pointy fangs. When she hisses, her goopy spittle launches my way and splatters on my clothes.

In the next breath, the silver blade of a sword catches in the sunlight. Thane steps between me and the creature, bringing the edge of it to the green thing's throat.

"She's not yours to have," Thane growls, pressing the sword deeper into the creature's skin and conjuring thick, inky blood. "Now leave us alone or I'll cut your damn head off."

The creature backs into the nearest wall, thin-slit nostrils flaring as a murderous look consumes her.

Lowering the sword and gripping my upper arm, my protector hauls me away from the scene. "I told you to keep your eyes ahead. All you had to do was keep walking."

"W-what was that thing?" I stammer.

"A skrellin," he says, picking up the pace, "and if there is one here now, believe me, there are more on the way."

A skrellin? Right. I've heard about them. They always travel in groups, inhabit some of the forests, and blend in as mortals by adjusting their skin. I didn't realize their natural form was like *that*, though. Skrellins love eating *anything* with flesh…including mortals.

I peer back to look at the skrellin girl. She shoots me a scowl before morphing back into her mortal form and scurrying away.

I bend over the lake, perched on my knees as I scrub the skrellin spit off my brown leather bodice. My hands are trembling, making it harder to remove the stains, but hey, at least I've gotten most of it off my satchel and the straps of my rucksack.

I still can't believe what just happened. I have no doubt Thane would've beheaded that thing if it hadn't backed off, and then it might've been blood I was cleaning off my clothes. It's been a while since I've seen anyone bleed from a wound inflicted by someone else. I haven't witnessed such a thing since Ruvain attacked my kingdom when I was a child.

My chest tightens at the reminder of my past.

I force myself to breathe a little slower, to take a second to calm down. The last thing I need is an attack of anxiety. Those memories still live in my head, though.

All that blood and destruction.

Friends decapitated.

Soldiers hanged from trees.

Others floating in the ocean face down.

Running for my life to reach safety.

Covering my ears while in the bunker to block out explosions and screams.

I concentrate on my reflection in the water in an attempt to rinse the traumatic memories away. My coils are slightly more untamed because of that encounter, and the gold streaks within them appear dull. My face is ashen, drained of most of its color. My deep, sienna-brown skin has seeped away—left on the filthy streets of the Scraps. I'm unintentionally clenching my jaw, so I soften it, taking careful breaths through my nostrils. I scoop more water from the creek onto the bodice and scrub harder with my fingers.

Thane is leaning against a nearby tree, waiting impatiently for me with his arms folded. How can he just stand there like nothing just happened? What if that thing shows up again?

When most of the slime has been cleaned, I dry my bodice off with a cloth from my bag.

"A clearer warning would've been nice," I say, side-eyeing him. I slip into the bodice again, then tie the strings, but I suck my teeth when I spot droplets of dried yellow goop on my beige chemise. Ugh. All of it didn't come out. Great. One of my favorite tops is now ruined. "And how can you stand there all nonchalant? I was just attacked. You act like this is some kind of game."

"No," he says, dropping his arms and pushing off the tree. "Clearly, this is a game to *you*, oh sweet one." His steps are heavy as he approaches me. "Everyone knows not to be friendly or to show any signs of vulnerability with people in the fucking Scraps."

"*I* didn't know," I counter.

But I've heard stories about the Scraps. In all my years being a citizen of Meriva, I've never visited that area before. Many say the people there are assholes but generally mind their own business. Others say the Scrappers are thieving monsters who only look out for themselves. Coming from the Commons, I didn't know what to believe.

"Is this how it's going to be during this journey?" Thane asks, frustration lacing his voice. "You getting all friendly with everyone, and me stepping in so you don't get yourself killed? Because if so, I need more coin for that. Looking out for a person like *you* with no combat skills who trusts way too easily will require double the work and double the patience."

"I told you I didn't know that would happen! She looked like a child—how was I supposed to know she would become that *thing* and attack me simply for waving?"

"Look, this isn't the Commons or even the Prospers, okay? This journey is deadly enough as it is, so from now on, I want you to follow these two rules. Number one," he says, raising a stern finger in the air as he steps closer. "Keep your kind gestures to yourself. They'll only get you killed. Number two"—he adds another finger—"stop being so sympathetic. People are poor, and children are starving. None of that is new and you can't change any of it, so learn how to accept it and move along. Plant those rules like seeds in your friendly, innocent brain and let them take root because if you die over feeling sorry for someone else, that's on *you*."

I glare at him with a grimace. "Fine." *Asshole.*

He strides past me, leaving behind the scent of cedar and leather. I collect my bags and catch up to him.

Begrudgingly I ask, "Where to now?"

"Redclaw."

I stop dead in my tracks. "You're joking, right?"

"No," he answers, still moving ahead. "We need a horse, and they sell them cheap."

"But Redclaw is ten times worse than the Scraps. My sister told me about it. I heard they buy dead bodies and sell the organs to the beastials who'll eat them."

"Even if that rumor is true, it doesn't have a damn thing to do with me buying a horse."

I draw in an unsteady breath as Thane breaks through a thicket of trees.

This is for Analla. Just push through for her.

With that in mind, I curse under my breath and follow him into the depths of the forest.

Chapter 9

"You act like you're not afraid of anything." I shove a branch out of the way, catching up to Thane. We've been walking for nearly half an hour now, weaving through the forest and crossing through fields of dirt.

"I'm not," he says back.

"I don't believe that. Everyone's afraid of something. Are you not scared of dying? Actually, I don't even know why I bother asking. You look like the type to invite trouble instead of running away from it."

He turns his head a fraction of an inch. I can't see his entire face, but I do see a lifted eyebrow. "Has anyone ever told you that you talk too much?"

I shrug. "My sister likes to say so occasionally."

"Well, she's right."

I roll my eyes, falling into step beside him. He takes long strides and moves at a rapid pace. Seeing as he's nearly twice my height, I damn near break a sweat trying to keep up.

He finally slows down to tug his mask up, covering half of his features as we approach rusty arched iron gates built into black brick walls.

"Oh, no." A guard standing at the gate in red buffers widens his stance and plants his hand on the handle of a sheathed sword at his waist. "The fuck do *you* want?"

My pulse quickens as my eyes swing from the guard to a bored-looking Thane.

"Let me through, Chaun."

"And why would I do that after what you did during your last visit?" Chaun steps forward, and another man emerges from a line of trees to our left, gripping the pommel of his weapon, too.

Oh, gods. I'm never going to make it to Elphar at this rate. I probably won't even live to see the end of the day with Thane swinging his dick around at every stop.

"I'm not here to cause trouble," Thane replies. "I'm here to buy a horse. Now let me through."

"Thing is, Valkor, Garyn is still pissed at you." *Valkor?* So that's his last name. Or maybe it's his first and he goes by the last? I don't know. "Do you know how long it took to clean up the card tables after you left? They were covered in velvet, and blood was *everywhere*, you piece of shit. We had to replace over half of them and bury those men."

Thane offers a shrug. "My condolences." He strides toward Chaun as he sticks out his hand. Thane drops several gold coins into Chaun's palm.

Chaun makes sure the other guard isn't looking before counting them. With an annoyed exhale, he shifts backward. "Go through the back gate. But I'm warning you now, don't let Garyn catch you. You get a horse and get the fuck out." He bobs his head at the other man. "Take them 'round."

The other guard leads the way, skirting the perimeter of the brick wall until a smaller gate appears. It creaks on the hinges as the guard unlocks the doors. I follow Thane closely, ignoring the stranger's obvious annoyance.

Redclaw isn't really a town, more like a small settlement. The dirt streets ahead are bustling with bodies. Copious treetops hang over the brick walls, as if they're proud to keep this place a secret. The sky is hard to make out, so it appears darker here than outside the gates. Shabby huts line either side of the street, and as we pass through, a few people peep out of their windows.

I grip the strap of my rucksack tighter as I notice a group of men standing near a tavern, smoking brimsticks. Ahead of us, in the heart of the village, is a half-circle of dirt-stained pavilions.

Merchants stand outside of them, shouting prices as we pass, insisting that we step in to look at what they're offering. Most of them smile and wave. Oh, no. I'm not falling for it this time. I keep a good pace with Thane as he remains intent on finding a horse.

Finally, we arrive at a stable made of tin walls and worn wooden beams. A man with a massive, wide-brimmed hat sits in an enclosed booth built in front of it, chewing disgustingly on a mouthful of seeds.

When he catches sight of Thane, he spits to the side and sighs. "Shit. Not *you* again."

"Yes. *Me again*." Thane stops short of his booth, waiting for him to come out.

He's a short man, ruddy with a pot belly. His bones pop and crack as he climbs off the stool, wiping the back of his hand over his mouth to clear the seed shells. "What happened to your last horse?"

"Sold it."

"You don't get attached to anything, do you?" Big Hat asks, cracking a grin.

Thane doesn't smile. Instead, he gestures to the stables and says, "Best horse you have."

"That'll be a pretty coin," Big Hat replies.

Thane digs into his pocket, producing a handful of coins. He shoves them into Big Hat's hand and demands, "Horse. *Now*."

"All right, all right. Take it easy, killer." The man takes off after counting the coins and enters one of the stables with a chuckle.

Okay, first Chaun mentions blood on velvet tables and buried men, now Big Hat is calling him *killer*? I start to ask Thane what he means by that until someone else's voice overpowers mine.

"I know that's not who I think it is!" a booming voice calls from behind us.

I whirl around while Thane inhales and exhales slowly like he's been expecting this man but had hopes of dodging him.

"Garyn." Thane finally turns to face the person wearing a red vest and matching gambler hat. His skin is purplish-brown, and he has thick, silvery-white braids that stop at his shoulders. He wears a black eyepatch over his left eye, but his right eye is alarming. The pupil is large and seems to absorb the color of his iris.

People who have eyes like theirs do the nastiest kind of drugs. Kopa is the worst of them because it's created with beastial blood and makes mortals feel invincible, like they have speed, flight, or can climb walls, too. And maybe they can. I don't know for sure. Analla spoke about kopa all the time, but only to serve as a warning for me to never, *ever* do it.

That creepy eye of Garyn's swoops toward me. He flashes what I assume is meant to be a charming smile. I step back as Thane shifts forward, partially blocking me from Garyn's view.

"We're getting a horse and leaving," Thane tells him.

Garyn keeps that twisted grin plastered on his face, fixing his attention on Thane again. "What? No fight in you today?"

"No time," says Thane.

"Right, yeah." Garyn sniffs as Big Hat returns from the stables guiding a black horse with a silky ivory mane by the reins. "But see"—Garyn waves a finger—"I don't think I should just let you leave. Last time, you ripped through my tavern, and I lost eight good men. You disappear for weeks and now you're back, prancing through *my* territory and buying horses like you own the place."

Thane tilts his head. "Horses in Redclaw are the cheapest. Plus, I figured your people would need the coin after what happened during my last visit—you know, the one you all so eagerly keep bringing up in conversation?"

Garyn's smile vanishes, and he works his jaw, inching closer to us. I ball my hands into fists, and my nails bite into my palms as I back away. More men line up behind Garyn, each one more menacing than the next.

"Maliek's been looking for you. Did you know that?" Garyn runs his tongue over his yellow-stained teeth.

I don't miss the way Thane curls his hand into a tight fist at the mention of this Maliek.

Garyn notices as well and sneers. "So how about this," he says, waving that same annoying finger. "You pay me for destroying my tables and killing my men, and I *won't* tell Maliek I saw you here."

Thane's silence is deafening as he gives Garyn a lethal stare. Then he scans the men gathering behind Garyn. There has to be at least a dozen of them. Each one holds a weapon of some kind. Seeing the blades, axes, and hatchets twists my stomach into knots.

"Maybe you should just pay him," I suggest. Surely, he has enough coin for it. I've given him a full pouch—and if he doesn't, I have some to spare, too. Not many gold coins, but it's still something.

"Get on the horse," Thane orders me without taking his eyes off Garyn.

"What?"

"Get on the fucking horse, Quinlocke." Hearing him say my last name causes a spiral in my belly…and not a bad one, despite the knots of dread that are developing. It's good to know he remembers part of my name, at least.

I turn for the horse to do as I'm told, swinging a leg over its bare back. Only then do I realize Big Hat is no longer around.

Shit. That can't be good.

"Come on now, Valkor! Let's not make this harder than it needs to be!" Garyn bellows after a haughty laugh.

"It can be simple if you fuck off and let us walk through those gates with my horse," Thane shoots back.

"Without my retribution?" Garyn makes a *tsk tsk* noise. "Not happening and you know it. I suggest you cough up the coin now before you lose a few limbs and, if I'm lucky, an eye."

Thane squares his shoulders and deepens his defensive stance. "Let's be honest with ourselves, Garyn. We all know that after today, you'll be telling everyone you went blind because of me."

A shadow runs over Garyn's face, his skin tightening behind the eyepatch. "Well, if you want it that way, I hope you make it to the Crystal Realm, though one of Xaimur's hells seems more fitting for a fucked-up soul like yours." The men behind Garyn swarm me and Thane with tight grips around their weapons. Garyn snaps his fingers. "Kill him and bring that pretty girl to me."

"*What?*" I shriek. What in the shadows do I have to do with any of this?

I give Thane a death glare, waiting for him to do something. He doesn't budge.

Why is he just standing there? Why isn't he trying to get us out of here?

"Oh, Orvena." I grip the reins to guide the horse away from him, ready to gallop to the gates and take off because *fuck this*. I am not about to die because of some man's ego.

A battle cry erupts, and one of Garyn's henchmen rushes forward with an ax in the air, taking a swing at Thane. Thane dodges it with ease, and a dagger materializes in his hand. He stabs the man in the chest, twists him around to slice his throat, then kicks him into another man charging his way. He performs all of this in movements faster than I can blink.

I back away on the horse, searching for a way out. The only exit I can spot is the gates we snuck through. I start for them as more men swarm Thane, but someone yanks me backward by the rucksack before I can get anywhere and slams me to the ground.

The horse whinnies and wastes no time clomping away as the breath whooshes out of my lungs. I cough as a man appears above me with a hatchet in hand. He swings down, but I roll out of the way just in time and hop to my feet.

"Come on, pretty girl," he taunts, licking his lips. "I won't hurt you if you make this easy."

"Uh, Thane!" I call.

Just as quickly as I say his name, a dagger whizzes through the air and jams straight into hatchet man's temple. Well, damn. I guess he is worth the coin.

When the man drops to his knees, the dagger is magically snatched back out and returned to Thane. Blood dribbles from a hole in hatchet man's head before he collapses. If this had been performed during target practice and not on an actual mortal, I'd find it pretty damn impressive.

I put my attention on Thane again. He fights off every man using one hand to slice and stab and the other to blast incomers away with gold whorls. Each strike is done with perfect precision. Not a single slip or fall happens. No one can land a punch or even a finger on him. If a sword swings his way, he ducks or dodges it and then retaliates.

Honestly, he isn't even breaking a sweat. He makes it look easy with how relaxed he is, yet every blow is vicious and deadly. Every move practiced, premeditated.

Too good with his magic.

Too good with his swords and daggers. Not like The Divine soldiers but more like a natural killer. Like a...

He spins and blocks another attacker with his blade as he shoots a whorl of magic from his hand. I squint, unable to breathe as I watch the golden trails of his power dissipate, leaving behind black wisps in their wake.

It's now the reality of what I'm facing hits me like a ton of stone.

The way Thane effortlessly fights, swinging his blades in the air, decapitating and stabbing men through the heart. Using magical daggers for those he can't quite reach and then signaling them back just to finish them off.

When we first met at the Tilted Crystal, he struck fear into every heart.

He jumps off dangerously high roofs and lands without a sound.

Threatens to behead vicious skrellins.

Blood on velvet tables.

Men having to be buried because of *him*.
Take it easy, killer.
And the black shadows clinging to his magic.
Thane is no ordinary sorcerer wearing a mask and buffers.
He's a sorcerer conjuring darker magic to kill.
He's a shadow assassin.

Chapter 10

But how is that possible?

Sure, I've heard rumors about some of these elite killers still lingering around. I've heard stories about fights in the streets and how many became bloodbaths because of the assailants they called shadow assassins, who were far too impressive with their blades.

But the stories were hard to believe. Assassins who wielded black magic? They were once called Nightcarvers and were outlawed shortly after the war between Meriva and Ruvain centuries ago because of how lethal they were.

They first originated in the red sand kingdom of Quamira to protect the royals from wicked sea beastials able to walk on land. The only way to truly defeat the beastials was to conjure darker magic.

But then the Nightcarvers used their black magic to take control…all for destruction and power.

In an attempt to overthrow Ruvain's kingdom, the Nightcarvers killed the ruling King Murren. The crown prince managed to escape, traveled straight to Meriva, and as Ruvain's newly appointed king, he made a treaty with Meriva to end the war *if* they helped stop the Nightcarvers.

So both acting kings of Meriva and Ruvain made it law that sorcerers caught using black magic alongside combat in their kingdoms would be killed without trial.

With Quamira's aid, the Nightcarvers were caught one by one, given muting elixirs to tamp down their magic, and were all either beheaded or hanged.

That put an end to the dark sorcerer-assassin era...and made it abundantly clear that anyone else who tried to replicate that behavior would face the same fate.

And yet, here is Thane—just as destructive as the whispers and rumors.

The Divine soldiers have a certain code of conduct. They fight with specific trained techniques, and their skills are uniform, at best. I've gone on many tours of the Crystal Palace grounds and witnessed some of their training. None of it comes close to the tricks Thane is performing right now, and it's both remarkable and terrifying.

What I pay attention to most from Thane's magic are the black shadows trailing the gold streams after every blow. Each sorcerer has their own color-coded essence, but the use of white magic never comes with a trail of black.

Where the shadows did this man come from? And who am I really dealing with? If he is some kind of assassin, where does that leave me? A combination of dread and fear wraps around me like a snake and squeezes tight.

If I could capture him and turn him in, the queen would pay handsomely for it. There is a bounty on the head of any shadow assassin. That must be why Garyn tried to take him down. And whoever this Maliek person is, it must be why he's searching for Thane, too. They know all about his power or are at least suspicious of him and want to exchange him for coin.

Regardless, what I realize is that hiring Thane was a mistake.

I've *really* fucked up.

As the fighting and killing continues, I snatch up my rucksack and run toward the gate in a panic, dodging Garyn, who is too busy watching *more* of his men get slaughtered.

The shock of it all has my whole body feeling cold. I have to get out of here.

When I make it out, Chaun is still at the front gates, but he doesn't bother chasing me. Instead, he busts out laughing as he watches me run toward the forest that leads back to Meriva. It's almost like Chaun knew Thane would start a fight and is glad he doesn't have to be a part of it.

I stumble on an uneven patch of ground and stop for a moment to catch my breath before taking off in a full sprint again. Even though I've gotten farther away, relief is nowhere to be found. Will it ever be found again, actually? Thane knows my name. My face. Where I live. Where I work. Now that I know who and what he is, he might kill me just to tie up loose ends.

Bile rises up my throat, and it burns. I swallow it back down. *No time for throwing up, Zaira. You gotta hide.*

If anyone catches me with a possible shadow assassin, I'll be strung up right along with him. I mean, it's clear that Thane's a fighter.

Or defender?

A brute, if you will.

Anyone who wears buffers daily does so because they expect to be in brawls and altercations involving weapons. I know that.

But *this*?

No. There is no way I can be a part of this. I have to hide. Figure something else out—*anything* else.

I don't stop running until I make it to the dirt field just outside of Redclaw. I plant a hand on a tree trunk, sucking in gulps of air as I peer over my shoulder.

Then I hear something.

Rapid clomping.

Horse hooves beat into the ground, coming closer, growing louder by the second.

My heart plummets when I spot the line of people on horses galloping in my direction. I take off again, running full speed as my satchel slaps against my waist, and the straps of my rucksack dig into my shoulders. I kick up dirt, racking my brain to remember how to return to Meriva.

What was I even thinking following him into Redclaw? I must be losing it. That or I've gone full-blown delusional. Trusting a stranger with swords and too many daggers to help me cross the world. Did I really think this was a good idea?

Under so much duress, it's nearly impossible to retrace my steps.

The galloping beats through me, rattling my bones.

I run harder.

Faster.

But it's not enough.

In one smooth movement, I'm swept off the ground in a magical grip. I scream as I realize Thane is the culprit. He's riding the black-and-ivory horse mere feet behind me. Just as quickly as I was picked up, I'm placed down on the horse's back and planted firmly behind him.

"Orvena help me!" I cry, locking my arms around Thane's middle so I won't bounce off the horse and fall to my death. I mean, really. I've made it this far. It would be anticlimactic to die in a mere horse-riding accident.

I glance behind us, and there are people chasing us. Seven of Garyn's men ride horses, too, weapons raised and teeth bared.

"Look out!" I yell.

I duck as one of them rides to our side and swipes at Thane's head with an ax. Thane ducks in time and throws up a hand, sending the man flying off his horse with a strong burst of gold.

Another appears, and Thane conjures a dagger, flicking with a flourish of his wrist and stabbing it into the man's forehead. I gasp as I watch blood gush around the blade. Then Thane's magic yanks it out and returns it to him. The man falls off his horse and slams to the ground.

"Oh, gods. I'm gonna be sick," I groan.

"Throw up on me, and I'll shove you off this horse," Thane threatens over his shoulder.

One by one, Thane finishes them off.

When the last man standing quite literally loses his head, we come to a halt and survey the damage. We've left nothing but innocent horses wandering an open field among the littered remains of dead riders. Not an image I ever thought I'd see and surely not one I'll ever get out of my head.

The horse beneath me grunts as Thane whips the reins.

We ride off, leaving destruction in our wake.

It's not until we reach the bridge outside Meriva that we come to a full stop. I immediately climb off our steed and stagger away, bile rising in my throat. Eventually, I can't hold it in anymore. I turn and vomit on a pile of silver rocks. Farewell to the bread with raspberry spread I had for breakfast.

I spit the acidic taste out of my mouth as Thane swings a leg over the horse and hops to the ground. "You ran the wrong way." His tone is much too calm for my liking right now.

I swipe the arm of my tunic over my mouth while holding up my other hand, waving him off. "You need to stay away from me!"

He stops and crosses his arms over his chest. "So you *purposely* ran the wrong way?"

"Yes!" I shout. "I was trying to get away from *you*!"

He looks me over, mildly confused.

"What was that?"

"I was protecting you."

"*That* back there? That was a *massacre*!"

"Is that not what you paid me for?" he asks, genuinely bewildered.

"No!" I run my fingers through my hair, only for them to get tangled in the curls, which frustrates me further. "Don't tell me you're what I think you are." I pant raggedly as I drop my arms. "There's no way those rumors are true. It's illegal for your kind to exist!"

Thane moves closer—so close I can feel the heat radiating from his massive body. "What is it you think I am, Quinlocke?" His voice is an ominous warning as he searches my face, daring me to say it.

"There has only been one group of people known to fight like you do, but they were outlawed a very long time ago, way before you were ever even born. I've heard stories that they're still around but…you're *young*," I breathe. "You can't be older than, what? Your twenty-fourth or twenty-fifth year? So how do you know how to fight like that?"

"Twenty-fourth," he confirms. "And how do *you* think I know how to fight like that?"

I take a second to form the words.

"You're a shadow assassin," I whisper, like there are other people around who might hear. "A sorcerer-assassin…like the Nightcarvers in the past. Tell me I'm wrong. Tell me you're just a person who wields magic and is unbelievably good with a sword. Tell me the black shadows in your magic were all my imagination."

I search for any tells I can make out, but with his mask in the way, it's tricky. His eyes, though…they harden at the nearly forbidden words.

Sorcerer.

Nightcarver.

Shadow assassin.

"I asked if you were sure about this before we left. You said yes. Should've asked your questions then." He yanks his mask down, revealing scars that seem much more sinister now. "*This* is what you paid for." He jabs his thumb to his chest. "*This* is what you get."

"So it's true?" I ask.

He shakes his head, working his jaw. "The less we talk about it, the better, Quinlocke."

"I—I just don't understand—"

"There's nothing to understand," he counters. "You paid me for a service and I'm doing my part, so just drop it and come on. We need to make it over the bridge before nightfall."

"I don't know if I can do this." My mouth goes so dry that when I swallow, the spit goes down rough. "There are already people coming after you, and if more people see you fighting like that, they'll come for you, too. Do you know how much the queen pays in bounty for people like you?"

"I don't care." He mounts the horse, facing forward. "Get on."

"No. Are you out of your mind?" I protest. "I'm not going anywhere with you! I'll just have to find another way." I twist around, ready to storm back to Meriva and forget all about this murderous man. Being around him any longer will get me killed.

"You either get on, or your sister dies," he says matter-of-factly. I freeze in my tracks. "There is no one else out there with skills like mine who will agree to help you. You'll never make it through The Shallows alone, and without a prosperity stone, you will never break that curse. You go back now, and you might as well start picking out flowers for her grave."

Balling my fists, I twist around as tears well in my eyes. "Fuck you!"

I can't believe it, but the asshole actually smirks. I want to slap it right off his face.

"You're acting like I can't go back and report you to the queen *right now*," I shoot at him.

The smirk vanishes. With a growl, he's off the horse and standing in front of me, towering above like a ruthless giant. Seething, he grips my face between his thumb and forefinger. His hold isn't tight, but it's firm, like he wants to make sure I look nowhere else but at him. He breathes as hard as a bull, his amber gaze penetrating mine.

"You could report me, but you won't," he rasps. "I just saved your life and am risking everything so I can help *you* get across the fucking world to reach a place hardly any man has survived." His grip tightens a bit more, his face mere inches from mine. My heart bangs chaotically in my rib cage. "You turn me in, and you'll never see your sister again. Do you understand that? Without *my* help, your sister will *die*."

I'm fuming now, my fists clenching tighter.

"Shove those fears aside, Quinlocke, because this is happening whether you like it or not." He studies my eyes, my nose, my mouth, his breath grazing my skin as my breathing shallows. "I don't take you for a quitter, so I expect you to follow rule number two and get your ass on that horse before Seferin destroys everything you have left."

My fists slowly stop clenching with the sudden realization of how much truth rings in his words about Seferin and with how close we are. My chest brushes against him. His presence is powerful, and his fingers on my face make me hyperaware of that. I stupidly look from his eyes to his mouth.

He does the same.

But just as quickly, he releases my face and steps back. I jerk myself away from him and widen the distance between us by stepping back, too. Jaw ticking, he awaits my next move, his irises sparking with warning.

I have two options to choose between.

Option one: report him to the queen, possibly get paid a shit ton of coins, but lose my sister in the process or...

Option two: swallow my good morals, suck it up, stick with him, and save my sister's life.

I chew on my bottom lip so hard I can feel my teeth piercing the flesh inside of it. I taste blood as I adjust the strap of my rucksack.

I hate admitting it, but he's right. I'm not a damn quitter. But I'm also not delusional enough to think sticking with a killer like *him* is even remotely okay. This goes against everything I stand for. I can be killed just for associating with him.

But this is about more than me and my perception of right and wrong. It's about my sister's very survival. I can't make it to Elphar alone, and if I fail, my only remaining family will die.

I stare at the tree line as the horse huffs next to me. The urge to climb on, dig my heels in, and gallop away hits hard, but I push it down. I'm not a coward, but I *am* scared. This isn't a case of choosing the lesser of two evils. It's knowingly choosing the greater evil for the greater good.

I shoot a glance at Thane, who is scanning for danger while impatiently waiting for my decision.

It's decided. From this point forward, there's no turning back. I'm going to save Analla or die trying. And my best hope—no, my *only* hope is this man. So I climb onto the horse's back and stiffen my spine as I accept my fate.

Thane evidently senses my resolve because he mounts the horse and sits behind me, his broad chest grazing my back. He lets out a deep sigh and chills run over the nape of my neck. Goose bumps prickle my skin, despite my fury.

Why in the shadows is my body reacting to him? I hate him for what just happened. Hate him for leaving me no choice. Damn it, I hated him from the moment he uttered "fuck off" to me.

Yet, with his chest against my back, his warm thighs wrapped around mine, and his arms reaching past me to control the reins, my heart can't help but beat a little faster.

Some part of me deep down is intrigued by this man—has been since I first laid eyes on him…and that does *not* sit well with me one bit.

Chapter 11

Being outside of Meriva feels odd. I've never left the kingdom since moving there as a child. I never had any reason to, seeing as I had everything I needed.

The gravity of that realization weighs on me as I stand on the other side of the Everwalk. I stare at the towering pillars on the other side of the stone road that are keeping the bridge intact. Fog clouds the area, thick enough to drown the lanterns in murky light.

The Everwalk has been around for ages—famous for its reliability and safety, and commonly used by traveling peddlers in mule-drawn wagons and royals in carriages who require safe passage to Meriva by land.

Many people pass Thane and me as we carry on. None bother us or toss suspicious gazes. Eventually, my shoulders loosen and my breathing relaxes, despite Thane's nearness—or maybe because of it, which would be ridiculous. He's a menace. It shouldn't be possible to feel safe around him.

Thane hardly speaks, and for once, neither do I. All I can think about is the fact that this murderous man is my only saving grace.

If my mother could see me now, she'd laugh and say, *"You sure know how to muck things up, Zaira."*

I always do, even when it isn't intentional. I muck shit up.

Once over the bridge, I breathe a sigh of relief that there weren't any threats or interruptions along the way.

"This way." On foot, Thane leads the horse away from the bridge, veering toward a forest instead of taking the cobblestone path lined with more lanterns. I'm certain this path leads to the capital city of Ruvain Kingdom. "We can't continue traveling at night in this area. We'll have to find a place to wait until morning."

I look at him in disbelief. It took us nearly four hours to cross the bridge. We took two short breaks—one so Thane could summon water from the river to hydrate the horse, and another so we could eat. I sat against the wall of the bridge and ate a bit of the bread from Ellanoch while Thane snacked on strips of dried meat. Both of us avoided looking at each other.

I have to see this through. No going back now. Stick with the shadow assassin. Get the stone. Save Analla. That's the plan, though a part of me despises every step I take with him.

This mission is one I can't butcher, and if that means working with an outlaw to save her life, I'd do it again and again. That much became clear to me on our quiet trek on the bridge.

I catch up to Thane as he nears the edge of the forest, where bushy-topped trees are lined up and built like towers. Though gray light still lingers in the sky, it's dark between the gaps of the tree trunks.

"We're not going in *there*, are we?" I point to the ominous woods.

"Yes. So stay close." He clicks his tongue at the horse and ambles forward. Nervously, I watch him disappear into the darkness for a beat before rushing in after him. I can hardly see him or the horse—that's until a glowing gold orb appears above his head and illuminates our surroundings.

"Thank you." I sigh, catching up to him.

He looks at me skeptically. "This won't last if you're scared of the dark, you know?"

"I'm not scared of the dark," I retort. "Light is necessary to see where I—or any mortal—is going. Besides, it's not like I could pack a lantern in my small-ass rucksack."

"Yeah, yeah. Just keep your voice down."

"Why?" I ask, lowering my voice.

Thane shakes his head. "The wilder beastials and other dangerous creatures wander through here sometimes, and believe me, they're much worse than skrellins or any of those men we encountered in Redclaw."

My pulse quickens as I peer into the darkness that surrounds us. "How much worse?" I whisper.

"'Skin you, eat your flesh, and then behead you' kind of worse." Of course his tone is nonchalant.

I clamp my mouth shut and place a hand on the horse. Not that the horse can protect me, but it's nice feeling a warm body next to mine. The temperature is dropping the deeper we walk into the forest. Every rustle of leaves and snap of a twig has me flinching.

Thane, however, seems completely unbothered, so I think it's safe to assume I'm being paranoid. That, or he simply doesn't care if something comes out of nowhere to snatch me away. He'll have coins, a pretty new horse, and one less mortal to deal with.

Relief washes over me when we reach a small clearing in the forest where the sky becomes clearer through a gap in the treetops above. He guides us toward a four-story brick building half swallowed in ivy and moss with shattered windows on every floor. It's clearly abandoned and likely has been for years, yet Thane keeps walking toward it.

He stops next to a tree, securing the horse's reins to the trunk of it. Then he drops his rucksack on the ground and says, "Wait here."

"What?" I ask, alarmed. "I'm not standing out here by myself."

"You have the horse. You'll be fine. I need to check inside, make sure no one is already camping here."

I draw in a ragged breath as he enters the building that, mind you, has no door. The darkness consumes him in one gulp. My heart begins beating twice as hard as a chill bites at my skin.

I keep watch.

Wrapping my arms around myself, I rub my hands up and down to stay warm while the horse nibbles grass. "That guy is one hundred percent unhinged," I murmur to the horse. She keeps grazing, and I rub her side, soothed by her calmness and warmth. It placates me enough until Thane returns.

I perk up. "Is it clear?"

"Is now."

A slow frown takes over my face as I look from him to the leaning building. Hesitant, I ask, "Did you just…?" I make a slicing motion across my throat with my index finger.

He snatches up his rucksack. "There were rats inside. I got rid of them. Or would you have preferred I leave them so they could eat you alive, oh sweet one?"

Irritation courses through me. "Why are you always making threats about being eaten alive?"

"Because it shuts you up."

I narrow my eyes and throw my middle finger at him.

Ignoring me, he removes the horse from the tree and circles the building. I follow, watching as he places her beneath an awning with a thick bundle of bushes surrounding it. No one can see her from here if they pass by.

He digs into his rucksack, retrieving two apples and feeding them to her. As she eats, he strokes the side of her head, and I swear I see his mouth twitch, like he wants to smile.

Wow. It's nice to see he actually cares about *something*...whether he wants people to know it or not.

"We should name her." I step closer, stroking her silky mane.

"I don't name my horses."

"Because what Big Hat said is true?"

He frowns. *"Who?"*

"Big Hat. The one who sold you the horse. He said you don't attach yourself to anything, which makes it abundantly clear to me that you have commitment issues."

"Could be that, or maybe it's because I know the horse might die during our journey and I'm sparing my feelings and hers."

I gasp. "Wait. You have feelings?"

He sighs, not at all amused by my little joke.

"She won't die." I give my head a confident shake. "But if you won't name her, I will." I study her in the dark, her glossy black coat and the beautiful ivory mane and tail. Her mane has a shimmer to it.

"Pearl," I say, finally. Her mane reminds me of the color of pearls.

Thane closes his eyes and rubs his forehead.

"Yeah. I'll name her Pearl. To replace the one I lost."

"Don't get too attached," he mutters, giving me his back. "You might lose this one, too."

"Don't listen to him, Pearl." I run a palm along her jaw, and she chuffs like she, too, is annoyed with his remark. "He's just a grumpy asshole."

Thane finds a back door and kicks it open, disappearing inside again.

After giving Pearl two more love pats, I trail Thane as he sends up another orb of light to illuminate the interior of the building. The room is empty, minus a few broken chairs and random pieces of furniture spread throughout. Some objects are covered with dingy white cloths. The hearth is full of soot and ash, and cobwebs drape the walls. There's also a mildew smell mixed with what is probably the scent of rodent pee.

Just lovely.

He rounds a corner and starts to climb the stairs. They creak under our weight, and I swear they're about to splinter in half with how soggy the wood is. One look up reveals a massive hole in the ceiling. When we reach the third level, Thane pushes one of the doors open and gestures inside the empty room.

It isn't any cleaner than downstairs, but at least there aren't any cobwebs or disgusting smells assaulting my nostrils. A single window is built into the north wall. A hearth is on my right, and Thane stands in front of it, rubbing his right thumb across the pads of all his fingers to conjure a ball of fire in his palm. Bending down, he tosses the fire into the hearth, and the flames swell.

"You can stay in here," he says, stepping out of the room.

"Oh. Where will you be?"

He points at the door next to mine.

"You swear you won't leave?"

"Are you serious?"

I shrug because how in the shadows am I supposed to know if he'll stay or leave? For all I know, he's keeping me holed up in here so he can lessen my chances of survival and run off with the coins I paid him.

When I don't budge, he releases a tired sigh. "You paid me for a service, and I'm seeing it through. Doesn't matter what you think about me being—" He clamps his mouth shut. *A shadow assassin*, I'm sure he was going to say. "Doesn't matter what you think about my *lifestyle*. I'm getting you to that temple, so just relax and get some rest. We'll pick up first thing in the morning."

"Okay." That's slightly reassuring. *Slightly.* I still don't trust him. He starts to walk away, but I hold up a hand. "Actually—wait."

He halts mid-step and turns to me.

"I know this is a lot to ask, but do you think we can, like, *not* be in separate rooms?"

His brow furrows as he looks at me like I've lost my mind. Maybe I have. It's been a long day.

"It's just that we're so close to Ruvain, and this is unknown territory for me. I won't really be able to sleep if I'm in this room by myself. We don't have to talk—and I'll be on the opposite side, as far away from you as possible. You can even sleep closer to the fire if you want so you can stay all warm and cozy."

He sweeps his eyes around the room that's already swimming with comforting heat.

"Come on," I tease, smiling. "You know you want to."

"I really don't." He draws in a reluctant breath and then exhales, eyes closed, practicing that patience again. "Fine. Whatever gets you to relax."

I ignore the relief and mini wave of excitement coursing through me. Excitement is the last thing I should feel about us sleeping in the same room. But if I wake up and he has stuck around, does that mean I'll be able to trust his word a bit more?

I suppose we'll see.

Thane ambles in and closes the door.

Dropping my rucksack, I lower into a squat and dig through it. I pull out a quilt as well as a shawl. As I begin spreading the quilt out on the side of the room farthest from the fire, Thane clears his throat.

"Take the spot near the fire," he insists.

I look from the flames to him. "Are you sure? I don't mind being over here…"

He gestures to the area with a simple nod.

I collect my things and spread the quilt out next to the wall where I can feel the heat. I now realize my teeth are chattering. I wonder if he's noticed, and that's why he's offered me the spot.

That's…*nice* of him.

Oddly, he doesn't seem to be cold at all.

I settle onto the quilt. It smells like Analla's perfume—sweet florals and lavender. I may or may not have taken it out of her room because I didn't want to dirty mine. Who cares? If I save her life, she'll owe me more than a pleasantly scented quilt.

I remove my bodice, tuck it under my head, and lie down while Thane takes up the corner on the other side of the room across from the window. A few silent seconds tick by as I listen to the fire roar. I'm getting warm, but not warm enough. I wrap the quilt tighter around me just as the flames in the hearth grow bigger and brighter.

I shift my focus to Thane, whose eyes flash gold while staring at the fire, then dim softly.

"Thanks," I whisper.

He bends his legs and rest his elbows on his knees, peering out the only window in the room.

"So...*Valkor*?" I adjust my head to see him fully. "Is that your first or last name?"

He remains quiet.

"How did you even get into the whole sorcerer-assassin thing anyway? I keep thinking about it, and unless there's a super-secret society lingering around, it doesn't make sense. You know people can take one look at you in action and report you based on suspicions, right? Are you not worried about that?"

Again, nothing.

"Who is Maliek? Is he a shadow assassin, too? Or just someone wanting to collect a bounty?"

That garners me a side-eye, but still, his mouth remains shut.

"Okay, well what about Seferin?" I prod.

His jaw steels.

"When I said his name at the Tilted Crystal, you reacted to it. You seemed to get angry about it, so I assume you don't like him much, either—especially if you're willing to risk your life to help me get a stone. Is this going to be one big *fuck you* to him once we get it and save Analla?"

"I thought you said we *didn't* have to talk," he says in an annoyingly grumbly voice that makes my stomach do all sorts of weird rolls and flips.

"If we're traveling together, it's only right that I know *something* about you, Thane. Or is it Valkor? I should at least know which one is your real name."

He grinds his teeth. "You're insufferable."

"And you act like a withered dick."

That earns me a mouth twitch, like he wants to laugh but won't dare give me the satisfaction. "If I tell you my name, will you stop asking questions and go to sleep?"

"I'll leave that up to Orvena. Maybe I will. Maybe I won't."

Sighing, he stretches his legs out and loosely folds his arms over his chest. "My name is Thane Valkor, but if you've been put on my shitlist, you'll only refer to me as Valkor. You aren't on that list *yet*, but keep talking and you will be."

"Okay, okay. Sheesh." I stifle a laugh. "So grouchy." My shoulders relax when I finally stop shivering. My eyelids droop as the warmth of the fire wraps around me like a second blanket.

"Tomorrow's journey will be much harder than today's," Thane says after a silent minute or two.

"Because we're going into Ruvain territory now?" I take my spectacles off and place them next to my head.

"Exactly."

Yes. The land is littered with thieves, cons, *more* murderers, and of course, the flesh-eating beastials living in their forests. And that's only the tip of the iceberg. Though some of the beastials live in the wild, there are feral beasts and monsters throughout Thelanor who are born only as that, and most of them lurk along Ruvain's borders.

They're not like the beastials that live among the mortals, sorcerers, and charmers. They are simply animals who understand we are the prey, and they are the predators.

Xaimur, the god of corruption, made some of the beasts and monsters to try and outnumber Orvena's creations. Orvena was the goddess who created all living things in Thelanor. She wanted her creations to be peaceful and to roam freely and happily. She even provided some of us with magical abilities, hence the sorcerers.

To protect us all from Xaimur's wrath, she trapped him in one of his darkest, lowest hells and sacrificed her physical form to grace all of Thelanor with her essence. Yes, monsters and beasts still linger, but her creations prosper and outnumber his immensely.

You'd have to visit some of the wickedest places and the darkest pits of the forests to encounter such monsters, but the distance never stops some of them from coming closer to inhabited lands if they're hungry enough.

Many people go missing or are attacked and eaten on the odd night, which makes being in this old building with no locks a bit distressing. Who knows what's lurking out there right now, sniffing us out.

"The fire won't burn all night." Thane's voice sucks me out of my thoughts. He's been quiet for so long, I almost forgot he was there. "I don't want anyone noticing the light."

"Yeah. I understand. Thanks for warming us up a bit." I close my eyes, reminding myself that if anything does try and attack us, Thane will handle it. He's here to protect me...

Or rob me, kill me, and leave me in this building to rot.

I guess I'll find out.

Chapter 12

"Make a peep and I'll kill you."

My heartbeat thunders rapidly in my ears as a man crouches above me. One of his hands is clapped over my mouth while the edge of a blade is pressed into my throat with his other hand. He pushes it deeper to shush me when I whimper.

Without my spectacles on and the room being half bathed in morning light, his features are a blur—that is until he leans in closer and reveals warm ochre skin behind a slightly turned-up nose, dark-brown eyes, bushy eyebrows, and hair styled in individual plaits.

"Do you understand?" he asks.

I nod behind his hand as my eyes burn with tears. So many thoughts run through my head: *Who is this man? Where is Thane? Oh gods. Is this a setup? I knew I shouldn't have trusted him!*

"I'm just gonna rummage through that cute little rucksack and lady bag you have over there," he says, gesturing with the hand holding the knife to my bags in the corner. "Well, actually, I'm not gonna do it. Zephra is."

My brows dip with confusion. *Who?*

As the thought erupts, a creature appears on the man's shoulder with the body and wings of a miniature dragon. Its pink fur looks as soft as a bunny's with the pattern of dragon scales. Its nose resembles a bunny's as well, while pointed ears sprout from either side of its head. Its amber eyes are too big for its face...but in an adorable way.

"Zephra, girl, check her bags for me, will ya? See what you can find." The man gestures to my bags, and his little creature hops off his shoulder to skitter toward them.

With her little paws, Zephra opens my rucksack, then buries her head inside. When Zephra whips out one of the half-eaten loaves of bread I got from Ellanoch, she joyously chitters.

"No—no, Zephra. You already ate!" the man scolds with exasperation. "You devoured a whole roasted turkey and didn't bother saving a bit of it for me. Let's not be greedy. Come on, I need you to remember your job. Coins, jewelry, yeah? Are there any in there?"

Zephra chitters again, buries her head inside, then comes back out with the strings of a pouch in her mouth.

"That's it! Good girl!" the man praises as she hurries to him, dropping the pouch into his palm. She crawls to his shoulder again and stares at me briefly before swiping the backs of her paws over her snout.

"Don't move. Got it?" the man advises.

I bob my head. Like I'll dare move. I can't even see clearly enough to know where to run.

He removes his hand from my mouth to open the pouch and dump the coins into his palm.

"Ah, look at that, Zephra. We'll be eating good for at least a week with this."

I reach for my spectacles, and the man points his blade at me.

"You can take it all," I tell him, throwing my hands up. "I don't care. Just take it."

His brows pucker. "Interesting. I expected more of a fight from you."

"Yeah, well, I'm not a fighter."

"That's strange coming from a person camping out near Ruvain." He dumps the coins back into the pouch. "You know what you're doing is dangerous, don't you? I mean, I literally walked right up the stairs and saw you sleeping like a sweet little princess. Almost didn't want to startle you because you looked so precious but, well...the coin calls." He shakes the pouch, giving the coins a light *clink clink* with a mischievous smile. "Someone like you, out here all alone, is not smart, I gotta tell ya. If I were anyone else, I'd have done—"

The man's words come to an abrupt stop as the door of the room flies open and Thane appears. With his sword in hand, Thane rushes the man, who scrambles to get up, and slams him into the wall, pressing the edge of the blade to his throat. Zephra flies off and blows a small gust of fire at Thane, who deflects it with an invisible shield before wrapping her in a gold bubble.

"Hold on!" the stranger yells, tossing his hands in the air.

Thane's eyes widen, and the blade at the man's neck slacks as he studies his features. "Are you seri— *Algar*?"

Algar?

The man cocks his head, confused, until Thane steps back and pulls his mask down. When Algar sees his whole face, his eyes light up.

"By the Crystal, I don't believe it! Thane Valkor? Is that really you?"

"Yes, it's me," Thane retorts, sheathing his sword. "What the shadows are you doing in here? I almost killed you."

Okay. What is happening? I hold my breath as I watch this strange reunion unfold.

"Where were you?" My voice comes out shrill, nearly hysterical.

"I was finding water for the horse. I was only gone for a few minutes." Thane points a finger at Algar. "Were you spying on me?"

"Well, yes. I couldn't tell who you were with the mask and all. And look at you! There was no way I was about to take a man your size down on my own. I wanted to see if you'd left anything behind, and it turns out you did. A whole *woman*."

"Give the *whole woman* her coins back." Thane huffs.

"Oh, right." Algar shoots me an apologetic grin as he tosses the pouch my way. I scramble to catch it. "My apologies if I scared you, princess. If I'd known such a pretty lady was with *this* twit, I wouldn't have tried to rob you."

"It's fine?" I look from him to Thane, positively baffled by what's happening.

Algar marvels at the sight of Thane.

"I can't believe it's you, my friend!" Algar releases a hearty laugh. "Holy Orvena. You've gotten taller, yeah?"

"Who is this, Thane? How do you know him?" I ask.

"Old friend," Thane answers, raising an eyebrow at Algar.

"Old friend? Please," Algar scoffs. "We're practically family! We go *way* back. To wee little children whose heads used to be too big for our bodies."

Thane sighs. "You're still thieving, I see."

"More like *thriving*," Algar replies, puffing out his chest.

Thane glances at Zephra, who is snarling in her bubble with her claws up. She slashes at the bubble, but it doesn't budge. "What in the shadows are you doing with *that* thing?"

"Oh, Zephra? She's my partner. Assists me in the *thieving*, as you like to call it. Set her free, though, yeah? She *hates* being trapped."

Thane makes a throaty noise of disapproval and waves his hand, removing the bubble. Algar reaches for Zephra, and she hurries to him, climbing up his arm until she's settled on his shoulder.

"Don't those things carry diseases?" Thane looks from him to the pink creature.

"Not my Zephra," Algar says. "I found her in some bone merchant's shop. He was going to kill her and drain her blood, sell it to the beastials."

"Hm." Thane puts his attention on me. "All right, grab your things. Let's go."

"Wait—now hold on," Algar calls as I collect my quilt, shawl, and rucksack. "Aren't you going to tell me what you're doing? Or where you've been for the last couple of years?"

We follow Thane down the wet, creaky stairs and out of the building and don't stop until we're close to the awning where Pearl is tied up. While we walk, I notice a limp in Algar's step.

"I'm sorry." I throw up a hand to pause the situation as the sun warms my skin. "Algar, how did you even notice us?"

"Well, that's a story, isn't it? I was on my way to Meriva—figured I'd try my hand at the gambling tables for some coin. Gotta feed Zephra and all. Right, girl?" He gives her furry chest a scratch, and she squeaks. "Anyway, I passed by here and heard the horse. Figured whoever was hiding away in a building this shit and staying so close to Ruvain was asking to be robbed—that, or they have something to hide." He shrugs. "If it wasn't me, it'd have been someone else. Best for both of you that I was around, huh?"

Thane shakes his head as he tosses his cloak on. "Last I heard, you were locked away in one of Ruvain's prisons for cheating their prince out of his coins."

"Um, two things. One: that was nearly three years ago. Two: their evil little prince is full of himself so, in my opinion, he was asking for it. And as you can see"—he raises both of his hands in the air—"I broke out."

"Broke out?" Thane arches a brow. "From a *Ruvain* prison?"

"It's easier than you think when you're fooling around with one of the lady guards—especially one who *doesn't* make you take your assigned muting elixir." Algar winks at me.

"Muting elixir?" I whisper to myself. I'm pretty sure those are only used for sorcerers and charmers to dim their magic. Most elixirs are taken orally, and if Algar was in prison, they probably had a lineup and forced the prisoners who held magic to take it.

Other times, if one wants to be sneaky about it and overpower a person with magic, they can douse an object in the elixir and offer it to them. A necklace, a stone, a cuff—anything, really. As long as the object touches their skin, it's effective for several hours. The downfall is that it has to be used the same day it's doused.

All of this leads me to wonder…is Algar a sorcerer, too?

"You didn't break out," Thane says. "That's never been done before—not without a person getting caught."

"Okay…you're right. I did my time. But I *almost* did." Algar scratches the top of his head. "Didn't quite work out, though."

"Right. Well, I'm glad to see you're still alive." Thane's voice drips with sarcasm as he tosses his rucksack over his shoulder while walking my way. He requests my bag, too.

"It's not like you to travel with someone, Thane." Algar watches as I hand my bag over. "Especially a woman. Is there something I should know?" He looks from Thane to me, waggling his eyebrows and grinning.

"It's not what you're thinking," Thane assures him.

"So you're *not* boning this pretty lady?"

My jaw drops.

Thane stops dead in his tracks. "No."

"Can I?" Algar asks, trailing after him, limping.

"It'd be nice if you ask me what I want," I interject.

But there's no need for me to bother because Thane lifts a hand and flicks his wrist. The smile slips from Algar's face as he loses his footing and lands on his side with a heavy thud. Zephra flies up, flapping her wings before she hits the ground. As she stares down at him, I swear the noise she makes is similar to a laugh.

"Must mean you want her, then." Algar grunts, propping himself up on his elbows with the biggest shit-eating grin I've ever seen. My lips twist as I hold back a smile.

I watch as Algar struggles to stand. "Here, let me help you." I grab his hand, and he rises, but not without hobbling to his left a bit.

"How sweet. I didn't catch your name, princess," he says, dusting himself off.

"I'm Zaira."

"Zaira. Gorgeous name. Tell me, Zaira, what in Xaimur's hells are you doing with *this* xerven?" He jerks a thumb at Thane, who is approaching Pearl. I can't help laughing at that remark.

"He's, um…assisting me. On an important journey."

"One that doesn't concern you," Thane tosses in. "Quinlocke, let's go. The sooner we move, the better."

As Thane ties our packs to Pearl's saddle, Algar staggers toward him. "A journey where?" he asks, ignoring Thane's impoliteness.

Thane shoots me a look of warning before focusing on Algar again.

"Elphar," I answer.

Algar's eyebrows dip as he looks between us. "The temple? In *The Shallows*?"

"Yep," I confirm. "That one."

Algar stares at me incredulously, as if waiting for me to say something else. When I don't, he limps toward Thane. "Have you lost your rocks or what? There's no way you're making it to Elphar."

Thane unties and guides Pearl away from the tree. "Please indulge me as to why I can't."

"I can give you a million reasons, but a major one is that you'll get killed before you can ever set foot on that bloody island."

"Wait." I frown, and Algar turns back, his plaits flying over his shoulder. "What island? What are you talking about?"

"Oh. Do you not know, princess? The Shallows separated from the mainlands four years ago. Some of the maps still show it connected to Thelanor, but it isn't anymore, and if you ask me, that's a good thing."

"Oh," I mumble, defeat settling in my gut.

"Most people who go there die. *Literally*," Algar says.

"There's something there that we need," Thane informs him. "Doesn't matter what you say, you can't convince us to not go."

There's a long pause.

I put my attention on Algar, whose eyes lower to the ground, as if he's thinking something through. Then he looks up and says, "Fine. I won't try to stop you. But I *am* coming with you." Algar puffs his chest. To enhance the theatrics, Zephra lands on his shoulder, and her pastel fur catches the sunlight as her ears twitch.

Thane looks his friend up and down as he pulls on a pair of gauntlets. "No, you're not. You'll only slow us down."

"I beg your finest pardon? Just because I have a limp doesn't mean I'm slow. You know what I can do." In a flash, Algar disappears from my side just to appear again on the other side of Pearl.

I gasp when he waves at me.

"You can teleport," I breathe.

Thane provides the slowest eye roll ever.

"A charmer's trick." Algar winks yet again. "Took me years to master." That explains the lady guard giving him muting elixirs in prison.

"Why would you put your life on the line by going with us to The Shallows?" Thane demands.

"Everyone knows there are treasures in and around Elphar that are enough to make a man and his next five generations rich. With even a handful of it, I'll be set for life."

"That sounds desperate." Thane cocks a suspicious eyebrow. "What kind of trouble are you in?"

"None at all!" Algar counters, but I notice the lilt in his voice. "Well, I do owe a few debts, and one of them I do have to pay within the next two weeks, or I'll be thrown into prison again, but other than that, I'm all good." He flashes a confident smile.

Thane sighs. After a few seconds, he says, "You'll get yourself killed, Algar."

"Let me worry about that."

Thane shakes his head. "If you die, I refuse to live with the guilt of your blood on my hands."

Algar gives him an almost devious smile. "Of course not, old friend. My blood, my fate. So, what do you say? May I join you on this quest of death?"

Thane grips Pearl's reins and guides her farther away. "It's your life."

"Hold on. Where are you going?" Algar calls.

"Around the perimeter of Ruvain. She doesn't have papers to pass, and a woman can't just waltz through."

"Hmm. Good point. Those Ruvain bastards." Algar scratches his chin.

"Hey, what do you mean?" I'm annoyed I don't understand what they're talking about.

"They get a whiff of a new woman's scent, and they're like hounds," Algar clarifies. "They'll sniff you out, tie you up, and have their way with you. They're ruthless bastards."

My throat thickens with dread.

"Regardless, going around the perimeter will take far too long," Algar goes on, marching toward Thane. "I assume you're trying to reach Gadonia, and lucky for you, I know a quicker route."

Thane comes to a stop. "Is it a *safe* route?"

Another one of those mischievous smiles sweeps across his face. "Define safe."

Zephra makes that laughing noise again. Only this time it sounds like an evil little cackle.

I have a bad feeling about this.

Chapter 13

"You're a fool, Algar." Thane grimaces as he peers through a gap in a thick wall of bushes.

I look, too, taking note of the dark stone streets and thousands of shacks and houses. At the far end of the street nearest to the wall is the king of Ruvain's castle, made of black marble with a cracked gray sundial attached. The tips of the castle stretch high, like thick spears ready to murder anything flying past.

While Meriva has light and hope, Ruvain is bathed in gloom and misery.

"How is this route any safer?" Thane demands, whipping around to face Algar, who is on the other side of me.

"Trust me, it is," Algar returns with a confident tone. "All we have to do is go behind that long row of buildings there, past the pillars, and make it to the tunnels. It's a little gross down there, and it may take a while, but it'll lead us to the other side of Ruvain's perimeter, and we'll be in Gadonia in no time. That way, no one is checking for passes, and pretty women aren't getting kidnapped, raped, and killed."

I groan. "Can you *please* stop saying stuff like that?"

"Sorry—but it's true."

Oh my Orvena.

"And what about the guards, wiseass?" Thane gestures to the numerous men patrolling the streets in onyx armor and helmets.

They're built like giants, and none of them look kind enough to let outsiders simply *pass* through their kingdom.

I know it for a fact when a feathery beastial runs through the street and one of the guards stops him with a solid hand to his chest. The guard sticks out a palm and shouts something in his face. The beastial tries backing away as he pleads his case, but this clearly doesn't satisfy the guard.

Another guard emerges and uses magic to lift the beastial into the air. Then he slams him against the nearest wall. He rams him once more, making the beastial bleed as the other guard bellows with laughter. The magical grip holding the beastial midair vanishes, dropping the being to the ground with a loud thump. When the beastial remains flat on the ground, the one wielding magic jerks his hand and twists the beastial's neck so hard it separates from his body.

I cover my mouth to fight a gasp.

My gods. He killed him. Just like that.

A growl escapes Thane's lips.

"Just conceal yourselves," Algar murmurs, waving his fingers, as if we all didn't just witness an unnecessary murder. "Thane, do your sorcery shit to keep yourselves covered and I'll teleport in between. As soon as we make it to the tunnels, you won't need to conceal anymore. No one walks through them except people without homes, and they won't mess with you. Trust me. Most are too hungry or strung out on kopa to do so anyway."

"That would require the whispershade spell, and that's *not* how it works," Thane grumbles through gritted teeth. "I can conceal myself for a lengthy period of time, but two people *and* a horse will drain me of energy very quickly."

"So take breaks." Algar shrugs like it's no big deal.

I have a feeling it's a *major* deal, considering Thane's frustration.

"We'll find places to hide for a few minutes, and when you're revived or whatever, we'll move again."

"No." Thane straightens to his full height. "This is a foolish plan. We'll just walk the perimeter. It'll take a little longer, but at least we'll have a careful eye on our surroundings."

"We'll lose time, Thane." I catch him by the arm before he can get away. "The sooner we can get through Ruvain, the better. I don't want to linger around this kingdom any more than I have to, and I definitely don't want to be near the forests. Plus, we're already here." I point a thumb over my shoulder. "I agree with Algar. We should just do this—take our chances with your whispershade spell, and when you need breaks, just tell us." I pull my hand away.

He breathes hard through his nose, jaw ticking as he looks through the bush again. The guards are now drifting away, heading toward the heart of the city.

"Fuck. *Fine.*" Thane pulls his mask up, then grabs Pearl's reins. "But we need to do it now, while those guards are gone."

I follow him and Algar, pushing through branches and thick bundles of leaves until we reach an opening. Thane steps out first, making sure the area is clear.

"Aren't you going to use your magic so we can't be seen?" I ask from the shadows of the branches.

"Not yet. Not until it's absolutely necessary." When it's clear, he gestures for me to follow before he runs the short distance to hide behind the first building, Pearl in tow. I jog after him.

"Great," I breathe, pressing my back against the stone wall. "Only, like, a hundred more to go." Somewhere in the distance, men's voices rise and fall in conversation. I fight the urge to peek around the edge of the building.

"Keep still." Thane's amber irises flash and become liquid gold. A blanket of heat wraps around me, making my skin prickle as the whispershade takes effect. "Stay close."

Thane looks a little blurry, like he's surrounded by a heat mirage, but I can still see him. I know the whispershade makes it impossible for those outside the spell to see us—including Algar, who nods in our direction before vanishing and reappearing behind the next building.

Thane moves ahead with Pearl while I stay close behind as instructed. We pass three more buildings before I feel the heavy heat around us ebbing.

"Whispershade is wearing out." Thane huffs, gluing his back to a wall.

"It's okay," I assure him. "Just take a moment to restore some of your strength."

His eyes connect with mine, the skin around them softening. I smile at him before shifting my attention to Pearl. Too much eye contact with him stirs something up inside me, and I don't quite know how to embrace it.

I feel him look away, too.

When I steal a glance at him moments later, though, his fiery eyes are on me again. If I'm not mistaken, he's admiring my body. Realizing I've noticed his staring, he clears his throat and snatches his gaze away.

I suppress another smile. I'm not sure whether to be annoyed that he was looking or flattered that he has even an inkling of interest in me.

I believe ten minutes or so pass before Thane stands taller and the whispershade wraps around us again. This time he moves faster, passing by four more buildings. I spot the black pillars wrapped in ivy a short distance away. If we can reach those, we'll be closer to the tunnels.

Algar was right. This *is* fast.

Hope blossoms in my chest, and my heart races a bit quicker…until the whispershade fades again.

"Hold on," Thane calls, pressing his back to the nearest building.

"Damn it, Thane!" Algar hisses, immediately rushing over to stand next to him.

"Hullo," a small voice says seconds later.

I gasp, and Thane yanks out his sword, spinning to find the source of the voice.

A man emerges—no, a *boy*. He can't be any older than his fourteenth or fifteenth year. He's wearing a ratty linen tunic that touches his knees and a faded blue scarf on his head.

"Who are you?" Thane angles his sword at him.

The boy studies Thane's sword before blinking at me and Algar. When he sees Pearl and Zephra, his eyes sparkle. "Is that a maobi?" he marvels.

Thane drops his sword a notch. "You need to go."

"I have never seen one in real life." The boy ignores Thane as he takes a step closer. "I've only ever read about them—in the library usually. One of the sorceress teachers used to create images of them with her magic."

I look between him and Thane, who is gripping the hilt of his sword hard enough to make his knuckles protrude while surveilling the area. He seems unsure whether to treat this boy as a threat or deem him innocent.

"Would you like to pet her?" Algar asks, stepping in front of Thane. He's also noticed how uneasy Thane is with this whole situation.

"Algar, we don't have time for this," Thane hisses.

"It'll only be a second. You have to restore your energy anyway." Algar shrugs him off, and the boy lights up even more as he brings Zephra closer. She clicks her teeth when the boy sticks out a hand.

"Easy," Algar whispers. "Slow movements—and only rub her body. She's picky about how her head is touched."

"Right. Of course. Sorry." The boy reaches in slower this time, and Zephra cocks her head. His smile widens as his tan fingers find their way to her fur and caress it. "Wow," he breathes, laughing. "She is so soft. You are such a lucky man."

I can't help smiling at the exchange as a warm feeling comes over me. Seeing the proud smile Algar wears. The brightness in the boy's eyes. Their shared interest in Zephra. Perhaps I've read Algar all wrong and shouldn't write him off as some lowly thief. He seems like a person who genuinely cares about others in need.

"What's your name?" asks Algar.

"I am Dulan."

Zephra bounces up to Algar's shoulder, and he folds his arms. "Are you going to snitch on us, Dulan?"

Dulan's excitement morphs to pure shock. "Of course not."

"How can we be sure?" Thane narrows his eyes at him. "You turn us strangers in, and you could get a good bit of coin." He may as well have stabbed the boy with how sharp his tone is.

"Well, in that case, I should turn myself in, too." Dulan releases an anxious laugh. Then he gestures behind him. "My nan lives in that building. She is sick, but the medicine she needs is not allowed in Ruvain. They don't want us getting better on our own, you see? They want us to keep paying their healers more and more money so they can pocket it. So sometimes I have to sneak to Meriva or Winstoft to get it." The boy digs into his pocket and fishes out a glass vial with shimmering green liquid in it.

Thane studies it while Algar mumbles, "I see."

"Are you trying to reach the tunnels?" Dulan asks.

"We are." I move past Thane. "Is that where you're going?"

"I just came from there. But I have to say, this route you are taking is risky. Many watchers in the towers. Follow me. I know a quicker way."

"No, we're good," Thane retorts.

"Sure," I respond at the same time.

Thane glares at me. "Come again?"

"Well, he clearly knows what he's talking about," I murmur, gesturing to Dulan.

"Yes, but at what cost? People around here don't help others unless they want something out of it." Thane bumps Algar out of the way and closes the gap between him and Dulan. "So either this is a setup, or he wants something from us. What is it that you want, Dulan?"

"Absolutely nothing at all," he pleads, looking at me and Algar for backup. "I—I just know what it is like to need help. And this is not a safe place for such beautiful creatures. Believe it or not, a lot of us Ruvainers are not as bad as other kingdoms think." He eyes Zephra and Pearl. "The sooner you get them out of here, the better."

Oh my goodness. He's so sweet.

Thane doesn't ease up on him, though, despite how genuine he sounds. I want to punch him for being such an asshole...but I can understand his defensiveness. Dulan is a stranger...and Thane clearly has trust issues.

"I know a liar and a con when I see one." Algar gives Dulan a thorough scan. "I don't think he's lying. If he wanted to rat us out, all he'd have to do is scream and the guards would come running. He's willing to help. Some people do that, you know? Help others because they're nice."

"Yeah." Thane shoots me a pointed look. "I've witnessed it with her firsthand."

I scowl at him. "I don't regret being a nice person, *Bane of My Existence*."

"Ha! That's a good one." Algar chortles. "Bane of My Existence. I'll have to use that one."

I smirk.

"Well, come along," Dulan urges, marching past us. "If we go toward the forest, it's much quicker. There is another entrance to the tunnels. It's sort of a secret passage only the lower-bred Ruvainers know about. We do lots of trading and meetings there."

Thane exhales deeply behind his mask while Algar trails Dulan. We near the forest again and cross a creek, approaching a different set of pillars. They stand before us, giants in black, split and chipped from all directions. I'm positive they won't stand for much longer, but they are majestic, nonetheless. Too marvelous to be in a territory this shitty.

"Just over there." Dulan points ahead. My eyes follow his finger, and I notice a gap in the trees. At first glance, I wouldn't have been able to make it out, but as I stare harder, I notice curved branches crafted into a makeshift passageway.

The opening is shrouded with bushes and vines, and the passage is much too dark to see very far in. This area doesn't seem like the sort of place where people congregate. It's desolate and swarming with wasp nests.

"This better not be a trap," Thane grouses as Dulan ducks under a few nests clinging to the trees. Irritated, Thane jerks on Pearl's reins, but she clearly doesn't like that because she snorts and then whinnies, stomping her front hooves.

"Easy," Thane whispers, holding a hand up to her. "Easy, girl. I didn't mean to startle you."

"Thane!" Algar whispers. "Keep her quiet!"

I notice him peering past Thane. A few yards behind is a gap revealing the center of the city. And in the middle is a group of Ruvain guards.

Pearl whinnies again and jerks forward, dragging Thane with her.

My stomach hollows, then drops. *Oh no.* She's running *toward* the city.

Thane grips hard, digging his heels into the ground to try and stop her, but he's no match for a horse that solid. She gallops loudly, drawing attention to herself. I gasp as the guards whip their heads to find us.

"Hey!" one of them barks.

"Intruders!" another one roars as they storm in our direction. "Sound the alarm!"

When bright lights flash and bells ring, my heart thunders in my chest. The ringing bells are so loud, my ears ache.

When Thane has finally gotten a hold of Pearl, he hops on her back. Algar's whole face drops with shock. And it's his words that spark the fire in me. "*Run*, Zaira."

I look for Thane again.

He nods. "Go!"

"Quick! Follow me!" Dulan shouts, waving a hand as he stands behind the trunk of a tree.

He speeds away in a flurry. I chase after him, zipping past Algar and running through thorny bushes. Algar is right behind me, limping quickly and teleporting in between to catch up. Zephra flies near the treetops, safe from attack. Thane gains on us as the Ruvain guards storm behind him with swords, spears, and bows at the ready.

Dulan looks back after jumping over a root. "When we make it into the tunnels, I can show you a hiding place where they'll never find—"

An arrow penetrates the center of Dulan's back.

I suck in a sharp breath and come to a screeching halt as he staggers a step or two, then turns around to face me. Blood drenches his tunic, and he points at the arrow protruding from his chest, as if he's trying to make sure it's real.

"No!" I cry as he falls to his knees. His glossy eyes pin on mine, desperate and afraid, before he tips over and hits the ground.

I start to run to him, but Algar yanks on my arm, dragging me away and shouting, "We have to keep moving, Zaira!"

Clearly, the adrenaline is fueling me because I grow steady on my feet and reality becomes clear again as I run with him. I have no chance to check on Dulan or come to his aid, even. He's dead because he tried to *help us*, and we'll be next if those Ruvainers catch up. That fear is enough to push me. I can be devastated later, once I reach safety.

Algar remains hot on my trail, pretty damn fast for someone who has what I assume is a permanent limp. Thane is right behind us, mask up and eyes sparking gold as he rides Pearl.

As he nears me, he scoops me up with one muscled arm and cranes it with just enough force to swing me up so I'm seated sideways in front of him on the horse.

Damn. That was smooth.

"What about Algar?" I call, looking behind his shoulder to see if the guards are gaining on us.

Algar shows up a millisecond later, now several feet ahead.

I lean over to peek around Thane again, and a lick of heat sears my arm, followed by flurries of fire zipping past us. I yelp as an arrow wrapped in flames flies by, stabbing into a tree trunk.

"Thane!" I yell as more dart in our direction.

"Take over the reins!" he commands.

I swing my leg over to straddle Pearl and keep her as steady as I can. Thane twists in the saddle, lifts a hand, and sends a fiery gold cannonball toward the men who are launching the arrows. Several of them are beastials in uniform running on all fours, dodging logs or skittering up tree trunks to leap to the next. Thane's fire blazes bright enough to light up the gloomy forest, singeing tree leaves, branches, and everything in its wake.

More arrows whiz by, and Thane blocks them with a glimmering shield. So many fires are growing, spreading through the forest like blazing rivers. Glancing over my shoulder, I witness Thane throw his hands up and grunt as he rips a large tree from its roots. He slams it to the ground to block the guards, then thrusts a hand forward, setting the tree ablaze, too.

Shadows.

The spread of flames is exactly what he wants.

The fire engulfs the forest behind us, swallowing it whole. The arrows stop, and the beastials come to a halt as some of them shout to retreat. I give my thighs a squeeze, urging Pearl to go faster as Thane twists around and faces forward.

We gallop through a clearing, past a roaring waterfall, and don't stop until we can see a two-story building, lit with gold lanterns in the distance—probably an inn. Thane climbs off Pearl's back first, reaching a hand up to help me down, but when I drop to my feet, I stumble.

"Sorry," I wheeze. I cling to his arm, trying to stand up straight, but dizziness takes hold of me.

"Quinlocke," Thane says. "Can you stand?"

"Yeah, I'm fine." I let go of his arm, but that's a mistake because I crumple. Well, would you look at that? Turns out I'm not fine.

"Hey, hey! What's going on? Where are you hurt?" Thane yanks his mask down and drops to his knees next to me.

Another person appears above me, panting wildly.

"What happened to her?" Algar asks.

My arm. It burns. It burns so much. I groan in pain as Thane touches the arm of my shirt where the fiery arrow cut through. He rips the fabric open wider.

"Shit." He presses his fingers to the wound. I cry out as the pain heightens. The dizziness becomes stronger, bile climbing up my throat. I'm going to vomit. I can feel it.

"It's poisoned. We have to get it out of her system now," Algar urges. "Pick her up. I know the owner of that inn up ahead. She can help."

"Okay," Thane replies quickly. "Get the horse while I carry her."

He sounds almost...concerned.

"Thane." My voice comes out a whisper as he lifts me up and carries me in his arms. I try speaking again, but my tongue feels heavy and thick in my mouth. I look up at Thane's face and notice that darkness has started seeping in at the edges of my vision.

"Hold on, Zaira," Thane encourages.

I hear a door creak open, and Algar's voice booms as he calls for someone.

"Rynthea! Has anyone seen Rynthea?"

The dizziness transitions to blurriness. My eyelids droop, and my heartbeat reduces to a terribly slow rhythm.

"Zaira, look at me. I need you to keep your eyes open." Thane's deep voice echoes in my head. He repeats himself with a firmer tone, but I can't fulfill his request.

I close my eyes and let the darkness consume me.

Chapter 14

The sound of crowing roosters pulls me out of sleep.

Wincing, I roll onto my side as sunlight stretches over half of my face. Oh gods. Why does my head feel so heavy? I try moving again but hiss through my teeth and flop onto my back.

"What the..." Hot, fiery prickles course through my right arm. I give it a look to find it wrapped in bandages. Confusion plagues me. I have no clue as to why I'm bandaged...

Until it hits me.

The men chasing us through Ruvain.

Dulan dying.

The fires the arrows started and that Thane made worse.

The nausea.

The dizziness.

I catch movement in my peripheral vision and gasp when I spot Thane standing in the corner of the room. His mask is lowered and arms folded as he leans against the wall—a shadow in daylight. I don't even want to know how long he's been standing there, all quiet and lurking.

"Thane." I blink at him before taking in the unfamiliar details of the room. A fire gently crackles in the hearth. The walls surrounding us are made of deep-brown wood. Beige curtains hang on either side of the two windows to my right, where rays of sunlight stream in through the gaps. Dust motes float in the filtered light, and there is a sweet berry fragrance wafting in the air.

It's all so cozy and comforting.

"Why are you standing there?" I ask.

"Waiting for you to wake up," he answers.

"If it wasn't so creepy, I would think it's sweet. How long was I out?"

"Three hours that we'll never get back," he deadpans.

My mind circles back to Analla.

The stones.

"At least it wasn't three days," I reply as he uncrosses his arms and steps away from the wall. "It's not my fault I needed time to recover from who knows what."

"The cerwen."

"The *what*?" I wheeze. "Cerwen? But that's only used for—"

"Poison, yes," Thane confirms. "You were shot with an arrow doused in cerwen. You're lucky it was only a minor graze on the arm."

"Yeah, lucky me." I refrain from rolling my eyes at him.

He shrugs. "Just letting you know."

"Well, thanks," I mutter, shoving the quilt off my legs. I slide to the edge of the bed and stand, or at least try to, but I'm met with dizziness.

"Better that you slow down for at least half an hour. The cerwen is still wearing off."

I press a hand on the nearest wall, drawing in a few deep breaths to relax my body.

"Where are we?"

"A little beastial-owned inn, right on the edge of Winstoft. We're not far from Gadonia. We can head south in the next couple of hours or so. Then we'll be out of Ruvain." He grabs my good arm to remove the bandage wrapped around it.

When he does, I see the shallow wound the arrow created. "Looks better." He puts the bandage back in place, then drapes my arm over his shoulder to help me. The reach up is uncomfortable, seeing as he's *much* taller than I am, but when he presses my side to his, I instantly feel better... at first. His proximity catches me off guard once again. It should annoy me or, at the least, make me feel awkward, but it doesn't. He's closer than usual, and I'm surprised I don't hate it. "Once you eat and are stable enough, we'll keep moving."

"Where are my things?"

"In there." He nods his head toward a wardrobe painted white with intricate pink floral designs. With my arm still around him and his hand at my waist, he makes his way to the door. Butterflies flutter in my stomach as I try ignoring the hand he has close to my hip…and how good he smells—all leather, cedar, smoke, and a hint of something woodsy. How can he still smell so nice after setting a whole forest on fire?

As we leave the room, I hear music trickling through the hall. Thane keeps me steady as I limp. In the hallway, I notice portraits of all sizes tacked to the walls.

Many of them are images of minotaurs in all shapes and sizes. A few mortals are included as well, but there is one painting that stands out most of all—a mortal woman and a rather large male minotaur in front of a ship. The minotaur has his arm wrapped around the woman, kind of how Thane's is around me right now, and they're looking at each other with bright smiles and gentle eyes. The painting appears so vivid and alive, I can imagine them stepping right out of the canvas.

"How are you feeling?" Thane asks. It sounds like a genuine question—so genuine, in fact, that I have to check his eyes for any hint of sarcasm.

"Could be better," I offer, softening.

He nods.

We finally enter a spacious hall made of wooden columns with beams spanning the vaulted ceiling. Round wooden tables are spread throughout. A long bar counter is to my left, wiped clean and topped with bowls of roasted nuts. Barrels of ale stand next to built-in shelves that are neatly lined with rustic mugs.

A carved wooden sign is tacked to the wall above the bar that reads *KAMTAUR INN*, painted in blue lettering. The paint is chipped and worn, giving a hint to its age. Across the way is a set of stairs that probably lead up to more rooms where people can sleep.

"There you go, Zephra." Algar's voice catches my ear. I find him sitting at a corner table with Zephra perched in front of him. He tosses an almond into her mouth, and she chomps it rapidly before opening wide for another, revealing sharp little teeth.

There is someone else at his table, too—a beastial with shaggy brown hair and large horns protruding from either side of his head. A silver hoop hangs from one of his bull-shaped ears, and he smiles as he watches Zephra eat. Other than his horns, the light patches of fur, and ears, every other feature of his is mortal, down to his tan skin, wide nose, full lips, and the softness of his eyes.

Holy Crystal. He's a real-life minotaur.

Well, he appears more like a cross between mortal and minotaur, but regardless, he is a sight to behold. Minotaurs of any kind are rare among beastials now. In fact, this is the closest I've ever been to one.

"Yeah, it's been dry around here lately," the minotaur says as he leans his upper back against the nearest wall. He's sitting on a barrel, chucking almonds into his mouth. "Rynthea won't admit it, but we won't stay afloat for much longer. We'll have to sell this place soon."

"No—you can't do that." Algar gapes at him. "It's been in your family for decades. You can't just give that up."

"Well, a lot of beastials are afraid to come in here now. Look at it." The minotaur raises a hand, gesturing around. "It's constantly vacant. We have a few people pass through while they travel, but ever since Ruvain gave permission for the mortals to hunt wild beastials, it's been sparse. Because you know the Ruvainers don't just hunt for the wild ones. They hunt *all of us*, then strip us of our clothes and try and claim us wild when they turn us in for coin. They're full of shit, all of them."

Thane sits me down at a table close to theirs, then takes a seat in the chair opposite mine.

When Algar spots me, he grins. "Well, if it isn't our sleeping princess. I swear you love resting those pretty eyes of yours."

"It wasn't my choice this time." I laugh, rubbing my arm. It's not burning as much as before.

"'Course not. How are you holdin' up?"

"My arm hurts a little, but I'm all right." I glance at Thane, who's grabbed an almond from the bowl. Zephra's nose twitches as she eyes him. With one quick motion of his hand, he tosses the almond at her as she opens her mouth. The almond sails smoothly into her mouth, and she eats it right up. He smirks, grabbing another and levitating it in the air, mildly teasing Zephra now. Her head moves up and down, round and round, as she watches the snack and waits for him to toss it.

I look at the minotaur, who is already eyeing me while chewing.

"Name's Torjack." He extends an arm and offers me a hand swathed in brown fur.

I reach out with my good arm and give his a shake. "Zaira."

"Nice to meet you, Zaira. I have to ask—why under the Crystal Realm are you traveling with a thief like Algar?" He chortles.

I smile, looking between him and Algar, who tosses his hands in the air like he's claiming innocence.

"I just met Algar today, and he decided to join us. Before that, it was just me and Thane."

"I see." Torjack leans forward to study me a bit more intently. "And is it true you're going to *The Shallows*?"

Everyone says "The Shallows" as if it's a cursed word.

I nod. "We are."

"Good luck getting anywhere near it," a lighter voice calls out behind us.

Another hybrid minotaur shows up, clearly a female based on her full, feminine physique. Wisps of curly brown hair frame her face, the rest collected into a thick braid resting down the middle of her back. She wears brown leather buffers and pants to match over two insanely muscled legs. Her tan biceps are just as defined, brown fingerless gauntlets occupying both forearms.

Just like Torjack, she has the horns and ears of a minotaur. Her nose is slightly smaller than his, turned slightly up, and as mortal as ever. However, her eyes are fiercer—black pupils surrounded by honey-brown irises. And I hadn't noticed it on Torjack because he was sitting, but she has hooves for feet. Other than those features, the rest of her is undoubtedly mortal.

"Rynthea, how about another on the house?" Algar lifts his wooden mug and waves it in the air.

"I don't think so. You can pay for the next. I know you've got coins on you, you little bandit." Rynthea approaches our tables but doesn't look at anyone else but me.

She's tall, strong, and carries a formidable grace that can't be ignored.

"Nice to see you're awake, Zaira." She quirks a half smile. "Would've been unfortunate if you died under my care."

"Oh yeah, if it weren't for Rynthea, you'd probably be dead," Torjack announces, tossing another almond into his mouth. "Rynthea's really good at creating healing elixirs. People come to her all the time for her remedies. You wound up in the right place at the right time, you lucky mortal."

"I am very lucky," I breathe. "Thank you so much for helping me, Rynthea. I would stand and shake your hand, but apparently, I need another half hour or so to let the cerwen wear off."

"Don't worry about it." Rynthea places a flat hand on her chest. "Rynthea Kamtaur. If he hasn't said so yet, that's my twin brother, Torjack

Kamtaur, and the spiky beastial behind the counter is Penju." She jerks her thumb over her shoulder to where a porcupine-like beastial is now wiping mugs with a cloth at the bar.

"Yeah, hard to believe we're twins, right?" Torjack wiggles his eyebrows. "Our mum used to tease us about how Rynthea stole all the strength and beauty while I was left with the brains."

I laugh at that as Rynthea huffs.

"Or maybe you were just destined to be feeble, little brother."

Torjack chuckles, shoveling more nuts into his mouth.

"You know you can't stay here long." Rynthea turns to Thane, and I swear her whole demeanor changes. There is more ice in her voice, and she clearly wears a grimace. "People like *you* always cause a shitshow."

"People like *me*?" Thane repeats with a frown.

My heart thumps faster. Wait...does she know he's a shadow assassin?

"Yes. Sorcerers who dress like you and carry all those weapons are notorious for picking fights," she goes on. "I always have to toss your kind out for causing a ruckus and manipulating people."

A bit of relief courses through me. To her, he's just a trouble-making sorcerer. I bet there are many of them in Ruvain who pass by here.

"Well, it's a good thing I'll be out of here soon, isn't it?" says Thane.

"A *very* good thing." Rynthea's eyes flash as she looks Thane over with a scowl.

"A bit prejudiced, no?" Algar mumbles under his breath.

"Never understood how people like you live with yourselves," Rynthea says.

Thane drops his folded arms and pushes to a stand so he can match her glare.

"Go on, then," she challenges, clenching her fists and smirking. That action alone makes the veins in her arms bulge.

"Oh, come on now." Algar springs up. "Let's not get hostile, friends. Rynthea, we're not looking for trouble, and I promise you this sorcerer knows when and where to behave. Give us a few and we'll go. I'll even keep my eye on the sundial."

Rynthea doesn't back down. Neither does Thane. They stare into each other's eyes, Thane with his jaw ticking, and Rynthea with that challenging smirk. Something tells me she loves confrontation. Based on the buffers and wrist gauntlets she wears, I would bet good coin on it. I would also bet that she's won every fight she's ever been in...or every fight she's had to finish because of sorcerers she couldn't stand.

"Rynthea, Torjack tells me Kamtaur Inn might be closing soon?" Algar steps between her and Thane. After a handful of seconds, she finally wrenches her gaze away from the sorcerer. Algar is good at that—interfering. Changing the subject. A proper mediator.

"That's not definitive, and I really wish you'd stop saying that shit, Tor." Rynthea pins her brother with intense eyes.

"Well, it's true, Rynthea." Torjack throws his hands in the air in a guiltless gesture. "Kamtaur is going to shit because we're too close to Ruvain, and I've reviewed the books. If we don't pack it in now and sell it while it still has some dignity, this place will crumble."

"It's really that bad, huh?" Algar murmurs as Zephra climbs onto his shoulder.

Rynthea exhales as she takes a step back and plants a hand on her waist. "It's...not the best it's been. Business has declined since Ruvain has started doing whatever they want to the beastials again. Couple that with Torjack's trips to the healer, and our coins are sparse. We've had to cut down to two kegs of ale per day."

"His trips to the healer?" I look from her to Torjack. He seems completely healthy to me. The only reason a being takes frequent trips to a healer is if they're injured, sick, or born with an incurable disease.

"Stiff Ditheria," Torjack answers with a shrug. "Sometimes my spine locks up on me. Occasionally, my hands won't work for hours and seizures take over. There are days when I'm trapped in bed because my legs are utterly useless."

"Oh," I murmur. "I'm really sorry to hear that."

"Ah, it's all right. We can't all be perfect, can we? If that were the case, Orvena and Xaimur never would've gotten into feuds and separated themselves as gods. Besides, the healers help—oh, and Rynthea created a medicine that eases the pain whenever we can't make it to the healer."

"Don't worry, Zaira." Algar reaches over and gives my shoulder a gentle squeeze. "Torjack's a tough one."

I give a half-hearted smile. It amazes me how the frailest of people smile the brightest. I can't help but gain more respect for Torjack.

"Can I get you something to eat, Zaira?" Rynthea asks. "I just made a pot of vegetable stew, and I have some chocolate oat crisps if you'd like some. On the house." She winks.

"If it's not too much trouble, yes please."

"None at all."

"In that case, I'd love some. Thank you, Rynthea."

She nods and turns away, her hooves thumping on the wood.

As she slips through the swinging kitchen door, a man enters through the front door of the inn wearing a gray cloak and hood on his head. Tensing, Thane watches the stranger stroll through and take a seat on the opposite side of the room.

Penju leaves the counter to approach the man and take his order. When Penju returns to the bar, the man shifts his stare to us. He scans Algar, Torjack, and me with disinterest, but when he locks on Thane, his eyes narrow with recognition.

Oh, fuck.

A dagger materializes in Thane's hand as he uses his other to pull his mask up to the bridge of his nose. Oblivious, Torjack and Algar resume conversation again, discussing Zephra's fur and eating habits.

"Thane," I whisper. "Do you know him?"

"No." He grips the handle of his dagger tighter. "But I don't like the way he's looking at me."

Penju returns to the man and sets down a mug of ale on his table. The stranger picks it up and takes a few deep gulps. Maybe he recognizes Thane from somewhere else—like Redclaw or the Scraps. Maybe he saw him in action and is trying to figure out if he's a shadow assassin? Either way, I'm relieved that he doesn't bother setting his sights on us again.

Rynthea returns with a wooden bowl full of stew, a cup of water, and a tray of chocolate oat crisps. My belly grumbles when she places all of it on the table before me. I don't even realize how hungry I am until I see the hearty meal and inhale the delicious aromas.

I dig in.

Once I'm finished, there isn't a single drop of broth left in my bowl.

"Did that help any?" Thane asks.

"Yes. Very much so." I place my spoon down and pick up an oat crisp. It crunches as I bite into it, and the chocolate explodes on my tongue. "Mmm. That's so good."

Crumbs tumble to my chest, and Thane's eyes follow them.

I swipe at the crumbs, my cheeks heating. "Gods…I love food."

"Didn't ask, Quinlocke." He sighs, looking away from me.

"If I were you, I wouldn't take *anything* he says personally." Algar tips back in his chair, balancing on one leg and locking his fingers behind his head. "He's a dick to everyone."

"Yeah." I huff a laugh. "I gathered that."

"I've known him since his sixth year, and he's always been uptight."

"Algar." Thane glares at his friend with an inclined eyebrow, as if telling him to proceed with caution.

"You've known him since your *sixth* year?" I ask, surprised to hear that.

"Oh, yeah. He was my neighbor, actually. Lived two houses away."

"Wow. So you two really *did* grow up together?" I thought he had been exaggerating before.

"Yeah. We were like brothers." Algar flashes a smile at Thane.

Thane shakes his head and peels out of his chair, like the last thing he wants to discuss is his past. "Going to the toilet," is all he says before trudging away.

"You'll have to tell me all about your childhood with Thane," I say, biting into another crisp. "Surely he couldn't have been *this* much of a grump back then."

"Nah." Algar considers that. "He could be serious, but he wasn't an absolute jerk like he is now. There are so many good things I remember about him."

"Well, that's good. I'd love to hear what they were."

"I'd tell you now, but he might overhear and put a spell on me." He winks. "Soon."

I laugh, then glance at the counter, where Penju is checking the barrels and reading something, while Rynthea holds a clipboard and is marking things off.

But then there's a thud in the distance.

And that's when I notice the hooded stranger who walked in is no longer at his table.

Rynthea places her clipboard down on the counter as the thudding grows louder along with deep, muffled grunts. Her ears twitch, as if sensing something.

Then the double doors to the entrance fly open, slam into the walls, and reveal a group of masked men.

Chapter 15

Algar and Torjack shoot to their feet. I stand, too, glad most of the unsteadiness has faded from my system.

"Absolutely not! Get out!" Rynthea bellows as she rounds the counter. "There will be *no* fighting in *my* inn!"

"There doesn't have to be a fight," the man leading the group says as he steps deeper into the tavern. "We just want the sorcerer."

Rynthea raises her chin as Algar slips his hand down and snatches a knife out of the holster at his waist. "I don't know what you're talking about." Rynthea squares her shoulders as she inches forward. "There is no sorcerer here. I don't like them in my inn."

"Cut the shit, *minotaur*!" the man barks. Rynthea's brows knit together as her eyes flare. "Give us the sorcerer or we'll destroy this whole fucking building *and* set it on fire!"

One of Rynthea's eyes twitches as she glares at him. Then, oddly, almost eerily, a smile sweeps across her face.

"Okay." She throws her hands in the air. "Fine. He's not worth my business being destroyed. Let me go and get him."

She wanders behind the counter again, past Penju, who is grimacing at the men, his spikes standing on end, appearing twice as lethal. When Rynthea disappears through the swinging door to the kitchen, I hear another door creak open in the distance.

Thane appears around the corner with his buffers splattered in blood. His sword, the blade dripping crimson, is in one of his hands. But the object in his other hand causes my breath to hitch.

It's a man's head.

And not just *any* man.

The stranger in the gray cloak who'd, only moments ago, been sitting on the other side of the inn staring at Thane.

"I believe this is yours." Thane chucks the man's head at the masked men. It hits the ground with a sickening splat and rolls to a stop at the feet of their leader.

The leader takes a step back from the head and rapidly draws a sword. "*Valkor,*" he growls, raising the blade in the air. "We've been looking for you."

"I can see that, jackass." Thane locks his eyes on me. "Go out the back. Get to Pearl and ride to safety with Algar. I'll find you."

"Fuck that," Algar counters while Zephra flies out the nearest window. "I'm not letting you fight alone."

"He won't be!" Rynthea's voice cuts through the room as she storms out of the kitchen, slides over the counter, and lands on the other side with the long handle of a scythesword firmly in her hand.

With one solid swing, she takes the leader's head off with the curved blade, then swings around and slices through another one of the men, separating him clear in half.

"Gods. Not again." I back away as a stunned moment of silence stretches through the inn and blood pools on the floor.

"Get outta here, Torjack. And take the girl with you," Rynthea orders, disrupting the quiet. That's enough to send the room into an absolute riot.

Thane zooms past me, joining Rynthea in the slicing and butchering, while Algar throws himself into the brawl with a battle cry. His limp doesn't hold him back from a damn thing. He's good at killing—maybe not as talented as Thane and Rynthea, but he damn sure knows how to defend himself.

"Come with me!" Torjack presses a hand to my back and guides me toward the hallway.

As we pass, I spot Penju whipping out a dagger with a sneer. He jumps on the counter and plunges it into the top of a man's head.

Torjack runs with me through the hallway and makes his way toward the back exit.

"Wait!" I call. "My bag! I need my things." I don't know if I'll ever get the chance to come back for them, especially if the building ends up being set on fire. I have important items in there. Coins to get me through the rest of my travels. A map. Allergy elixirs in case the pollen becomes unbearable.

"Hurry!" Torjack orders.

I dash into the room I woke up in, throw the wardrobe doors open, and retrieve my rucksack and satchel. After I strap them to me, I turn to face Torjack. A sharp gasp escapes me when a masked stranger appears behind him.

This person isn't dressed like the others in the main area, who wear simple black masks and buffers. This man's buffers and mask are stitched with red. His hair is as black as ink and slicked back, his skin nearly as white as the snow in Velkana.

With a flick of his hand, the stranger suspends Torjack in the air and throws him into the wall.

"No!" I yell. "Torjack!"

"A friend of yours?" The man cocks his head as he looks me up and down. "You're the noble one, I see."

I back away as he inches closer.

With a twist of his hand, a cold, solid grip of power wraps around my throat, and I'm suspended in the air once again. He pins me to the nearest wall, choking and squeezing as I struggle against his magic, desperate for breath.

Darkness seeps in around the edges of my vision as the man watches me with blazing blue eyes. I don't think I can take it anymore.

Damn it.

I'm going to die afraid, alone, and useless. Choked to death by a man I don't even know.

I'll be dead.

Analla will be dead.

All of us will be dead and—

Rynthea appears in the doorway and stomps in, kicking the pale man in the lower back with a hoof.

He grunts as he stumbles forward, and his grip around my throat loosens. I collapse on the ground, landing on my hands and knees and gulping down as much air as physically possible.

Rynthea looks from the man to her brother, who is groaning in the corner of the room, struggling to get up. A growl builds in her throat as she whips her scythesword in a motion way too quick to capture and swings at the man.

The man dodges her strike with ease and kicks at her ankles, but she doesn't buckle. Instead, she kicks him straight in the chest. His body crashes through the glass windows as I stagger to a stand, watching him land outside and flop a time or two.

"Torjack," she breathes, rushing to her brother. She taps his cheek as he groans again. "Hey, Tor, you okay?"

"Yes, I'm fine. I'm fine."

"I told you to get your ass *out of here*!"

"She needed her bag!" Torjack retorts.

Rynthea looks back at me with a frustrated huff.

"I'm sorry." My voice wavers as guilt consumes me. I didn't mean for Torjack to get hurt. He could've died because of me.

Rynthea sighs. "It's fine. Just get out of here. Both of you. Take the back exit and get to the bunker. I'll meet you there when this is settled."

When Torjack is on his hooves again, Rynthea leads the way out. Before we can even reach the middle of the hallway, though, another one of the masked men appears. She doesn't hesitate taking him out. After cutting through him like warm butter, she storms ahead of us and shoves the back door open.

"Go!" she orders.

I run outside after Torjack but end up tripping over something and falling flat on my stomach. My spectacles slide off the bridge of my nose as I land on the ground. Then an unknown object wraps tightly around my ankle. I look back and see the blur of the masked man with the red stitching again. He holds up a stiff hand and reels me toward him like I'm a fish on a hook.

Rynthea roars as she jumps over me to attack him. An onslaught begins as three more people appear. Somehow, through all the mayhem, the man with red stitching holds my ankle steady while fighting Rynthea off with whorls of blue and smoke.

"Come on, Zaira!" Torjack yells.

"I can't!" I scream. "He has my ankle! I can't move!"

"Shit!" Torjack curses.

Someone flies out the back door, across the field, and slams into the ground with a thud only a few inches away from me. They're bloodied and dead…definitely dead. My hand searches desperately for my spectacles, but the body has landed on top of them.

"No!" I wail. "No, no, no!" I shove the man's leg off of them, only to see shattered lenses. I start to grab them, but someone beats me to it and snatches them up. Another masked person. A woman.

She tugs her mask down to sneer at me. "Can't see? What a shame." She tosses them in Torjack's direction, then lifts her sword, about to bring it down on me until another sword penetrates her chest, driving straight through her heart.

"Get out of here, Quinlocke!" I hear Thane shout.

Of course he's killed the woman with precision like that.

The woman crumples to her knees, then her head slams into the ground.

I feel the grip around my ankle weaken when someone lets out a loud yell. I'm not entirely sure, but based on their blurry silhouettes, I think Rynthea has just injured the man with red stitching.

When the grip completely vanishes, I crawl around the dead person who taunted me to find my specs, spreading my fingers over the cold dirt in search of them. Finally, I spot them, but someone else picks them up before I can reach them.

My heart drops, until I quickly realize it's Torjack.

He offers me a hand. "Come on. I'll guide you. Just hold my hand."

Torjack helps me up, and we scurry away. I steal a glance over my shoulder and am almost positive I see Thane snatching a sword out of the woman who just teased me about not being able to see.

What a bitch.

Not my fault Orvena gave me eyesight that's weak at best.

We can't all be winners.

Fortunately, the man with red stitching is nowhere in sight.

"Bunker is right over here," Torjack says, panting. He points ahead, but it's useless. I can't see anything clearly past his arm. The towering trees are a blur of green and brown, the sky seems farther away, and the sun feels twice as bright.

The commotion behind us has doubled.

Wood splinters.

A man cries out.

Someone hollers in pain.

Fortunately, it doesn't sound like any of the people fighting *for* us.

Finally stopping, Torjack bends down and touches the ground, swiping leaves until he comes across a metal handle. I make out a hatch covered in moss and grass. He hauls it open, and I squint my eyes, trying to see what's down there, but it's completely dark.

"We have to go down the steps one person at a time as there's not much room." Torjack faces me. "It'll be a little dark, but there's nothing terrible down there, I promise. You go first. I'm right behind you."

I place my feet on the first stone step.

"Just grip the rail there. Yep, right there," Torjack instructs as I reach for the built-in railing. I hold on tight, taking each step one at a time, until the soles of my boots meet softer ground.

Torjack joins me after shutting and locking the hatch. Darkness consumes us. I feel him slip past me, his fur brushing my arm, before he rummages around a bit. A clicking noise echoes, and the bunker flickers with light.

"How long has this place been here?" I squint, trying to decipher what is what. I move closer to a towering piece in the corner to see it's a shelf lined with books. Next to it is a table for four. I run my fingers over the smooth top and rub the tips together. They're free of dust. Used recently.

"A while. This is the Kamtaur bunker," Torjack says, and based on his tone, it sounds like he's smiling. "We hide out here when we get news about riots happening in Ruvain, or when an alert goes out that beastials are being hunted. Rynthea hates it down here, but it's saved our lives more times than I can count."

"That's awful, living that way. Being hunted and all."

"Yeah. It is. Sadly, you get used to it." Torjack shifts closer and pulls a chair out for me. "Go on, sit. Rynthea will show up. I'm sure she'll slaughter the lot of them. Same for that dark, grumpy friend of yours. Hope Algar makes it out, though. He thinks he's stronger than he actually is."

"I hope so, too," I murmur, clinging to faith they'll make it out alive.

Torjack takes the seat next to mine so I can better see his face.

"Here." Torjack opens his hand and holds up my specs. He helps me slide them on.

"Yeah. I can't see a damn thing," I gripe. "Everything's a kaleidoscope."

"Just means you get to see multiples of this handsome face," Torjack teases. I don't know how he can joke during a time like this, swarmed by chaos and madness. Then again, it's like he said. He's gotten used to it.

I yank the shattered specs off, fighting the stupid urge to cry. If I can't see, how am I going to make it to the temple now? It's not like spectacle designers are on every corner of Thelanor, and even if there were, they don't come cheap.

The floodgates of frustration open. I might as well give up and return to Meriva. Maybe if I go back now and request new spectacles, I'll still have time to make it to the Temple of Elphar.

But I don't want to go back. And I definitely don't want to go through Ruvain again.

"Hey," Torjack calls.

I look at him.

"It'll be okay."

I shake my head. "Not if I can't see." I sink my teeth into my bottom lip, blinking my tears away. As badly as I want to, I can't do so here. I'll think of a solution. I always do. But I won't be able to proceed without that ruthless shadow assassin at my side.

I strain my ears, wishing to know what's happening at the inn, wishing I could do something. The feeling of helplessness has my stomach twisted in knots. It's probably twice as bad for Torjack, though he doesn't show it.

I swallow down the feeling and focus on what I can control.

"Why don't you and Rynthea move to Meriva instead?" I ask. "Or another kingdom that doesn't allow the hunting of beastials?"

"Well, Kamtaur has been in our family since before we were born. My mother and father opened it together." Torjack sighs and clears his throat. "My mother grew sick and died when we were in our eighth year. My father became sad thereafter. He showed us the ropes of running Kamtaur when we were in our fourteenth year so we could take over one day. He died when we were in our eighteenth year, and ever since then, Rynthea has been trying to keep the place alive. She has way too much hope for weak or failing things, despite how powerful she is."

He shifts in his chair uncomfortably, and my heart aches for him.

"But I know a lost cause when I see one," he continues. "My sister believes Kamtaur Inn should stay open, despite the danger, but I tell her all the time it won't stand for much longer. Sooner or later, they won't care for the rules and will burn that place down just to get to us."

"That's so unfair. You shouldn't have to live like this."

"That's life for you, huh?"

A thump sounds at the hatch door. Our eyes widen as we look at each other. He stands up and reaches for what looks like a pitchfork in the corner, then remains a few steps back from the opening of the hatch.

I stay seated with bated breath.

Chapter 16

Torjack's nose and ears twitch. Just as quickly as his defenses rose, he drops the pitchfork as six rhythmic knocks sound on the door.

After he climbs the steps and unlocks it, Rynthea staggers down, a massive blur in the sunlight without my spectacles. Behind her are two more shadowy figures. Based on their stature and the color of their clothes, I assume they're Thane and Algar.

Thank Orvena.

"Are they all gone?" Torjack asks.

"Yes. Dead or they've run off." Rynthea claps her brother's shoulders. "Are you all right?"

"I'm fine. Good thing I'm not stiff today, huh?" He huffs out a laugh.

"Oh, shut up, you fool." She sighs as she reels him in for a tight hug.

Thane walks around her to reach me. "Quinlocke, are you hurt?"

"No, I'm okay," I answer when our eyes connect. His warm, concerned tone is a surprise to hear.

Algar crouches next to me. "Where are your specs?"

I press my lips and pick them up from the table, waving them by one of the wiry arms. "Broken."

"Damn," Algar mumbles.

"There's no way I can continue the journey like this. I can barely see."

Thane stares at the spectacles a beat before holding out a hand. "Let me see them."

His change in tone makes me hesitate. I really don't like how demanding he can be, but I place them in his palm anyway. He closes his hand around them, and a flicker of light illuminates the space between us. When he opens his hand again, the spectacles are surrounded in a powdery gold aura.

I lean in closer and squint. I can't believe it. They're like new again. Actually, they're *better* than new. The previously black frames have transformed to a gleaming gold, and I can't make out a single scratch on the lenses. There were many scratches before, but that was of my own doing.

Thane settles the specs gently on my ears, his warm fingers brushing the sides of my face. Goose bumps sweep over every inch of me, but I pretend the reaction didn't happen.

"Better?" he asks.

Once again, the urge to cry is nigh. But they're happy tears I want to shed. Tears of hope. "They're perfect."

For a moment, we look into each other's eyes, and I swear I see a softness in his that I've never seen before...

But the moment passes when Thane coughs and looks away.

I look around and take in the crystal-clear details of the bunker—wood paneling on the walls, gas lanterns hanging in a row on thick rope above, shelves stacked with books, wide glass jars stuffed with peeled fruits and vegetables.

"Wow, they're so clear." I smile at him. "Thank you."

He nods. "Don't mention it."

Something seems to be happening right now. A shift—a change. As our gazes linger yet again, I have the irrational thought that this assassin might not be all that bad. He's protected me from a lot so far, waited for me to heal in the inn, and has just restored my spectacles.

But it's just a thought. Reality still rings like a bell in the hollows of my mind. Despite the kind gestures, he is still a *very* dangerous man.

As if Thane senses the disruption in my thoughts, he says, "We should get going if we want to make it to Gadonia at a decent time."

"Are you seriously going to The Shallows?" Rynthea asks, glaring at Thane, Algar, and then me. Before I can speak, she's flaying Thane again. "You realize you're leading her to her death, right?"

"She wants to go," Thane replies in a low rumble. "She asked me to escort her."

"For a stone that may not even be there?" Rynthea places her attention on me now. "You'll get yourself killed, Zaira."

"That's why she has me," Thane counters. "So she can make it there alive."

Rynthea's eyes burn with irritation.

"Traveling with you is the true death wish, and we all know it," she rants. "There is a clear target on your back, and you brought it straight to *my* inn. Do you know how long it will take me to clean up all that blood? To replace or repair the broken tables and chairs? It's bad enough our business is going downhill. Now we'll have to shut down for days."

"There's treasure near that temple, Rynthea." Algar interferes once again. "All sorts, I've heard. Coins, jewels, crystals—you name it. They don't call it Elphar's temple for nothing. He scoured these lands and buried all he found there. He was Azidel's brother, so everyone believes the legends to be true about the treasures because Azidel was capable of protecting it. If we get a hold of some of it, you can rebuild Kamtaur and your financial burdens will be washed away."

"Yeah, if I'm not dead first," she shoots back. "Making it to The Shallows is a fool's dream."

"Then I'll go with them," Torjack blurts out. "I'll bring some of the treasure back, and we can get on our feet again."

"Like shadows you will!" She turns her head slowly to face her brother. Hot, visible breath might as well be coming out of Rynthea's nose. "You can hardly even walk half the time, Torjack! What the shadows are you getting on about?"

"If I take the medicines with me, I'll be fine." He shifts on his hooves with a weak shrug. "You don't want to sell Kamtaur even though we're drowning in debt, Rynthea. I think if we travel as a group, we can make it. That guy there is pretty lethal with his swords and daggers"—he points at Thane—"and Algar is a good scrapper himself. Zaira seems to have done her studying and is quite clever. Our chances are much higher as a group."

"Lots of groups go to The Shallows for treasure, and hardly any of them leave the island alive," she says. "And if they do, they either die on the way back to the mainland or make it back crippled. None have returned with treasure."

Torjack throws his arms wide in frustration. "What does it matter if I die? And I'm already crippled, so that means nothing to me. I can't have you looking after me for the rest of my life, Rynthea. That's no way for you to live. I'm the one who's sick, and I'll never get better unless we do something about it."

She clamps her mouth shut and stares at him with glossy, honeyed eyes.

"I know you want to look out for me," Torjack goes on in a gentler voice, placing a hand on her shoulder, "but one day my life might come to an end, and not only will you be out of a business, but you'll have no brother, either. You'll have no family left. You'll have no money. There will be nothing to hold on to, all because you wanted to play it safe. Why not take a risk—a chance for the better—instead of sitting here waiting for my final breath?"

"Tor, you're talking nonsense." She shakes her head and pushes his hand away. "You're not going to Elphar, and that's final."

Torjack steps back with a deflated sigh.

The rest of us remain silent as Rynthea breathes in and out rapidly, one of her fists clenching and unclenching. Finally, she spares us from the tense silence and looks between the three of us.

"Do you even have a plan?" Her question is drowned by reluctance. "The Shallows is not an easy place to navigate."

Algar looks at Thane, who replies with, "We're making it to that temple."

"Well, if you're going to make it, and *if* I decide to join you, I need to hear a fucking plan." She scans all of us with narrowed eyes. "I know only one man personally who made it out of The Shallows alive. If we can speak to him, get some clear guidance, and figure out our chances of survival, then I'll see if it's worth joining you."

"Really?" Torjack's eyes light up as he gawks at his sister.

"Not now." She points a stern finger at him. As she stomps up the stone steps to leave the bunker, Torjack grins as if he's just won a grand prize.

Algar and I look at each other at the same time. He shrugs while I bite my bottom lip, unsure what to make of this whole situation.

We follow Rynthea out, and Torjack shuts and locks the hatch behind us before covering it up with leaves. When we near the inn, Penju is coming out the back exit, dragging a body by the ankles. He grunts as he places it on top of two other bodies to start a pile.

"Who were these people anyway?" Rynthea asks when we're all inside the inn again. Her question is one I've been wanting to ask, too, but I can't form the words while staring at the wreckage.

Orvena's sake.

The place is a mess. Blood is sprayed on the walls, and nearly all the furniture is ruined. Several of the glass windows are shattered, and I don't even want to count how many dead bodies are lying around with puddles of blood and guts surrounding them.

"They're most likely with the Grim." Thane steps over a headless corpse on the floor. I refrain from gagging at the smell of iron in the air and choose to stare at the barrels behind the bar instead. That doesn't help much, though, considering there are streaks of blood there, too.

"Why are you mixed up with the Grim?" Rynthea stares at him like he has two heads.

"I'm not mixed up with them," he retorts.

"And what about the one who got away?" Algar cuts in. "The one who wielded magic like you? Do you know him?"

"Maliek," Thane grumbles, jaw clenching.

Wait...Maliek?

"What does this Maliek want with you?" Rynthea continues her interrogation.

"I don't know," he says, and I'm positive he's lying.

Rynthea glowers at him, not buying it, either.

"So what will it be, Rynthea?" Algar probes. "You joining us or what?"

She places eyes on Torjack, who is examining the mutilated bodies, half disgusted, half fascinated.

"I'll only agree if we speak to the survivor of The Shallows," she answers. "But *only* because I'll have to close the inn for now *and* because I don't want Tor going with the likes of you. *If* this survivor can help us and the odds are in our favor, I will take the journey. He's not far—only a couple of hours away, in Bernwood."

"Fucking shadows." Thane sighs. "As if we need more of our time wasted. We aren't even supposed to be *here*."

"It is wise to have a solid plan before reaching The Shallows," Algar chimes in.

"I agree," I toss in. "If it'll only take a few hours to reach this person, I think we can spare it. Better to be safe than sorry."

Thane gives his head a slow shake. After several seconds tick by, he says, "Fine."

"So be it." Rynthea sighs.

"We'll clean up the place a bit, then we go," Thane says. "Algar, help me get these bodies outside so we can burn them. Once we're done, we're leaving to find your little survivor, Rynthea, and we'll have to make it quick because time is dwindling." He eyes the lady minotaur before gripping an armless body by the feet and dragging it toward the hallway, leaving a trail of smeared blood behind.

"I don't know how any of you can trust him," Rynthea says when Thane disappears behind the wall. She inspects her fingernails with a frown. "Great. Those scoundrels made me break a nail."

"Thane's not all bad." Algar shoves one of the bodies onto its back with his foot. "He just has to warm up to you. But for the record, he hates being challenged. I know you have your scythesword and all, but don't go swinging it at him, all right? I don't want him killing you in your sleep."

Torjack blanches. "He'd do that?"

Rynthea tosses her head back to laugh as she moves past Algar. "I'd love to see the fucker try."

When she enters the kitchen, I realize that I've been silent during the majority of their conversations. As I absorb my surroundings, I feel nauseated, and a tight sensation is developing in my chest. They all proceed with their tasks, moving the bodies or dragging them, as if this is a normal occurrence. There has to be close to fifteen of them.

So much blood. So much *death*. Is it really going to be like this the whole way to Elphar?

My throat thickens with unwelcome emotions.

Dread. Uncertainty. Fear. None of this is normal.

"You okay, Zaira?" Algar pops up on my left, startling me.

"Yeah." I force a nod. "I think I just... I think I need some air."

"Oh, okay. Would you like me to—"

I hurry past him to reach the front door before he can finish. Once outside, I scurry around a corner while sucking in rapid breaths. When I find a wooden bench, I sit immediately and pull my knees up to my chest, breathing in and out with my head buried in my lap.

Just focus on your breath. Okay, Z? Breathe in and out.

That's what Analla would tell me. But she isn't here, and knowing that makes the breaths harder to control. Knowing I'm surrounded by a group of killers makes my body swirl with anxiety. I have no idea what kind of mess I've thrown myself into, but my mother was right. I'm in the muckiest muck of all, and there is *no* going back now.

Stuck. I'm stuck with my decision.

I don't know if I can do this. Surviving seems even less likely now, and that terrifies me.

Hot tears fill my eyes, but I close them to soothe the burn. I want to tell myself I can make it work—but I've seen the worry in Rynthea's eyes. If a minotaur as strong as her doesn't believe she can make it through The Shallows, how can I? I don't have a fraction of the strength she has, and I don't know a damn thing about using weapons or combat. I'm an ordinary mortal in my twentieth year, who spends most of her life reading, sipping tea, volunteering at refugee centers, and baking. I'm much too simple for such madness.

And then my mind circles back to Dulan, another ordinary mortal. For some reason, the memory of him strikes me hard, to the point I feel stabbing pains in my stomach. That poor boy was murdered in cold blood because he helped *us*. What will his grandmother do once she realizes he's missing? How will she get her medicines now? Who will look for his body? Or has it been burned by the fires we left behind? Or worse, picked up by the Ruvainers and hung in the city center for all to call him a traitor?

I press the heels of my palms to my temples and squeeze my eyes shut.

Gods, this is too much.

I genuinely don't know how I'm going to survive this journey. I'll be lucky if I survive another hour of it.

Something soft rubs against my arm, then I feel dulled claws dig into my shirt as they climb their way to my upper body. I lift my head to see Zephra now perched on my shoulder. Her head is cocked at an unnatural angle as she ogles me. Her big eyes bore into mine for a few seconds, then she brings her head closer as I sniffle. Her furry crown rubs across my cheek to wipe some of my tears away.

"Oh, goodness." I sniffle again, reaching for her with both hands. She settles into my cupped palms, peering up at me like she has a million questions she wants to ask. Dulan was right. She *is* really soft, and her pink fur is beautiful. "You're the cutest thing, thief and all."

She chitters, pointing her little paws to my left. I look in the direction she's pointing and spot Thane standing next to a nearby post with his mask down and his eyes trained on me.

Oh, gods. Don't tell me he saw me crying.

As he approaches, Zephra hops out of my hands and scurries toward him. I quickly wipe my remaining tears away. For some odd reason, Zephra climbs up his body to reach his shoulder and stares at him expectantly. Thane lifts his hand, offering her a mound of almonds.

"Good girl," I hear him murmur as she devours them.

Zephra hops off his shoulder and scampers away.

"Did you tell her to come and do that?" I ask.

"Not exactly." He steps closer. "I told her to run over and smack some sense into you. She chose a nicer deed."

I fight a smile, lowering my chin so he can't see my puffy eyes, but I don't stop side-eyeing him.

"You know you don't have to do this, right?" His face turns serious, eyebrows knitting, jaw setting.

"Yes, I do. I refuse to let my sister die."

"That minotaur woman is right." Thane blows a breath, standing close enough to block the sun from my view. "Taking this journey with me at your side *is* deadly—"

"Yeah," I scoff. "I learned that back in Redclaw."

"It's *deadly* for the people who cross me," he finishes. I meet his gaze. His eyes aren't as serious as usual. There is a tenderness to them. Possibly a touch of sincerity. Or maybe I'm just imagining it, just like I had in the bunker, and hours before that, when he was using his whispershade. "I won't let anyone or anything hurt you during this journey, Quinlocke."

With a hard swallow, I ask, "How can I be sure of that?"

"Because I wouldn't have agreed to do this if I didn't think I could succeed. If there's one thing you should know about me, it's that I *hate* failing."

I purse my lips together while staring at my lap. My clothes have so many holes and rips in them now. It's all a sheer reminder of the chaos surrounding me. I definitely need a bath. And possibly a nap. My adrenaline is slowly seeping away, leaving behind only weariness.

"Can I ask you something?" My voice comes out softer than expected.

He lifts a brow of approval.

"You seem really determined to make it to Elphar, and I know it's not just for my sake. Is there something there that you're after, too? Do you want treasure like Algar?"

He's quiet for a second, eyes drifting to focus on a cluster of trees in the distance. "There is one thing."

I perk up a bit. "What is it?"

He seems to contemplate telling me. "The Tome of Azidel."

"The *what*?"

He sighs. "It's a book of spells written by the firstborn sorcerer."

"Oh." I pause. "Why do you want it?"

"Because there are spells in there that can increase the power of my magic."

I chew on the corner of my bottom lip. "You seem pretty powerful already. Why do you want to increase it?"

"I have my reasons."

I wait expectantly for him to continue.

"I don't care to explain them right now."

"Of course not," I mumble. "It would be nice to know, though. Might make this journey of ours a bit easier."

"How so?" he asks, lowering those amber eyes to me again.

"Because we both want the same thing, and that's to reach the temple for something we desire. Better to work *with* each other than against, right?"

"Hmm." I can't tell if that's a positive or a dismissive "hmm."

"Don't get me wrong, I still loathe that I'm doing *any* of this with a person like *you*," I say, teasing, "but if it's my only option, I may as well accept it."

"You're basically saying you hate me."

"Hate is too strong of a term."

His mouth twitches at the corners.

I smile a little. After a few seconds, I ask, "So what happens if Maliek finds you again?"

His jaw ticks this time.

I push my specs up the bridge of my nose. "He caught me and Torjack in the inn before we made it out the back door. He was…choking me with this invisible grip—almost like the one you used when you tossed me out of the Tilted Crystal. Only his felt colder and sharper." I shudder at the reminder of Maliek's harsh magic, the fierce look in his eyes. "He came after me and called me *the noble one*. I don't understand what he meant by that."

Thane looks back toward the inn. "You don't have to worry about Maliek or anyone else while you're with me."

"Because you won't let anyone hurt me?"

"Glad you're finally catching on."

"Why does he want *you* so badly, though?" I prod.

Thane presses his lips firmly together as he steps back.

I stand up to scan the details of his face—those jagged scars and the dark flecks embedded in his irises. The hardness of his prominent features, the slightest hook in his nose, his sculpted lips.

"You're a man of many secrets, Thane," I murmur. "I knew that when I first met you. You were this big, blinding mystery, and I'm realizing you like it that way. You like that people don't know much about you—you don't want anyone to figure you out."

"Your point?"

"I just can't imagine all the things you're hiding. Or who you *really* are under all that black and leather."

He matches my stare, allowing several quiet seconds to tick by before stepping in closer. Leaning down, he brings his lips so close to the shell of my ear that a chill runs down my spine, and a tingle slinks from my stomach to my inner thighs. I clench my fists to chase away the illicit feelings that one action alone has brought me.

His warm breath spills down my chest, causing my nipples to pebble beneath my bra. I contain the desperate sigh brewing inside me as he says, "Don't pretend my so-called secrets don't intrigue you, Quinlocke."

I close my eyes and swallow, ignoring the delicious stir in my stomach.

When I open my eyes again, Thane leans back with a faint smirk on his face and gives me a full once-over. He then marches away, and perhaps it's my imagination, but I swear I hear a dark rumble of a laugh leave him before he enters the inn, as if he knows his words and proximity have gotten the best of me.

I sit on the bench again with a huff.

What the shadows is this man doing to me?

Chapter 17

It takes longer than expected for them to clear the bodies, drag them to the middle of the forest, and burn them. Despite them going deep into the woods, I can still smell the scent of burning flesh, and it's putrid. It's so bad it makes me want to throw up.

By the time most (but not all) of the blood is cleaned up and broken tables are hauled out and tossed in a pile, the sun is setting. I didn't expect it to take so long, but what can we do now? It isn't wise to walk through any forests at night.

"Just stay the night," Rynthea says when I make a mention of it to Thane. She's working on starting a fire behind the inn. "There are plenty of rooms. I already have some dough rising, so I plan on baking bread and making more soup for everyone."

"Oh—I'll be happy to help you bake it," I offer, tossing up a hand. "I work in a bakery in Meriva, so I'm basically married to bread."

She laughs, and when the flames ignite and the wood crackles, she says, "Come on, then. You handle the bread and I'll make more soup."

Within the next couple of hours, the bread is fresh out of the oven and the soup is piping hot. We eat around the fire, perched on thick logs that connect around the firepit to form a square.

Rynthea, Torjack, and Algar chat away about Kamtaur Inn—future plans, fond memories, and past guests.

Thane is quiet...and I realize I am, too.

Baking bread took my mind off the massacre for just a while, but even now I can still smell the burned corpses lingering in the air.

A rustling noise sounds behind me, and Pearl groans a short distance away. I stifle a gasp as I look over my shoulder to where she's tied to a tree next to a water trough. I forgot she was there for a second.

Calm down, I think to myself.

But how can anyone be calm? I'm so jumpy after all the fighting and bloodshed I witnessed earlier. Thane said Maliek got away. What if he comes back to finish us all off? Not that I think Thane would allow it, but still. That man has magic, too. And he seems powerful.

I glance at Thane. He's already looking at me, studying my face with slightly narrowed eyes, as if he's trying to read my thoughts.

I look away, putting my focus on the fire instead, hoping it'll rid my mind of all the worries.

After dinner, Rynthea and Penju heat up water from their well and fill the washbasins in each room being used for the night. I study the basin on the stand, the ewer below, and sigh. At least I get to clean myself up a bit. I've been dying to wash the grime of today away.

After dipping my hands in the water and washing my face, I remove my clothes, then grab one of the cloths from the armoire. There's a small block of soap Rynthea left as well that smells like a mixture of spices and florals. It smells nice.

I wash with it while releasing a slow and steady breath. The water feels good on my skin. Refreshing.

As I dunk the cloth in the bowl again, I catch my reflection in the mirror connected to the washbasin stand and pause.

I look so...stressed.

All of my features are tense. And it's now I realize how much my body aches. Every limb feels heavy and every joint tight. I notice my shoulders are a little too close to my ears, so I relax them. The action does nothing to ease my mind, though. How can I relax when I'm traveling across the world with a shadow assassin? One who's being hunted by equally dangerous people?

Shaking my head, I finish washing, then strip out of my undergarments. There's a clean ivory gown in the armoire that I assume the inn offers to guests. I put it on. It's baggy and stops at my knees.

I go for my rucksack and take out my brush, then sit on a stool in front of the washbasin mirror to work through the kinks in my hair. The flames of candles in brass candelabras—one on a bedside table and the other on a windowsill—dance and sway, casting the room in a warm glow.

When I'm done, I put all my things away, then peruse the sparse bookshelf. I spot a book about minotaur origins and scoop it up so I can settle on the bed with it. It soothes me, hearing the pages flip. Feeling the paper under the pads of my fingers.

I'm about halfway through the book and yawning when I hear a knock at the door.

I freeze. It must be nearing midnight by now. Who could that be?

I blink at the door a few times. Maybe Rynthea wants to ask me something. Or Algar needs a word. Or we're about to be under attack again and they're trying to warn me as quietly as possible.

I climb off the bed, fully alert now as I head to the door.

My eyes widen when I crack it open and see...

"Thane?" I whisper.

His buffers are gone, and he's swapped his black tunic for a fresher one without sleeves. The muscles of his arms ripple under his warm, brown skin as he reaches up to scratch the back of his head. He's not even wearing his mask. He looks...normal. Almost mortal, really.

"Is everything okay? Are we in trouble again?" I ask, ready to gather all my stuff and run if so. We can hide in the bunker again.

"Everything's fine," he says, holding a hand up to calm me.

"Oh." I wrap my fingers around the edge of the door, opening it a bit wider. "Do you need something?"

His throat bobs up and down as he sighs. "I'm really not good with this sort of stuff."

"What sort of stuff?" I ask, and it's now that I notice one of his hands is hiding behind his back.

"I just came to give you this." He brings his hand around and offers something wrapped in a white cloth. I grab it, open it a bit, and a flood of warmth rushes through me. I can't help but smile when I see what he's given me.

"Honey loaf?" I look back up at him, tears springing to my eyes.

"I, uh…I asked Penju right after dinner if they sold any in Winstoft. He said they did, so I rode there to grab a slice. That was the last one their bakery had." He shrugs a shoulder. "I thought it might cheer you up a little, since the maobi didn't do the trick earlier."

A soft laugh escapes me. "She helped a little." I study the honey loaf again. It's cold, but it looks soft and delicious. "You went all the way to Winstoft for this?"

"It wasn't a long trek with Pearl."

I smile even wider. "Aww, you just said her name. Someone's getting attached."

"Okay, don't lose your mind over it." He rubs the top of his head with a small smirk.

I step closer, taking his free hand in mine and squeezing it.

"This is really sweet, Thane." Our eyes connect again. "Thank you."

He seems coy all of a sudden—gaze drifting, features softening. He's clearly not a man who receives lots of thank-yous. "Just making sure you're, you know, okay and everything. We still have a long journey ahead. It won't get any easier from here."

"I know." And yet I'm still committed, albeit terrified. I'm not giving up on Analla. I release his hand, studying the honey loaf again. "Do you think they'll come back?" I murmur, lifting my head. "The people from the Grim."

"I don't know, but I've cast a few spells around the inn to protect us. I'll know if someone approaches."

"Okay." I breathe a sigh of mild relief. "Good."

"I'm not going to let anything happen to you, Zaira." His face is serious again, determined. I can tell he means it.

"I sure hope not with all the coin I'm paying you," I tease.

I expect a laugh, but he only stares at me a moment or two before nodding. "Get some rest," he murmurs. "I'll see you at first light."

"Okay."

I watch him drift through the hall. He stops at his door and is about to grab the handle, but he pauses. He turns his head, looking in my direction again. Looking at *me*.

I wave. "Good night."

He opens his door. "Good night, Zaira."

When he disappears inside, I close my door and press my back to it. As

I look at the honey loaf again, a huge smile sweeps over my face.

I'm not even sure I can eat this with all the butterflies flapping around in my belly.

He went all the way to Winstoft for a single slice of sweet bread—and not just any sweet bread, one of my absolute favorites. He brought it by so he could check on me and see if I was okay. I might as well melt into a puddle of goo because that's the sweetest thing a man has ever done for me.

I laugh softly as I break off a piece of the loaf and pop it into my mouth.

Maybe the assassin has a heart after all.

Chapter 18

After packing rucksacks with supplies and water, then locking up the inn, the group of us who slept at Kamtaur Inn make our way to a small, rustic village called Winstoft. Apparently Rynthea and Torjack have a cabin outside of this village that their parents built before they were born. Penju owns a hut in the heart of town, and it has been decided by Rynthea that Torjack will stay with him until she returns.

"I wish you'd change your mind, Ryn. I'm sure I'll be fine if I travel with you—at least during this first part." Torjack shifts on his hooves as he stands in front of Penju's hut.

The hut's roof is swathed in vines and ivy, the exterior a combination of stone and wood painted a light blue. The door has been crafted into an arch that I'm not so sure Torjack will be able to squeeze through with his wide frame. Flowers are planted in stub barrels, and clay pots surround the hut, ranging in various colors and sizes.

Despite its washed-out, rustic appearance, Penju's hut has a charming appeal. It embodies a real home—a place I'm sure he cherishes and respects. I can tell by the swept stone steps, rocking chairs, and hanging lanterns on the short porch.

Rynthea glances sideways. I don't want her to think I'm eavesdropping, so I look away. Even though I am...unintentionally, of course. She told us earlier to wait at the end of Penju's walkway, but I can still hear pretty well from here.

Not too far away, Algar stands in front of a merchant stand, buying fruit, jerky, and nuts. Zephra rests on his shoulder, eyeballing all the food.

Thane is a few feet away from me, leaning against the wall of a cobblestone building with his mask in place and his arms folded. He remains vigilant as he keeps watch of our surroundings. I don't think he has very much to worry about in Winstoft. There are a few mortals, but most dwellers here are peaceful beastials. Pearl is right behind him, drinking from a bucket of water he's collected for her from the village well.

"We agreed. You'll stay with Penju where it's safe," I hear Rynthea say to Torjack. "No one should come for you here. And if I don't like what I find out about our odds, I'll be back soon anyway."

I bite into a juicy white snow fruit, focusing on the chipped statue of a beastial in a combat uniform in the center of the village.

Torjack groans with reluctance. "Fine. But be careful, Ryn. I *need* you."

"I'll be okay. Just make sure you take your medicines and let Penju escort you to the healers. If you feel stiff anywhere, rest and relax."

I glance their way as I finish off my fruit. They're hugging. When Torjack turns and ducks his head to enter Penju's hut, Rynthea stares at the spot where he'd been standing for several seconds with sorrow twisting her features. Her grip tightens around the handle of her scythesword, then she turns around and stomps down the steps.

"Let's go," she mutters, brushing past me.

"All set?" Algar calls after her.

Rynthea doesn't answer, just keeps marching.

Thane pushes off the wall to grab Pearl's reins and waits for me to pass. When we walk through the wooden gates of Winstoft, I can't help giving the quaint village one more look before continuing on.

I know how Rynthea feels. Leaving someone you love behind to do something incredibly dangerous yet could potentially save their lives? It's a hard decision to wrap your head around. None of it makes sense, but it feels necessary. I should know. I'm in the same boat.

Not that Rynthea *has* to do this, but if there is treasure in Elphar, she and Torjack could live the rest of their lives in peace. Torjack could have as many treatments as he wants. They could probably find a permanent healer for his disease. Kamtaur Inn would be restored. They could hire protection so no one would attempt to destroy it again. So many possibilities are ahead if this works out.

A forest looms before us. Rynthea clomps through a gap between two trunks, and her large body disappears as she goes deeper. I hurry to catch up with her.

"We need to be careful walking through here." Rynthea's voice is low as the forest becomes dense and thick with trees. Sunlight becomes scarce, and several crows perched on nearby branches flap away. "There are paths in Delchester Forest that you do *not* want to encounter. Do you see that?" She pauses for a moment, pointing at a fork in the trail ahead. "*Never* take the left or right. *Always* stay on the middle path."

"You've been through here before, too?" Algar asks.

"Twice," she answers. "And only during the day. I've heard stories about people veering off. They never return."

I look both ways as we press forward. The left path doesn't seem too bad. More light is coming from that way than the middle; however, the right is ominously dark. Clumps of long moss hang from the branches, floating like bodies that have been maliciously strung up. Branches croak, and the wind carries an eerie melody from that direction.

Out of instinct, I move closer to Rynthea but end up bumping into her arm. She glances at me with a note of concern.

I force a smile. "Sorry."

"All good." She says that, but her scythesword is gripped tighter in hand now, like she's expecting something to attack at any minute.

Up close, I see that the scythesword's blade is made of gleaming silver with a clean-cut edge and a dangerously sharp tip. It isn't your typical farmer's scythesword. Hers is crafted delicately, the polished black handle half of its usual size. The handle is crafted in a rope-like design and is truly impressive, especially since not many people fight and kill with scythesswords. They are much heavier than your usual sword and require not only great strength, but a unique set of skills.

"So why are we going through Delchester Forest if it's not safe?" I ask. "There are other routes, right?"

"Delchester is the quickest route from Winstoft to Bernwood," she answers. "We could have traveled to Junsho and hiked the mountains or waited at the ports, but the steepness of the mountains would slow us down, and who knows how long it would take just to get someone to let us ride their ship? Junshorians keep to themselves and aren't always inclined to go out of their way. If you want to beat that curse you mentioned, we can't afford to spend time begging for a ship ride to Bernwood ports. That could take days."

"Oh." I try matching my pace with hers. She has long strides, and her hooves stamp into the ground hard enough for me to consider being careful where I step. I'm lucky to not have broken spectacles. The last thing I need is a broken foot.

"I've heard way too many stories about Delchester," Algar says behind me. "Where I'm from, they call it *Death*chester."

"For good reason," Thane mutters, leading Pearl, who is packed up with our rucksacks and satchels.

"It's not too bad if you know where you're going." Rynthea scans the area ahead as she steps over a thick tree root.

"How long will it take to get to Bernwood from here?" I ask.

"Two hours, give or take."

"Hmm." Silence lingers between us before I clear my throat. "Well, while we're having a rare moment of tranquility, I was thinking I might need a weapon of my own."

"For what?" asks Thane.

I glance over my shoulder at him. He's frowning.

"Because if I'm traveling with people like all of *you*—"

"Whoa! Come on now!" Algar says as he feeds Zephra a slice of jerky.

"No offense," I add, looking between him and Rynthea, who simply laughs. "But we have to be honest here. You're a thief, Algar—not to mention you have an incredibly rare creature occupying your shoulder that people will pay a lot of coin for, especially when they realize she can steal on command. *You* told me that."

Zephra squeaks and bobs her head as Algar shrugs. "Fair point."

"And Rynthea, you're part minotaur." I gesture to her as she looks down at me again through the corner of her eye. "If the wrong people come across you, they'll try to kill you on sight."

"In their dreams," she grumbles.

"And Thane, well…you know what kind of threat you bring."

He provides a jaded blink.

"My point is, I'm traveling with a targeted group of people. We could be attacked at any time. I want to be able to protect myself somehow. So, if any of you have a spare dagger, a knife, or anything, I'll be happy to take it."

"Would you even know how to use it?" Thane chimes in.

"I can try," I shoot back. "I'm a quick learner."

"Okay. Say someone is about to kill you. Would you be willing to kill *them* to save yourself?" he asks.

I hesitate with my response, holding his gaze.

I can tell he's smirking underneath that damn mask.

"You don't strike me as a person who can steal a life and live with the consequences afterward, sweet one. If we give you a weapon, the enemy will likely turn it against you if you hesitate. There's no point in having one if you don't know how to use it or if you're not *willing* to use it at all."

"Then show me how," I counter. "You're the savage sorcerer with the blades, right? Show me where to strike so I can save myself."

Thane contemplates this as he rearranges Pearl's reins in one of his gloved hands.

"If he doesn't teach you, we will." Algar gestures between himself and Rynthea, tossing me a wink. "We've got your back, princess."

I smile. "Thanks, Algar."

"Okay, fine." Thane comes to a halt, and Algar follows suit. When I stop, Rynthea blows out an agitated breath and pauses, too. After digging through his rucksack strapped to Pearl's saddle, Thane takes out a sheathed weapon and hands it to me handle first.

"I was going to throw this one out anyway," he says as I close my fingers around it. "Don't let the size fool you. It's small but lethal."

I unsheathe it to reveal a black blade with silver lining the edges. Engraved in the hilt is the symbol of a familiar *D* with pointed edges.

"The Divine?" I swivel my eyes up to him again, but he's already backing away to take hold of Pearl.

"We should keep moving," he says.

"Gladly," Rynthea mutters.

I study the letter on the handle again as I follow along.

How did Thane get this? I mean, he could've stolen it from one of the soldiers...or killed one of them and taken it. But if he'd done that, he wouldn't have gotten away with it. The Divine are heavily protected and very close to the crown. One can't die without another knowing.

That leaves me wondering if they're after him, too. But what would possess him to attack one of The Divine? And why wouldn't a soldier have detained him when we were in Meriva if that were the case?

I peer over my shoulder at him, but now he's avoiding me altogether. He knows I have questions, and *I* know he isn't going to answer them...

at least not right now. I have the urge to slow my pace so I can match his.

He was right yesterday at Kamtaur. His secrets *do* intrigue me. I need to know who he really is beneath the mask and buffers. I want to ask so many things about the dagger, about Maliek, about who he *really* is. I'm so close to doing so…until I hear a voice cry out in the distance.

Immediately, Thane draws one of the swords strapped to his back. Rynthea comes to a halt, ears perked, and the handle of her weapon gripped tight in hand. Algar freezes along with Zephra as their eyes dart toward the sound.

"What was that?" I whisper, clinging to the handle of my new dagger.

"Shh." Rynthea steps past me and sniffs the air. Narrowing her eyes, she peers into the darkness, searching for the culprit. The cry pierces the silence again, sounding much closer this time. It's coming from the darkest path.

"Please," a small voice whimpers. "I need your help. I have—I have been badly hurt. Someone, please help me. I am begging you."

My heart drops. I know that voice. I turn to Algar. "That sounds like Dulan."

His eyebrows bunch together. "Impossible. Dulan died. We saw him go down right in front of us."

"Yes, we saw him go down, but that doesn't mean he died. He could've survived and now he's on the run." I turn to face the dark path again.

"Quinlocke, what you hear isn't real," Thane warns as gently as he can. "That's a trick of the forest. Don't fall for it."

"How can it be a trick? That sounds *just* like him."

"He's right, Zaira." Rynthea's eyes stretch wider as she shakes her head. "We should keep moving. That isn't whoever you think it is."

"Please help me. I will bleed to death. I—I just need help, *please*. I ran away from the guards. I held on for my nan because she needs me. I am wounded very badly. *Please, Zaira.* Help me."

Hearing him say my name sends a burst of cold through my veins.

And then I see something deep in the forest. A murky light growing brighter…and within it, a silhouette of a person stumbling toward us.

"Dulan," I whisper.

"That *isn't* him." Thane says the words through gritted teeth.

"It is him, Thane!" I look at Algar, whose eyes are swimming with apprehension and confusion. "We have to save him, Algar! He tried to help us!"

Algar puts his focus on Thane and Rynthea, who shake their heads at him in unison. "Zaira, we have to keep walking. If that *is* him, he'll find Winstoft and someone will assist him there." Algar grabs my shoulder, but I shake out of his grasp.

"Zaira, look at me." Hearing Thane say my first name again steals my attention away from the silhouette. He hardly ever says my first name unless he's serious—or taking me seriously. I look into his eyes, my heart rapidly beating. "This is not the time for saving people, do you hear me? You must let that part of you go during this journey. Not everyone can be saved. *Trust me.*"

My eyes burn with tears. I glance over again. The silhouette is closer now. Thane is right, but why can't I move? My eyes are locked on that dark outline—on Dulan limping toward us. His pleas for help eat at my heart. All I can think about are the children at the refugee center. The cries for their parents in the middle of the night. A new child joining the center with trauma pouring off them in waves. The horrors they likely witnessed just to escape. Survivor's guilt as they grew into teens and then adults... just like me.

My homeland—Ember Coast—was attacked by Ruvainers. We were victims of their madness, abuse, and anger. We only escaped because there was someone out there willing to help us.

I was lucky to find a new home in Meriva, despite being a refugee child. Not everyone gets that chance—especially innocent Ruvainers like Dulan. It will only take a few seconds to grab him and get back on the middle path. Only a few.

As my thoughts race, I feel a clench in my stomach. Something changes. I can feel it. It tugs at every sense and nerve, luring me toward the path to the right, sucking me in like a vortex. There is no resisting it.

Save him. You have to at least try. The whispers enter my mind and tickle my brain.

Before I know it, I'm running toward Dulan.

Thane shouts my name as he chases after me. I run faster.

"Zaira, stop!" he shouts.

The warm light burns brighter, and the silhouette grows in size. Dulan's pleading voice becomes closer. I hear water sloshing and gurgling in the distance. The scent of wet wood along with a rancid smell is strong enough to make me gag, but still, I don't stop.

Actually, no. I *can't* stop. Not until I realize Dulan's silhouette isn't forming into a person. It remains as just that. A dark figment of him. A *shadow*.

Something isn't right.

And then I wonder…

If Dulan escaped, why would he be here? Why would he not stop somewhere closer and ask for help? Why…

As the questions plague me, I come to an abrupt halt several feet away from the shadow as Thane rushes around to face me. "It isn't real, Zaira!" He points sternly toward the silhouette behind him. "It's a trick of the mind! Delchester Forest is notorious for it! It preys on the vulnerable so the creatures living here stay fed. It steals your thoughts, your worries, your *fears*, and turns them into something it can use to consume you!"

"But I—I swear I thought it was him." I can still feel that heaviness in my stomach, the words echoing in my brain to *come closer*, to *save him*. Something is continuously urging me forward, demanding that I keep moving. "I don't know what's happening, Thane. I'm sorry. It's like…like I can't control my body."

Help your friend. It's the right thing to do. Just take a few more steps. A few more steps, it repeats.

I squeeze my eyes shut, trying my hardest to ignore the voice, but my feet move anyway. One step followed by another.

Thane presses a firm hand to my chest to keep me still. "What do you mean you can't control your body?" His voice is laced with confusion.

I hear footsteps behind me and open my eyes again as Rynthea and Algar approach. They left Zephra and Pearl where it was safe. "We need to get back on the middle path *right now*." Rynthea glares at both of us, clearly irritated.

"Zaira, let's go." Thane wraps a large hand around mine. It's the first time he's touched my hand and held it in a protective way. I look up with a quickening heartbeat, wanting to see if he's aware of it, too, but I gasp instead because the shadow is closer to us now. My heart booms as the silhouette grows larger, *larger*, until it towers right behind Thane.

"Thane, look out!" Algar crows.

But it's too late.

The shadow forms into something else entirely, and the glow of the light fades, wrapping us in thick, foggy darkness.

Releasing my hand and turning, Thane swings his sword, but the shadow rapidly descends to the ground and fastens around his ankle. That's when I realize it isn't a shadow at all but a tentacle—slimy, gray, and barnacled.

"Fuck," Thane mutters as he looks down, as if he half expected this to happen.

With a yank from the tentacle, Thane falls to his stomach. And in the blink of an eye, he's dragged away, disappearing into the darkness.

Chapter 19

"Thane!" I scream.

"No!" Algar roars.

"Zaira! Get back!" Rynthea grabs my arm and tugs me aside just as another tentacle comes flying out of the darkness. She cuts it in half with her scythesword before locking eyes on Algar. "Take her and hide!" She stomps past us and runs into the fog after Thane.

Algar catches my wrist and runs, guiding us between a thick cluster of trees and boulders. He aims for the middle path where Pearl and Zephra are, but something slams into the tree in front of us. I scream, and Algar ducks as another tentacle blocks our way.

"This way!" Algar releases me, running in the opposite direction. The ground starts to turn to mush beneath my feet the farther we run. When we reach a large boulder, Algar tugs me aside so we can hide behind it.

"What the shadows is that thing?" My breaths come out swift and heavy as my heart hammers against my rib cage.

"I don't know!" Algar scans the perimeter with frantic eyes. "Gods—see, this is why I hate this death forest!"

In the distance, Rynthea unleashes a battle cry. As the fog begins to clear, I peer around the edge of the boulder to see if I can spot Thane and Rynthea. I shouldn't have, though, because what I see causes fear to swallow me whole.

Sickly, glowing yellow eyes burn through the remaining wisps of fog. Attached to those eyes is a monster that emerges from the cloudy waters of what appears to be a marsh or swamp stretching beyond it. Its skin is a thick, blotchy, grayish green. With broad shoulders, it's built like a giant, and its arms are the size of tree trunks. Worst of all, it has tentacles coming from all areas of its body, even its head. Some of the tentacles end with claws. Others don't. One of the clawless tentacles has Thane wrapped up tight by the midsection. He dangles upside down, grunting as he continuously swipes his sword at the tentacle but misses each time.

The monster gnashes its overly sharp teeth at Thane's face, but Thane prevents the incoming bite by hurling a blazing gold sphere at its head. With a deafening screech, the monster drops him, sending him plummeting into the swampy water.

While the monster is distracted, Rynthea lunges into the air and cuts several tentacles off with her scythesword. The monster roars as the severed tentacles create loud splashes and sink into the water. She darts around the border of the swamp, slicing at several more.

Breaking through the water's surface, Thane swims toward the nearest edge and catches his breath. When he manages to climb out, he's covered in swamp weeds and slime. He shoots to his feet, then snatches out his other sword with a scowl. The monster attempts to grab him again, but he dodges each tentacle, cuts at the ones in his way, and doesn't stop until he mounts a boulder and flies toward the beast with a whisper of gold and shadows guiding him. He lands on top of the creature's shoulder.

One of the monster's tentacles slaps down on the boulder Algar and I are near, and as if it can sense us, it reaches in my direction. I scream as the tentacle unfurls, revealing bumpy, undulating suction cups. Algar grunts as he stabs it with a dagger, and the monster screeches again.

I jump over the gushing tentacle, fleeing with Algar. There aren't many places to hide, though. The swamp extends in all directions, each path blocked by random tentacles, and the other boulders are much smaller. The tree trunks are too thin to hide behind, but something tells me if we keep running in random directions, we'll encounter monsters much worse than this one.

How the shadows do we get back to the main path from here?

We stop behind a tree that barely hides us and listen to the unnerving sounds of the monster squawking, Rynthea hollering, and Thane yelling as he fights.

"We have to help them." I focus on Algar, my heart racing madly. "They aren't going to beat that thing on their own. Do you have any grenades on you?"

"Grenades? Have you lost it?" he yells. "No one carries grenades on their person unless they want to die."

"I mean, I just assumed, since you're a thief who likes to break into things and all…"

He cocks a brow. "I don't use *grenades* to steal, Zaira. Much too obnoxious. Besides, the sorcerers who spell them charge way too much."

"Right. Okay, um…" I peer around the tree, gripping the damp bark as Thane struggles to gouge one of the monster's eyes out. Rynthea's lower half is now wrapped up in a tentacle, while another with a claw tries taking snaps at her head. She punches the claw away each time, but I'm not sure how long she'll be able to keep it up with the lower one squeezing tighter and tighter around her midsection.

I look at the monster again…and that's when I see it.

Just below the right side of the swamp creature's head are gills. From what I studied—no matter if it was a fish, beastial, or even a monster—the gills are a sure way to weaken a water creature.

"There!" I point. "The gills! They need to puncture the gills!"

"What?" Algar turns his head, utterly confused.

"The gills! They have to— Ugh! Never mind! Just follow me!" I grip the handle of my new dagger and pray for Orvena to protect me so I can, with her favor, save Rynthea and Thane.

I dash around the tree, and Algar shouts my name, demanding that I come back. I ignore him. If I don't save them, they'll die a horrible death because of me. And on top of that, there's no way I'm making it to Elphar without the minotaur and the assassin. I need them.

I climb over jagged rocks and slide down a short, mossy embankment. My feet land in a deep, slushy puddle and nearly get stuck in the muck. As I grunt with frustration, struggling to free my boots from the mud with each step, I notice the monster is so much uglier up close. And it smells like pure shit.

"Thane!" I yell once I'm on stable ground again.

Thane whips his gaze in my direction. "What the shadows are you doing?" he shouts. "Get back to safety!"

"The gills!" I yell. "Stab it in the gills!"

His face warps with confusion. Either he can't hear me, or he doesn't understand what I'm going on about.

"Damn it," I hiss.

I look in Rynthea's direction. She's now bound in *two* tentacles. She bites one of them with a growl, but that does nothing to the monster. Rushing her way, I clumsily dodge and duck tentacles until I stumble across her scythesword lying next to one of the trees and grab it.

It's heavier than I expected.

Rynthea grunts, trying to break free, but the monster only squeezes her tighter. Her agonized cry makes my heart sink. One of the tentacles rises behind me, but I hold the handle of the scythesword in a firm grasp and use all my strength to swing. To my surprise, I chop the thing in half.

"Oh shit." I pant, astonished.

The monster screeches once again, just as Algar appears in front of me.

He sticks his hand out. "Give me that damn thing before you cut your leg off!"

I place it in his hands, and he teleports to the other side of the tentacles that are death-gripping Rynthea. With a mighty holler, Algar swings the scythesword and cuts through both of them, sending black blood spraying toward the trees as Rynthea collapses on the ground.

"Rynthea." I dash her way, trying to help her stand.

"I'm fine, I'm fine." She presses her knuckles into the mud and pushes herself up.

We look for Algar. His clothes are now stained with inky blood. "Fucking disgusting!" he shouts.

"Give me my scythesword," Rynthea demands.

Algar tosses it to her, and she catches it with one hand just as another tentacle aims straight for us. She whips the scythesword by the handle and slashes through it before it can strike.

"You both are meant to be hiding!" she barks at us.

"Well, if we'd kept on hiding, your precious guts would be spread all over this swamp right now, wouldn't they?" Algar fires back.

Her nostrils flare as she glares at him, shaking her head.

"Rynthea, listen to me." I grab her arm and force her attention on me. "You need to aim for the gills. A monster that size must have lots of them, and they're probably close to its hearts. If you can strike some of the gills, you can weaken it even more and finish it off."

She stares at me for a fleeting second. When my words sink in, determination settles on her face, and she nods. Stomping past Algar, she charges toward the beast and leaps into the air. Her scythesword swings downward, and the tip lands close to the monster's ribs, piercing right through one of its gills.

The monster belts out a scream that seems to shake the entire forest.

Tentacles flail as blood oozes down its side.

Algar wrenches me toward him, and there is a sudden drop in my stomach as he teleports us away from the battle area. The ground feels unsteady beneath me as we wind up next to another boulder, this one smaller than the previous.

"Whoa." I throw my hands out to steady myself again, blinking several times to clear the short spell of dizziness. "I didn't know people could teleport *with* you."

"Yeah," he replies, panting. "Wears me out, though, so I don't do it often."

"But you kept telling Thane constantly to use his whispershade in Ruvain, even though you knew it would wear him out. That's a bit hypocritical, don't you think?"

"Excuse me. If I hadn't insisted that he use it, those Ruvainers would be fucking you in a dungeon right now! *To death!*"

"Orvena help me," I groan.

The monster howls again, drawing my attention back to the onslaught. I look in its direction. Thane has caught on to what Rynthea is doing as she runs along one of the thicker tentacles before it can descend and penetrates another gill. He swings one of his swords at an angle to stab the set of gills on the other side of its neck.

The monster roars in agony.

Thane and Rynthea don't relent.

They manage to reach the monster's shoulders as it throws up all of its remaining tentacles in an attempt to stop them. The two of them bob and weave, look at each other, nod, and then jump off either side, but not without piercing their blades into the creature's neck. With their descent, the blades drag downward and slide right across the monster's throat. Two cuts interconnected.

Thane and Rynthea plunge into the gooey water as the cries of the monster cease. The large head topples off and drops into the swamp, causing an even greater splash. The ground quakes when the body of the monster descends backward and slams down.

It's gone...and so are Thane and Rynthea.

The atmosphere quiets. Water gurgles. My pulse thunders in my ears.

I step around the boulder, waiting with bated breath for them to resurface.

Algar joins me at my side, and our faces seem riddled with the same anxiety. I fear they might be dead. The seconds feel like hours as the swamp water conjures up slow, slimy bubbles.

And then a sharp, loud gasp breaks through the air. Thane has emerged, and right next to him is a massive gold bubble floating on the surface of the water. Rynthea is inside that bubble, and Thane grunts as he holds one hand out to keep her steady while swimming with his other arm to reach the nearest edge.

Algar and I rush over to assist. When Algar offers him a hand, Thane grips it tightly and is hauled out of the water.

As soon as he's on land, Thane collapses, sucking in deep, rapid breaths. Rynthea is still in the gold bubble, floating on the surface, but the light is fading. Raising a weak hand, Thane grunts as he guides the bubble out of the water. Then his arm falls, the bubble dissolves, and Rynthea drops like a stone on the ground.

"Rynthea?" Algar hurries to her side, giving her a shake. "Are you all right?"

She doesn't budge.

"The monster's head landed on her." Thane flips onto his back with his eyes shut. After a second or two, he sits up. Though he's weak, he seems fine. He isn't the one who needs me right now.

I rush to Rynthea's side.

"Hey. Rynthea. Can you hear me?" When I get no response, I hover my ear above her nose. "She's not breathing."

I study her face. Her lips are tinged blue. I press my ears to her chest and listen for a heartbeat. It's barely there, but there, nonetheless. I sit back on my heels and sigh with relief, glad she's not dead. Yet.

I'm not sure if I'm strong enough to resuscitate a minotaur, but I have to try. I place my hands under her neck, which is thick with muscle, so tilting her head back to open her airway takes effort. I place my mouth over hers and give her several strong rescue breaths.

"Come on," I whisper.

Nothing.

I press my hands firmly to her chest and start compressions. Over and over again, I push with all my might, but I'm not sure it's enough, considering her size.

"Do you know what you're doing?" Algar asks.

I ignore him and give her a few more breaths, then place my hands over her sternum and pump again.

"Come on, Rynthea," I rasp, my vision blurring with tears. This wouldn't have happened if I'd listened to her and if I'd stayed on the middle path. If I'd used my head instead of my heart, she would be fine.

My arms tremble from the strain and exhaustion. Maybe I'm not strong enough. I'm just about to ask Algar to try compressions when she twitches. Then her chest expands and her eyes pop open.

Oh, thank Orvena.

I turn her head to the side, and water spills from her mouth. "Algar, help me," I say, trying to roll her over. Algar joins, and we manage to get her onto her side. He shifts back just as she coughs and sputters, gagging up swamp water, chunks of weeds, and who knows what else.

"Orvena's sake, Rynthea," he mutters, staring at the mess she's created.

I laugh with relief as I help her sit up. "Are you okay?"

After a few deep breaths and another bout of coughing, her eyes turn to mine, burning wild with confusion. "Did you just save me?"

I smile. "I did."

"Where did you learn?"

"I was born in Ember Coast so…" I shrug. "Sort of mandatory to know this kind of thing when you live near the sea."

Rynthea just stares at me. The longer she does, it feels like she's seeing me as an entirely different person. Like I'm not just some simple, useless mortal. Before I know it, she's locked her massive arms around me to collect me in a hug.

I giggle as her damp vest and hair press to my cheek.

"Thank you, Zaira."

"You're welcome. But I wouldn't have been able to resuscitate you at all if Thane hadn't brought you to shore."

When I gesture to Thane, Rynthea peers over to where he's still sitting with his legs spread wide and knuckles planted into the ground. He blinks with damp, feathery lashes.

"Thanks to you, too, I guess." Rynthea stands up slowly.

"You guess?" He grunts as he hoists himself up, too.

She takes a beat. "*I guess* I appreciate you saving my life." It looks like she wants to say more but thinks better of it, and Thane knows it. "I just mean…thanks for…helping me out and everything." Her words are strained. Does she really not trust sorcerers that much? I can't help thinking something must've happened in her past for her to feel so strongly against them.

Rynthea steps back, searching for something. Her scythesword is floating near one of the swamp edges. When she snatches it up, she inspects the blade. "We need to get back to the middle path. That swamp monster was only a sample of what lurks in Delchester."

She gives Thane a sideways glance before walking past him.

Thane motions his hands toward the water to call his swords. They fly out rapidly, the hilts slamming into his palms before he tucks them away in a seamless motion.

Algar meets up to Thane. "She'll learn to trust you. You just have to give her time."

"Was saving her life not enough?" Thane's question is genuine.

Algar offers a helpless shrug before following Rynthea.

When they're out of earshot, Thane tilts his face to the sky, takes a large inhale, and exhales.

"You saved her. She won't forget that." I step closer to him, watching as he rakes his fingers through his soaked hair. "I didn't think either of you would— I mean…" I sigh. "I'm just glad you made it out alive."

"Yeah." His gaze shifts to me. "Smart call on the gills."

"Yeah, well, it's a good thing I love reading about beastial anatomy."

Thane quirks a brow.

I cough up an awkward laugh, realizing that sounded cheesier than I expected.

He narrows his eyes at me. I can feel the heat of his body as those bold irises focus on my lips. When his fingers clasp my chin, I hold my breath, focusing on his lips, too.

My mouth tingles, anticipating something I'm not sure I need but know I *want*. My body is *craving* his touch. *Why?*

When his lips are only a hair's breadth away, he says, "You disregarded rule number one."

I blink, confused. "What?"

"*'Keep your kind gestures to yourself because they'll only get you killed,'*" he reiterates.

Oh.

"You have to stop trying to *help* people, Quinlocke. You do realize that if you'd stayed on the main path, none of this ever would've happened, right?"

Ah. So we're back on a condescending last-name basis. Gods, he's so confusing. Frustrated, I try to pull my face out of his hands, but he won't let go.

His eyes spark with gold, burning with a hint of frustration, too. "You could've died," he rasps. "All of us could've died for someone *you* thought you could save. Even if he had been real, how were you going to help him? How, when you can't even save *yourself*?"

We stare at each other, me fighting the urge to cry again, and him seeming more disappointed by the second.

Finally, he lets his hand drop away, and my stomach sinks. His clear disappointment bothers me more than it should. Why do I care what he thinks of me? He has no right to judge.

He looks me over from head to toe while shaking his head. "Sometimes it's hard to remember that…" He pauses. "That you're this sheltered woman who doesn't understand the true dangers of this world. Algar and Rynthea? They know what it's like to be threatened—to try and help someone, only to be fucked over. But you… *Fuck*. You wear your heart on your sleeve, Quinlocke, and that'll get you *killed* one day. You may think your bravery will save you, but it won't. This I know for a fact."

"How would you know anything about bravery?" I retort as heat rises to my cheeks. "You live your life as an arrogant *assassin*." I whisper-hiss the last word, not wanting it to carry to Rynthea and Algar. "All you care about is killing, shutting people out, and making others feel inferior to you. You wouldn't understand what it's like to care about others because all you care about is yourself, Thane."

His mouth opens, as if he's about to say something in defense, but just as quickly, it snaps shut and he steps back. Jaw clenched, he closes his eyes and inhales. After exhaling, he peels his eyes open and settles them on me again.

"I don't have to explain who I am to you," he responds in a lower voice. If I didn't know better, I'd say he almost sounds hurt. "You didn't pay me to be your friend. You paid me to keep you alive." He shoves a dagger into one of the sheaths in his vest. "What does it matter? There's no point in arguing with a naive woman."

My eyebrows incline. *"Naive?"*

"Yes, naive."

"I'm not as naive as you think," I counter as he turns his back to me.

"Whatever. Let's just go."

I steel myself as he treks forward and start to say something else just to have the last word, but he stops and says, "For once, listen to me, and return to the middle path."

He stands sideways, pointing in the direction Rynthea and Algar have gone, jaw flexed, nostrils flaring. With a grimace, I storm past him, but not without purposely bumping into his arm. He doesn't budge, but he does release an irritated huff.

The worst part about that conversation with Thane is that he's right. Had I just left the situation alone, had I just kept walking, Thane never would've been snatched away by that monster. Rynthea wouldn't have almost drowned. I risked all of our lives because my soft, empathetic heart couldn't handle leaving a stranger behind. A stranger who was never even there.

Thane's words sting, only because I can't help the way that I am. But if I don't toughen up, my empathy will certainly be the death of me...of all of us.

Chapter 20

I feel nothing but pure relief when I see we're nearly out of Delchester Forest. As soon as the break in the trees comes into view, along with the sunset bathing the green pastures ahead, I quicken my pace.

Algar had a point. Delchester should have been named *Death*chester instead. The swamp monster was the worst thing we faced, but eerie sounds from deep in the forest accompanied us all along the way.

None were like the false cries of help from Dulan that made me lose control of my body as I was lured in the monster's direction, but there were whispers. And on the left path, I heard a woman scream like she was being brutally murdered. It sent chills up my spine but didn't seem to affect the others as much. I suppose the swamp monster had done them in.

Courtesy of that awful attack, it takes us closer to three hours to get completely out of the forest. My feet were killing me on the path, so I climbed onto Pearl's back to rest them for a while. I took turns with Algar, whose limp had become more pronounced the longer we walked. We took one break when Rynthea complained about pain in her ribs.

Now we're clear of that damn forest.

As soon as I feel that first sip of sunlight, I hop off Pearl's back and jog toward the center of the grassy field.

I toss my head back to peer up at the open sky, admiring the beautiful swirls of pink and orange as well as the flat white clouds scattered throughout. A ten times better view than the dark, hovering treetops of the forest.

In the distance is a gray stone mountain flanked in greenery with an abundance of lush, leafy trees spread throughout its rocky paths. The peaks seem to touch the sky while the broad bodies of mountains run east and west for miles.

Zephra flies past me, and her transparent pink wings catch in the light as her fur and tail sway with the wind.

Rynthea staggers past. "Let's keep going." Her left leg is injured, too, a small gash, but she wrapped it in bandages before we continued on the middle path. "Bernwood's gates are not too far away, and it's best to get there before dark."

"Don't they lock their gates after a certain time?" Algar asks.

"Yes, to keep pests like *you* away," Rynthea throws at him.

Algar snorts. "One day you'll be kind to me, Rynthea."

"This *is* me being kind to you. Now hurry up."

I laugh as I trail behind them.

Thane is in the back, guiding Pearl again. I haven't spoken to him since our argument near the swamp...if I can even call it an argument. It felt more like a scolding. Regardless, I don't see the point in apologizing for something I had absolutely no control over. He knows this, too, yet it feels like he's blaming me for every single thing.

Sure, a part of it was my fault, and I do feel terribly guilty that they were hurt, but I literally felt helpless in that moment. I was under some kind of trance, and like he said—the forest preys on the vulnerable.

I suppose that's why he's truly upset with me.

Because he thinks I'm this weak, pathetic mortal—the complete opposite of him and his unyielding power. I bet he's having second thoughts about this journey, too.

I try not to let those thoughts weigh me down and enjoy this moment of walking through the knee-high grass. Even the air feels cooler and less stiff now as a sweet hint of jasmine and honeysuckle drifts past my nose. A low trickle of water sounds nearby, likely from a brook.

My mouth dries. The sound of water reminds me of how thirsty I am. Rynthea offered us individual canteens before leaving Kamtaur, but we ran out shortly after the swamp.

Eventually—and much to my relief—we reach a wall of stone. Built into the center are two towering iron gates with the letters *B* and *W* engraved in the handles. Four guards stand before it while two more gaze down from watchtowers on the opposite side of the wall. All are beastials of various species.

One is built like a bear. Another has green fish scales on its face but seems mostly mortal. The beastial farthest to the right has the broad stature and fur of a gorilla, and the other has the eyes and skin of a snake. The two in the watchtower have eyes like owls with brown feathers protruding out of vents in their silver helmets.

"Permits," the bear beastial demands as we approach.

Rynthea digs into her rucksack to fish something out. While she does, the other guards scrutinize us. As Rynthea hands the bear her permit, he wrinkles his nose and says, "What the shadows is that *smell*?"

"Swamp monster," she responds with a shrug.

The guards look at one another, disgusted. "A *swamp monster*?" the bear scoffs.

"Yes. Look at us." She gestures to her filthy clothes before showing him her injured leg. "We're hurt, covered in slime, dirty water, and monster blood, so the sooner you let us in, the quicker we can make use of the baths. Gods know I need one right now."

The bear sniffs the air again, then turns his head away to dry-heave.

"Stop trying to smell it, then," the gorilla grumbles to the bear.

"I can't help it. They smell like wet shit."

Rynthea growls, and the bear straightens his back. I stifle a laugh, which earns me a glower from the bear.

"What is the purpose of your visit?" he asks after clearing his throat.

"The Autumnal Beast Fete," Rynthea replies.

"Are you on the guest list?"

She stacks her spine. "Ask your king."

I frown, confused. She has to be bluffing.

The bear inclines an eyebrow beneath his silver helmet. "The king isn't to be disturbed tonight."

"Just tell him my name. Rynthea Kamtaur. He'll be happy to welcome us in."

The bear narrows his eyes at her before studying the rest of us again.

"For Orvena's ssssake, Yelahn!" the snake guard hisses. "Jussst let them passss and we'll deal with it inssside!" He covers his narrow nostrils with a gloved hand. "I can't take another sssecond of the ssssmell!"

All the guards howl with laughter at the snake's outburst.

I sputter a laugh myself, looking from them to Algar, who's found the situation just as comical as I have. Thane and Rynthea, however, are not tickled in the slightest.

"Fine. Go on. Ask for the king, but you'll get nothing of it," the bear instructs with a dismissive wave of his paw. "And I beg of you. Wash four times and then burn the clothes. You smell like you've been rolling in a pigsty."

The scaly beastial hurries toward the gates, shouting for them to open it from the inside. To my relief, the gates spread apart, creaking mildly at the hinges as they open at a snail's pace. As we pass through, the fish-scaled one covers his nose again, which I think is hilarious, seeing as his lineage is likely connected to the sea and, last I checked, fish don't have a pleasant scent.

"Okay, either they've all been drinking, or they're insanely bored at those gates," Algar chortles as we stroll in.

"They're all ridiculous," Rynthea mutters. "Poor excuses for guards."

As we walk deeper into the village, I have to take a moment to appreciate the beauty of this place. On the outside, the kingdom of Bernwood doesn't appear like much, but the inside is charged with life. I have a feeling it's because of the fete Rynthea mentioned.

Beastials of all species wander about, carrying sacks full of clothing, silk, and other materials. Beastial children run around giggling with sticks of colorful, oversize sugar pops in hand, and in the distance is a stunning view of the ocean with half of the sun nestled beneath the horizon. Several speedships are lined up at the ports with people carrying barrels and crates on and off.

We trek across an ivy-clad bridge arching over a river that connects the modest homes to the bustling attraction of the marketplace. Stalls and tables overflow with silk fabrics, rare spices, and ripe fruit. A wagon piled with red and lilac flowers is carted along the cobblestone streets, zipping right past us. Gorgeous horses clomp along with carriages attached by breeching straps. One of the beastials guiding a carriage tips his hat at us.

I can't help but smile.

Deeper in the village, wooden merchant stands painted deep purple or navy blue are built between stone boutiques. Each one has a line of eagerly waiting beastials. A gentle breeze carries the scent of roasted meats and vegetables from a food alley. It's enough to make my mouth water and my stomach growl.

But the village is no competition for the towering castle in the distance. Built into the mountains and made purely of stone is a castle just as tall as the Crystal Palace in Meriva. A sundial to match is attached to a thick tower on the left.

Wow.

Bernwood is beyond *gorgeous.*

I've read many things about this kingdom. It's where the famous alvanite stone originates. Alvanite is used to construct the sturdiest buildings, homes, and ships. Bernwood often trades it with other kingdoms, which makes this a generally wealthy settlement.

It's why no other kingdom has ever started a war with them. Not only does Bernwood have a massive army with some of the strongest beastials in all of Thelanor, but any kingdom willing to ruin their healthy supply of alvanite stone would be foolish. Alvanite is nearly as valuable as gold.

After collecting our gear from Pearl's saddle, we drop her off at a stable where Thane pays a stable boy for her food and water. She is worn out from the journey, just like us.

We then walk across a towering bridge with royal purple flags attached to thick posts. I notice each flag has the symbol of a black lion standing on all fours, its mouth ajar and its tail erect. Nearing the end of the bridge, I realize we're within walking distance of the front doors of the castle.

Wait. Is Rynthea really going to try and talk to the king? Was it not a bluff?

This close, I can see silvery flecks in the stone, shimmering from the remnants of sunlight. I imagine Analla being in complete awe of this place. She loves castles and has always dreamed of stepping inside one. One of her lifelong dreams is to attend a ball and dance the night away in a beautiful silk gown.

The thought of her causes a bittersweet feeling to stir in my gut. I smile at the idea of her in a gown, yet my heart aches when I think of her never being able to live out that dream if I fail.

I shove my emotions aside as we approach a set of colossal wooden doors. More beastials patrol here, well suited, heavily armed, and not looking nearly as silly as the set at the front gates.

"All of you wait here." Rynthea drops her rucksack on the ground close to my feet. She gently places her scythesword down, too, then marches toward the guards. They stiffen when they notice her coming and tighten their grips around the handles of their spears.

Well, all but one — a female white tiger beastial whose silvery eyes lock on Rynthea as she saunters forward. Two beautiful ears spring from her head, and her fur and hair are an even mixture of white with black stripes. That same hair on her head is braided neatly and laid over her shoulder.

Her deep-purple military uniform is capped with gold at the shoulders and decorated with medals. She carries a sheathed sword at her waist with a gleaming gold hilt. Her boots make deliberate thuds as she marches across the walkway until she's face-to-face with Rynthea.

They stare at each other for a while, eyes narrowed, heads tilting as they size each other up. Then a sharp-toothed grin spreads across the tiger's face as she throws her hands in the air.

"Rynthea Kamtaur! It's been far too long! I didn't think I'd ever see you again!"

Rynthea smiles back, seeming relieved. "How are you, Sheera?"

"I'm well. I would hug you, but you smell *awful* and look like you've been dragged through the Shadow Realm." She looks at Rynthea from head to toe. "What happened to you?"

"We were attacked by a swamp monster, and before you ask" — Rynthea throws up a hand just as Sheera is about to interrupt — "*yes*, I'm serious. We walked through Delchester to get here."

"Why on Thelanor would you do that?" Sheera asks with utter disbelief.

"Quickest route. We don't have a lot of time to spare."

"I see." Sheera peeks over Rynthea's shoulder at me, then Algar, but focuses the most on Thane. He hasn't put his mask on since the swamp (probably because of the smell), but his swords are still strapped to his back and his buffers and dagger-lined vest are a clear indicator that he's the fighting type. He looks like a walking weapon. "Surely you wouldn't have traveled through Delchester unless it was urgent. Why are you here?" She places her attention on Rynthea again. "Is Torjack okay?"

"Yes, Torjack is fine. I'm just hoping to have a quick word with King Draedor."

At that, Sheera stiffens, her smile lost. "The king is preparing for the fete. He has requested that he not be disturbed unless the matter is urgent."

"I wouldn't be asking if it weren't important, Sheera."

The tiger shifts on her feet, studying Rynthea for several seconds. She sighs, shoulders softening. "Who are the travelers with you?"

Rynthea gestures to us. "They seek his help and insight, too."

Sheera's brows knit together. "Rynthea, you know that I always want to help you, but the king does not care for strangers. Especially not tonight."

"Not even if these strangers require his help about a journey to the Temple of Elphar?"

"*Elphar?*" Sheera's striking eyes expand. "Did that swamp monster eat your brain?"

"King Draedor is the only person I know who has survived The Shallows," Rynthea goes on.

"Yes, *barely!*"

"He *still* survived, and that's what matters."

Sheera steps back. "It isn't wise to pester the king with those troubling memories."

"Just tell him I'm here. *Please*, Sheera?" Rynthea pleads. "He'll make time. Plus, he owes me."

Sheera lifts her chin. "Owes you *for what?*"

Rynthea crosses her arms with a smirk. "Ask him and find out."

Okay...now I know she can't be bluffing.

Chapter 21

"It's been over an hour." Thane stands with his back against the wall and his arms crossed tightly over his chest. He gives his head a shake, staring out the nearest window. "If we wait any longer, it'll be too late to leave, and we'll waste hours of the journey."

He always seems annoyed, but I think he's even more so now because Sheera took his weapons and vest as a precaution. She even found the dagger strapped to the inside of his boot and another tucked into a leather band under the sleeve of his shirt. He won't get them back until it's time for us to depart Bernwood altogether.

"You can go on if you want, but I'm not going anywhere near The Shallows until I see King Draedor," Rynthea says.

"How does a king owe *you* anyway?" Algar asks. He's lying on a divan with a sleeping Zephra on his belly. I can't help but think about how a servant is going to have a really hard time getting the stench out of that upholstery.

"His son nearly drowned, and I was there when it happened." Rynthea leans back in her chair. "I saved him."

"Really?" My brows arch. "How old were you?"

"I was in my fourteenth year. The prince was in his eleventh."

"Wow."

"The tide came out of nowhere and was stronger than anyone expected. Apparently, Prince Kelrean had snuck out of Bernwood to have himself a little fun at the nearest shore with a few friends."

"And if it weren't for you, I wouldn't have my heir." A booming voice travels through the room.

I turn my head to find a man standing near the double doors.

Well, he isn't exactly all man.

He has the mane of a lion, fur on his hands, claws protruding from his thick fingertips, and skin of a mortal—bronze-like skin, as if he spends the majority of his days basking in the sun. His eyes, however, are just as fierce as a lion's. Equally as tall as Rynthea, he wears an ivory suit embellished in gold, and a purple tie with the letters *BW*. An emblem is pinned to his suit, the same lion shape on the flags I saw outside. With a warm, sharp-toothed smile, he approaches Rynthea and releases an exhilarated sigh.

"King Draedor." She drops to one knee, bowing her head.

"Oh, don't you dare." He chuckles. "Rise and let me look at you!"

Rynthea hurries to her feet as an elegant woman breezes into the room in an ivory silk gown with a gold crown atop her head. Her thick hair is pulled back in an elegantly coiffed puff with purple jewels pinned to one side. Her eyes are a sparkling brown, her lips painted the color of black cherries, and her skin a lovely shade of brown with copper undertones. She is utterly breathtaking.

"Rynthea, you're here!" the woman chimes as she aligns herself with the king. "I think this may be the best fete yet, darling. All of our favorite people have come."

"Indeed," King Draedor replies.

"Queen Jenia." Rynthea bows her head, but Draedor is still insisting she stand up straight so he can study her. He seems fascinated by her. I can't blame him. Minotaurs are beautiful, intellectual creatures.

"To what do we owe this pleasure?" Queen Jenia asks, clasping her nimble fingers together. The jewelry on her wrists tinkles, pearls entwined in gold bands. The sight of those pearls sends a pang of guilt through me that lands right in the pit of my stomach.

Knowing I'll never see the necklace my mother gave me hurts all over again. Not only that, but I can no longer tell how Analla is. Is she still hanging on? Is she weaker? Has the necklace grown hotter because Seferin is physically hurting her?

If it were with me and still warm, I'd assume she's still alive. But I suppose I should consider it a good thing that it's out of my possession. It'd cause me to lose my mind. If it were with me now and decided to return to regular temperature, I'd know I've lost her. I'm not sure I can fathom that while being so far away from home.

"I apologize for the inconvenience," says Rynthea, her voice cutting through my thoughts. "I understand the Autumnal Beast Fete begins tonight, but this couldn't wait. We're traveling to the Temple of Elphar, and I need your guidance on getting through The Shallows to reach it."

King Draedor's face becomes as hard as stone as he glares at Rynthea. "I told you and Kelrean the story about The Shallows out of sheer boredom and for entertainment purposes, Rynthea. You'd be mad to travel there, especially now that The Shallows has drifted farther away from the mainland."

"I know, but you survived it, and we *really* must get there."

"What for?" King Draedor asks incredulously, looking from her to us, the other supposed lunatics in the room.

"She needs one of the prosperity stones." Rynthea gestures to me before pointing to Thane. "And he's traveling with her as her protector. Algar there…well, he and I are after the same thing. We want some of the treasure in Elphar's temple so we can better our lives. As a group, I believe we can make it."

"You'll *lose* your lives by going there. You should reconsider." King Draedor raises an eyebrow, glowering at each of us. "You're all children who clearly think you're invincible. You don't understand the true dangers of The Shallows."

"We understand enough." Thane's voice has a hard edge to it as he steps forward. He acts like he's speaking to a commoner and not a *king*.

"You understand *nothing*." King Draedor stares him down before settling his gaze on Rynthea again. "I'd have to either hate you or be a fool to give you guidance about that island, and neither of those apply. I'm sorry, Rynthea, but I cannot do it. If it is currency you seek, my offer still stands for you to become one of my guards."

Rynthea groans. "The hours would be too long and inflexible, Your Majesty. I have to be around for Torjack and to keep Kamtaur Inn alive."

"We have wonderful healers," he adds.

"I know, but I can't let Kamtaur shut down. That place is all I have left of my parents."

King Draedor sighs, then purses his lips, as if he understands exactly where she's coming from.

"Please," I beg when Rynthea hesitates on what to say next.

The king and queen place their attention on me with stunned expressions. "It's a lot to ask, I know. But it's for my sister. She's been cursed by a Grim sorcerer and will die if I don't get one of the prosperity stones to save her. It's my only shot at setting her free." I pause, feeling the weight of everyone's eyes on me. "I know I'm simply a mortal, and I understand there are risks, but I'm willing to take them if it means there's even a *slight* chance to break that curse and get her back."

I try not to let my bottom lip tremble as King Draedor scans me. "Your name?" he inquires, eyes softening.

"Zaira," I answer. "Zaira Quinlocke."

Draedor raises his chin. The room falls into a thick silence.

"It's honorable what you're doing for your sister. I've not seen such nobility in a mortal in a very long time." He looks at his wife, who gives him a *please help them, darling* expression.

"Nonsense. You encounter nobility every day when it comes to me." Another beastial saunters into the grand room in a mauve suit, similar in height to the king, only leaner and with slightly less muscle. *Slightly*. His well-tailored clothing does absolutely nothing to hide his toned arms or the definition of his chest. Unlike Draedor, almost everything about him is mortal minus his eyes, which are the color of a lion's as well. "Although I am only *half* a mortal."

I've never seen a man like him before. There is a controlled demeanor about him, as if he walks into every room knowing his place, confident in where he belongs. And yet...there is also a hint of something feral and untamed within those deep lion eyes. He has the loveliest shade of ochre skin, with hair shaved short on the sides, a sharp contrast to the riot of curls atop his head—thick, natural, and effortlessly regal. Beneath the power of his crown, it seems even his hair refuses to be subdued.

He is easily one of the most beautiful beastials I've ever seen—if he is beastial at all. There is something unique about him and the king. They aren't fully lion or mortal, and they are much taller than any other beastial I've seen, excluding Rynthea.

"Kelrean, you were supposed to be here half an hour ago." Queen Jenia gives him a stern eye.

Ah. The prince. This makes sense.

"My apologies, Mother. I had a rather important *meal* to eat."

I can't help noticing the mischievous smirk that settles over Kelrean's lips.

"Very well." King Draedor's voice bellows through the room again, stealing my attention back. He continues on like his son and wife haven't spoken at all. "I will tell you all what I know about The Shallows, but it will have to be *after* the fete."

"The Shallows?" Kelrean frowns as he looks from his father to Rynthea. "Why on Thelanor are you going there? Are you suicidal?"

"Not even close," Rynthea says.

The prince's golden eyes land on mine. He flashes a lopsided smile.

I blush as I smile back. There's no way a prince is flirting with me. *Me*, a woman who's just walked for hours, smells like swamp, and looks like a pile of horse droppings. Nope. Absolutely no way. I avert my gaze, only to catch Thane in the corner, glaring at the prince with heavily knitted brows.

He looks ready to kill.

Clearing my throat, I listen to Rynthea explain for the second time why we're going to the island of death while Queen Jenia tosses in my reason behind needing a prosperity stone.

"You were right, Father." Kelrean sweeps his eyes up and down the length of me. "She *is* noble."

"Indeed," responds the king. "Very brave. A true example of Orvena's courage."

"And what is your name?" Kelrean asks.

"Zaira."

"What a beautiful name." His compliment is smooth. "So full of character."

Like a fool, I blush again as the prince reveals a charismatic smile.

"As I informed you, we must go to our people for the Autumnal Beast Fete," King Draedor announces. "I encourage you all to be our guests and join us for the merriment. You may make use of our guest chambers so you can refresh yourselves before meeting us in the village square. Feel free to make use of the baths, and you are welcome to anything in our wardrobes."

"Well, that is terrific." Algar hobbles past me with Zephra cradled in one of his hands. "I'd love to take a scalding-hot bath in a castle this divine, Your Majesty. I'm honored to be your guest."

"Is that a maobi?" Kelrean ogles Zephra with burning curiosity.

"She is."

"Beautiful creatures, they are. But rare. A female?"

"Yes."

"And she allows you to just *hold* her? I hear they don't care for mortals and bite hard enough to take off a finger."

"Well, I've had her for two months, and she hasn't bitten me yet. What can I say? She's my better half." Algar holds her up a bit higher in his cupped hand, removing lint from her tail. "I've seen her bite others, though, and it is not pretty. She's a little savage when she wants to be."

"Kelrean, why don't you lead our guests to the main halls and inform the helpers that they'll need assistance?" Queen Jenia offers.

I like that they call their people *helpers* and not servants. There's something cozy—no, kind—about that. Commendable. These are good people.

"With pleasure, Mother." Kelrean places his attention on me again, offering me an elbow. "My lady?"

I smile, looping my arm through his and leaving the room at the prince's side. When we pass a set of guards, I look over my shoulder to see Rynthea still chatting with the king and queen.

Algar is following us, as well as Thane.

But Thane's eyes are now burning gold as he glares invisible daggers at the back of the prince's head.

Chapter 22

Before we're given access to the chambers, we have to partake in one of Bernwood's traditions for new guests.

According to this tradition, I'm told to take a gold coin, then they prick my forefinger, and I smear a drop of my blood on the coin. After that, we're given individual crystal bowls with shards of alvanite stone inside them, and I place my coin in my bowl.

If the gray stones stay their natural color, it means you have good intentions for the kingdom. If it turns black, however, it means your intentions are malevolent and could lead to being detained or, worse, *executed*.

Everyone passes the test…but then it's Thane's turn. He's the last to go, and to say I'm nervous for his outcome is an understatement. I watch with bated breath as he drops his bloodied coin into the bowl. The stones go unchanged, and I blow a sigh of relief.

After that, Kelrean takes pride in showing us the interior of the castle, pointing to certain doors and letting us know what lies at the end of the ornate hallways.

"If you follow that corridor," he says, pointing to a stretch on our right, "it will lead you to a steam room." He winks down at me.

I bite my lip, fighting yet another blush.

When we finally reach our designated floor, the women are split from the men. I walk with Rynthea and Kelrean to one of the four doors at the end of our wing.

"When you're done, return to the main hall on the first floor and take the right corridor all the way down," Kelrean instructs as he watches me push the door handle down. "The side entrance will be there, and a chariot should be around to take you to the village square."

"Thanks, Kelrean."

"Of course, Zaira." He strolls away. It's hard to ignore how great his ass looks in those fitted pants.

"Don't do it."

I turn to the sound of Rynthea's voice. "Do what?"

She stands in front of the door across from mine, the handle of her scythesword relaxed in her palm. Sheera had taken her weapon, too, but, unbeknownst to his father (or Sheera), Kelrean found it and gave it back to her. He trusts Rynthea a lot, I realize.

"Don't bother with Kelrean. He's charming, sure, but also the most conceited person I've ever met. He'll sleep with any woman who has legs."

"You don't have to worry about that." I laugh. "I don't have time to sleep with charming, conceited princes right now. My mind is much too crowded with the idea of my sister being on the brink of death."

"Well, just so you know, this fete is all about drinking and partying. Good times are bound to happen." Her eyebrows do a little wiggle. "It's easy to slip up and do things you never thought you'd do."

"Have you been to one of the fetes before?"

"Only once. That was enough for me."

"So you're not going tonight?" I ask.

"No. I'll probably have a bath, then find a place to practice with my scythesword afterward."

I'm a little disappointed to hear that. I was hoping to hang out with her a bit more. "You should have some fun, Rynthea. At least while we're stuck here waiting for the king to give us the details about The Shallows."

She turns to fully face me, seeming disheartened. "You probably haven't noticed, but a lot of beastials aren't partial to minotaurs."

I frown. "Why wouldn't they be?"

"Because they know how sacred we are. Envy, I think, and also greed. Whatever their reasons, they hold bias against us. I've visited Bernwood three times. The last time I came was about two years ago to obtain medicines for Torjack. I traveled to the borders, so it took longer to get here, and because the trip was so long, I stayed a few days in the city to rest. While I was here, a group of beastials attacked me in an alley and called me an abomination. They broke two of my ribs, one of my fingers, and nearly broke off one of my horns. If Sheera hadn't shown up to stop the attack, I'm certain I would've died and that horn would've been sold."

"Oh, Rynthea. I'm so sorry. I didn't know it was like that for you or other minotaurs." I shift closer to her, wanting to hug her, but she turns her body sideways and her shoulders tense, like a hug is the last thing she wants. "I always assumed minotaurs are highly respected among the beastials."

"We used to be. But when our numbers dwindled and the healing properties in our horns became more important than our existence, we became nothing more than prey to many." Her head drops as she studies the hardwood floors. "There was a time when beastials used to look out for each other. There was hope, you know? But now? Now, we just turn against one another for something as simple as a coin. It's beastials who'll sell each other out quicker than the mortals will."

I stare at her, unsure of what to say. The chandeliers highlight her thick, pointed horns as she lifts her chin and draws in a breath.

"Anyway." She exhales through parted lips. "Enough about that. You should know that I won't be able to thank you enough for saving me in that swamp, Zaira. King Draedor is right. You *are* noble." She gives my shoulder a gentle squeeze. "I pray to Orvena you never lose your principles."

She smiles, and my heart warms for her. Rynthea truly is beautiful. She appears so strong—so indestructible—yet there is a softness to her. One that makes me want to get to know even more about her.

I place my hand on top of hers. "Get some rest, Rynthea."

With sagging shoulders, she enters her chamber and shuts the door behind her.

I don't allow myself much time to take in the silk curtains and oversize canopied bed when I step into my room. The moon has made its debut, and its silvery light floods through the double doors leading to a stone terrace.

I drop my rucksack on the floor, not daring to touch anything for fear I'll soil it with the stench of swamp monster.

Now that I have a moment to myself, my thoughts are much louder. I think of Analla trapped in Seferin's keep, of her fear as she realizes her life is coming to an end. Is he feeding her at least? Giving her water? He can't be *that* cruel to deprive her of mortal necessities, can he?

My hands shake as I recall the attack in Kamtaur, the swamp monster, and Dulan's death. The urge to cry is at an all-time high, but I swallow it down and lift my head.

"Okay," I breathe. "Come on, Z. Pull it together."

I make my way to the washroom to start a bath, cleaning myself up thoroughly by using the luxurious soap that smells of lavender and a hint of spice. I give my hair a good wash, too, threading my fingers through the thick curls to detangle them before I comb out most of the kinks. Afterward, I moisturize it with a smooth hair butter that makes my curls look luxurious.

"Wow," I murmur, studying the glass container of hair butter. "Royals have the best hair products."

The queen mentioned there being clothes we could select in the wardrobes. I didn't expect them to be filled to the brim with gowns, skirts, corsets, and bodices.

There are too many options to choose from. A person living in this castle is one thing. But deciding what to wear on a daily basis is another entirely and has to be mind-boggling. All the garments are high quality and bursting with color.

Since it's the night of the fete, I decide *not* to go with my usual leggings, tunic, and earth tones and instead pluck out an ivory underdress with threaded gold-and-purple flowers embellishing the hem. It pairs well with a rich purple bodice and overskirt that's laced with delicate gold ribbons.

I slip my arms into the billowy sleeves of the underdress, then put on the underskirt, allowing it to flow in waves to my feet. Next, I toss on the bodice and tie it as tightly and comfortably as possible.

Standing before one of the mirrors, I grab a handful of the skirts and twirl around with a grin. I've never worn a gown this lavish—so vibrant and full of life. I could never afford one as gorgeous as this.

I feel royal myself right now.

There are several jeweled clips in one of the drawers of the wardrobe. I select a few that match, do a quick braid design on the right side of my hair, and pin the ends with the clips. As I gaze into the mirror, I can't help but wonder who this room belongs to. Are all these clothes Queen Jenia's? Perhaps they're all outfits she no longer cares to wear…or maybe there's a princess around somewhere? That can't be likely, though. I assume she'd have made an appearance downstairs when Kelrean did. Plus, the king said

Kelrean was his only heir.

Once I find a pair of boots my size, I leave my room feeling ten times more relaxed. I pause in front of my door and stare at Rynthea's. Through the gap at the bottom, I spot her shadow.

"I can hear you breathing, Zaira," she calls.

I stand taller. *Right*. Beastials have impressive hearing.

"Sorry." I laugh nervously. "Are you sure you don't want to join us?"

Her door cracks open, and she sticks her head out. Her hair is loose, damp, and curly. She appears so innocent this way. "I'm fine." She laughs. "Have fun. I'll see you tomorrow, after the king has a hundred drinks and is ready to spill his guts. He's surprisingly more lenient when he's hungover."

I smile. "Okay."

She closes the door, and I drift through the corridor to reach the intersecting hall. As I approach the carpeted area, I spot a familiar person in all black on the opposite side.

Thane.

And, of course, my traitorous heart thumps several beats faster.

He's wearing a laced-up black leather waistcoat over an ivory tunic with the sleeves rolled up to his forearms. The tunic has a shallow V-cut at the chest that reveals a slice of his silky brown skin. He looks refreshed.

"What, no buffers tonight?" I ask as I approach.

"They're being washed." He taps his waistcoat. "And this has buffers sewn into the lining. It's the only one I could find in that wretched wardrobe," he grumbles. "I don't understand how anyone can wear such colorful clothing every day."

"Not everyone wants to live out their days in all black like you." I do my best not to focus on the broadness of his chest. The tunic he's wearing right now is much more fitted than his other clothes. His pecs are... Well, let's just say he takes *great* care of his body.

He's wearing a necklace I hadn't noticed before, a round black pendant with a scorpion in the center attached to a silver chain.

I start to ask about it but decide against it. He'll probably give me a smart remark or ignore my question altogether, and I'm not about to let him ruin my mood or my night. Plus things are still a bit weird between us since the swamp.

"Well...I should get going. Getting kind of hungry." I pass him and start for the curving staircase.

"I'm waiting on one of the helpers to bring me a pair of boots that fit," he says, as if noticing my hesitation.

I nod. "See you at the chariot, then."

"Yes. Unless, of course, you need me to guide you down the stairs, oh sweet one?"

"I'm certain I can handle a flight of stairs," I call over my shoulder, but I still take each step down carefully, clinging to the handrail. I can hardly see the steps beneath the skirts. If I trip, it's a long way to the bottom. Breaking my neck falling down a flight of stairs is not how I want to die after everything I've already gone through.

I look back to find Thane still watching me.

He looks disturbingly handsome with his freshly washed hair—all thick and coiled—his clean skin, and non-threatening attire. Even the scars on his face aren't as menacing, but more so just a part of him. He's much more relaxed, too—still vigilant, of course—but not as tense as he was outside of Bernwood.

That could be because we're tucked away in a kingdom that's far too busy celebrating a fete to bother with us. The front gates are guarded, and I'm certain the village is swarming with soldiers keeping an eye on their people as well as the royals. We're as safe as we can be…and if anything happens, we know damn well to run.

I finally turn my eyes away from him when his gaze becomes too much.

Stop staring at him, Zaira. Don't be ridiculous.

I feel like I walk down a hundred steps before finally making it to the first floor. As I look for the chariot, each step feels heavier than the last without Thane escorting me.

I can't believe I'm this hung up over a man like him.

Chapter 23

"They have the Autumnal Beast Fete every year, you know?" Algar says during the carriage ride.

"Do they?" I ask.

"Yep. I remember reading about it somewhere. It always begins on the twenty-third day of autumn, and lasts for about three days, I think."

"Hmm. I'd never heard of it until today." I point my gaze out of the carriage window. "What are they celebrating?"

"Apparently, it's tradition for the beastials of Bernwood to come together and give thanks to Orvena for allowing them the opportunity to flourish near the Alvanite Mountains."

Ah, yes. Orvena, the goddess of life and prosperity. Makes sense. It surely is a blessing to have direct access to one of Thelanor's greatest resources. Many would kill—literally—to have it.

The fete is celebrated in expansive courtyards in the heart of the village. I see the raging fires licking the sky as our carriage approaches. The music grows louder, as well as cheers and laughter. I'm so intrigued that I slide closer to the edge of the bench to get a better look outside.

Once we're out of the carriage, we take a path that leads us directly to the heart of the event, which is in a massive square surrounded by towering bushes and trees peppered in gold-and-purple flowers. Colored crystals and lumps of alvanite stone sit at the base of the various fires.

"Oh, I forgot about that." Algar's voice is loud as he speaks over the music. "Every person in the kingdom brings their own crystal to place around the flames so they can receive a blessing."

"Oh! Maybe we should've brought one out of respect."

I take a look around. There's food, drinks, desserts, music—and I love it. For the first time in a while, I'm actually feeling *joy*. I almost forgot what that emotion feels like. Joy. Such a simple three-letter word that many, including myself, can't seem to keep ahold of. It's only been a few days since I left Meriva, but it feels like so much of my peace has been destroyed already.

A sister slowly dying in a dungeon.

Attacks in Redclaw and Ruvain.

Getting nearly choked to death by a murderous Grim sorcerer.

Almost eaten by a damn swamp monster.

Truth be told, this journey is triggering me. The Ember Coast attacks from my childhood linger in the back of my mind during every hardship.

The reminders of being forced out of my kingdom. Watching the fires swallow our homes and demolish everything we owned. My fingertips lingering on my father's just before he pulled away to save more people— never returning.

And Mother promising to find us but—

Someone bumps into me, snapping me out of the tragic memories.

"So sorry, love!" A woman giggles as she clutches the hand of her lover and melts into the crowd.

I clear my throat and anchor myself in the present moment.

Beastials make up nearly the entire population here. It's such a rare sight. Meriva has a diverse blend of all living beings—mortals, beastials, charmers, and sorcerers. Apparently skrellins, too. I spotted a few mortals in the castle working as helpers, but as far as the festivities are concerned, I can only spot three other mortals around—one selling hot honey cakes, a charmer making candies levitate for children before giving them away, and that woman who just passed by.

I smile when I catch sight of a beastial with charmer magic as well. He throws his fingers into the air to light up the sky, creating mini, vibrant fireworks. The children squeal while the adults applaud. Some of the beastials who already seem drunk stare up in awe, their glistening eyes reflecting the bursts of colors.

Algar catches up with me in the crowd, now carrying a tin mug of ale in hand. He walks by my side as we pass a band playing a lively tune on string instruments and flutes. A woman with gray feathers on her arms offers us skewers stacked with roasted meat and veggies. I take mine gratefully and bite into it, moaning as the savory flavors explode on my tongue.

I could get used to this.

"Have you ever been to a fete like this?" I slow my pace so Algar can catch up again.

"The closest thing to this that I've been to is the Crystal Festival in Meriva." He scans the crowd as he bites off a chunk of meat.

"Oh, I love that one. They always have so much honey loaf and wine."

"I *do* love wine." Algar raises his mug to his lips.

"Where's Zephra?" I ask.

"I left her in my chamber," he says. "She's got a load of food and a comfy bed. She's in the Crystal Realm right now."

I laugh.

From a short distance away, I spot Thane walking into the courtyard. He scans the whole area, assessing, before pressing on.

"Wonderful. The sorcerer has arrived," I announce sarcastically.

He spots us rather easily. I mean, it's not hard to find a mortal and a charmer in a scattered crowd of beastials. The woman who offered us a skewer also gives him one. He accepts it and bites right into it.

"What's the story between you and Thane, anyway?" I ask as we approach one of the fires. I sit on a smooth slab of stone, and Algar joins me, taking another hefty sip from his mug.

"The story?" he repeats. "We're friends—well, we *were*. That's all there is to it, really."

"Close friends, right?" My eyes dart to Thane, who now has his back to us while he requests an ale from one of the stands.

"We used to be. Before I stumbled across you two in that leaky building, I hadn't seen Thane in almost three years." The flickering flames make Algar's face seem fiercer, as if it has hardened all the features that make him appear kind and approachable. "When we bumped into each other the time prior to this one, he'd changed. I could see it in his eyes. He wasn't the same person from all those years ago."

"What do you think changed him?"

"I don't know." He takes another gulp before consuming more meat. After chewing and swallowing it down, he goes on. "Truth is, Thane didn't have a great life when he was younger. We were neighbors living in the Scraps. Neither of us went to school, so we spent most of our days teaching each other stupid things, like how to strike with cheap wooden swords, or throw rocks at wealthy people in the Commons so one of us could keep them distracted long enough to steal their food."

I chew slower, too busy digesting his words.

"My mum, Orvena rest her soul, was a good person." Algar's smile is soft, eyes lost in the fire, as if he's remembering her. "She knew Thane was troubled and that his father wasn't a good man, so she'd tell me to sneak food through his window. If you'd seen him then, Zaira, you would've wondered how he was even breathing. He was skin and bones, that one. Being so naive back then, I used to wonder why I could see the imprint of his ribs on his body. In fact, at one point, I thought it was interesting that they were so visible, so I poked them, and it made him incredibly angry. As I got older, I realized it was no interesting feat at all. He couldn't help it. I mean, we were both poor, but my mother never allowed a night where we didn't eat *something*. Even if it was half a loaf of bread." Algar presses his lips together as he darts his eyes toward Thane, who is swapping coins for the ale.

"His father was a shit person who was even shittier with his coins. His mother wasn't around at all. During his ninth year, I stopped seeing him altogether. Weeks went by, and it got to a point where I had to knock on his front door and ask for him. I received a rather ignorant greeting from his drunk father, who shouted in my face for me to fuck off."

I lower the skewer as my stomach churns. "Did you find out where he went?"

"Didn't find out for a few years," he says, along with a humorless laugh. "Not until I spotted him one day. This was back when I was trying to live a decent life by making my coin the ethical way, yeah? I was hired as a tour guide for the Crystal Palace grounds. Showing people the gardens, courtyards, and what have you. But on my first day of work, I saw Thane marching *with* The Divine."

I blink at Algar, stunned. "Wait…are you *serious*?"

"I wouldn't lie about this. I saw him but couldn't bring myself to go over and speak to him. I walked away instead. No one approached The Divine without consequences anyway. Five years later, I stumbled into him again, only this time he wasn't wearing the same white uniform The Divine wear. He was in all black. He didn't have those scars on his face that he has now, but his eyes were lost. There was still some innocence left in them, like what I saw when we were children, right? But he tried *really* hard to hide that softer side of him. He hardly spoke to me that day. He kept looking over his shoulder every few seconds like someone was coming after him. Then he disappeared when I offered to buy him a pint, and I never saw him again. At least not until yesterday. And, oddly enough, he was with *you*."

Algar turns his head so his hazel eyes lock on mine.

My heart drums a beat faster.

"I saw him with you and had even more questions than before. But I have to tell you, Zaira, I look at him now, and I don't see that lost boy anymore. I see someone who's been hardened to the core. Someone carrying way too many secrets. I see a person willing to risk his life over and over again just to prove something to this world. I don't know what that *something* is, but I know it's dangerous, and that's why I worry for you."

"For *me*?" I gape. "Why?"

"I worry about your safety. I don't think he agreed to travel with you all the way to The Shallows just because he got a few coins from you." Algar's head shakes gravely as he stares into my eyes. "I think he's doing it because there's something he wants. Something he's chasing. And he needs *you* to obtain it."

A nervous warmth coats my throat. I recall the conversation I had with Thane after the brawl at the Kamtaur Inn.

I lean in closer to Algar. "I thought the same thing, so I asked. He said he's looking for a tome of some kind…" I snap my greasy fingers. "The Tome of Azidel. Apparently, there are spells inside it that can increase the power of his magic."

"Ah. I knew it was something."

"But it's just a book," I say. "He could've gone at any time to get it if he wanted to. Why would he need me if that's all he's after? I'm no more than a mortal."

"You'd be surprised how valuable a mortal can be under the right circumstances."

I turn my attention to Thane, who tosses his empty skewer aside while walking toward us.

"Just be careful with him, Zaira." Algar places a hand on top of mine. "You're a good person, and you don't deserve to get dragged into whatever mess he's created."

With that simple statement, Algar pulls his hand away, stands, and flashes Thane the largest of smiles as he approaches. "How's the ale, my ruthless friend? Thinking about grabbing another for myself."

Thane lifts the mug and gives it an approving tilt. "You should. It's better than most."

"Will do. I'll catch you both at the castle once the fete is over, yeah? I hear Bernwood brothels are like being sent to the Crystal Realm." He shoots me a wink before disappearing within the crowd.

Thane drops his eyes to me, amber irises glinting from the fire. It's like he's trying to read me, trying to figure out the conversation I just had with his childhood friend.

"Wanna sit?" I tap the spot Algar just vacated.

Thane thinks on it for a second, sighs, then claims the spot next to me. His knee brushes against my leg, ruffling my skirts. I ignore the tingly feeling the movement creates. With him this close, smelling like spice and leather, pretending that electricity isn't there is futile.

I allow us a moment to sit in silence, him sipping his drink, me finishing off my meat skewer.

"So…" I start. "Will you tell me more about that tome you were talking about earlier?"

He stares into the fire. "It's a long story."

I throw a hand up with a shrug. "I have time."

"It's…a lot, Quinlocke. Way too much to explain right now with all these people around."

"Just imagine we're the only people around this fire. No one else can hear us. They're not worried about us anyway. They're all too busy having fun."

Without thinking, I place a hand on his arm for reassurance. His gaze falls to my hand, and he studies it for a second or two, not knowing what to do about the small gesture. I jerk my hand away and clear my throat, realizing how intimate the action was.

Thane leans forward, planting his elbows on his knees and wrapping both hands around his mug. "Fine," he sighs. "What do you want to know?"

"You said you wanted to retrieve the Tome of Azidel from the temple. Why is that particular tome so important to you?"

"I told you why. To increase the power of my magic."

"Okay…why?"

"To defeat Seferin."

I blink at him. "So I was right before. You hate Seferin."

His jaw clenches. "With every fiber of my being."

"Care to explain?" Not that Seferin is a hard man to loathe.

"That's an even longer story...and tonight is not the night to go over it. It'll dampen your spirits and mine."

I allow his words to steep, mulling over each one. "Well, if all of this is true, and you want that book so badly, why haven't you gone after it before now?"

His throat bobs. "That's the tricky part."

I adjust my position on the slab, waiting for him to speak again.

"In order to get the tome, I need a *mortal's* blood. And it can't just be any mortal. It has to be a mortal who is *one hundred percent* willing to go into the Temple of Elphar and help me retrieve it." He takes a long pause, drawing in a deep breath before delivering the last sentence. "Most importantly, the mortal must be noble, kind, and willing to risk—possibly even sacrifice—their life with the sorcerer they traveled with."

I blink at him a few times before staring at the ground between my boots. He said the words, but it takes a moment for me to digest them. Yes, I am willing to take the risk going to Elphar, like he said, because of my sister, but the word *sacrifice*...that's something else entirely. He's supposed to protect me. That's our agreement. So how can he possibly protect me *and* help break my sister's curse if there is even the slightest possibility that I'll have to sacrifice myself?

I relax my shoulders, trying to see this from his perspective. He acknowledged he's taking the same risk, and that's fine. What isn't okay is that he's kept the truth from me this whole time—since the beginning.

"So you think *I'm* the mortal that can help you?" I ask through partially gritted teeth.

He nods. "Yes, I think you could be..."

"How do you even know the tome is still there? In the temple?"

"It is. Some sorcerers, if strong enough, can track certain objects and artifacts. Last I checked, it's still protected in the temple. Trust me, many sorcerers have attempted to go after it, and all of them have failed. I assume none have been able to come anywhere near the tome because the mortal they've chosen would instantly back out before reaching the island...or die before even setting eyes on the place. If they have managed to make it there but left without the tome, it's because it didn't deem that mortal's blood worthy enough."

The mortal they've chosen. No, no. I chose him. He didn't choose me.

I frown as I stare harder at the ground, now gripping my skewer tighter. He should have told me this up front. *Why* didn't he tell me this before?

I meet his eyes. "How much blood is needed?"

"Not much."

Another cryptic, evasive answer. I narrow my eyes at him. "What if mine isn't worthy enough, either? Will I die if I offer my blood and it's rejected?"

"No. It's been a while since anyone has tried, but I assume those who were rejected probably left the temple just fine. It's getting off of the island that they most likely didn't survive. But I'll make sure that you do." He pauses as he studies my profile. I look away to stare at the fire, trying not to lose my temper. "I think you come as close to worthy as possible considering all the sacrifices you've already made, Zaira."

"Right." His flattering words should soothe me, but I find myself growing angrier instead. He even used my first name, but that does nothing for me right now. "So…the morning at the Tilted Crystal when I gave you the coins…you already had this plan in mind?"

I look at him, and he nods, seeming mildly sympathetic now.

Wow. This lying, scheming asshole. "Don't you think you should've mentioned it to me, then? We could've made an agreement, considering how desperate I am to reach the temple." I stand up and throw my skewer stick into the fire, trying not to explode on him in front of all of these people. "You took my money when, in fact, you needed me as much as I needed you. I sold my necklace—the last thing I owned from my mother—so I could get you those coins! Who does that to someone?"

He remains seated, noticing my balled fist and the look of anguish on my face. "I had to be one hundred percent certain that taking such a dangerous journey was what you wanted. You were drunk that night, so I couldn't go based on that. I told myself if you returned the following morning still wanting to save your sister, that it could work, and that it was possible I could get the tome while we were at it. All I had to do was keep you alive long enough to reach it. A slim chance, yes, but it makes sense to go after it if I have everything I need."

Finally, the missing puzzle pieces are sliding into place. "That's what Maliek meant, then." I gape. "About me being the noble one?"

"He knows what I'm after now. Fortunately, he'll never be able to get the tome unless I have it in my possession, and I wouldn't let him come close to it. He's been chasing me for a very long time."

"Why is that?"

"Because I stole something from Seferin."

Great. So is the whole kingdom hunting him? Hunting *us*?

"And that is…?"

"A crystal. A powerful one that he needs."

"You stole a crystal, too?" I exclaim. Why the shadows isn't he locked up in Seferin's keep like Analla, then? "Do you have it with you?" I ask, scanning him with wary eyes.

"No. I hid it. It's far away from here."

"So not only do they want the crystal back, but they now know you're after the tome?" I glower at him, shaking my head. "Why are you mixed up with Seferin anyway?"

"Many people get mixed up with him, only to realize it was a mistake later. Fortunately, I escaped him. Your sister would know all about what he's like, considering the situation she's in."

I swallow hard, still shaking my head. That I can't deny, but I refuse to give him the satisfaction of agreement.

"It's easy to fall victim to a wicked fucker like him," Thane adds.

A woman begins to sing loud and proud behind us on a platform stage, and the villagers cheer. Before long, she begins dancing with a chimp-like beastial. Other people begin to dance, too. Everyone is truly enjoying themselves, oblivious to the storm raging between me and Thane.

"Now I see why you agreed to risk your life to go on this quest with me," I say, focusing on him again. "It's not about doing the right thing or helping someone else. It's all about getting what you want."

"The only noble thing about this quest is you," he says, pushing to his feet. "I never indicated otherwise. I haven't lied to you. Not once."

"But you withheld the truth. That's the same thing in my opinion." I raise my chin to meet his eyes. "Why are you only telling me this now?"

"Would it have made a difference? Would you have decided not to make the journey if you'd known about all this before we left?"

I study him for a moment, my anger cooling a bit. "No. I would have made the journey regardless. But I wouldn't have had to sell my necklace."

He releases a short breath. "The coins you gave me for that necklace have been used to make this journey easier for you, Zaira. They've benefited you most. And I figured I would tell you more about the tome and the blood the closer we got to the island."

"I would have agreed to help you regardless of if you were willing to help me."

"I know that now...but I can't just take people at their word. Actions speak much louder." His lips twist before he adds, "And this must stay between us—*only* us." He leans in close—so close, I can feel the heat rolling off his body. "I don't want a single word about us going after the tome to spread. Algar is a blabbermouth, and Rynthea...well, you know how she feels about me—about any sorcerer, really."

I start to tell him that Algar already knows but think better of it. I'll just have to talk to Algar later, beg him not to tell anyone. As for Rynthea, I understand. I'm not a huge fan of this particular sorcerer myself at the moment.

"You better hope that broker still has my necklace," I growl as I poke a finger into his chest. "And I expect you to repay me for every fucking coin I gave you."

Thane doesn't even react to my finger. He sighs instead. "I'll pay you back with any treasure I get from the island. That'll be worth way more."

I scoff and roll my eyes. "Yeah, if we even make it there."

A body brushes against my right side, and I startle when an arm drapes over my shoulders.

"Zaira the Noble. My goodness, you clean up so well." Kelrean smells of *way* too many pints of ale. "Have I told you how beautiful you are?"

I let go of some of the tension in my body and smile, flattered. Kelrean lowers his hand to squeeze my upper arm. I steal a glance at Thane, who is now glaring at the fire with a frown and a ticking jaw.

"I love mortals." Kelrean hugs me from the side with a wide smile. "You're all so...*simple*."

"Um...thank you?"

"It's a compliment, trust me," he assures me. "Question for you: have you ever tried talmoon?"

"You're joking," Thane counters, cutting a glare at the prince.

"Not at all." Kelrean's eyes turn to the assassin. "There's a tent a short walk away with loads of it. Would you like to join me, Zaira?"

"Not wise," Thane grumbles.

"Let her decide, yeah?" Kelrean gives him a smug grin.

"I'm her protector, so I can chime in. It's not wise to do talmoon when we're in the middle of a quest, Quinlocke. Anything could come up, and you'll be too high off your ass to handle the situation. You shouldn't go."

My eyebrows knit together as I focus on Thane. I intended to tell Kelrean that I would pass. I wanted to talk with Thane a bit more, possibly even hammer down on him about withholding the truth about the tome, but now that he's pulling this shit, I don't want to be anywhere near him right now.

Yes, he was hired to protect me on our journey, but he has no right to tell me what to do during my free time, and he *definitely* doesn't have the right to make any personal decisions for me.

Algar's warning from before replays in my mind. *"Just be careful with him, Zaira."* I know a bit more about Thane now, but I still have so many questions.

How did he go from marching with The Divine to getting involved with Seferin and the Grim? Why does he want to take Seferin down so badly with the tome?

There are still some missing pieces to this giant puzzle, and I doubt he's going to explain any more of it any time soon. Staying here with him will be a waste of my time and energy anyway. I have no intention of doing anything foolish, but I refuse to allow Thane to dictate what I can and cannot do.

I settle my expression into one of indifference, face Kelrean, and say, "Let's give it a try."

Chapter 24

"Clear out for the prince, won't you?" Kelrean's deep voice swims through the broad tent. The individuals inside quickly stand up and bow to him before exiting.

"It's that easy for you, huh?" I ask, drinking in the interior in awe. This tent is colossal, made of purple silk with a high, pointed ceiling and chandeliers hanging from the center beam. Dripping pillar and taper candles flicker throughout, casting a romantic glow.

"Oh, come on. Why be a prince if not to request a whole tent for myself?" Kelrean flashes me another one of his crooked smiles as he sits down on an oversize floor pillow.

I sit on the pillow next to him as he reaches for a stick of talmoon. A pot of burning coals is on the short table as well. He presses the end of the talmoon on the coals, letting it spark before bringing it to his lips and taking a strong pull.

"Rynthea says she saved your life," I say when he passes the stick to me.

"Dear Orvena." He rubs his forehead. "She'll never let me live that down, will she?"

"Probably not." I stare at the stick, and Thane's words run through my head. *Not wise.*

Yeah, well, neither is hanging out with an assassin.

I raise the talmoon to my lips and take a tentative pull. Smoke instantly fills my mouth and lungs, tasting as hot as pepper. I blow it out just as quickly, coughing and sputtering.

Chuckling, Kelrean gives me a pat on the back. "You all right?"

I nod, despite the fact I'm still coughing.

He smiles. "You get used to it."

I raise it to my lips again, but Kelrean slips it from my fingers before I can take another pull. "That's probably enough. Talmoon is powerful and takes effect quickly." He takes a draw from the stick again and exhales in the opposite direction from me, then reclines back on an elbow. "First, you'll feel your heart racing a bit, but that's normal, I promise you. Your body is getting acclimated to the relaxing properties of the plant. Then your body will feel like it's melting—but in a good way. Your mind will soften around the edges, and everything will feel both heavy and weightless. With a soft mind and soothed body, all your worries and anxieties are allowed to drift away. Seems like you need it after the journey you've had so far."

He's right.

My heart *is* racing, but I'm sure it's due to the rush of the fete and this moment.

Alone.

In a luxurious tent.

With a handsome *prince*.

But just as quickly, the beating settles, and my limbs feel loose as relaxation takes over. The worries are melting away.

I study my palms.

Then I giggle for absolutely no reason at all.

"About Rynthea," he goes on, ignoring my silliness. "Don't get me wrong, I'm grateful she saved my life. But it's an embarrassing story for me because I'm a shifter, for fuck's sake, and I couldn't even shift to save myself because I was quite literally *scared for my life*."

Wait. What?

"You're a *shifter*? What are you talking about?" My words come out much too slowly. Even my mouth is relaxed.

"Oh, you didn't know?" He smiles as he places the talmoon down on the table. "My father is a full-blooded shifter. I'm his son, so his genetics are passed down to me, obviously."

That explains why they have minor lion features but look mortal otherwise.

"So, you choose to look like…*this*?"

His teeth glisten in the candlelight. "Like a sexy lion heir?"

I burst out laughing. "Sure. That."

"It's my father's choice. Lions are the strongest of the land beastials, and shifters are rare, so we have to display our dominance. He insists I keep this form a majority of the time unless he needs me to leave the kingdom to do some spying."

"You're a spy, too?"

"I am, and I make an impressive mouse. Would you like to see?"

My eyes expand as I wait for him to magically shapeshift into a rodent.

"Oh, please! I'm joking." He chuckles. "We don't shift often. It hurts too much. Feels like every bone in the body is breaking. We only do so when necessary."

"Interesting. I've heard stories about the king of Bernwood being a shifter but had a hard time believing them. I always figured it was a myth."

He takes my hand and gives it a soft squeeze. "Do you feel that?"

His hand is warm and only slightly callused. I nod.

"We're *very* real, Zaira." He holds my gaze for a few seconds, smiling. When he releases my hand, heat rushes to my cheeks, and I look away. I can't deny that Kelrean is sexy. He truly is, and interestingly enough, his animalistic features make him even more attractive. He seems far too majestic for Thelanor, as if he's meant to exist in an entirely different realm.

His attentiveness is beyond flattering. I'm just not used to so much of it at once.

I've had two boyfriends in my lifetime. One was during my tenth year. I met a boy at the refugee center whose name I can't even remember. It was a simple childhood crush.

The other was during my seventeenth year, and he'd taken my maiden's mark. That courtship was fleeting.

"I find you so interesting," Kelrean says with a lazy smile.

"Do you?"

"Yes. There's something about you…" He leans closer. "There's this light—a certain pull to it. Or perhaps I'm simply drawn to you." His nearness makes my skin hum. He studies my eyes while I absorb the depth of his. He smells nice, like pine and an elevated scent only a royal can carry.

He takes my hand and brings it to his lips. When he kisses the back of it while holding my gaze, I tingle all over.

"What do you think about meeting me for a drink in the castle after the fete?" he asks in a smooth, low voice. "I can show you around a bit more, take you to the gardens, lead you to my favorite waterfall so you can see the view."

Surprise bubbles up inside me. "Oh. Um..." I snicker. The talmoon is taking full effect now. "Are you sure? Is it wise to spend so much time around a common mortal?"

"It's only up to us." He shrugs and then whispers, "No one can tell us what to do."

That's true.

Not wise, Thane's deep voice warns in my head again. *He* certainly wants to tell me what to do. I close my eyes and see his face...his chiseled features...his full lips...his...

No. I will not think about Thane. I'm alone with a handsome *prince*, for shadow's sake. It has to be the talmoon warping my thoughts.

"No pressure," Kelrean murmurs. "We have all night. Give it some thought." He leans in and presses his warm lips on my cheek.

Heat floods every sensitive part of my body as I open my eyes. My thoughts jumble and my vision blurs around the edges. His eyes are soft as he smiles.

"Come," he insists, climbing to his feet. "I'd hate to overwhelm you. Let's return to the festivities. I'll show you where the best wine is."

I grin as he helps me to my feet. "Wine sounds lovely."

Chapter 25

Kelrean leads me to a nearby stand stacked high with barrels of wine. We each drink a goblet as we wander through the village, my arm looped through his, laughing over silly things.

He points out several stands that have his favorite foods, shows me the statue of Orvena in the middle of the village and another of a beastial who reigned several hundred years prior to King Draedor, and then takes me to the outskirts away from the village. There, we continue sipping wine while gazing at the stars, which seem closer here.

"With how brightly you shine, you'd fit right in with the stars," Kelrean says, turning to me with a soft, crooked smile.

I shake my head. "You're just saying that."

"I'm serious, Zaira. Don't discredit yourself. You're beautiful."

I feel my cheeks heat up as my heart picks up in speed. Being romantic seems natural to him, as if he practices exactly what to say and when to say it. Or perhaps he's just a really good flirt.

To distract myself from the wave of excitement and desire swirling within me, I take a hefty sip of wine. Some dribbles down my chin, and he releases a soft laugh.

Reaching up, he wipes it away with his thumb in slow, careful strokes. Our gazes lock as that same thumb travels up to my cheek to caress it, then glides along my jawline. This simple act makes the small hairs along my spine rise.

"Fascinating," he murmurs, studying every feature of my face. My body.

I start to ask him what, exactly, is so fascinating about me, but someone approaches, and he looks their way.

"Our Majesty is looking for you, Your Highness," Sheera says, stopping only a few steps away from us.

"Of course he is." Kelrean looks at me, huffing a laugh as he lowers his hand. "Just when the fun was starting."

"It's okay," I assure him. "Go ahead. I should find my friends anyway."

"Would you like me to lead you back?" he offers.

"That's okay. I can find my way back."

He nods. "I'll find you afterward, then." He excuses himself, and I watch him stride away.

A freaking prince. Flirting with me. Maybe the swamp monster actually demolished us and I'm dead right now. Or perhaps the talmoon is making me imagine all of this? That's the only thing that makes sense. Fascinating? Beautiful? I must be dreaming.

I head back to the village square, polishing off my wine and then grabbing another meat skewer. I watch a man play a flute on the stage as I eat it.

My body still feels weightless from the talmoon, my mind so utterly relaxed that I can't help smiling as I wander about. Everything seems much more vibrant—the moon fuller, the heat of the fires warmer on my skin as I pass them.

After discarding my empty skewer, I stop at a cart for a sticky roll and bite into it. It's not honey loaf, but it's just as delicious and warm. I notice all the children have disappeared, likely sent home to bed. The remaining beastials hang around eating, drinking, and…making out. Some dance together to the music, while others drunkenly sway alone to their own rhythm.

I start to feel the talmoon ebb away as the wine creates a soft buzz.

In the distance, I spot Algar and Thane standing between two buildings a few paces from the courtyard. I bite into my roll as I stroll in their direction, but the longer I watch them, the angrier Thane becomes as he speaks to Algar.

When Algar points a finger at Thane's chest, Thane shoves it away, then yanks him forward by the collar. I gasp, walking faster. As I approach,

Thane releases Algar, mutters something in his face, then storms off.

"Algar? What just happened?" I ask.

Algar whips his head around so hard the ends of his plaits fly over his shoulder. "Where the shadows did you come from?"

"I saw you and Thane arguing," I reply, ignoring his question. "What was it about?"

"It was nothing," Algar grumbles as he hobbles past me. "Just Thane being *Thane*."

Confused, I watch him go. Before I can follow him, I notice Kelrean coming from the opposite direction.

"There you are," he says. "Shall we pick up where we left off?"

"Um, sure. I just need to check on someone really quickly."

He blinks at me a few times, seeming confused. "Is everything okay?"

"Yeah, I just—"

I clamp my mouth shut as Thane makes his way toward us with heavy steps. He's the person I wanted to check on.

"We should get back to the castle." Thane says the words to me while glowering at Kelrean.

"What's the rush?" I ask.

"Your sister's imminent death." Thane finally eyes me.

I scowl. *Jackass*. "I'll go back when Algar does. Or just return with Prince Kelrean." I shift closer to the prince, demonstrating once again that he doesn't dictate my decisions.

"I don't think you'll be seeing Algar anytime soon," he returns.

"Why? Because you've pissed him off?" I quirk a brow, testing him.

Thane tenses.

"Hey." Kelrean puts on a smooth smile as he claps a hand on Thane's shoulder. "She'll be taken care of, my friend. Don't you worry."

"I'm *not* your fucking friend," Thane growls, swiping Kelrean's hand away.

Shock fills Kelrean's eyes before his face settles with a frown. "That swamp has clearly shaken you up. Perhaps you should return to the castle and have a lie down."

"And leave her with a man who is intentionally drugging her and drowning her in wine?"

"What are you talking about?" I cut in, mildly annoyed. "I *wanted* to try the talmoon, and I grabbed my own wine. Besides, I'm nowhere near drunk, and the talmoon is already wearing off."

"Right," Kelrean adds, "and I would never do such a thing anyway. She only had one pull of the talmoon, and that was it. I wouldn't have let her try more." Kelrean sizes Thane up as he puts on a knowing smile. "You know what I think it is? I think you're jealous, my friend. I can't blame you, truly. She is unbelievably gorgeous. I've been drawn to her all night."

My heart thumps faster as heat crawls up my neck.

Thane grimaces. "Call me friend *one more time*, and I'll punch you in your fucking nose."

I gasp. "Thane!" What is it with him *always* choosing violence?

Kelrean throws his head back to laugh at the audacity of Thane's words. "Right. You know what? You're a bit too hostile right now, and frankly, even if Zaira were ready to go, I wouldn't trust her running off with the likes of you. Leave her with me. She said she's fine, and I believe we should respect the lady's wishes. Okay...*friend*?"

Before I can blink, Thane slams his fist into Kelrean's face. Kelrean howls, and I gasp as his nose immediately starts gushing blood.

"Ow! *What the fuck?*" Kelrean roars—literally—as he clutches his face. "You nearly broke my nose!"

Thane looks the prince up and down. "Sorry about that...*friend*."

"What the shadows is wrong with you, Thane?" I snap, setting my wine down to assist Kelrean. "Kelrean, are you okay?"

Two guards appear with swords in hand, pointing the tips of their blades at Thane's back. "Are you all right, Your Highness?" one of them asks.

"Give the order and we'll detain him, sir," the other guard says.

Kelrean raises a patient hand as bystanders swarm, murmuring among themselves with worry as they focus on their prince.

Oh my gods.

This is so embarrassing. This reckless assassin just punched royalty. Perhaps it will be Kelrean who causes Thane to finally meet his demise. What a twist that would be.

"I'm all right, I'm all right," Kelrean announces, sniffling as he swipes a hand under his bloody nose. "Our friend here has suffered a rough journey. He had a few drinks, and I believe he needs rest. Mercy is needed here." He fixes the lapels of his suit, then brushes imaginary dust off his shoulders. "Guards, please escort our *friend* to the castle so he may reorient himself."

The guards go for Thane immediately, grabbing either arm.

"Get the fuck off of me." Thane manages to maneuver himself away from them and storm off.

"Kelrean, I'm *so sorry*." I clasp my hands together, looking at his bloodied nose. "Are you sure you're okay?"

"I'm all right, Zaira. He got me good, I must admit."

"I'll talk to him. I'll make him apologize," I swear. "That was unbelievably rude of him."

"Yes, it was, wasn't it?" Kelrean accepts a handkerchief from another guard. When the blood is cleared, he sighs. "I should calm my people. See you at the castle?"

"Sure. Yeah." When Kelrean saunters away, I chase after Thane and the guards, making sure to catch up before they reach a covered carriage. The guards shove him inside and demand the coachman take him straight to the castle.

"You're lucky the prince is forgiving, otherwise we'd hang you on the mountain for what you've done!" one of the guards spits out.

"Just wait 'til the king hears about this," the other one snarls.

When they storm off, I climb into the carriage and sit on the bench across from Thane. I hold on to the edge of the seat as we lurch forward. It's only us in the dark, velvet confines—our bodies jostling with every dip and bump over the rocky path.

"I cannot believe you did that," I finally mutter when we're a third of the way there. "It's like you *want* someone to kill you."

He doesn't dare look at me. Instead, he peers out the nearest window, watching the courtyard glow from a distance.

I scoff. "I don't understand you at all."

"I never asked to be understood," he returns, eyes still focused out the window.

"Whatever." I fold my arms. "You need to apologize to Prince Kelrean."

"Apologies are only necessary when regret is felt." He turns his dark gaze to me. "I don't regret making your pretty prince bleed."

"You know what, Thane? You are being beyond childish right now. You just punched a *prince* in the face in his own kingdom! They could've killed you for that!"

"They wouldn't have succeeded."

"He was being kind to you!"

"He's full of shit."

"You think that about everyone!" My voice rises a few notches. I don't even fully understand why I'm yelling. Probably because I'm pissed that he's keeping his voice so calm while I'm getting worked up. That has always irritated me. Analla would do it all the time whenever we had a disagreement. "I'm capable of making my own choices. You know that, right? I hired you to protect me when there's danger. I didn't ask you to watch me like a hawk during the times I'm actually enjoying myself."

"I'm watching you because you trust too easily," he fires back. "That heinous trait of yours is why you're in this situation now. Because you hired a man you *hardly* know and put way too much faith in him."

"And every step I take with you makes me regret that choice a little more," I say under my breath.

After a stretch of silence, I sigh and lean forward, cradling my chin in my hands.

His eyes narrow, and he leans in, too, as he studies all the features of my face. "Are you sure about that, Quinlocke? Because when I look into your eyes, I don't see regret."

"No?" My pulse quickens. I hate how sexy he looks with the moon bathing half of his face, revealing the wicked scars I want to trace with the pad of my thumb. "What do you see, then, *Valkor*?"

He doesn't flinch at the name like I thought he would. "I see hope, even when matters are unfavorable. You reserve it for me because you're hoping you can find the light in my soul, but there is no light." He pauses. "Do you want to know what else I see?"

I hold my breath as his face comes closer. "What?"

"Passion," he murmurs. His lips are only inches from mine. "Hunger. *Desire*. You hate yourself for wanting a person like me, don't you?"

He's just as close as Kelrean was earlier, only with Thane, I can feel my pulse in places I never thought it could pump. "I never said I wanted you."

"You don't have to say it." His eyes drop to my lips, then slowly to my breasts, lingering for just a moment before climbing right back up to my eyes. "It's very clear."

I clench my teeth together, refusing to look away even though he's right.

Gods, I hate that he's right.

"Going to that little prince's chambers will be nothing more than a distraction for you, and we both know it."

"How did you—"

"He's not hard to read, Quinlocke. Everyone saw the way he stared at you. Treating you like you belong to him. The night was bound to end in one way—with you in his chambers."

"So you're jealous, then? Is that it?"

As rare as it is, his lips quirk up on one side, amused. "Not jealous. Territorial, more like."

"I'm not your property," I bite back. But why do I feel a delightful twist in my belly? Territorial. Of me?

No. Stop it. Don't fall for it.

"You may have tossed me those coins, but as far as I'm concerned, *I'm* the one in charge. Which means during this journey, no matter where we fucking are or how safe you feel in the moment, you're *mine* to look after and *mine* to keep close." He scans my face thoroughly, then slowly drinks in the rest of my body, searing me with his gaze. I have to clench my thighs together from that action alone.

I fidget in my seat.

"Like I told you before, oh sweet one," he continues in a silky, deep voice, "I don't like to fail, and if that means stopping you from making a reckless decision with a prince who might have beast warts, so be it. I'll be right there protecting you. *Watching* you. *Keeping you safe.* Is that clear?"

I refuse to answer him, not with that smug face and entitled attitude. I want to slap him.

He lifts an eyebrow, focusing on my mouth.

"I'm literally starting to hate everything about you," I whisper.

He says nothing, which only irritates me more. The carriage jostles us around, but I remain steady, matching his stare, waiting for him to lean back first.

But then something tight wraps around me and pulls forward, guiding my bottom closer to the edge of the bench. My breath hitches when I realize it's Thane's magic. He stares into my eyes as an invisible hand digs into my waist.

An unavoidable sigh slips out of me as his lips graze mine. A rush of tingles sweeps over my entire body, and heat pools between my legs, hotter than ever before.

My mouth aches for him—no, my *whole body* aches for him. Why didn't I feel this way toward Kelrean? During the moments alone with him, I wanted him. But my desire for the prince wasn't nearly as frustrating. How is it possible to want to slap Thane's beautiful face and kiss it at the same time?

I have to be under some kind of spell. I've never craved defiant, broody, dangerous men like Thane Valkor before. Men who are clearly no good for me. And yet, here I am.

Craving.

Wanting.

"Interesting," he rasps. "What I see in your eyes right now doesn't look like hate."

"Oh, shut up," I mutter, breathless. And instead of slapping him, I grip a handful of his waistcoat, yank him forward, and kiss him.

Chapter 26

It's happening.

This kiss. This *moment*.

Yes. Without a doubt.

I want this so badly that I can't stand another agonizing second of resisting him.

I pull my mouth away, and he looks at me—*really* looks at me—before cupping the back of my head and pressing my lips to his again. He groans as I straddle him and clasp his face in my hands. He tastes like ale and mint and smells so good, like firewood, leather, and spice.

The stubble along his jaw is coarse beneath the pads of my fingers, a contrast to his soft skin. Our breaths thicken between the slightest breaks, and he clutches the back of my bodice with one hand while I thread my fingers through his silky hair.

"This doesn't mean anything," I say, panting when his hot mouth claims my throat. He presses a kiss there, causing a soft moan to escape me. I tingle everywhere.

"Liar."

"I'm serious." I grip a handful of his hair and tug on it, forcing him to look at me.

He stares up, his mouth as damp and swollen as mine feels. "You really don't know how to stop talking, do you?"

Cradling the back of my head, he guides my mouth back to his, much gentler this time. I melt in his lap, moaning into his mouth, ready for more. Our tongues collide as we wrestle with each other's clothes. That invisible hand of his skims down my spine as his real hands perfectly cup my ass.

Flipping me onto my back on the carriage bench, he shoves my skirts up and guides the lower half of his body between my thighs, and when his mouth claims mine again, I savor the taste of him. I lace my arms around the back of his neck, bringing his chest closer as he grinds his hips up and down, creating a steady friction. I feel him hardening, digging into my pelvis and lower belly as deep groans form in the hollow of his throat.

I never want this ride to end. I want this moment to last forever, with his lips on my throat and his erection rocking against me, making me wetter by the second.

"So you *were* jealous," I say as his lips plant kisses down my chest.

"Fuck the prince," he growls, kissing the swell of my breasts.

His words send a twisted thrill through me.

"Take off your trousers," I demand.

"No."

I pause, frowning. "Why not?"

"I'm not fucking you in a carriage."

"What does it matter? This won't ever happen again after tonight."

"I really wish you'd stop lying to yourself."

"Thane," I snap.

"Zaira," he snaps back.

I huff and start to sit up, ready to push him away, but he forces me back down with a forearm to my chest.

"I said I'm not *fucking* you in this carriage. I never said I couldn't please you in it." He scans my face with blazing gold eyes. "That's what you want, right? For me to please you?"

I'd be a fool to deny it. My body is way too worked up for my own good.

I nod eagerly. "Yes."

"So *you* were lying." His deep chuckle fills the coach. "This does mean something to you."

Holy Crystal. The Shadow Realm must be bathed in light right now because Thane Valkor just laughed. Out loud. Should I point it out to him? No, no. I won't mention it. He might not ever laugh again just to spite me.

I want to hear it again, though. Many more times.

To keep us in this moment, I say, "If you keep talking, I'm going to shove you out and hope you hit your head on a rock."

I watch him fight a smile as something tugs at my underpants. It keeps tugging; however, when I look down, I don't see a thing.

"Tilt your hips," Thane instructs. That magical hand of his is clearly at play again. I lift my hips so he can lower my underwear just enough for the magical hand to have access.

I gasp when I feel the warmth of it skim through my delicate lips. Thane's eyes burn bright gold as he kisses me again, massaging one of my breasts with one hand while the other cradles the side of my head. As he does, the invisible hand dips inside me before pulling back out and circling my most sensitive spot until I buck beneath his hardened body, gasping.

Caging my bottom lip between his teeth, he keeps the magic going, rubbing my swelling bundle of nerves before allowing it to take careful thrusts inside me. I hold on to him as he releases my lip to give me a tender kiss. My moans grow louder, and he disrupts the kiss to drag his mouth to the shell of my ear.

"You're so wet for me, Zaira," he rasps.

I suck in a breath, clenching my thighs around his magic. Hearing him say my name drives me crazy.

"No. Don't hold back now," he growls, spreading my thighs apart again. "I need to hear you come for the man you pretend to hate."

His words are my undoing. Never in my life have I had an experience like this, but that magical hand keeps rubbing, keeps dipping, keeps pleasing with perfect pressure, and sure enough, I detonate.

I begin a cry of ecstasy, but he crushes my lips and swallows the noise. The carriage is slowing down, but his magic is still finishing me off, grazing, teasing, making me twitch while his hands roam my body in soothing strokes.

Pleased, he watches me writhe and gasp a few seconds longer before he finally takes it all away.

"Damn." He kisses the bend of my neck twice. "I can only imagine how amazing that would've felt around my dick."

When the heat of his body is gone, I sit up and breathe as evenly as possible, closing my legs and adjusting my skirts. Orvena's sake. That was... *too good.*

The carriage slows to a complete stop. I stare at Thane as he side-eyes me with that same smug smile from earlier. My heart still thunders as the coachman opens the door and helps me out of the carriage. His assistance is definitely needed. My knees are so weak that I'm not sure I can walk down the steps on my own. I wonder if he may have heard my sounds of pleasure, but based on his simple smile, I assume he hasn't. That, or he's used to hearing people get naughty in his conveyance.

As Thane and I make our way to the massive doors of the castle, neither of us says a word. Even when we enter and carry ourselves through the corridors, I still don't bother saying a thing.

I take the stairs ahead of him, aware of his dominant presence more than ever now. I swear I can still feel the heat of his body pressed against mine, his lips on my skin, his hands roaming every curve, the invisible one inside me. The words he murmured in my ear before making me come.

Good grief, Zaira. Stop thinking about it.

When I reach the landing to our floor, something slips up my dress and between my thighs. I yelp as my body is carefully guided to the nearest wall.

Thane stands before me, his eyes illuminated as that same *something* presses on my sex, pulsating and teasing. It's only now that I realize I haven't put my underpants back on. I accidentally left them behind in the carriage.

I clutch Thane's arm, trying to level my breathing. Gripping my face between his thumb and forefinger, he pins me to the wall. He kisses me again, a carnal moan rumbling in the base of his throat.

"Listen to me carefully," he rasps when our mouths briefly part.

I sigh as his mouth hovers above mine and the magical thing between my thighs becomes firmer, now sliding up and down, purposely grazing that spot that makes me squirm. "I'm listening."

He graces me with another deep kiss, coaxing my lips apart to plunge his tongue into my mouth. I clutch tighter at his tunic, wanting more than what just happened in the carriage. I want him—*all of him* in *every* way. Am I foolish for wanting to have sex with an assassin?

Yes.

Do I care in this moment?

No.

Tearing his mouth away, Thane keeps hold of my face. "If you let that cocky little prince into your room tonight, I'll stab his fucking eyes out, Zaira." There's no smile or smugness this time. He's not joking. Of course he's not. Even if it means adding another mob of angry people to his shit list. It's not a question for me anymore about whether or not he wants someone to kill him. This man clearly has a death wish.

I stare into his eyes. "Why do you care if he comes by or not?"

"You deserve better," he says.

I scoff. Who is better than a sexy prince? "And you think a wanted shadow assassin is better for me?"

He doesn't answer, but he does release my face and make the naughty bit of his magic disappear.

I straighten myself up, clinging to some kind of decorum. "Why didn't *you* actually do it? I mean, why use magic instead of…well, your *you know what*?" My voice is lower as my eyes dart left, then right. Anyone could be around to hear.

"You mean *my dick*?" Thane asks with a tilted brow.

I blush and fidget with my bodice, smoothing out the wrinkles. "Any other man wouldn't have cared where it happened. And I no longer have my maiden's mark…if that's your concern."

Thane offers a dark chuckle before bringing his mouth to the shell of my ear. "I didn't fuck you in there because if I had, these mountains would've crumbled from how loudly you screamed my name, *oh sweet one*."

I blink at him, clenching with need, as he takes a step back.

"Better to save all those innocent lives in the courtyard and in the castle." He drinks me in, smirking. "You wouldn't want to be the one responsible for all those accidental deaths, would you?"

I fold my arms, giving my head a slow shake. He's such an arrogant bastard.

"Sleep the rest of the talmoon off," he orders, walking backward. "I'm looking forward to seeing the regret in your eyes when the high wears off and it sinks in that you let an *assassin's* magic fuck you." He strides away while chuckling to himself.

That laugh again…only this time I'm annoyed by it.

Like a lustful fool, I stare after him, hoping he'll turn around and kiss me once more, or at least use his magic again for another round…

But he doesn't. He rounds a corner and disappears, leaving me sexually frustrated.

And the worst part about it? I can still hear him laughing.

Chapter 27

There's a pounding in the distance.

Groaning, I turn onto my side, begging for the sound to die. It doesn't. The pounding resumes, growing much louder this time.

"Zaira! Get up! It's first light!" Rynthea shouts on the other side of my door. "King Draedor is ready for us!"

I spring up with a gasp, swinging my legs to the edge of the bed. That's a mistake, though, because as soon as I'm on my feet, I stumble sideways and have to catch myself on the nearest storage chest.

Shit.

Maybe I shouldn't have had another glass of wine as I settled into the chamber last night. I needed something to distract me from the constant thoughts of Thane, though. It helped for the most part. Helped me go straight to sleep.

I'm regretting it now, though. I hold on to the smooth wooden edge of the chest, breathing evenly as I squint at the closed terrace doors. A bold stretch of sunlight streams in through the gap in the curtains, highlighting clean wooden floors. Even without my spectacles on, I can make out silver flecks in the stone walls.

"Zaira!" Rynthea calls again, banging on the door. "I can hear you moving. Don't make me break this door down."

"I'm coming!" I release the chest and throw my arms out to my sides to balance myself. When I feel stable enough, I head to the door as steadily as possible, unlock it, and pull it open.

"Orvena's sake," Rynthea says as she looks at me from head to toe. "You look like pure shit."

"Ugh." I press a palm on my throbbing right temple. "I feel like it, too."

"I should've warned you that Bernwood's wine is strong. Takes more for most beastials to get drunk, so they enhance it. One glass is enough to knock a mortal on their ass."

"It could be an aftereffect of the talmoon I smoked with Kelrean last night, too," I say with a pathetic wince.

"I told you not to get mixed up with that goof. Was he here last night?" She scrunches her nose, peeking into my room for signs of him.

I glance back. All she's gleaned, I'm sure, is an unmade bed and my filthy rucksack on the floor.

I recall last night's events with the prince. Going to the tent. Taking a stroll with him. The heat of the flames on my skin as I sat by the fire. The taste of sweet, spongey bread and wine. The feeling of talmoon coursing through my bloodstream…and of course Thane punching Kelrean square in his face.

It was all so very interesting. However, what I remember most is how it felt being with Thane in the carriage. And then on the stairs. Followed by his threat to gouge the prince's eyes out if I let him into my room.

To my surprise, Kelrean never showed up at my door. I was partially relieved by that, honestly—not that I really think he has beast warts, like Thane said. I just wasn't sure if I was up for hanging out with him after the naughty things I'd done in the carriage with Thane.

Knowing Kelrean is attracted to me, and I to him, leaves me unsure of what might've happened between us. Would Kelrean have tried to kiss me? If so, I don't think I would've denied him.

But what does that make me? A woman thinking about kissing two men in one night? I have a feeling that, if something were to happen between me and Kelrean, I would have been comparing his kiss to Thane's the entire time.

"He wasn't here," I tell Rynthea, shifting on my feet.

"Good. Well, hurry up." She rests the handle of her scythesword on her shoulder, the edge of the blade mere inches from one of her horns. "Everyone's already downstairs."

"Shit."

"Yeah. *Shit.* Wash your ass and get dressed so we can go."

Rynthea stalks away, and I close the door, hurrying to find my specs before searching for a proper outfit from the wardrobe. I decide to go with tan leggings and a burgundy tunic. We still have so much ground to cover in order to break Analla's curse. We can't afford any more delays after this.

I go to the washroom, glad one of the helpers has already been here to fill the washbasin. I give my teeth a solid brush as well as my hair before collecting my things and hurrying out of the chamber…all while fighting dizziness.

Downstairs, I catch Rynthea and Algar standing in front of a broad glass window that reveals distant mountain peaks and fleecy white clouds. And off to the right, cloaked in his familiar black garments and buffers, is Thane.

It takes everything in me not to react to the sight of him.

Externally, I succeed. Internally, not so much.

My heart races, and I feel these odd flutters in the pit of my belly. It doesn't help that when our eyes connect, amusement swirls in his, and a faint smirk tugs at the corners of his lips.

Yeah. He's going to hang last night's events over my head for as long as he possibly can.

"You're all here! Wonderful!" Queen Jenia's voice echoes through the main hall, bouncing off the rotunda and stained-glass ceilings. I wince, turning to find her. It's still too early for me. "I hope you have time for a quick breakfast before your departure." She saunters in our direction in a powdery pink gown, her crown glinting in the sunlight. And just behind her, dressed in a dark-purple doublet and beige trousers, is Kelrean. His eyes instantly land on mine.

I smile and wave hello, feeling a blush blooming under my brown cheeks again.

When Rynthea confirms that we have time to eat, Queen Jenia leads us to a dining room so large, it could fit at least three of the dining halls in the Meriva refugee camp. There are four lengthy tables in the room. The one she's chosen could seat twenty people.

I pull out one of the high-backed chairs and sit. Rynthea takes the seat left of me, Algar to my right, and Thane sits directly across from me. Kelrean and Queen Jenia take seats at the head of the table. Kelrean, of course, is still ogling me and smiling, despite the redness around his nose that comes awfully close to a bruise. You'd think after being punched in the face over me that he'd lose interest. I suppose it only intrigues him more.

Thane glares at him with his arms folded, not even trying to hide his disdain.

When the helpers pour us goblets of fresh pomegranate juice, I grab mine and take a few sips. It's good, but I wish it was tea. I need the jolt of caffeine so I can snap out of this haze.

"Ah, you're all still here." King Draedor's voice booms through the dining hall. My head throbs once again. Were they this loud yesterday? "Suppose you younglings are as foolish as I thought."

"Sweetheart," Queen Jenia titters.

He takes the seat next to her but not before dropping a kiss on her forehead and the top of Kelrean's head.

"Yes, Your Majesty, we're still here. Are you going to tell us how to get to Elphar and back safely?" Rynthea asks.

"I made you a promise, didn't I?" The king grunts as a plate full of food is placed in front of him by one of the helpers.

After the royals, plates are set in front of us guests, piled with steaming chopped apples in cinnamon sauce, sweet rolls, strips of meat, and poached eggs. My stomach grumbles but not as loudly as Rynthea's. She digs straight in, and I follow suit, resisting a moan as the flavors burst on my tastebuds.

Algar's delighted moan, however, fills the dining room, and the king and queen laugh at his unconventional flattery.

"As I'm sure you all know, the journey to The Shallows is one of the most dangerous," King Draedor says, chewing. "There are vicious creatures of all kinds and many less desirable paths. I nearly made it to the Temple of Elphar. I was so close I could taste it. But then I came across a creature I'd never seen before. There was no way I could beat it alone." He eyed each of us. "And not to boast, but if a shifter such as myself couldn't find a way around it, I don't think the lot of you will, either."

"We'll take our chances," Thane says.

King Draedor scans Thane thoroughly before sipping from his goblet. "I hear you struck my son last night," he says, but I don't miss the hint of venom in his tone.

"Accidentally," Thane replies, as if bored.

"How do you accidentally punch someone in the face?" the king counters.

"Your son just has one of those faces, Your Majesty." Thane shrugs. "Very punchable up close."

"Thane," I hiss with a frown. He's going to ruin this for us if he doesn't shut his mouth.

Surprisingly, Queen Jenia stifles a laugh.

King Draedor zeroes in on Thane with a growl as he tightens his grip around the handle of his fork.

"Now, now. It's quite all right, Father." Kelrean interrupts their stare down. "Our *friend* here was drunk and exhausted last night. In fact, I believe he was bordering on delirium, so I offered him mercy. All is forgiven." His teeth glint as he flashes an arrogant smile at Thane.

"You're correct, Your Highness." Thane takes a bite of his eggs. "I was a fool who had way too much to drink last night. And perhaps a little too much fun." His eyes slide to me as he chews. My cheeks turn hot. "I appreciate your forgiveness."

Well…that was the worst apology I've ever heard. The king and prince seem to accept it because they grunt and nod, holding their heads up high.

"As I was saying," Draedor goes on, giving Thane a pointed look, "I wouldn't have made it so far through The Shallows without the Kelvanite Sphere."

"What's that?" Rynthea asks around a cheek full of food.

"There is only one in Thelanor, created by an ancient sorceress named Frevella. She lives a short hike from Bernwood, higher in the Alvanite Mountains. She's been a wonderful ally of mine for quite some time, and had it not been for her, I wouldn't be able to tell you any of this."

"What exactly does the sphere do?" Kelrean inquires.

"It guides you, shows you to the safest routes," his father answers. "It was a valuable resource…until it wasn't."

Wait…what does *that* mean?

"If you stand any chance of making it to that island and back," the king continues, "it can only be accomplished with the Kelvanite Sphere."

"Is it here with you?" Rynthea probes, scanning him.

"No. It always returns to its creator after use. That is how the true essence of its power is restored."

"So, we have to make a stop to see this Frevella person first?" Thane asks. I'm glad Thane is able to lose the sarcasm. I suppose even he knows the royals of Bernwood have their limits and shouldn't be pushed past them.

"That is correct." The king runs a thick claw over the edge of his goblet, making a light scraping noise. "But be warned, my friends. Though Frevella and I are allies, she will not allow you to have the sphere without a price. And I don't mean with coin or treasure."

My chest tightens at that. What could she possibly ask for? Blood? A limb? One of our hearts? I glance at Thane, who doesn't seem the least bit concerned about King Draedor's warning.

"We defeated a swamp monster," he reminds the king. "I'm sure we can handle an elderly sorceress."

"An arrogant one you are," King Draedor counters with a chuckle. "It'd be wise not to underestimate Frevella. Besides, she will not see you all without confirmation that I sent you."

Thane frowns as he looks from the king to Rynthea, who also appears confused.

"My son and two of our finest guards will travel with you up the mountain to see her." He gives Kelrean's shoulder a squeeze.

Thane stiffens. Oh, *now* he's concerned.

"It is truly my honor," Kelrean declares with a cheery disposition. Then he aims his focus on Thane. "I hope me taking this brief journey with you doesn't present any issues."

"Shouldn't be a problem," Thane says. Right after the words leave his mouth, I feel something warm skate up my inner thigh and give it a squeeze. I stifle a gasp as I jump in my chair. I look to Thane, but he's too busy staring down the prince. There is a small challenge in his eyes as his magic hand inches higher up my thigh.

I shove it away, flustered, and the sensation vanishes.

"You all right, Zaira?" Algar murmurs.

"Yeah—I'm fine." I force a smile at him as I pick up my goblet and take a nervous sip.

Thane clears his throat, finally looking away from the prince to finish off his food.

"Very well!" King Draedor's voice reverberates through the room as he rises from his chair. I squeeze my eyes shut and wince once again as my ears ring.

Kelrean and the queen stand with him, and we follow suit, raising our goblets as he does.

"Though it pains me to see you all make such a grave decision, I wish you nothing but success on your quest," the king declares. "We'll pack food and supplies to last you the duration of your travel up the mountain. Kelrean will direct you straight to Frevella's cave with a scroll of my consent. And crew?" He assesses each of us with his impenetrable feline gaze. "No matter what happens, guard your heart and protect it at all costs. Because once you make it to The Shallows, your entire life will change. And believe me, it will *not* be for the better."

Suddenly, the king's face contorts, transforming into something completely unexpected.

My eyes widen with shock.

Rynthea's shoulders tense.

Algar hisses through his teeth.

Thane narrows his gaze.

The right half of King Draedor's face, which was once picture perfect in its human-lion form, is now thick with scars that have clearly been created by claws. The vicious marks start at his forehead and stretch all the way down to the middle of his throat.

And the worst part about it?

His eye is missing—a gaping hole now in its place.

Chapter 28

"Well, that was rather dramatic." Algar walks with me through the gates of Bernwood with Zephra curled around his shoulder.

With his weapons now returned, Thane inspects each one thoroughly as we pause to get our bearings.

"What do you think happened to his face?" I ask when I meet up with Rynthea. "What kind of creature could have done that?"

"I'm not sure," she murmurs, stuffing a canteen into her rucksack. "But it clearly didn't want visitors."

"It had to be massive." Algar shudders as Zephra clicks her teeth and shakes nervously.

Rynthea's focus travels to where the trail up the mountain begins.

"How long is the walk to Frevella's?" Rynthea asks as Kelrean saunters through the gates with two guards in eggplant-purple buffers trailing him.

Each guard carries a sword at their waist and a spear in hand. The prince nonchalantly totes a double-sided battle-ax with a thick wooden handle. In the center of the ax is the head of a snarling lion with a smooth mane made of gleaming silver. Kelrean also has a sword attached to his hip.

"Should be no longer than an hour," he answers. The curved blade of the ax glimmers in the sunlight as he gives it a smooth swing and then rests the handle on his shoulder.

"Show-off," Algar mumbles.

"Great," Thane mutters sarcastically under his breath.

"What was that, my friend?" Kelrean flashes a cool smile as he turns his attention to Thane, who is tucking the last of his daggers away in the designated slots of his vest.

When his swords are sheathed on his back, he marches past Kelrean and says, "We need to get moving."

Kelrean chuckles as Rynthea, Algar, and I follow suit.

"I agree," says Kelrean. "We *should* get moving, but you're headed in the wrong direction, I'm afraid."

Thane pauses, fists clenching. With a reluctant turn, he grimaces at Kelrean, who is already walking past the left gate.

"Just remember if you kill a prince, you'll be beheaded," Rynthea teases as she passes Thane. Algar side-eyes him with a slight frown before walking faster. I think he's still angry about last night.

I sigh, glad my headache is passing because dealing with men whose egos are as large as the mountain we're about to climb is going to require a lot of patience and effort.

When we round the wall built around Bernwood, we start up a rocky path. We aren't even five minutes in, and my thighs are burning. The interiors of my boots are rubbing against my pinky toes, and my heels ache.

Blisters are bound to come, but I stick close to the group and suck on a hard lemon-and-honey candy to distract myself.

Algar slows his pace to match mine, and we look down at Bernwood, which now seems like a blotch in the distance.

"Did you have fun last night?" I ask.

"Oh, *too much* fun," Algar answers. "They were gambling in one of the tents. Let's just say I may owe one of those beastials one hundred gold coins."

"*One hundred?* That's a lot of coin, Algar." I laugh.

"Yeah. But I don't plan on returning anytime soon so, in my mind, I'm debt free."

An ache develops in my lower back. It would've been nice to ride up the mountain on horseback, but Kelrean warned us earlier that the mountain becomes very steep, plus to reach the other side, we have to cross a bridge that can't bear the weight of a horse. So, to my disappointment, we left Pearl in Bernwood. I swear I'll go back for her one day. I've already lost one pearl. I'm not about to lose another. Queen Jenia promised me that she would move Pearl into the royal stables so no one would steal her.

"What were you and Thane arguing about last night?" I ask Algar in a low voice. Thane is several paces ahead, closer to Rynthea, who is shaking her head at something Kelrean is chortling about.

Exhaling, Algar digs into his pocket and pulls out a strip of dried fruit. He offers it to Zephra, who eagerly takes it with both her little paws and nibbles on it.

"I asked him why the attack in Kamtaur happened and if he was involved with the sorcerer who got away. He said he wasn't involved with him, so I pushed for more answers because I know he's lying about something regarding those people. There wouldn't have been so many of them coming to kill him if he hadn't done something serious."

I nod, remembering Thane's mention of stealing one of Seferin's crystals. I also remember him requesting that I keep our conversation about the tome, Seferin, and Maliek between us, but Algar already knows about the tome. I just need *him* to keep quiet about it now.

"I talked to him about that a little more last night, too," I tell him in a lower voice. "He doesn't want anyone else knowing about the tome. Apparently, I wasn't even supposed to tell you."

Algar frowns a bit. "Why not?"

"He thinks you're a blabbermouth."

Algar rolls his eyes. "Yeah, all right. As if I'm out here shouting everyone's secrets to the gods."

"Just promise to keep the tome thing between us, okay?" I plead. "It might be the safest thing to do—for all of us."

"Fine." Algar releases a deep sigh, concentrating on Thane's back. "I suppose me being a blabbermouth annoyed him last night and that's why he grabbed my shirt and told me to fuck off in spectacular Thane fashion." He shrugs as if he doesn't care, but I can tell he does—that Thane hurt his feelings. I lock on Thane, too, who is now looking over his shoulder at me and Algar. He turns away, but I notice him slowing his stride.

"Just remember what I said last night, yeah?" Algar steps over a rock. "About being careful with him. I wouldn't lower my guard too much if I were you. Thane has never attached himself to *anyone*, and I doubt he'll start now." With a half-hearted smile, he walks faster to catch up with Rynthea.

Thane meets me at my side. I take a peek at him. It's always so hard to decipher his expression with that mask covering half his face.

"I'm amazed," he finally says.

"What are you talking about?"

"To not see any regret in your eyes." His moisturized, tight curls gleam under the sun. He must've taken a bath and worked some kind of hair butter into his tresses.

I clear my throat, fighting the urge to imagine him having a bath...

Naked and wet.

Sculpted.

Delicious.

I dig into my satchel for another honey-lemon candy, seeking distraction.

"There's no regret because I don't care," I tell him. "It happened, and now it's in the past."

"Still lying to yourself, I see."

I put my attention ahead as I pop the candy into my mouth.

"The prince didn't make it to your room." It's a statement—not a question.

"And how would you know that?"

"Because he's still looking at you like he wants to devour you. He probably would, too, seeing as he's half beast and all."

"First of all, he's a *shifter*. They're not the same as beastials. Second, jealousy doesn't suit you."

I swear he's giving his signature smirk behind that mask.

"There's nothing for me to be jealous of. I know whose dick you want, and it certainly isn't the prince's."

"Gods," I groan. I really hope Kelrean's hearing isn't as keen as Rynthea's. "You're so full of yourself."

"Am I wrong, though?"

I ignore him, almost glad the mountain is becoming steeper because the exertion shuts him up. I breathe evenly through my nose as the sticky taste of honey lingers in my mouth.

The high altitude makes my ears pop. The sun feels closer, beating down on the back of my neck and making my forehead slick with sweat, yet it seems to only be a struggle for me. Everyone else carries on just fine. Thane walks with so much ease, I'm envious.

After at least forty or so grueling minutes, Kelrean announces, "Only a few more minutes, my friends!"

Thank Orvena.

We travel around a bend in the mountain, and not too long after, we reach a dark tunnel. The edges of the tunnel are seamless, like they've been chiseled and sanded by hand. Carved into the edges are runes. It's so pitch-black within the tunnel that I can't see a thing.

"Here we are." Kelrean gestures to the cave. "Frevella's cave."

"I don't get good energy from a person living in a cave," Algar mutters.

Just then, purple flames flicker, illuminating an endless tunnel. They hover close to the walls, floating on their own like orbs.

Rynthea starts forward, but Kelrean sticks out a hand and presses it to her chest to stop her. "I wouldn't do that if I were you."

Rynthea quirks a brow. "Is she not inside?"

"Most likely, but my father mentioned that no one should enter her cave without permission." The prince bends down to pick up a jagged rock and tosses it toward the mouth of the tunnel. Before it can reach the darkness, though, the rock shatters with a burst of purple ripples and rains to the ground in shards.

Rynthea looks shocked as she steps back next to Kelrean. "I appreciate the heads-up. Should we call for her, then?"

"No need. I'm sure she knows we're here. I've heard she's a bit eerie that way."

In the brief moment of silence that stretches over us, I spot a figure at the end of the tunnel. Purple light dances on the edges of their frame. Just as quickly as I see it, it vanishes.

My heart races faster. "What was that?" I whisper.

Algar narrows his eyes, looking harder at the tunnel.

Then it happens again. The figure appears, but it's closer this time. Thane slowly reaches for one of the swords on his back, unsheathing it and bringing it to his side. Rynthea squares her shoulders, tightening her grip around the handle of her scythesword.

The figure, I realize, is a person. And they are moving closer with each reappearance until, finally, they're *right here*—right at the mouth of the cave with a cloud of gray smoke billowing around them.

"Why are you on my property?" The voice behind the smoke comes out as a thick croak.

"We're here to see you, Frevella." Kelrean steps to the front and holds out the scroll to the mass of fog before him.

Frevella. It's her.

She's quiet for a few seconds. "Prince Kelrean Shattore of Bernwood."

"Yes." He nods as the scroll floats from his hand to Frevella's. "It is."

"With guests," she notes with a hint of agitation, her spindly fingers clutching the scroll.

"With *harmless* guests," he assures her.

"You know to only speak the truth to me. One member of your crew is not as harmless as you claim."

Kelrean peers over his shoulder, setting his gaze directly on Thane. Out of instinct, everyone else does, too.

"Seriously?" Thane frowns, glaring at everyone. "Why are you all looking at me?"

Everyone looks away, clearing their throats or shrugging.

Yeah. Maybe he should've kept the mask off.

"If you'd like, we can secure their weapons." Kelrean is speaking to her again. The smoke spills from the cave and rolls toward us, swimming around our feet. "They seek your help reaching the Temple of Elphar."

At that, Frevella laughs, a drawn-out, peculiar sound that makes me cringe. Slowly, the smoke disappears and reveals a woman with frizzy, stark white hair and sepia skin. She wears layers of robes in dark colors—black, brown, green—and all swim around her feet. A black snake is draped over her shoulders, its beady, glowing eyes examining each of us.

But those things aren't what surprise me most about her.

It's the fact that she has no eyes. They're simply two thin slits, as if they've been gouged out and the eyelids stitched. The sight of her should terrify me, but instead, I brew with curiosity.

I wonder what happened to her eyes. Why is she in this dark, lonely cave, so closed off from the rest of the world? Who did this to her?

"The Shallows are not for the weak," Frevella informs us.

"I don't take them for weak," Kelrean replies, voice firm. "My father sent me here with his request. A favor to allow them use of your Kelvanite Sphere."

Frevella scoffs. "Why would I give my sphere to a group of travelers I do not know?"

"They're willing to pay."

"Do they know the price?"

I notice Kelrean's throat bob as he glances at Rynthea. He comes to her side and whispers something in her ear. She frowns at him before focusing on Frevella again.

"Secrets?" Rynthea repeats.

Frevella's wrinkled mouth twists into a sly smile. My curiosity about her fades as a cold feeling slithers down my spine.

"Fine." Rynthea bobs her head. "We'll tell you whatever you want to know if it means we can use your sphere."

"Oh, not you." Frevella gives her head a subtle shake, then lifts both arms and points her index fingers directly at me and Thane. *"Them."*

My heart plummets as all eyes turn to us. I look at Thane, and his jaw is clearly clenching behind his mask.

"Only them. No weapons." Frevella turns away and disappears in another cloud of smoke, leaving us no room to object.

I know we have no choice but to follow her. She's made up her mind. There aren't any other options.

Kelrean starts for Thane, but Rynthea stops him. "I've got it," she says.

Approaching Thane, Rynthea sticks out a hand with a dim smile. "Algar and I will hold on to your weapons."

Thane eyes her and Algar, who offers him a hand, too. Clearly annoyed, Thane pries off the leather straps holding his swords, then removes his vest, shoving it all into Rynthea's hands.

Before he can reach the cave, Algar clears his throat. "Forgetting something?"

Thane halts, and with a low growl, he yanks the dagger out of his boot and another from beneath the sleeve of his shirt, dropping them in Algar's hand.

"All right. *Now* you can go," says Algar.

I feel my chest constrict. What if I go inside and never make it back out? What if she has a collection of eyeballs and wants to gouge ours out just to add to it?

Oh Orvena. This isn't at all what I expected.

"Good luck," Algar calls as Thane and I approach the tunnel.

"We *need* that sphere, Zaira," Rynthea says when I give them one more look over my shoulder. "Tell her whatever she wants to know. And make sure the *sorcerer* doesn't fuck this up for us."

Chapter 29

My feet shuffle over rocks and piles of dirt as I scurry through the tunnel to keep up with Thane. I stumble and end up bumping into him because I keep glancing back at the mouth of the cave, which is now just a pinprick of light in the distance.

"What did Frevella mean by secrets?" I ask.

"I don't know," Thane grumbles. "But I know elder sorcerers like doing things the old-fashioned way. They don't care for debts. They just want to mess with your head."

He says that like it's a good thing.

When we reach the end of the tunnel, it feels twice as warm. I spot more flames flickering in the distance, but those are normal, not purple. We walk down three stone steps and round a corner, entering a room shaped like a half-circle with rocky gray walls peppered in silver. The silver catches the fire blazing in the hollow of one of the walls. The only sounds are crackles and pops, but there is no wood for the flames to scorch.

It smells like so many things at once—fish, spices, sulfur, flora, a *corpse*. I shudder at the idea that dead bodies could be hidden in this cave…and how easily we could be joining them. But hey, at least there aren't any eyeballs floating in glass jars.

I spot Frevella to our left, standing next to a table that's been built from alvanite. She slaps a thick book closed, startling me as she faces us. That snake of hers slides off her shoulder and slithers in our direction.

I draw in a breath as it coils around Thane's ankle. He doesn't stir, even as it creeps all the way up his body and winds around his shoulders. When it makes its way back down, the snake roams over my foot and slides up my leg. I fight a tremble as it circles my waist, then slinks to my chest with its tail wrapping around my ribs. It moves back so its face can hover in front of mine, eye to eye. I hold my breath, staring into its glowing red eyeballs.

Its black tongue rapidly flickers through its lips before Frevella says, "Good." And just like that, the snake drops to the ground and slithers back to her.

My hands shake so violently, I have to fold my arms and tuck them beneath my armpits.

"Sit." Frevella gestures to two rickety-looking chairs in the center of the room.

Thane goes first. I follow him. I hate that the chairs face each other. It's hard *not* to look at him, especially now that he has his mask lowered. His sharp jawline is peppered in stubble, his lips are pressed into a thin line due to his agitated mood, and his eyes dart from me to Frevella.

"How long will this take?" he asks as she glides toward us.

"However long it takes." She stands behind him, but the snake slinks closer, stretching up to his eye level. And then it dawns on me—she's seeing us through the snake's eyes.

The hairs on the back of my neck rise and a shiver rattles through me as she asks Thane, "Why are you traveling to Elphar's temple?"

"She needs a prosperity stone," he answers.

Frevella is quiet for a beat. "And what do *you* need?" she probes, walking around his chair. Her head is tilted up while her snake studies him intently.

"I'm simply her protector."

Frevella snorts.

He scowls.

"You. Girl. Why do you willingly risk your life going to Elphar's temple?"

"For my sister," I tell her.

"She needs your help, yes?"

"Yes."

"Oh, poor girl. You would do anything for her, wouldn't you?"

My heart drums faster as the snake studies me more closely. "Anything," I whisper.

The cave falls into a tense silence as she makes her way around the room, her fingertips pressed together. Sweat accumulates on my forehead and upper lip from the heat...and probably from the nerves, too. The fire is unnecessary, but perhaps she's cold. Or maybe the fire is her only source of light. Either way, I can feel my clothes sticking to me, like honey to my fingers. I swipe at the bead of sweat dripping down the side of my face.

"You want my Kelvanite Sphere." She stops between us. "Very well. I can give it to you."

I perk up a bit.

"But, as I mentioned, there is a price." Her snake looks between us, and my hope deflates. "Two secrets must be shared. One from each of you."

Thane frowns. "Seriously? *A secret?*"

Frevella doesn't answer. She remains completely still, her face pointed forward, the snake examining us for her.

"Fine." Thane's seat creaks as he adjusts his position. "I kept a dagger on me. It's tucked in my left boot."

Frevella's head tilts backward as she unleashes another one of her croaky laughs. He and I pass a look between each other. This woman is mad.

She faces Thane and leans in, coming face to face with him. "If only it were that simple."

"I don't understand what you want." His words come out through gritted teeth.

"I don't want your surface secrets. I want to know the deepest, darkest fear that you've never shared with anyone—the one that torments you so much, it turns your sweetest dreams into cruel nightmares." She turns her face toward me. "I want you to tell me about the fear that eats you up inside. That is the secret I want in exchange for my irreplaceable sphere."

When she moves out of the way, Thane's amber eyes clash with my dark brown. His teeth grind when he turns away from me, focusing on the fire instead.

"I've poured many of my spells, secrets, and energy into the very sphere you seek," Frevella goes on. "It is dear to me and has saved *countless* lives. You want it to save yours, then you must reveal yourself."

As she speaks, the cave becomes hotter. I'm dripping with sweat, and I'm certain the jagged walls are closing in on us. Everything, including the table and bookshelves, feels closer. Even the energy flowing off of Thane feels stronger, like he's right in front of me.

Frevella grips our shoulders, and a shock courses through my bloodstream. Thane clearly feels it, too, because his eyes ignite a fierce gold.

"Look at each other," the sorceress orders.

I stare into his eyes as he does mine. I can't look away even if I try.

"You speak first, *Thane Valkor*." I can hear the satisfaction in her voice. She's pleased to have us under whatever spell this is—to have us as pawns in her hands.

Thane grunts as he tries resisting, but Frevella grips him tighter, her nails piercing into his buffers.

Rynthea's words ring in my head. *Make sure the sorcerer doesn't fuck this up for us.* I try telling him to just reveal something so we can get the sphere, but it's not my turn to speak yet. Frevella won't allow me.

"My greatest fear is not getting vengeance," Thane confesses. He closes his eyes as if those words—that don't surprise me in the slightest—are an earthshaking declaration.

"That's a start," the sorceress says. "But you must give me more. I must know why. Continue."

Lips clamped tight, he takes several deep breaths through his nose as if he's fighting to keep silent. "I…had…a brother…" His words come out strained and painful. "He… *Fuck*… I can't."

I have the urge to reach out to him, but I still can't. My body is completely under her control. My emotions are not entirely my own, either. I can feel so much in this moment.

Anger.

Worry.

Fear.

Thane's emotions have entwined with mine. I didn't think he feared anything, but seeing him now in such a vulnerable state, fighting with his truths, makes me wonder…

"Do not resist," Frevella commands. "Speak your truth. Your greatest fear. Your pain, I must feel."

Maybe she feeds off emotions and gets her power from that somehow. I try to look at her, but the spell holds my gaze firmly on Thane's face.

He manages to close his eyes. Frevella hangs on, and the tension finally leaves his body as he parts his lips to speak again.

"His name was Koa. He was… He was my little brother. He was killed in his nineteenth year, and...it was my fault."

My throat thickens as I study the man across from me. His head sways with shame, and his mouth quivers. His eyes remain closed as he tilts his head back and swallows, the lump in his throat going up and down.

"I still see his face when it happened. I...I can't forgive myself or the people who killed him. I *never* will. He told me all the time that he wanted to be just like me, but...I'm the worst person. My existence is riddled with disappointment and bathed in blood. I come from *nothing*, but he had the potential to become *everything*. It's my fault he's gone, but I want to make it right. I *must* make it right. My greatest fear is that I will fail him."

Hot tears run down my cheeks as I watch him struggle with his secret.

His fear.

His *truth*.

Now I understand why he's so guarded and angry—not only because of the past Algar told me about, but this, too. Now I understand why he wants to increase the power of his magic. Did his brother die because he became a shadow assassin? Or did he become a shadow assassin because of his brother's death? How was it his fault?

So many questions run through my head, but they slip away as Frevella squeezes my shoulder and says, "Speak, girl."

I can only stare at Thane, whose eyes open to focus on mine. "My greatest fear is..." I bite my lip. It seems cruel to say "losing my sister" after Thane's retelling of his own brother's death, but whatever spell she has us under compels me to speak. I decide to start from the beginning.

"I still have nightmares about my last day in Ember Coast," I confess. "I'm a native. I loved it there and was so happy, but then the Ruvain attack happened."

Frevella's grip on my shoulder relaxes.

"I...I remember the explosions. The raids. The *screams*. Some of my friends' bodies on the streets...dead. There were fires everywhere, and I was so scared." My voice breaks as Thane's eyes soften at the corners. "I still remember the desperation in my father's eyes and the fear in my mother's before Analla and I were hauled away to safety by soldiers from Meriva. The attack had gone on for four days before they found us.

"We'd been hiding in a fortified building, and we were lucky because not many of us made it there. But when we were taken, my parents insisted on staying behind to help. My father was a doctor and my mother a nurse, so it was in their nature to take care of others. Meriva won and drove out the Ruvainers, but...I never saw my parents again after we were removed from the coast. My sister and I saw so many of our friends reunited with their parents, but it never happened for us. Instead, we were sent to a refugee center for orphaned children in Meriva."

I drop my chin as hot tears slide down my cheeks. "I know you think it's reckless, Frevella, that we're going to Elphar's temple, but this journey is important to me. I'm doing it because I had *everything* ripped away from me before, and I couldn't do a damn thing about it. Now my sister will be taken away from me, too, if I don't act. She's the only family I have left, and the truth is..." I fight through the emotions clogging my throat. "Well, the truth is I'm *afraid* to be alone. Without her, I'm afraid loneliness will swallow me whole. I hardly even have friends," I say with a humorless laugh. "I have no one else. I *need* her, and I don't care what I have to do to get her back. You ask what my greatest fear is? My greatest fear is not being able to save her. It's knowing that if I fail, there will be no one else left in this world who loves me back."

The cave drowns in a deafening silence.

Frevella releases our shoulders, and the shock coursing through my bones melts away. I draw in a full breath before exhaling, trying to calm myself. I can feel Thane's heavy gaze on me, curious, lingering. I'm sure he has a million questions just like I have for him, but I've revealed enough for one day. I'm too ashamed to look at him right now.

Talking about Ember Coast, about my parents, about my past...it's always been too much for me to bear. In the beginning, the mere thought of it made me curl over and weep. Each year, it becomes a little easier, but I still have moments where crying is the only way to cope with my reality.

I can't do that here, so I clear my throat and shove away my frustrations.

"Can we have the sphere now?" I ask in a softer voice.

Frevella angles her chin higher. "The sphere is yours."

Chapter 30

"My Kelvanite Sphere will detect traps and assist you in avoiding all dangers." Frevella places a pale-blue glass ball in the palm of my hand. "When you wish to activate it, you simply rub it four times and say *drusako*. *Drusako* means—"

"To guide," Thane fills in.

Frevella's snake turns its eyes to Thane. "You know Thelasian?"

"I've studied it," he answers, as if it's no big deal. But it *is* a big deal. Not many people know our originating language.

"Hmm." Frevella taps her chin. "You're smarter than you look, boy."

Based on his frown, Thane doesn't take her remark as a compliment.

"When you say the proper word, the sphere will spark with an arrow. If it's green, it means you are in a safe area," Frevella continues. "But if it sparks red, it means danger is nearby, or you're already *in* danger."

"Sounds easy enough." I weigh the sphere in my hands—it's light.

"There is something you should know," Frevella adds, a finger rising in the air. "All creations, no matter how powerful, have their limits. The Kelvanite Sphere will burn out. Its power usually only lasts about an hour."

I blink at her. "Only an hour?" I look at Thane, who shifts on his feet. "That's not enough time to make it through the whole island, is it?"

"No, it isn't," he mutters.

"Can you add more power to it?" I ask Frevella.

"That is my limit," she snaps, waving a flippant hand. "It feeds off of my magic, and anything more weakens me. I don't care to deteriorate my energy for people who voluntarily risk their lives. Use it wisely. Whether you make it off that dreaded island alive or not, the sphere will find its way back to me. *Eventually*. Now leave my cave," she demands with a sniff. "I'm ready to rid myself of this disturbance."

I feel nothing but pure relief when we make it out of the stuffy darkness of Frevella's home. Thane is now carrying the sphere in one hand and studying it thoroughly, as if he's trying to figure out how a simple glass object like that can hold so much power. When the others outside the cave see him with it, they huddle together for a closer look.

"Wow," Rynthea marvels. "Glad you didn't fuck it up for us, sorcerer." She always says that word like it's a dirty one, which really makes me wonder again what she has against sorcerers in general. Surely, Thane isn't the only one she doesn't like.

To my surprise, Thane doesn't react at all to Rynthea's comment. Not even one of his habitual grimaces makes an appearance. Instead, he tucks the sphere into the pocket of his trousers while sticking out his other hand. "Give me my weapons."

Rynthea gives him the vest. Algar gladly returns the sheathed swords and daggers.

"You know"—Kelrean smiles as he looks at each of us—"I was thinking I should journey with you all to the shores, at the very least."

Still, Thane doesn't react. Not even to Kelrean deciding to be around us longer? Now he's scaring me.

"You couldn't even save yourself from drowning," Rynthea counters. "Just take your royal, spoon-fed ass back to the castle. We can handle it from here."

"First of all, I was a *child*," he retorts. "Secondly, I am a *man* perfectly capable of traveling to the shores. You won't have to worry about saving me."

"We have orders to return you to Bernwood once the sphere is obtained, Your Highness," one of the Bernwood guards states.

"I'm well aware, but this is something I'm choosing to do for our friends," Kelrean asserts. "Something tells me this crew will need my assistance along the way."

Thane scoffs as he laces his vest. At least there's finally a reaction out of him, albeit a weak one.

"Tell my father I will return soon." Kelrean is already walking away from the guards. "I've done missions in Ruvain, for Orvena's sake. I'm certain I can travel around a mountain and take a gander at the Gadonian shores without issue."

Rynthea follows after him. "I'll only end up saving your ass again."

"Or perhaps I'll settle the score and save yours." Kelrean grins. "Then you can stop hanging your little badge of glory over my head."

Rynthea falls into step next to the prince. Algar and I join them. The guards hesitate as we march past. They blink at each other with apprehension, likely torn between following the prince and ignoring the instructions of their king. Neither outcome seems wise, especially the latter, because that would mean returning to Bernwood and explaining to the king why they left his only heir unguarded.

"They're following us, aren't they?" Kelrean settles the upper handle of his ax on his shoulder, giving me a lazy smile as he moves closer to my side.

I look over my shoulder at the disgruntled guards trailing a few steps behind Thane. "Yep."

Kelrean groans, tossing his head back. "I'm so tired of being treated like a child."

"They treat you that way because you *are* a child," Rynthea chides. "An annoying, spontaneous child in his twentieth year who can't stop playing with his own penis."

"Shadows! She's so mean, isn't she?" Kelrean winks at me.

I can't find it in me to smile as wide as him. My mind is still racing with thoughts from Frevella's hot and dark-ass cave. I glance at Thane again. He's staring off to his right, gazing at the lower peaks of mountains and forest tops. I slow my pace, feeling the need to check on him, but Rynthea slows her stride as well, taking up my right side as Algar flanks the left.

"What happened in there?" Rynthea asks in a low voice.

"Secrets," is all I can manage.

She's quiet for a moment. "Are you okay?"

I meet her eyes. She studies me with her eyebrows drawn together, seeming genuinely concerned.

"I'm okay. Thanks for asking."

"What about him?" Algar cocks his head, gesturing to Thane.

"I'm sure he's fine. Nothing bothers him, right?" I try to divert the question. I want to ask Algar if he knows about Thane having a brother. It didn't come up in the conversation we had during the fete. Now isn't the time, though.

"Suppose you're right." Algar swings his gaze to Rynthea. "Do we even know what's on the other side of this mountain, Ryn?"

As Rynthea fishes out a map from her rucksack, I slow my pace to match Thane's. When the group is a short distance ahead of us and the guards several steps behind, I look at him.

"Do *not* start with me," he grumbles, side-eyeing me.

"I'm not starting anything. Just trying to make sure you're okay."

"Would be a whole lot better if your little prince wasn't tagging along."

"Thane." He catches the sharpness in my tone, and his chin lowers. When his eyes latch onto mine, he stares into them for several seconds before finally looking away. I want to reach for his hand and hold it in mine but think better of it.

He sighs. "It doesn't matter."

"It *does* matter," I counter in a lower voice, hoping no one up ahead will hear. "You lost your *brother*, Thane. That matters a lot."

"Just stop."

"Why didn't you tell me about him last night?"

"Not right now, Zaira."

"Yes, *right now*," I insist. "This is important information, is it not? Why hide it? It's good that I know now because it all makes sense—why you want the tome and why you want to increase your power."

His jaw steels. "Just drop it."

He speeds up his walk again. I scurry to catch up with him. The mountain is finally sloping downward. We're getting closer to the other side.

"Did Seferin murder your brother?" I ask, catching up to him.

He's about to pause but keeps his stride steady as he shakes his head.

"If you don't talk about it and keep bottling it up, it'll make you rotten inside, Thane."

I notice one of his fists clenching. This time, he *does* stop walking. One of the guards almost bumps into him, but the guard catches himself and scowls at us before continuing his trek.

Up ahead, I notice the others have rounded a slight curve in the mountain. They're nearing the bridge.

Thane turns around and slowly closes the gap between us.

I back away from him, then feel the heel of my foot come perilously close to the edge of the mountain. My heart pounds when all I see below me are rocky cliffs and lush treetops. There would be no surviving a fall like that.

"Look, I don't need your pity," he starts. "Right now, all we need to do is focus on making it to Elphar so we both can get what we want. This thing between us," he says, gesturing back and forth with his hand, "shouldn't get any deeper because once it's all over, you'll never see me again."

My foot slips, and I gasp.

He clutches my arm and whirls me around, placing my back against the safer side of the mountain.

His body presses against mine as he holds me against the jagged mountainside, and as he regards me, my pulse quickens.

"You started this journey despising everything about me, Zaira." He studies every feature of my face, starting with my eyes, lowering to my nose, then my lips and chin. "I encourage you not to forget who and what I really am. I'm no good for a person like you, and definitely won't be after this journey is over."

"What if I don't despise you anymore?" I ask in a softer voice.

His hand circles my waist before skating up my spine. I feel it press to the back of my head and tug on my ponytail to angle my chin upward. As he hovers his mouth over mine, my breathing shallows. That silly heart of mine races faster.

Suddenly, I'm eager—desperate to know what he'll do next.

Desperate for him to kiss me once again.

"I suggest you reconsider," he rasps. "Because in all reality, I don't know you, and you don't truly know me. It's better to keep whatever this is on the surface. No point in taking it deeper."

All his words go through one ear and out of the other. I can feel the heat of his mouth, his breath dancing across my slick skin. I remember the carriage, his hands all over me, the taste of ale and mint on his tongue…

I want him to kiss me. I want it *badly*.

But he doesn't give me the satisfaction. He releases me instead and steps away. I can't stand how much my body aches at the loss of his touch.

"Let's keep going. When we cross that bridge, we'll be in Gadonia before we know it." He fixes his mouth like he's about to say something else, but just as quickly, his shoulders tense, and his eyes spark gold.

"Thane?" I call, concerned by his sudden change of mood.

Swiftly, he grabs my wrist and yanks me to the side as something silver and sharp flies through the air. The sight of the four-sided blade penetrating the mountain *right* next to my head makes my stomach coil. The letters *TSG* are engraved in the center. I don't know what they stand for, but I know whoever has thrown it is a real threat.

The air seems to grow stiffer with humidity as Thane turns his head a fraction to glare over his shoulder. That's when I realize we're not alone.

Coming up the mountain is Maliek and a cluster of assassins. Maliek narrows his blazing ice-blue gaze on us, weapons in hand, ready to attack. With the sound of a growl building in his throat, Thane lifts his mask and draws one of his swords. He stands in front of me to block me from Maliek's view. "Get to the bridge with the others," he commands, shifting to a defensive stance. His long fingers curl around the hilt of his sword as he grimaces at Maliek.

Before he can say anything else, Maliek lifts a hand in the air and points two fingers at us.

And with his silent command, the assassins rush in our direction.

Chapter 31

I should've chosen better shoes for this hike. I *definitely* would have if I'd known a dozen assassins would be chasing us. *Again.*

My rucksack, full of food, water, my satchel, and a bag of candies, slams into my back as I book it. With lungs that feel like they're about to burst, I run down the sloping side of the mountain; however, it's much steeper than I anticipated.

"Shit, shit, shit!" I leap over a large rock, but another comes into view, and the tip of my boot catches on it before I can jump again. I careen forward, sliding downward on my palms. I can feel the skin on my hands rip open as the gravel and dust cloud around me, invading my mouth and nostrils. I cough as I look back to see four assassins a short distance away.

I push up on scraped, stinging hands and stumble forward. "Rynthea! Algar!" I scream. They're ahead, nearing the bridge. They turn, along with Kelrean and the guards, and their eyes widen when they realize I'm being chased.

Something flies past me—another four-sided blade—and aims straight for Kelrean's head. He catches it between his fingers with a bored scowl before it can hit him. Chucking it aside, he swoops his ax in the air, unleashes a lion's roar, and sprints forward. Rynthea follows suit with her scythesword, and the guards storm after their prince. They all zoom past me to take on the assassins.

"Where the shadows did they come from?!" Algar shouts when I approach him.

"I don't know!"

We hurry toward the bridge with Zephra flying behind us, but as we near it, I throw my hands out and come to an abrupt stop.

No one told us the bridge would be an ancient, unstable rope suspension bridge, or that there are rapids beneath it roaring so hard and swift, they'll surely drown us in seconds if we fall.

"Oh Orvena," I breathe.

"We have to cross," Algar insists.

"It's missing so many slats!" I yell over the thundering water.

"Then be light on your feet! Let's go!"

"Why don't you just teleport us over?!" I ask.

Algar's eyes widen before he gives me a sheepish smile. "Oh, yeah. Spot on."

I feel the energy coursing through him when he takes my hand, ready to send us across the bridge to safety. But that energy instantly seeps away, and his hand falls out of mine when he cries out in pain.

"Algar?" I call as he falls to his knees.

He drops to the ground, curling into the fetal position, still screaming like someone is stabbing him.

"What's happening? What is it?" My voice is borderline hysterical. Gods, I *feel* borderline hysterical. His screams come to a rapid halt, and his eyes widen as veins bulge on his forehead and throat. He tugs at my shirt, struggling to breathe, looking at me to help him. But I don't know what's wrong. I don't know how to stop his struggle—the pain.

Panicked, I look for help, but Rynthea, Kelrean, and the guards are fighting off assassins. However, standing in the middle of the sloping mountain trail is Maliek with an arm raised and his hand balled into a fist. He squeezes his fist so tight his knuckles are the color of snow.

Algar wheezes, grabbing at his throat. Zephra squeaks as she lands next to Algar's head with big eyes full of worry.

That blue-eyed fucker is doing this.

"Stop it!" I shout. I hate how useless I feel.

Thane appears at the top of the mountain, stumbling as he takes in the scene. Someone materializes behind him, swinging a sword. He twists around and cuts them down before charging down the mountain and tackling Maliek.

The grip on Algar breaks, and he sucks in a sharp breath, clinging to his neck.

"Algar? Oh my gods. Are you okay?"

"Fuck. No," he croaks between several coughs. He rolls onto his side to drag in a few more breaths.

"Can you still teleport us over?" I ask, helping him stand up.

He swipes a hand over his nose. "I—I don't think I can. He nearly crushed my insides."

"Damn it."

Anxiety swells in my chest as three more assassins appear at the top of the mountain. Thane and Maliek have tumbled down to where Rynthea and the others are battling. Maliek is on top of Thane, punching him repeatedly with wisps of black shadows surrounding his fists. Thane shoots a hand up and blasts him toward the wall of the mountain. Maliek's back slams into the jagged rock face before he falls on his stomach.

Struggling to a stand, Thane throws up a hand and sends a wave of gold flames up the mountain. It engulfs the three assassins running toward him. I hear their wails of agony all the way from the bridge.

Thane is *pissed*.

I can see it on his face, the deep furrow in his brow, the bright flare of his eyes, his tightly clenched fist. All hallmarks of a very angry and very deadly Thane.

Another assassin darts for him, but he twists around, and in one swift motion, he slices all the way up until he's nearly split them in half.

Two more are fighting Kelrean, who's now lost both his guards. Kelrean swings his ax and chops one of them clear in half, while Rynthea gives her scythesword a twist and takes the other one's head off.

All of them are down, Maliek included. Thane is on his way to Maliek again, his sword ready, but he flies backward out of nowhere, flopping on the ground...and that's when I see more assassins at the top of the mountain. There has to be at least a dozen more of them.

Shit. Maliek came prepared this time.

They storm down the mountain, dodging Thane's flames and leaping over bulky rocks.

"Zaira! Get across the bridge!" Thane shouts, climbing to his feet.

His voice finally pulls me back to the present. I assist Algar, throwing his arm over my shoulder so we can get moving.

The first step causes the whole bridge to tilt and sway. My heart drops into my stomach. The wood feels brittle beneath my feet. There is no way this thing is going to hold us.

"How fast can you move?" I ask Algar.

"Probably a bit faster."

"Good." I pick up the pace.

Algar groans but keeps himself steady. About halfway, I feel the bridge shift like someone else has come on board.

Of course, it's fucking Maliek.

He grips one side of the rope railing with one hand and uses his other to send a blue beam of light toward us.

"Duck!" I yell, bringing Algar down to a squat with me.

The light sails across, slicing through the nearest boulder at the end of the bridge. That squat alone sends one of my feet plummeting through a soggy plank.

I shriek, trying to yank my foot back up, but my legging gets caught on one of the splinters.

"Come on, sleeping princess," Algar says in the most serious tone I've heard from him. He grabs me by the elbow and pulls, trying to assist.

Maliek closes in on us, lifting his hand again with his palm glowing a bright blue. Before he can shoot another beam, he hollers in pain. Behind him, Rynthea pierces through his arm with her scythesword. She grunts as she rips the scythesword out, causing Maliek to yell at the top of his lungs.

"You minotaur *bitch*!" Livid, Maliek whirls around and throws up both hands, sending her soaring off the bridge in a blast of light.

"No!" I scream. "Rynthea!"

She lands on a narrow, flat-topped stone jutting out from the wall of the gorge, close to the rapids. Her scythesword plunges into the rushing water, and my heart aches. One wrong move, one wrong turn, and she'll fall right in with her weapon. She's unconscious, completely still, but once she wakes up...

"Where were we?" Maliek taunts, running a hand over his shoulder and healing himself with a whisper of shadows.

Gods damn. How powerful is his magic?

Zephra pops up behind him, blowing a large stream of fire at his face. He yells and throws up his arms to block the flames with his gauntlets.

This is the distraction I need to finally free my leg. Hauling myself up, I wrap an arm around Algar again and guide us to the other side. But Zephra, as amazing as she is, is no match for Maliek.

Over my shoulder, I see him cross his wrists and grunt, shoving them forward and blowing Zephra away with a powerful surge of magic. She sails past us in a flurry of pink, landing on the other side of the bridge with a pained squeak. She tumbles a few times but recovers quickly.

"Stay there, Zephra!" Algar's voice is hoarse. "Don't you move, girl!"

Panicked, I cling to Algar and walk faster. There has to be at least twenty more slats before we reach the other side, not to mention some are missing.

"Don't look back," Algar pants. He uses the back of his free arm to swipe blood from his upper lip.

"You just keep breathing," I order, nearly breathless myself. We skip over a shattered piece of wood. Then the bridge sways and wobbles twice as much, causing us to clash into each other.

I don't want to, but I look back to see what's caused the commotion. I'd have been more relieved to see Thane walking onto the bridge if it weren't about to collapse. The more weight on board, the worse off we are. We *really* need to reach the other side.

Maliek freezes in place when Thane throws a hand up with his fingers spread wide. With a swift yank, Maliek is reeled backward. He slides off the bridge but catches the edge with one hand, using the other to shoot a fiery ball of blue at Thane. Thane deflects it with a glowing gold shield.

"Hurry, Zaira!" Thane calls. He steps on Maliek's fingers, raising his sword higher in the air. Maliek kicks his legs forward and backward in a swinging motion, rocking the bridge from side to side. Thane stumbles, tilting left and then right.

Then a loud *crack* sounds a short distance away. Ahead, the post at the end of the bridge is now tilting forward.

Shit. Not good.

"There's too much weight!" Algar winces as our backs slam into the thick rope. Maliek keeps swinging until he effortlessly flies up. His landing makes the wood beneath our feet rattle. The post tilts farther, now starting to split down the middle.

I hustle ahead with Algar while Thane faces off with his relentless nemesis. We're so close. I've never wanted to touch land so badly before. Only five more steps will do it.

I press my hand to Algar's back and force him to go in front of me. The post splinters more as he dives forward and makes it to land safely.

I'm ready to take my leap, but it's just my luck that the post gives out at this very moment, and with a quick *snap* and a jerk, it drags toward the rapids.

The bridge splinters apart.

I scream.

Algar calls my name as he tries to catch me.

But he's too late.

I'm falling.

Chapter 32

I've had many close calls with death since this journey with Thane Valkor began, but clinging to a rotted rope from a shattered bridge as water rushes beneath my feet has to be the closest yet.

I yelp as I dangle above daggerlike boulders.

"Zaira!" Algar peers over the edge, his eyes wide and panicked.

I breathe raggedly as my nails dig into the rope. My raw palms sear with pain as I hold on with all my might. Algar throws a hand down for me to grab.

I let go with one hand to reach up, my other arm burning under my weight, then yelp again as the rope shifts.

Snap.

"No," I whisper.

The rope is rubbing against a sharp edge of the gorge, the threads fraying one by one.

"I can't reach!" I wail.

"Just try!" Algar sticks his hand down as far as he can while pressing his belly flat to the ground. But right as our fingertips brush, the rope sways left from a rush of wind. My body hits one of the rocky walls, and I slide down the rope several feet.

Another *snap* splits the air like the crack of a whip.

The water sounds louder, or perhaps it's all in my head, or really, it's the drumming of my heartbeat. The rope has now severed almost all the way through. It won't hold me much longer.

"I refuse to let you die like this, woman!" Algar says. He shouts something over his shoulder. Seconds later, Zephra climbs down his arm with a thick, dark-green vine. Her eyes are desperate as she spits the vine out of her mouth and pushes it toward me. Algar grips the other end while I reach for it.

Two more *snaps* echo in the canyon.

The rope lurches downward. I can't help but scream as I drop several feet, panic rising in my chest. I try to steady myself before I reach up to grab the vine with both hands and hold on tight. As soon as I do, the wood and rope crash into the rapids.

Dangling from the vine, I gulp for air, watching the rope I was just holding hit the raging water and get swept away.

"There we are!" Algar grunts as he pulls me up. I imagine how hard this is for him to do at this moment, considering he's lost some of his strength.

I dig the tips of my boots into the slick crevices of the gorge, but I keep slipping. I can't get proper footing. My foot slips once more, my hands skidding down, blood now coating the vine. I look up at Algar, who curses as the vine slips farther out of his hand. He loses his grip on it, and I sail downward.

I plummet and scream until I'm jerked to a stop. The abruptness causes my back to slam into the jagged edge of the gorge with enough impact to knock the breath out of me. Hands stinging and muscles trembling, I focus on trying to find a toehold in the rocky cliff.

I can hear Algar calling my name, demanding that I keep hanging on as he tugs on the vine. As he does, I can't help wondering where Thane is. Is Rynthea okay? I hope Kelrean hasn't been killed by the assassins. King Draedor would never forgive us. Well...if any of us even survive.

I need to keep going. I have to keep going.

Analla needs me.

But I'm so lightheaded. I blink several times and breathe deeply, trying to pull myself together.

It doesn't work. If anything, I slip farther down the vine.

Just like the fraying threads of the rope before it snapped, my strength is failing. I blink back tears. This is it. *I'm sorry, Analla.*

As I continue slipping, something with dark, massive wings flies by.

The sun is too bright to catch it, but it circles around again, revealing outstretched talons.

Great. Something else wants to kill me.

It hovers directly above me and, with a screech, clamps its talons around my body. To my surprise, it doesn't pierce me with its sharp claws as it lifts me higher in the air. Its wings create their own wind as it squawks.

Breath fills my lungs again when I realize what's happening.

I'm being *saved*.

Spreading its talons, my savior drops me on stable ground at the top of the gorge, and I land on my back with a grunt. Finally able to get a good look at the creature, I see it's an oversize hawk with brown feathers and a sharp yellow beak. It circles above, cawing loudly, before landing near me.

It squawks again, only this time it sounds pained. Skin squelches and bones crunch like they're being worked through a grinder. I can't look away as the bird transforms, wings shifting into arms, beak diminishing to form a mouth and nose. It's turning into a familiar man with a full head of hair and the eyes of a lion.

Naked, Kelrean writhes on the ground with roars that sound as deep and ferocious as the king of the beasts. He's in pure agony, his claws digging into the dirt, bones cracking even more until, finally, the cries stop, and he settles on his stomach.

"Kelrean," I whisper, crawling to him.

He struggles to open his eyes. "Zaira. My favorite mortal."

A weak smile spreads across my lips as I reach for his hand. "You saved me."

He smiles, too. "Don't mention it."

I help him stand up.

Algar hobbles toward us while pulling a robe out of his bag. "Good grief! Put that thing away!" He tosses the robe to Kelrean.

Kelrean catches it right before it can slip out of his fingers. "Did you steal this from the castle?" he asks through labored breaths.

"Of course not," Algar says.

Kelrean points to the emblem engraved on the chest with his lips pressed together.

"Okay, fine! I did. There were three more in the wardrobe! You all can spare at least one."

I can't stop myself from looking at the "thing" Algar's talking about as Kelrean slips into the robe. The prince is... Well, let's just say I understand why he's so confident in who he is. There is absolutely *nothing* lacking in size there.

I turn away, giving him some privacy.

Zephra flaps above Algar as he moves toward me. "Zaira, are you okay?" he asks.

"I'm okay. Where are Thane and Rynthea?"

Algar looks at me, then at Kelrean, who is busy tying the robe at his waist. We bolt toward the cliff. As we approach, I spot a dark figure below. Thane clings to a ridge at the bottom of the gorge, barely hanging on. Water splashes over his head, trying to drag him down. Rynthea is only a few feet higher than him on the same ledge she fell on, still unconscious.

I look to my left at the vines clinging to the boulders before running to pry some off. Algar assists me until we have several in hand.

"Help me knot these," I say hurriedly, tying the vines together with my blistered, bloody hands. It hurts so much, but it has to be done.

Thane is going to fall. I can see his grip slipping.

All the other assassins are gone, likely taken by the rapids or dead on the opposite side. And just as I suspected, Thane hollers before being pulled underwater.

"This way!" I run along the edge of the cliff as fast as I can, watching Thane get dragged through the rapids. I hoped this would be my only concern, but of course my life is never that easy. The rapids end at a waterfall.

A steep, *steep* waterfall.

His body slams into boulders and sharp edges of the gorge. I see his head hit one of the rocks before lolling a bit, but he remains conscious, using every bit of energy to stay above the surface. Miraculously, he catches onto a slim stone outcropping in the water. He sputters, wiping his eyes before looking up at me. I slide down one of the ridges, keeping myself steady on a ledge.

I hold up the vine in both my hands, hoping he'll understand what I'm trying to say. As if he does, he nods, and I toss the vine in his direction. A gold hoop wraps around the end of the vine like a lasso and tugs me forward an inch. I pull backward against it, digging my heels into the ground.

"Algar! Help me pull!" I call.

Algar joins me on the ledge and tugs. The strain is enough to hurt my shoulders, and my palms are so raw and burning, but I keep pulling, finding relief the closer Thane comes to the gorge wall.

We're so close to saving him, and then we can get to Rynthea...only—Gods damn it.

Rynthea has fallen in the water, too.

She startles awake from the cold rush, unleashing a deep roar only a minotaur can produce.

"Oh shit!" Algar yells as we keep pulling Thane up.

She floats past Thane, who has already made it to a safe ledge and holds on to it with an elbow anchored on top.

My chest tightens when I realize I have no solution for Rynthea. There's no way we can toss her a vine, too. She's too far away and getting closer to the falls.

Thane breathes rapidly as he throws an illuminated hand up in her direction. With the remaining strength he has left, he manages to stop Rynthea from going any farther. He peers over his shoulder, curls flat on his head, water spilling over his lips as his arm shakes. He's doing his best to keep her steady. She's able to shift toward the edge and wrap her arms around a boulder. When she does, Thane's hand falls, his eyes close, and his head drops on the ledge.

And then something miraculous happens.

A bubble of water forms around Rynthea like a cocoon and carries her to our side of the rapids. Confused, I watch as she hovers in the safety of the bubble. Then I notice a group of people in brown and gray tribal clothing a short distance away.

One of them has his hands in the air as he manipulates the water, the muscles in his large, tan, inked arms flexing as he places Rynthea on the ground with a gentle splash.

The land quakes beneath my feet, and I back up as Thane's ledge breaks away from the gorge. Rocks and dirt descend, falling like rain as he and the ledge are transported around us to reach safety.

I climb back up and run to Thane, lowering to my knees and pressing a hand to his forehead. His skin looks a little gray, and he's hardly moving. But he's breathing. That's what matters.

The woman who controlled the ledge stands a short distance away. She drops her arms, and her deep brown eyes connect with mine. Her gown is beige and billowy, her face utterly flawless. A silver crown with golden flora sits atop her head.

The man who manipulated the water joins her, and both approach as the tribe members wearing brown masks with hollow mouth holes close in on us. Spears are in their hands, and every single tip is pointed at *us*.

I'm hoping Kelrean can aid us, but he, too, has a hand in the air. The other is pressed to his ribs. His eyes are closed, and his face looks contorted in pain.

"Speak," the woman with the crown orders with her eyes still trained on me. She has warm, wheat-like skin and hooded eyes. Her lips are plump, and pale-yellow lines are painted on half of her face. The loose waves of her hair are the darkest shade of black I've ever seen.

"We're not here to cause trouble," I say, holding my hands in the air. She studies my hand, tilting her head a bit. The tribe thrusts their spears forward, bringing them dangerously close to my head.

"Do you possess magic?" she asks, shoulders squaring.

"No—no! I'm just a mortal." I pull my hands down. "I have no powers."

She scans me before cutting her gaze to Algar and Kelrean. She pauses on Kelrean, studying his robe—mostly the engraved emblem on the chest. He's breathing much harder now.

"A royal," she says.

"That I am," he wheezes. "I apologize for my…my lack of introduction. I'm Prince Kelrean Shattore of Bernwood, and it is possible that I will bleed to death without your help." Kelrean lifts his hand, revealing a fresh bloody patch on the robe near his ribs. It's seeped right through.

"Kelrean, oh my goodness," I gasp. Algar and I rush to his side, catching him before he buckles.

"You are very close to Immalon borders," the woman says, like she couldn't give a damn that he's bleeding. "We nearly killed you."

"Well, I'm thankful you didn't." I cling to patience. "Can you *please* help us?"

She looks from me, to Thane, and then Rynthea. "They are with you?"

I nod. "Yes."

"One is a sorcerer with exceptional combat skills," she remarks, raising a brow. "A severe threat to my people."

"I guarantee he won't hurt you or your people. I can explain everything if given the chance, but *please* help us."

Thane is still unconscious on the rock. I really hope he's not drowning from fluid in his lungs. Rynthea is stirring, so I assume her lungs are fine.

The woman sighs, glancing at the muscled man to her left. She speaks in the native Thelasian language, causing the man to straighten his posture.

Then she shouts an order to her tribe, and they lower their weapons.

Two of them peel Kelrean away from us, while a few others lift Thane off the rocky ledge and assist a stumbling Rynthea.

"Follow," the woman commands with her back to us, sauntering away.

I glance at Algar, who gives me a *what the fuck?* expression.

I have a good guess which tribe this is... I just didn't know they still existed. But if this is the tribe my mother told me stories about, then I know we're in good hands. They exist to nurture and protect, especially when it comes to their own.

I use that as my sliver of hope and follow the elementalists into the forest.

Chapter 33

My mother used to tell me stories about the ancient tribes of Thelanor. We'd sit around a bonfire and listen to her exciting storytelling about how many of them possessed unique powers. Of course, there were those who carried magic like the sorcerers, but there were unique tribes who referred to themselves as elementalists.

I was told the elementalists divided themselves into distinct communities by their designated elements. They would often join together as allies when it came to external threats. As we follow them, I realize being separated by elements is no longer the case because this tribe has a mixture of all.

The tribe's queen takes us along a hidden path, where one of the elementalists waves a hand and causes a thick set of interwoven branches shaped like hidden doors to spread apart. We pass through three of them before ducking under the thick trunk of a fallen tree and walking through gates made of silver. This leads to a winding stone footpath, arched by greenery that's tangled in sweet-smelling flora. We don't slow down until we reach the hidden world of Immalon.

The first thing I notice are the steep mountaintops in the distance with peaks jutting toward the sky. Huts made of brick and wood with straw roofs are spread throughout the village. A dirt footpath connects them.

No matter which path you take, all lead to a crystal-blue lagoon reflecting a blue sky, mountaintops, and fleecy clouds.

White flowers embellish nearby bushes while gorgeous clusters of pink and yellow drip from low-hanging branches on surrounding trees. Bamboo stalks protrude between groves of trees. Everything is deep green and smells sweet here, like the air has permanently been fragranced with honey and flowers.

We pass the lagoon, where children play and giggle. Some levitate rocks in the air, while others fling splashes of water with rapid flicks from their dry hands.

Wow. The stories and curated art do not do this place justice. Not even the greatest artist in all of Thelanor could capture the grace and beauty of this place.

The tribe queen doesn't stop until we reach two interconnected huts built on stilts with cone-shaped roofs. The elementalists assisting Thane, Rynthea, and Kelrean lead them into the building.

I start after them, but the queen stops me with an arm to my chest. Her forearm is wrapped in a fingerless gold gauntlet. Swirls of ink on the warm skin beneath it flow to her nimble fingers.

"You two will stay with me," she says. Definitely an order and not an option.

I look from her to Algar, who now has Zephra cradled in his arms.

"Will they be okay?" I ask, glancing at the hut where the other three have now disappeared.

"They will be taken care of by our healers. Speaking of which…"

She gestures for a woman near the hut to come our way.

"Heal them, please," the queen commands.

The woman takes hold of my wrists. Her hands warm up like a stoked hearth, and the heat transfers to me. An odd tingling sensation crawls under my skin, and right before my eyes, the stinging scrapes and visible rawness on my palms disappear.

"Gods, thank you," I murmur in awe.

The healer bows her head before grabbing Algar's wrists and doing the same. Once finished, Algar thanks her as well. She gives a quick bow before returning to the hut.

"Better?" the queen asks.

"Yes," I answer, rubbing a thumb over my healed palm. "Thank you."

"Good. Follow me." The queen strolls past several more huts until she and the muscular man approach a stone building. The first floor of the building doesn't give much away, but on the second floor is a platform wrapped with wooden railing, along with several tables and benches for dining. The queen enters the building, and the muscled man (who I assume is her partner) holds the door open, waiting for us.

I walk past, forcing a smile at him as Algar trails behind. He unexpectedly returns a smile and a nod.

We're greeted with a dining hall, where nearly everything is made of wood and stone. A hearth is built into the center of the room, and an archway reveals a massive kitchen where a group of people cooks. Steam rises in front of their faces as they use fire from their hands to boil water. Delicious scents waft through the hall, teasing my nose.

"Please sit." The queen gestures gracefully to an open table. We pull out our seats, and once we're settled, she claims a chair on the opposite side of us. The muscular man joins her. "Shall we start with your names?" She examines Algar and me closely now.

I clear my throat before telling her mine.

Algar follows suit.

"Zaira and Algar." She stares at us, unblinking. "And the names of the others?"

"The prince is Kelrean, as he told you," I say. "He's from Bernwood."

She nods. "I am fond of King Draedor. We've traded with him many times."

"The minotaur is Rynthea Kamtaur," I add. "She's a good person."

"She must be if that combat-heavy sorcerer is willing to save her," the woman notes. "What is *his* name?"

"Thane Valkor," I answer, my voice a little quieter now.

"And why do you travel with him?" She looks at both of us expectantly, her dark eyes narrowing.

"He's helping me get somewhere."

"And I'm assisting," Algar tosses in.

The queen drops her eyes to Zephra, who is already studying her. "You care for creatures. For nature," she notes after a brief silence.

"Of course I do." Algar strokes Zephra's back. "Nature is beautiful, and creatures like Zephra are the best parts of it."

Her mouth twitches as she studies Zephra a bit longer. Then she sticks out her hand, and Zephra wiggles out of Algar's arms to climb onto the table.

As Zephra climbs up the queen's arm, the queen puts on a full smile — teeth and all. Not that I've known her for very long, but she doesn't strike me as the kind of person who offers lots of big smiles.

"What a beauty you are," she coos as she holds Zephra to her chest and strokes her soft head. Zephra makes a pleased, throaty little noise, and even the muscled man smiles at the maobi. I understand. It's hard *not* to adore Zephra.

"She should be roaming freely." The queen turns her attention to Algar, still rubbing Zephra's head.

"She chooses to stay with me," Algar returns defensively.

"It appears so." She pauses, smiling down at Zephra again. "You know, it is considered an honor for a maobi to ride the shoulder of a human. They haven't been seen doing that for many generations. In order for them to do that, they must see you as their equal. They are emotionally intelligent creatures. Some believe maobis understand our feelings more than we can understand them ourselves. The fact that she's attached to you is interesting. I'm sure you know how feisty and fastidious they can be."

Algar lowers his defenses, shoulders sagging a bit. "She's my best friend, and we get each other." He offers a half smile. It's so sweet, seeing the adoration in his eyes. "I love her."

Zephra squeaks and looks back at Algar. Then she wriggles out of the queen's hands and scampers across the table to return to her person.

"And she loves you, too," the queen replies.

Algar laughs softly as Zephra mounts his shoulder and nuzzles her head in the crook of his neck.

"You have questions." The queen's eyes are pinned on me again. So much for that smile.

"A few," I say.

"Ask away."

"Well, I think it's best to start with your name...right?"

Her chin inclines. "Xiaodera, Tribe Queen of Immalon."

"Nice to meet you, Queen Xiaodera."

"This is my husband, Jehon, Tribe King of Immalon." She gestures to her partner.

I smile at King Jehon, who gives me a curt nod.

"You nearly died on that bridge," she says.

"Yeah." I release a shaky breath, wanting to forget all about dangling from a fraying rope and then a slippery vine. "We almost did. How did you see us?"

"I have eyes at the borders. I was informed of a disturbance."

"Well, it's a good thing you showed up when you did."

Someone from the kitchen enters the dining hall carrying a tray with a teapot on top. He places it on the center of the table, along with four wooden cups shaped like miniature bowls. With a bow to the queen and king, the man strides away.

Queen Xiaodera picks up the glazed clay teapot and pours steaming hot liquid into each cup. King Jehon then places a cup in front of each of us. I pick up the tea with a grateful nod before taking a sip.

When the steam fogs my spectacles, I can't help but laugh. It's been a while since they've done that. It reminds me of better days.

Safer days.

They used to fog up all the time when Analla and I would have a cup of tea on our balcony that overlooked the canal. The air would be crisp and cool enough for a thick sweater.

"My people say they saw that sorcerer friend of yours fighting off attackers that looked like assassins," Queen Xiaodera says after a short sip of tea. "Do you know who they were?"

I glance at Algar. He bobs his head, insisting that I tell the truth. "They were coming after him…our friend. I believe they're with the Grim."

She narrows her eyes a bit. "So he carries trouble?"

I notice King Jehon's hand curling into a fist on the table.

"They've been tracking him, but we can't figure out why," Algar tells her. "We've asked, but he won't tell us what they want."

That's not all true, of course. He told me, but there's no way I'm about to inform the queen about his past or the links to Seferin. He looks trouble enough, and she clearly knows he's dangerous. She has no proof, but I'm certain she could find some if she really wanted to.

"So, he puts all of your lives in danger because he doesn't care to share why he's being hunted by a group of deadly people?" Queen Xiaodera scoffs as she sits back in her chair. "Wisest thing to do would be to leave him in the infirmary and carry on without him, no?"

"We can't," I counter quickly. "I paid him to protect me." I swallow hard, staring down at my teacup. "If it helps figure out who *they* are, one of them had a blade with the letters TSG on it."

Algar's chair creaks as he turns to me. "TSG?" He's frowning. "Are you sure?"

"Yes. Why?"

"Because if that's what you saw, it means that crew is from The Shadow Guild."

Confused, I ask, "The *what*?"

Algar releases an exhausted sigh. "People have made claims about there being an underground society recruiting the strongest sorcerers in all the kingdoms and teaching them black magic. From what I hear, most of the people who join are from the Grim. Either way, they are *not* good people."

"Yeah, I gathered that when Maliek almost turned your organs to mush."

"I've heard of this society," Queen Xiaodera says. "Many believe they're trying to become the next Nightcarvers, though there has never been any proof. Regardless, it is odd if this secret group is revealing themselves so openly just to get your friend. That leads me to believe your sorcerer friend is somehow associated with them and he's done something to wrong them."

"That doesn't make any sense, though." Algar folds his arms and shakes his head with tightened features. "He was a soldier with The Divine in Meriva. I saw him marching with them and wearing their uniform."

"The Grim is known to recruit all kinds of people," the queen informs him. "One can only assume they are manipulating as many people as possible and twisting their souls into complete corruption to join their devious society."

"That doesn't sound like Thane." Algar's frown deepens. "No, he wouldn't have joined people like them unless he had no choice."

Queen Xiaodera sips her tea. "Perhaps he didn't."

Her words instantly make me think of Thane's brother. He claims Koa's death was his fault. Did he willingly join The Shadow Guild in hopes of saving him somehow? But Algar said he saw him with The Divine. If he were with them, why would he leave? Surely, if anything had happened, The Divine would've protected him. They always protect their own. Gods, I have even more questions than before.

"Regardless, it will take quite a bit of time for your friends to heal." The queen's voice pulls me out of my thoughts.

"How long, do you think?" I inquire.

"Give them at least three, possibly four hours. Our healers are wonderfully skilled, but they work diligently and never rush their processes."

Okay. Four hours. Not four *days*. I can work with that. It won't take much longer to reach Gadonia. If we're only behind by a few hours, we could still make it to the shores before nightfall.

As if she's read my mind, Queen Xiaodera asks, "Where are you traveling to?"

"The Shallows," I reply in earnest. I'm tired of beating around the bush everywhere we stop.

Queen Xiaodera narrows her eyes at me while King Jehon's broaden. Then the king bellows a laugh that makes me flinch. He howls as he throws his bald, tatted head back. The queen rolls her eyes before placing a patient hand on his arm.

"Sorry, my love," he chortles. "But you are joking, right? *The Shallows?*" He shifts his gaze to me.

"She isn't joking," Algar responds.

Jehon's smile slips. He studies me more intently with misty hazel eyes. "You will surely die."

I wrap my hands tighter around my cup. "I'll take my chances."

"There is something there that you need?" Queen Xiaodera probes.

"One of the prosperity stones."

She blinks at me several times, sitting up taller in her chair. "Are you dealing with a curse?"

I nod.

"Placed upon you or someone else?"

"My sister."

"And there's no one in your kingdom who can help you break that curse?"

I shake my head. "No. The sorcerer who cursed her is powerful. The people I asked before Thane were too afraid to go against him. This was my last resort."

"I see." She taps her fingers on the table, studying me as I take my last sip of tea. "You don't strike me as foolish. I assume you have a plan to make it through that island."

I shrug. "Sort of."

Queen Xiaodera eyes me for so long, I fidget in my chair. It seems she's trying to read me now, searching for some kind of secret or truth like Frevella did. I don't think she can read minds, but it wouldn't surprise me if a woman of her power could.

"Brave." Her voice is soft, sympathetic. "But I was wrong before. You *are* foolish if you believe you will survive." She rises from her chair, and her dress flows to her feet. King Jehon follows suit.

"We will be preparing for lunch soon," she announces. "You are more than welcome to stay and dine with us, or you can join your friends in the infirmary. When you are ready to leave, my people will show you the way out. But I must warn you." She presses her palms flat on the table and brings her face so close to mine that I can see the faint brown freckles peppered across the apples of her cheeks. "You must tell *no one* other than the Gadonian council that you recovered in Immalon. And believe me, if you do tell, we will find out, and we will come for you." She scans my face. "You aren't the only people in this world being hunted."

"So the history is true?" I ask.

Her eyes narrow, only a touch. "What do you know about our history?"

"That your tribe sectioned themselves off from the rest of society because others assumed you were creations of Xaimur. They said the elementalists set fires to kingdoms and caused floods in others. Earthquakes destroyed many of the coasts and killed thousands of people."

She fights a smile. "For starters, we *only* praise Orvena here. She is our creator, and she provides us with our gifts. And it is true that our ancestors set fires and caused floods and earthquakes, but that was *only* done to protect ourselves from becoming slaves to those who considered themselves superior to us—those who wished to use their magic *against* us. Our ancestors were attacked, our people raped, and many children killed. They refused to bow to the enemies, so they retaliated." Her eyes harden as she looks deeply into mine. "Now, Immalon is protected, and no one can enter unless we give them that honor. You should be very grateful."

"Right," I murmur. "That's very wise. And I am...grateful, that is."

"Every story needs a villain, Zaira. The rest of the world can believe what they want, but do you believe we are the villains in this one?"

"No." I really don't. I know what it's like to be attacked—to be shoved into a corner with your back against a wall. If I had the power of an elementalist or even a sorcerer, I'd have done the same to protect myself and the people I loved in Ember Coast. Then maybe my parents would still be alive. Maybe our land would still be there.

"Wise answer." The queen steps back and links elbows with her partner. "Check on your friends. When you are ready to depart, come find us."

When she and the king head toward the exit, I look at Algar, who is watching them go with a blank stare.

"I think she wants to kill Thane," he utters.

I gape. *"What?"*

"She has a certain look in her eyes, one I've seen many times before."

He finally peels his gaze off the exit. "She doesn't trust him, and when it comes to people in power lacking trust, they eradicate the source."

"I don't think she trusts *any* of us."

"That may be so, but Thane is the biggest threat to their tribe." He leans in closer. "I didn't see that Maliek fucker go down. If he returns with more assassins and attacks her borders, she'll give Thane up in a heartbeat. She won't let him cause her people's downfall."

"Then we'd better get out of Immalon before that happens." I stand as Algar does. As he pushes his chair in and walks with me out of the dining hall, I say, "Algar, can I ask you something?"

"Sure."

I twist my fingers in front of me, suddenly anxious. "Is there anything else about Thane's past that I should know?"

His eyebrows dip. "Like what?"

"Has he ever mentioned having any other family? Talked about his father a little more, maybe? Or an aunt? Uncle?"

Algar thinks on it a moment. "Not that I can remember. Why do you ask?"

"Just curious."

He studies me with a slightly narrowed gaze. "You're asking for a reason."

Once outside, I keep walking until we're near the clearing. Flying fish leap out of a brook nearby, and several of the water elementalists catch them in wobbly bubbles before dropping them into woven baskets.

I face Algar, whose eyes swim with curiosity. My mind drifts back to last night, with Thane telling me about Azidel's tome, to Frevella's cave, when he confessed about Koa. He asked me not to tell Algar and Rynthea—or anyone else—about the tome, and other than Algar, I won't, but he never said anything about not discussing his brother.

For a moment, I toy with telling Algar what Thane revealed in the cave. I feel certain Koa's death is somehow linked to The Shadow Guild, but it also feels wrong to betray Thane's trust, even if he hasn't specifically mentioned keeping this a secret.

Algar grew up with him and knew his father, but there were twelve years when they didn't see each other, and a half brother with a different mother isn't out of the question.

I shrug, letting it go. "No reason. Just curious. I don't really know much about him, that's all."

"Well, the only way you'll find out more is if you ask him," Algar says. "He won't tell me anything about his life after he disappeared, but I see the way he looks at you, and I see the way you look at him."

Those words steal my attention completely. "It's not like that, Algar. He's just— I mean, we're—"

"I'm not judging you, trust me. Though I still urge you to be careful." He throws an innocent hand in the air. "All I'm saying is, at the end of the day, he's a man, and whether he admits it or not, he *is* interested in you. If you soften him up enough, you'll squeeze the truth out of him…eventually."

Chapter 34

The infirmary is much cooler inside than the dining hall. No doubt, the woven bamboo blades of the ceiling fans are fueled by elemental magic controlling the air. They whirl at a steady pace, providing a comforting breeze.

We're greeted by a woman with red hair wearing brown linen who guides us through a hallway to reach separate care rooms. There are eight rooms total with large, rounded windows overlooking the lagoon. Each room is equipped with two beds and washbasins.

Kelrean is in the first room with his eyes shut. A woman stands at his side, adjusting his bandages, while another woman rubs his temples with the pads of her fingers to keep him calm.

I smile at the healers—they're so gentle and attentive. I move on to the second room, where Rynthea is seated on the bed, sulking as she stares at the floor. Other than a bandage wrapped around her forearm and another on the top of her head, she appears fine.

"Should've known you two were coming," she says without looking up. "I could hear Algar's annoying voice when you were at the entrance."

"Yep," Algar says with a pop of his lips. "She's swell."

"How are you feeling?" I ask.

"I lost my scythesword," she grumbles.

"Yeah." I step into the room. "I'm so sorry about that."

She's quiet for a few seconds, then she exhales. "It was a gift from my father." She drops her head just enough for her hair to curtain her face. "I promised to *never* lose it."

My heart aches as I watch her continue to stare at the floor. After a while, she raises her head and meets my eyes. "I don't think I can continue this quest, Zaira. I feel like I've lost so much, and it's only been a *day* since I left Kamtaur."

"I understand." I lace my fingers in front of me, giving them a light wring. "You won't go back through Delchester alone, will you?"

"No. I'll return to Bernwood, go to the nearest port, and catch a boat that'll take me to Junsho. From there, I'll travel to Winstoft. It'll take an extra day or so, but it's much safer."

I nod, relieved. "I know we just met, but I'll miss hanging out with you," I murmur, sitting next to her.

She laughs. "You call being attacked every hour hanging out?"

I laugh, too. "Fair point. But it's better to face an attack with a fierce minotaur at my side than none at all."

She gives me a warm, genuine smile.

I look at Algar. "What about you?"

"I agree about the attacks. It's been gods-awful. But I'm seeing this through." Algar flashes a grin, and Zephra whacks him in the face with her tail.

I giggle. Even Zephra considers him a fool for not backing out. I won't blame him if he does. No one deserves to carry Thane's baggage—and heavy baggage it is.

Thinking of Thane, I stand up and say, "I'll check on our sorcerer."

Algar takes my place next to Rynthea, giving me a knowing look before he taps the patch on her head. She winces with a snarl. He chuckles, throwing his hands in the air when she raises a fist at him.

When I step around the corner, I take a peek into the next room. There is Thane, resting on his back and staring up at the ceiling. His mask, swords, and buffers have been removed and placed neatly on a corner table, along with his rucksack. There seems to be a cloud of gloom hovering above him. In stark contrast, there is a vase of bright-yellow flowers on his windowsill.

I clear my throat, and he lifts his head. When he sees it's me, he drops his head on the pillow again and puffs out a breath. "Surprised you stuck around," he says.

"Well, I don't hate you anymore, and you have Frevella's sphere, so…"

He doesn't respond.

My heart starts to beat faster. "You do still have it, don't you?"

"Yes. It's in my bag."

"Okay. Good." I breathe a sigh of relief and step deeper into the room. Then a cheeky smile sweeps across my face. "So do I get a thank-you?"

"For what?"

"Saving your life."

He snorts. "Are we keeping tallies? Because if so, I'd say we're about ten to one. Maybe higher."

"So you agree. It was my turn to save you, then?"

"Sure. There might even be a next time."

"So you admit it—I'm just as good at saving your life as you are at saving mine."

"Don't get carried away, Quinlocke." He smirks the tiniest of smirks.

I stifle a laugh. "How long do they say you need to heal?" I ask, moving to the side of the bed and looking into his eyes.

"I'm fine." He starts to sit up but hisses sharply and flops back down on the bed as he grips his chest. When he tugs the collar of his shirt down, I see a small stab wound close to his shoulder.

"What happened there?"

"Maliek," he mutters.

"It's bleeding."

"The healer gave me something and said the bleeding would stop soon."

"Well maybe if you stop moving and tone down the bravado, it'll heal faster." I scan the high shelves on the other side of the room. They're crammed with bowls, medicines, and glass vials. A built-in counter below them displays a stack of neatly folded towels.

"Where is the healer, anyway?" I ask.

"Don't know. She saw my gear and kept giving me funny looks. Won't be surprised if she doesn't come back. She probably thinks I'll cut her head off or something."

"Hmm. Can't say I blame her for thinking that. You *do* love cutting heads off."

I walk over to the shelves and read the etched vials. I spot one with porune oil, pluck it off the shelf, grab two clean towels, and carry both to Thane's bed.

"What is that?" he asks, fighting a groan.

"Porune. It's a numbing agent. It'll blunt the pain. Now lift up your shirt," I order.

"You'd like that, wouldn't you?"

"Get over yourself." I place the medicine vial down on the bed and tug his shirt up. It takes everything in me not to react to his rock-hard abs and impressive pecs. Even with a few battle scars, he's a delicious sight. Honestly, the scars make him sexier, though I'll never admit that out loud, and *especially* not to him.

"Stare harder, why don't you?" There's clearly humor in his tone.

I poke his wound. He grunts and swallows the pain through gritted teeth.

"Stop your shit talking or I won't numb the wound," I threaten politely.

"You're not as nice as I thought you were, oh sweet one."

"I *am* nice. Just not when it comes to dealing with jerks like you." I open the vial and press the towel to the mouth of it, allowing the translucent yellow liquid to soak into the fibers. I place it on his wound, and he winces, his muscles tensing before settling again.

I use the other towel to wipe sweat from his forehead, and in the process, his eyes latch on mine. I want to look away, I really do, but I'm stuck—lost in his deep, golden irises.

"I thought you were going to die." My words come out sounding more vulnerable than I expected.

"It'll take more than water to kill me." His hand curls around mine. I squeeze it as my heart flutters. His palm is warm with hardly any calluses, likely from those fingerless gloves he wears.

I've never seen so much of his skin before and find it hard not to absorb every detail. On his forearm is the letter *D*, but each point of the letter is sharp and jagged. It matches the same *D* on the dagger he gave me in Delchester Forest, only this *D* has a raised slash cutting through it. It's as if someone pressed something hot to his skin to try and burn it off.

The Divine.

"Thane?" I struggle with my next set of words, looking into his eyes for answers. He waits for me to speak. I chicken out, pulling my hand out of his. "Turn on your side," I murmur instead.

He hesitates before doing as he's told. When he flips over, I freeze again. On his back is the most intricate (and upsetting) ink design I've ever seen.

The hilt of a sword starts at the top of his spine and slopes downward just for the tip of the blade to end at the small of his back. Swirls of black ink wrap around the blade like whispers of smoke. In the center of the blade are the letters *S* and *G*. The letters are stacked, the bottom curve of the *S* bleeding into the *G* and ending with more swirls. It takes me a second to realize the whispers of smoke are meant to be shadows. And the sword is the letter *T*.

The Shadow Guild.

I have to look really close to make out the blend of the letters. But I'm not mistaken. I try to swallow as Thane glances over his shoulder. "What are you doing?"

"Nothing." Whatever Maliek used went straight through his body, so I grab the vial again, dribbling some more liquid onto the towel before rubbing it on his wound.

When I'm done, he rests on his back again and sighs as he tugs his tunic down.

"So just a heads-up, you should try and be still so you can heal faster. Xiaodera—the queen—is not a fan of yours. And Algar and I think Maliek will come back. If he shows up at Immalonian borders trying to attack, she won't hesitate to feed you to the wolves, so to speak."

He shifts on the bed. "Maliek won't be coming back."

"How do you know?"

"Because I drove my sword into his heart and threw his body into the rapids before the bridge collapsed. He's likely at the bottom of the waterfall now, food for the fish…or the monsters. Whatever deems him appetizing enough."

"Oh." He has no idea how much relief this brings me. "Are you sure?"

He looks me in the eye with certainty and says, "He's *dead*, Zaira."

"Okay." I release a steady breath. "I still think we should leave here as soon as possible."

"We will." He studies me as I study him. There are so many things I want to ask. So many things I want to explain.

He frowns. "I don't like when you look at me like that."

"Like what?"

"Like I'm fragile."

I shift closer. "Is it possible that you are?"

"Far from it," he grumbles.

"Broken, then?" I offer.

He swivels his gaze to the ceiling.

"Thane, I know you think we should keep things on the surface, but you can talk to me." I grab his hand and hold on to it, collecting his attention again. "I think it's ridiculous that you chose your line of work, and I think I'm ridiculous for embarking on this journey…and hiring you to accompany me…but that makes us both a little ridiculous. But, as ridiculous as this all is, I mean what I say. You *can* talk to me. I'm a pretty good listener and would never tell anyone your secrets."

He looks at me a beat longer before lowering his eyes to our hands. His thumb strokes my knuckles. "I don't want you putting too much faith in me, Zaira."

"Why? Because you don't want me to care about your well-being when you happen to kill for a living?"

"Precisely."

"Well," I sigh. "I think it's too late for that."

"Why?"

"It's kind of hard for me *not* to care about a person I've been traveling with for days who has saved my life on multiple occasions. I think you're starting to care about my well-being, too. That's why you keep trying to push me away."

"It's my duty to keep you safe," he says. "And I keep a distance because it'll be easier for us to part ways when this journey ends. There'll be nothing left to cling to. Trust me on that."

I can't deny that. Even if I decided I wanted to be with Thane and he decided to change his life, he'd still be a wanted man. What kind of future would that be for us?

But, for the briefest moment, as his thumb sweeps over the back of my hand and our eyes connect, I can imagine that future.

No mask.

No hood.

No swords.

Just a man living a normal life. But then I wonder…

"Is now a good time to tell me more about your brother?" I ask, studying the ink on his arm.

"There's too much to tell."

"Please, Thane," I plead. "I just want to understand you. That's all."

The knot in his throat bobs up and down, and he closes his eyes, drawing in a deep breath and following it with an exhale. He's silent for a few seconds.

"I hadn't known him my whole life, but I found out my father slept with a woman several years after I was born and left her pregnant. I only knew this because I saw him speaking to her in the city one day. She had a young boy with her. He looked to be only a few years younger than me. I got a closer listen to their conversation, and she was demanding coins from my father. Turns out he wanted nothing to do with Koa and was willing to pay her so she'd leave him alone."

I nod so he knows I'm listening.

"My father sold me to The Divine when I was only ten years old. I worked on the palace grounds and everything."

"Ten years old?" I gasp, eyes stretching. "He sold you like you were an object. What the shadows?"

"Yeah, well, my father was born with magic, and I inherited that magic. He was nothing more than a drunk, though, and shit with his gifts. He'd have never made it as a sorcerer with any special skills. But it doesn't matter. I'm glad he sold me off because when I was with The Divine, I had a bit more freedom.

"I'd always been curious about the boy I saw with that woman, though, so I found them. I showed up in my Divine uniform, introduced myself to them, and instantly took a liking to Koa and his mother." His mouth curves just a bit at the edges. Almost a smile. But even this half smile makes his face more beautiful...and he has no idea. I can only imagine what a fuller one would look like on him. "They liked me, too. And Koa was funny, bright in spirit, and could be a little mischievous...just like me."

I can't help but smile. Our hands still touch. I don't think he even realizes it.

"Anyway, I grew closer to him and his mother, Helena, and after just a few months, Helena began to feel like my mother, too. Koa looked up to me a lot, and Helena knew this. She appreciated me, said she was glad Koa had someone he could connect with. I never wanted him to look up to me, but he did, so when he turned sixteen, he decided he wanted to join The Divine, too."

"Oh. Did he get in?" I ask.

He nods. "Something in my gut told me not to let Koa join, but he was so eager. And truthfully, I felt safe with The Divine. I was fed every morning and night. I was trained to be the best of the best in all of Meriva. I was one of the queen's soldiers and proud to be. A part of me figured it couldn't be too bad if he joined, if that's what he really wanted. Helena knew she couldn't stop Koa from chasing his dreams, so yes, he ended up joining, did his training, and was eventually sworn in." An unexpected frown sweeps over his face, and his jaw ticks. His grip around my hand tightens. "Only a few months later, we met Seferin."

His hand slips out of mine. "Thane," I whisper.

"I..." He shakes his head and swallows. "I don't want to talk about any more of it right now. Not while I'm like this, lying on a bed, fucking vulnerable."

"What's wrong with being vulnerable? I'm not judging you."

He looks away, staring out of the window while clenching his jaw. Rage swirls in his eyes, tiny sparks of gold flashing deep in his irises. That's when I know the conversation about his brother is done for now.

An ache develops in my chest, but I give him his space. I step back and busy myself with closing the vial and picking up the towels. There is so much more I need to know. The ink on his back is a clear indication that he was with The Shadow Guild. But how? How did he go from being a proud Divine guard to *this*? This killer who wants revenge and has nothing else to lose?

It's become clear that Seferin is the reason for Koa's death. Thane blames himself because he influenced Koa to join The Divine...but what doesn't make sense is their link to Seferin. How did two Divine guards get mixed up with a Grim sorcerer?

"I'll get you some water," I murmur, starting for the door.

"Zaira," Thane calls before I can walk out.

I pause at the threshold.

"Thank you," he says.

I turn around. "For what?"

"If you hadn't thrown that vine to me, I wouldn't have had anything to hang on to," he says. "There was only so much I could do with my magic while being washed away. In that moment, I only focused on staying afloat and not drowning. Tossing the vine gave me another option. Same with the swamp monster. I was only focused on *my* way of killing it, but your advice saved us. So...if we're keeping score, you've saved my life twice. It's not every day a mortal saves a sorcerer's life," he admits. "You should be proud of that."

I grin, actually feeling a sense of pride. "And all this time you thought I was a useless mortal girl."

"I thought a lot of things about you when we first met." He studies my face, as if trying to memorize it. "Turns out I've been wrong about a lot of it so far."

Our eyes connect again, and a buzz charges between us that feels tangible. For a fleeting second, it's just me and him.

No running.

No fighting.

No danger.

Just two unique, beating hearts in one room.

I linger by the door. "I expect to hear more about Koa," I tell him, instead of focusing too much on how I feel in this moment.

He presses his lips together, contemplating it. "Sure, sweet one. Later."

"Okay." I blush at the nickname. I try to dismiss it—pretending his words haven't just twisted me into tender little knots or that my heart isn't pounding with excitement—but I can't stop the smile from spreading across my face.

I'm feeling things for him.

Things I never expected.

Chapter 35

"I'm afraid I won't be making it to the shores with you, my friends." Kelrean sits with a quilt around his shoulders in front of a gentle fire.

The group's healing time takes much longer than we anticipated. The sun is setting now, dipped halfway under the horizon. The sight of it increases my anxiety. If we don't get moving soon, we'll lose daylight.

Everyone from our crew is now seated around a firepit. Thane is better, but still a little sore, and Rynthea's arm has recovered completely from the healing elixirs.

Kelrean, on the other hand, needs more time before he can go anywhere, even back home. Apparently, the stab wound through his ribs and shapeshifting took a toll on his body.

"You should rest, *friend*. Looks like you need it." Thane's eyes catch the flames as he points his attention to Kelrean.

"You will learn to like me one day, broody sorcerer." Kelrean flashes a smug grin at him before looking at Rynthea. "You really don't plan on continuing the journey?"

"Not without my scythesword," she says. Then she smirks. "Unless you let me borrow your ax."

"Absolutely fucking *not*!" Kelrean shouts, then he winces and clutches his ribs.

"You don't even need it right now," she retorts.

"That doesn't matter! I had that ax handmade with alvanite and the finest steel in Thelanor. I'm the only one who has the honor and privilege to wield it. If I let you borrow it, you'll hold that over my head, too."

Rynthea scoffs and then bites into an apple.

Queen Xiaodera and King Jehon approach with three elementalists flanking them. My eyes stretch with surprise when I spot Rynthea's scythesword in Jehon's massive, inked hand.

"Rynthea..." I tap her arm.

She peers up from the fire. Then she gasps. She sounds so innocent, like a child who's found their lost toy.

"My scythesword," she says in awe as she stands and marches around the fire with heavy steps. "Where did you find it?" Her eyes sparkle as Jehon hands it to her.

"Washed up on the banks at the bottom of the waterfall while some of the tribe were fishing," he answers.

Rynthea inspects the blade, running her fingers over the thick handle. "Hardly a scratch." She looks at the king and queen. "Thank you."

"You can thank us by leaving Immalon," Jehon says, voice gruffer.

We all stand and meet at Rynthea's side.

"What my husband means"—Xiaodera gives Jehon a sharp look—"is that it's best for you all to leave while the sun lingers. If you have plans to reach The Shallows, you will need to reach Gadonia first, correct?"

"That's right," Rynthea answers.

"Gadonia is a straight path from one of our departure passages. Normally, it would not be safe to travel at night when creatures of Xaimur are on the prowl, but this passage will not throw you into any forests or imminent danger. It is relatively safe to travel on, and it's how we handle our trading with Gadonia. It is, however, seven hours by foot, and that doesn't include rest breaks. By horseback, you could make it within four or five."

"Do you have horses we can borrow?" Thane asks.

Xiaodera focuses on Thane. "Are you sure you won't endanger them with the burdens you carry?"

Thane fights a grimace. "I don't hurt animals."

"Well, there was that swamp monster." Algar raises a finger. "Technically, the monsters are like the animals. They're just wilder and—"

"Algar, *shut up*," Thane and Rynthea say at the same time.

I stifle a laugh as Xiaodera observes us, mildly amused. "It is a miracle you all have survived one another."

"Tell me about it," I mutter.

"Very well. We will see to it that you have horses to reach Gadonia," Xiaodera vows. "When you make it, I request that you give our horses to the owners of the Gadonian stables. They'll refresh them before we make our way over to collect them."

"Is your tribe close with Gadonia?" I ask.

"They are our closest allies. Just as we have things to protect, so do they."

I nod. "Well, thank you so much, Queen Xiaodera." It feels necessary to bow to her. When I stand up straight, she seems pleased by it, so I roll with it.

"Suck-up," Algar mumbles in my ear.

I catch him off guard and elbow him in the ribs. Zephra does her little maobi cackle as he grunts.

"When the prince is healed, we will escort him to Bernwood safely." Xiaodera walks toward Kelrean, who is sipping wine from a deep goblet. She snatches it out of his hands and tosses the remainder into the fire, causing a loud sizzle.

"Oh, come on!" he exclaims. "I was drinking that!"

"You'll never heal at this rate," Xiaodera scolds.

"Believe me, wine heals everything." Kelrean beams at her. She is not at all charmed.

"I will press on." Rynthea faces me, Algar, and Thane.

"Really?" I shrill. She has no idea how happy I am to hear that.

"I hate thinking about what other dangers lie ahead," she admits, stroking the handle of her weapon with her thumb, "but my scythesword has been returned, and we're very close. Torjack needs this. *You* need this, Zaira. We'll keep going."

I feel warm and gooey inside and want to hug her, but I know better than to get all mushy on her while we're around such a strong tribe. Rynthea seems to only reveal her softer side in private, likely with people she respects or trusts. I'm honored to be one of those people.

"Come back to visit me in Bernwood again, won't you?" Kelrean gives me a gentle hug as I rest my head on his chest and hug him back.

"Of course," I tell him. "I had a lot of fun there."

When I look up, he grabs my chin between his fingers and smiles down at me. "My favorite mortal. Travel safe."

"Thanks." I smile, giving him one last hug before turning for the horses.

"He's so desperate," Thane mutters as he offers me a hand to help me mount our horse. Queen Xiaodera gave us two horses, each equipped with a double-seated saddle. Rynthea and Algar share one horse, even though Rynthea isn't fully comfortable on horseback.

"I already told you before, Thane," I say, sighing. "Jealousy doesn't suit you."

"Take care of her, my friend!" Kelrean calls to Thane as our horse clomps ahead and follows several of the elementalists.

I look over my shoulder just in time to see Thane wave at the prince with his middle finger.

I shake my head and roll my eyes before giving Kelrean a friendlier farewell wave.

The departure passage is located just beyond a grove of bamboo. After we pass a clearing, a wide stone path made of glittering alvanite appears. There is hardly a crack in it. It's so smooth, it almost looks like new.

"Journey well!" Jehon calls out behind us.

I look back at the tribe and wave.

Queen Xiaodera waves back, but I don't miss the way her smile slips or how her head shakes with dismay before she turns away.

I can tell she doubts we'll survive. Honestly, I have my doubts as well, but we're in the thick of it.

Too late to turn back now.

Chapter 36

After several hours and two breaks, I see a towering gold gate with torches flickering ahead. The sky has long changed from the yellow-orange hue it was when we left and is now a velvety dark blue splattered with twinkling stars.

"We're finally here," Rynthea says after a deep sigh. Both she and Algar dismount their horse.

"Did anyone consider that they might not let us in?" Algar throws out there.

"They will." Rynthea wraps their horse's reins tighter around her hand and closes them in a fist. "We'll just tell their council where we came from and who these horses belong to. But first…" She pauses, giving Thane a critical once-over. "You need to put your weapons away. Gadonia is all about peace, and if they sense any sort of threat, they won't let us in."

"Says the minotaur carrying a scythesword," Thane retorts.

"My scythesword will be out of my hands and strapped to the horse. I'm not stupid enough to approach a kingdom's gates with weapons in hand as an outsider. It's not a good look. But I suppose you could care less about that."

"You *do* know that I've saved your life *twice* now." Thane tugs on the reins to slow our horse down. "Yet you still treat me like scum."

Rynthea rolls her eyes. "Now I see why Kelrean gets so pissy when I remind him that I saved his life."

Algar snorts.

When our horse stops, Thane slides off the saddle, and I follow, stretching with relief. My tailbone is aching and my spine feels stiff, but riding was better than walking.

"Stuff everything into your rucksack." Rynthea watches as Thane unties his vest and tucks it into his bag. In exchange for the vest, he pulls out his hooded cowl and slides it over his head.

"You just *love* being ominous, don't you?" Algar quips.

Thane ignores him as he removes the dagger from under his shirtsleeve. He wipes imaginary dust and lint off his clothes, then spins around slowly, showing off his new look. "Better?"

"Much," Rynthea says. "Let's go."

As we trail behind, I gawk at the arched gates made of pure, shining gold. Pearls adorn the edge of the gates, and two guards stand before them in sea-green uniforms. Their clothing is made of an iridescent material that shifts colors in the moonlight with every movement.

As we near them, they stand taller, square their shoulders, and place their hands on the hilts of their swords.

"Where are you traveling from?" the shorter of the two guards asks.

"Immalon," Thane answers.

The taller guard's eyes narrow as he scrutinizes us. "We are to believe the Queen of Immalon welcomed *you* four in?"

"Check the saddles." Thane gestures to the horses, and both guards make their way around them, studying the brown leather saddles. Each one has a symbol of a circle split into four, and each section of the circle contains an image of an element.

"How do we know they aren't stolen?" the tall one interrogates.

"How would we have stolen horses from a tribe of *elementalists*?" Rynthea asks with a scoff. "They'd have killed us before we could even blink at a horse."

"Magic," the shorter one shoots back. "I'm sure one of you wields it. Which one of you is it?"

"I do." The guards put their attention on Thane again, scanning him thoroughly, possibly seeing him as an even bigger threat. "And I didn't use any magic in Immalon. They helped us escape a broken bridge. We were wounded, and they healed us, then sent us on our way here, as we'd already planned." Thane pulls the collar of his cowl lower, revealing the fresh scar on his chest.

The guards look between each other but still don't buy it.

"Queen Xiaodera told us not to mention we were in Immalon to anyone but the Gadonian council," I say. "I assume speaking to the guards is safe, too. She values the relationship her tribe has with your city."

The guards' shoulders soften, but only a notch.

Then the short one says, "We'll need to run this by our council. Stay put."

"Great," Algar says under his breath as they march off.

After a quarter hour, the guards return with two people trailing them. One is a woman, the other a man. A very *familiar* man. He passes through the gates and looks at Rynthea in both shock and awe. Everyone is always surprised to see a minotaur. As I take in his wavy, dark-brown hair, bronze skin, and the cleft in his chin, there's no mistaking who he is.

"Enver?" I gape at the sight of my childhood friend.

He fastens his eyes on me.

"Love of Thelanor," he breathes. "Is that you, Zaira?"

We run toward each other, and he reels me in for a tight embrace. I nearly cry into his shoulder.

"I can't believe it's you!" He laughs. "My goodness, it's been so long!"

"It's me!" I confirm.

He jerks back with his hands gently squeezing my upper arms. "You look— I mean, how is this possible? You should be in Meriva. What are you doing here?"

"I still live there, I'm just...*traveling* at the moment."

"And you've come all this way to Gadonia?"

I nod, smiling. "Just for tonight."

I can tell he has more questions, but when he looks at my crew, he refrains. "Well regardless, this is wonderful. You'll have to catch me up on everything while you're here."

"Should we allow them entry, sir?" the tall guard asks.

"Of course!" Enver waves an inviting hand at us, gesturing for us to come inside. "Welcome them in and get them something hot to eat! This night has just become ten times better!"

Chapter 37

After eating, Enver leads us out of the dining hall and through the city, where the shops, taverns, and merchant stands are still very much alive.

Each building is adorned with brilliant glass bulbs of light humming with magic—a Gadonian invention that only their citizens are able to produce.

Gadonia is charged with life, light bathing exterior walls and gold trails. Ivory-and-green sails are draped from roof to roof like canopies between the buildings. I think they might reflect and amplify the light from the bulbs at night. Riders on trikes with wooden boxes attached whiz past us on the cobblestone streets.

"Fish," Enver says, as I watch one of the riders descend a hill. "There are fish in the baskets. They deliver them to the families. We like to make sure everyone is fed, no matter how much coin they have."

"It's getting late." I watch a woman offer a beaded bracelet to Rynthea, who gratefully accepts it. "I'm surprised to see it so busy."

"Ah yes. Gadonia, the city of daydreams and light," Enver replies, indulging me.

We continue down the hill the trike riders took moments earlier. The dark-brown roads are slightly damp but likely not from rain. I can imagine all the families coming back and forth from the coast, their hair and clothes drenched, sand sticking to their skin, and exhausted laughs as they find their way home.

I make out the ocean ahead. The water stretches far beyond the never-ending horizon, soft waves rippling silver beneath the crescent moon. At the shore are rows of docks with bobbing boats, where merchants likely sell items, too. Some are built with stands that are now covered by thin sheets to protect them.

It reminds me of Ember Coast—the idea of sellers leaning over the edges of their boats to offer freshly caught seafood. The nostalgia is hitting me so hard right now. No wonder Enver moved here.

I look at Thane, Rynthea, and Algar. Algar and Rynthea are absorbing the ivy-wrapped buildings, but Thane is studying Enver with a frown. When his eyes find mine, they're filled with…curiosity? Jealousy? Both? He tears his hot gaze away and clenches his jaw before I can decipher what it is.

"How long do you all plan on staying?" Enver stops in front of a two-story inn with light pouring through stained-glass windows. Music trickles out of the swinging front door, along with laughter and other joyful noise. The vibrancy of the stained glass reflecting on the streets is inviting enough for me to want to join.

I stand next to Rynthea, whose eyes bounce between me and Thane.

"If you're not sure, we have several inns you can use with wonderful accommodations," Enver suggests.

"Actually, Enver, we don't plan on staying too long," I tell him. "We were hoping you could help us with something, though."

"Of course. What is it?"

"We're looking for someone who can sail us to The Shallows."

Enver's eyes widen, and the color drains from his face. "I believe that is the first time *anyone* has ever asked for my help getting to The Shallows." He gives Thane a solid once-over. "Does this have something to do with *him*?"

"What? No!" I counter.

Thane chuckles darkly.

"So why on Thelanor would a girl like *you* ever want to go to *The Shallows*? There is nothing for you there."

"There is, and it's very important that I get it," I reply, slightly annoyed by his remark. I don't like how he makes it seem like I'm a child incapable of making my own decisions. He's literally only a year older than me.

Enver narrows his eyes at Thane.

"Look, are you going to help us or not?" Rynthea demands, clearly fed up with his questions. "We can always find our own way. We've worked through situations much more difficult than this."

"I—I want to help, I do. It's just..." Enver sighs and drops his head. "I assume you'll need a ship?"

We all nod.

He eyes each of us carefully. "There is only one captain I know who travels anywhere near The Shallows, and he doesn't come cheap."

"Coin doesn't matter." Thane's voice is raspy. "Where is this captain?"

"His name is Captain Solyen Terrick. He owns a speedship. He lives here, but right now he's likely on his way to Junsho ports. He handles many of our overseas trades."

"When will he return?" Thane asks.

"That depends." Enver drags the pads of his fingers over his forehead like he's riddled with unfathomable stress. "Sometimes Solyen makes stops at other cities for leisure before he returns. Could be within a few hours. Could be a day or two. I've not known him to be away from Gadonia longer than three days at most."

"Damn it," I mutter as Rynthea curses under her breath and Algar sighs. "Three days is a long time, Enver."

"I'm not understanding the rush, Zaira." His face is drowning in concern. "No one is ever this eager to go to The Shallows. Literally, no one."

"Never mind." I step closer to him, sighing. "We'll take a room for the night. If the captain isn't back by morning, we'll find another way."

Enver raises his chin with a mild flare to his nostrils. "Very well," he says tightly. "This way." He walks away from the boisterous inn, leading us to a smaller one that has potted plants and rocking chairs on the porch.

Entering the building, he greets an older woman with blond hair who stands behind the front counter. She blinks at all of us, surprised. Mostly by Rynthea, of course.

After a few minutes, Enver returns to us with three keys in hand.

"If you truly want rest, this is the best place to stay." He blows out a weary breath. "The other inns closer to the city are loud and usually packed with travelers. Irina has three rooms available for the night. Will that be enough?"

"It's fine." Rynthea takes one of the keys from him. "But just for the record, I don't share rooms," she says, eyeing our crew. "I need my privacy."

"What?" Algar's mouth hangs open. "Well, if you need privacy, so do I!"

"No. No fucking way," Thane growls, grabbing both keys out of Enver's hand before Algar can. "It doesn't make any sense for me to share a room with Zaira."

"I agree," I add rapidly. I couldn't even imagine that. My stomach flutters at the mere idea of it. "If anything, the men should share, and the women should have their own rooms."

"Let me tell you something. Zephra will literally bite through or burn those fancy swords and weapons of his if Thane is in the room with us. I'm telling you, she hates other people in her space for too long, and she *especially* doesn't like him. She won't make it comfortable for him."

"Then let her sleep outside where she belongs," Thane says with a smirk. He's trying to rile Algar up.

It works, because Algar's jaw drops as he pulls Zephra from his shoulder to cup her head and shield her ears. "How dare you! She is an *indoor* sleeper."

"I also beg to differ about Zephra's tantrum. She's starting to adore me." Thane reaches forward to scratch Zephra's chest with a finger. "Right, girl?"

Zephra chitters a noise of pleasure.

Algar raises her in the air to look her in the eyes. "You little traitor."

"Okay, you know what?" I sigh. "We don't have time for this. I'll just hang out with Enver around the city. I'll take a quick bath here and then properly catch up with him." I turn to Enver for approval. "If that's okay."

Enver eagerly nods his assent. Thane looks between me and Enver before gesturing to the lounge area. "You can have the room, Zaira. I'll stay in the lounge, sharpen my blades, or have a drink at one of the taverns. Doesn't matter."

"No." I wave a hand at him, dismissing the offer. "You need rest, too. It's fine, really."

Algar plucks one of the keys out of Thane's hand and hobbles after Rynthea. I watch both of them disappear around a corner before putting my attention on Thane again.

"We can share the third," Thane says suddenly, shifting on his feet. "I'll take a spot on the floor. Shouldn't be any different than the time we stayed in that shabby hut bordering Ruvain. Just promise you won't snore this time."

I can't help smiling as I playfully bump against his arm with my shoulder. "No guarantees."

"Z, can I have a word with you outside really quick?" Enver steps forward, slicing through our conversation.

"Sure. Be there in a second."

Enver smiles at me before glancing at Thane again. His features harden for a split second, then he presses his palms together, nods, and strolls out of the inn.

Thane sits on a worn brown couch across from a hearth, dropping his rucksack on the floor between his feet. "I don't like him."

I roll my eyes. "You don't like anyone."

"Well, I *really* don't like him." He plucks a dagger out of his bag, then takes out an angular rock. "Who is he to you?"

"He's a friend from Ember Coast. He was one of the kids that was rescued alongside me and Analla. He lived in Meriva for a time with his parents until one day they moved." I let the information soak in for him. "Anyway, please feel free to make use of the room. You need rest."

He starts sharpening the blade of the dagger. "Fine."

As I begin to trot off, I glance over my shoulder, not missing the way his gaze lowers to my butt and lingers before shooting up to my face again.

Smirking, I saunter toward the exit with an extra swing in my hips.

Chapter 38

The streets are a bit quieter near this inn. I spot Enver hovering a few paces away and descend from the porch to meet him.

"Zaira," he breathes, smiling.

"Hi, Enver. Thank you for arranging the lodging for us. I was hoping we wouldn't have to stay overnight."

"Yes, well, it's better to have somewhere to rest your head. There is no telling how long it will be before Captain Solyen returns."

"Hopefully soon. How long do you think it takes to get to The Shallows from here anyway?"

"About two days' journey on a regular boat, but since Captain Solyen has a speedship, you'd probably be there in a matter of hours."

"Okay." Hours, I can do. "That's good." I smile and look out at the sea, as if the captain will be returning any minute.

"So…listen. I hate to pester you about this, but I'm deeply worried about you. Why are you traveling with that crew of random people to The Shallows?"

I sigh. "Because Analla is cursed."

"Cursed?" His brows pucker in the lamplight. "How?"

"She got mixed up with a Grim sorcerer near Meriva."

"Oh." Enver's face is stricken with concern. After all, he was Analla's friend, too.

"Long story short, no decent sorcerer in their right mind is willing to go against this evil sorcerer, so I found another way to lift the curse…but it requires a trip to the Temple of Elphar."

"Ah," Enver says, as if things suddenly make sense. "What is it that you need from there, exactly?"

"There are prosperity stones in the temple. I just need one of them."

"I see." He frowns, staring at the cobblestones under his feet. "That seems a bit risky, don't you think, Z?"

"It *is* risky. Life-threatening, actually. But it's the only way I can think of to save her. That's why Thane, Rynthea, and Algar are with me—well, it started with just me and Thane. I paid him to be my guide and protector, so he can help me get through Thelanor and reach The Shallows in one piece—"

"Wait a minute." Enver throws up a hand, pausing me. "You *paid* him to protect you?"

"Well, yeah." I shrug. "I was willing to pay anyone who agreed to protect me on this journey. So far, he's done a great job. We've been through some insane situations, and miraculously, I'm still alive. You wouldn't believe the half of it."

"So prior to Analla's curse, you didn't know him at all?"

I hesitate. "No…"

"You're traveling with a *stranger*." It should be a question, but it isn't. It's a solid statement. Enver is no longer smiling. "Look, I didn't want to say this around him, Z, but there is something about him that I don't trust. Knowing you paid him, and that he's agreed to a journey so dangerous, makes him even more suspicious to me, I won't lie."

"Thane just has that look about him." I shake my head, hoping he'll back off.

"You mean the look of a cold-blooded killer?" Enver counters.

I stifle a laugh. *If only you knew.*

"Listen, I can help you find another way to save Analla. I know many sorcerers who might be able to help." Enver sighs. "I just don't think it's wise to be traveling to such a dangerous place with a man you've only just met."

"We're too far in, Enver, and too close to stop now. We plan on finding a boat and going tomorrow, regardless of if Solyen arrives. Do you have anyone who can help us that soon? Anyone who will agree to risk their lives facing one of the strongest sorcerers in Meriva? One who uses black magic, might I add, to handle most of his affairs?"

"I..." Enver's throat bobs as he looks out at the watery horizon. "No, I don't."

An awkward silence swells between us.

"Do you like him?" he asks after a few seconds.

"What?" I sputter.

He stares at me, waiting for an answer.

"He's— It's complicated."

"I suspected as much." He shakes his head. "I mean, the guy has not just two but three swords, and don't think our guards missed the countless daggers when they checked his bags. He doesn't seem like the kind of person you'd normally associate with."

"He's only around right now so we can reach The Shallows. Once he helps me get what I need, we'll part ways. It's as simple as that." Saying it out loud feels like a lie. In fact, it hurts my heart a little to admit it.

Enver scoffs. "I'm sorry, but I just can't believe that a person like *him* would willingly risk his life for coins just to get you to the deadliest place in Thelanor. Either he has a death wish, or there is something else in it for him."

I drop my chin and wring my fingers together.

"Look, Z." Enver grabs my hand and gives it a squeeze. When I meet his eyes again, he places his other hand on top of it, sandwiching it. "I only want the best for you." He pauses to choose his next words carefully. "I mean, if I'd never left Meriva, maybe none of this would be happening."

"What do you mean?" I have the urge to pull my hands away.

"There is so much that could've happened between us. I hate that I had to leave you."

"I hate that you left, too. I lost a really good friend." I emphasize the last word. "But you seem to have made a great name for yourself here. You're on the Gadonian council. I'm sure that was no easy feat."

"Yeah." He finally releases my hand, smile fading. "Just...promise me something, Zaira."

"What?"

"Promise you'll reconsider going to that island."

I stare into his brown eyes as I shake my head again. "I can't promise you that, Enver."

"I figured you were going to say that." We fall into another awkward silence. "It's just kind of hard to accept," he says, half laughing. "It's like accepting notice of your death."

"Enver, promise me you won't do anything to hold us back."

"Anything like what?"

"Like send inquiries out to other kingdoms about my group—especially Thane. I don't want any of my crew getting distracted or detained. As long as you keep the peace, they will, too."

He gives me a hard look. "I would never do that to you."

"*Promise* me."

He lifts his chin. "I promise, Zaira. You're all safe here."

I bob my head. "Okay. Thank you."

A balmy breeze drifts by, making me want to stick outside just a few seconds longer, and a sigh escapes me. "I can see why you stayed here."

"Yeah?" He tucks his hands into his pockets. "It's a beautiful place, isn't it? Almost reminds me of Ember Coast…just with more light."

"Yep. I get that same feeling. All that's missing are the pearls." I look past him to the glittering waters in the distance highlighted by the moon. "I miss it every day. Life felt so much simpler there. I mean, don't get me wrong, Meriva is nice, and I appreciate them for giving us refuge, but nothing can ever replace our home."

He nods in understanding, then leans in closer as I take a minor step back. "Anyway, I should go inside and get some rest. Whenever you hear from Captain Solyen, will you let us—"

I don't get the chance to finish my sentence.

Enver has leaned in completely to press his lips to mine.

Shocked, I pull away with a soft gasp. "Enver." My cheeks burn as I shift backward. "Why did you do that?"

"I— Zaira, I'm sorry," he stammers. "I just… It's been so long since I last saw you, and all of these old feelings are rising up again. I've always felt something for you. I never thought I'd see you again and…well…"

I keep quiet for a few seconds, unsure what to say to that. "I'm…going to go in now," I murmur. "To get some sleep."

"Yes." He nods quickly, taking the hint and stepping away. "Yes, of course. I'll, uh…I'll let you know when I hear from Captain Solyen."

"Thanks." I warily look him over once more before turning a fraction. "Good night, Enver."

"Good night."

I give him my back before he can say anything else, and hurry to the porch. Gripping the door handle, I glance over my shoulder to watch him walk away with his head hung and his shoulders sagging.

I didn't give him the wrong impression, did I?

No, I'm *positive* I didn't. He kissed me without permission. I'm sure his intentions were good, but still…

He's just a friend. He's always been a friend and nothing more. I suppose Gadonia has made him bolder.

"Now I see what he is to you."

Startled, I gasp when I hear another deep voice come out of nowhere. Emerging from the shadows at the farthest end of the porch with a furrowed brow is Thane.

Chapter 39

Thane's sleeveless black tunic shows off his muscled arms and a glimpse of the Divine tattoo on his forearm. In his left hand is the handle of one of his swords. The sharp silver blade gleams in the moonlight.

"Thane?" I look around, confused as to where the shadows he came from. "What are you doing out here?"

"About to train."

"On the porch?"

"Behind the inn."

"Oh."

He steps closer, his boots thumping on the wooden floorboards.

"Were you eavesdropping?"

"Wasn't intentional. I stepped around the corner, and there you two were."

"You saw him kiss me?" I ask, avoiding a wince.

"Saw that. Heard everything. No wonder he's been eyeing you like a desperate stray. He's always loved you." Thane is only a step away now, peering down at me with tense features. His hair looks curlier, moisturized, like he's made use of the bath or has at least given himself a quick wash. "Even more reason for me not to like him."

I fold my arms. "It isn't like that with him."

"He doesn't seem to think so."

"I don't feel like talking about this." I drop my arms and reach for the door handle again, but before I can open it, Thane's hand wraps around mine, and he pulls it closed.

"Why didn't you run off to his hut after that kiss?"

"Oh my Orvena." I whirl around. "Stop it, Thane. I don't care for him in that way."

His eyes narrow. We stare at each other for several seconds, and when he realizes I'm not going to back down, he drags in a breath through his nose and exhales. "There's something I want to show you."

"I'm ready to lie down," I protest.

"I have a feeling you'll like it."

He steps off the porch, giving his sword a swing over his head to sheathe it in the holster on his back. He stands sideways and looks at me, cocking his head. "Stand there any longer and I'll force you to come."

"I'd like that again, actually," I tell him, biting my bottom lip to suppress a smile. "I bet that would help me sleep like a baby."

When he smirks, his eyes flash gold, and I yelp as my body elevates.

"Not in the way you're thinking," he says. "But we can make that happen, too."

I hover in the air as he guides me toward him. Once I'm at his side, he places my feet on the ground, and I stumble a bit before gaining my footing.

"Tag along," he calls over his shoulder.

I scoff, watching him drift farther away. I could ignore him, waltz right into the inn, wash, and go to sleep…but of course my foolish heart won't allow that. Not only am I intrigued by whatever he has to show me, but I also want to be near him. Why that is, I have no clue. I choose not to question it and jog after him to catch up.

"You know it's wrong to use magic just to get people to do whatever you want, right?" I ask.

"What's the point of having magic if not to control others?" he responds with a corner of his lips quirked up.

I try not to react to that darkly alluring smirk by putting my focus ahead instead. We walk for a handful of minutes until we reach a footpath lined with cream stones. That's when I notice a building in the distance.

Separated from the rest of the village, the roof is domed while the body beneath is covered in the same stone that lines the path. The portico is made of glazed wood, and oddly, there are no windows.

"What is this place?" I ask as we approach the arched double doors.

Instead of answering, Thane raises a hand above one of the handles, and a flash of gold leaves his fingertips. The light melts into the handle, then he grips it, pulling the door open with ease.

"Was that door *locked*?" I whisper-hiss.

"Yep."

"So we're breaking into places now? I'm sure it's locked up for a reason."

Thane slips right in, blending into the darkness. With a reluctant groan, I take one last look behind me before following him inside.

The door booms as it shuts, creating a hollow echo around us. The only form of light spills from a dim spotlight in the center of the room that highlights the glistening marble floor.

With a snap of his fingers, Thane sends up several gold orbs of light. They hover above our heads, emitting enough luminosity for me to see exactly what surrounds us.

"Oh *wow*."

This isn't just an ordinary building.

Paintings of all sorts hang on spackled walls while marble sculptures of Orvena tower on either side of the room. One of her hands reaches to the rotunda above as she stares up at the sky, her hair falling in waves long enough to cover her breasts.

Crystals of all colors are embedded into the edges of the rotunda, and Thane's orbs allow them to create a gentle kaleidoscope on the walls and glass ceiling.

"I visited this gallery years ago, back when I was with The Divine," Thane says. "We had to escort the queen and several other elites. A group of us stayed in Gadonia for a few nights." He looks all around him, seeming content. "The best art travels here."

"This is…" Words fail me. All I can do is drink it all in. My breath catches as I lock eyes on one of the art pieces. "That's a Bruvo Devell piece," I say, rushing toward it.

Thane stands next to me, studying the details of the painting: deep-brown branches swathed in gold-and-white flowers with a frothy teal ocean in the background. The ocean feels more like a distant view, as if the person studying the art is standing behind branches and flowers with the ocean slightly blurred in the distance.

"I love his work. His art is never straightforward." I smile. "Did you know he was from Ember Coast?"

"Was he?" Thane asks with genuine curiosity.

"Yeah." I peer up at him. He's still examining the portrait. He seems so bare without his mask and buffers, like a part of him is missing. But he's so very handsome. I wonder if he realizes just how beautiful he is.

I turn away before he can catch me ogling.

"My favorite is over here." Thane turns on his heels and strides across the room, stopping in front of an oil painting: a boy dressed in all white with floppy brown hair. Gold rings of light surround him, and though he's smiling, tears are in his eyes.

I lean in for a closer look. "This one kind of hurts my heart."

"What do you see when you look at it?" he asks.

I pause, giving it a harder look before answering. "A sad boy who needs a hug."

He tilts his head, analyzing it.

"What do *you* see?" I ask.

He's quiet for a moment, eyes roaming the art. "I saw the same thing at first." He takes another pause. "But now I see a boy clinging desperately to hope."

"Hmm."

"Perhaps he does need a hug," Thane says absently, still staring at the boy. "But it's clear he has resilience. The world is bright and beautiful around him, he's upset and hurting, yet he smiles through it. He perseveres because he knows there is better for him out there. He just has to find it."

A calming silence wraps around us like a cocoon. Who knew he had such poetic thoughts in that dark mind of his?

One of Thane's orbs hovers above my head before bouncing toward a sculpture of Orvena. She's a beautiful goddess. All the stories and art depict her as a woman with umber skin and wavy, ebony hair. The stories say she radiated like a crystal in sunlight. That's sort of how the sculpture looks now with the orb floating around it.

Radiant.

Hopeful.

When I stop in front of Orvena's sculpture, I can feel Thane's eyes on me from across the room.

"Is there something you want to ask?" I ask over my shoulder.

"No."

"Has to be something. You're staring."

He strides up behind me, the heat of his body now on my back and his powerful aura wrapping around me.

"Why did you turn Enver's kiss down?" His voice is low and deep while his lips are close to my ear.

Goose bumps crawl up my arms. "You were watching way too closely." I try keeping my voice steady.

"Was it because it held no comparison to ours?" Something wraps around my middle and tugs me backward.

Hello, invisible hand.

My back presses to his chest, and I sigh, squeezing my eyes shut.

"Did you turn him down because I was on your mind, Zaira?"

"You're overconfident."

"You're not denying it."

The invisible hand slides up my belly and palms one of my breasts. I suppress a moan and instead open my eyes. When I twist around to face him, he's already looking down at me, watching me with heated eyes, as if I'm something to behold.

"We're not supposed to be doing this," I remind him.

"Doing what?" The invisible hand cups my ass.

Thane lowers his head, and I angle my chin upward. For a moment, we stand like this. Staring at each other, trying to fight the pull. Lips only a hair's breadth away.

Then he cradles the back of my head with his real hand, and his mouth claims mine.

Chapter 40

This time, I let the moan take over—even more so when he forces me to walk backward so that my back is pressed to the wall.

He drops heated kisses on my throat as I lace my arms around the back of his neck. As he starts to pick me up, coaxing my mouth open a bit more with his tongue, we hear a solid thud sound in the building.

I gasp and drop my leg. Thane freezes, looking toward the sound. His orbs disappear.

I hear footsteps click along the marble floors, coming from the hallway.

"Who's there?" someone calls out.

Thane takes my hand, and I immediately feel warmth coating my skin as a guard steps around a corner and marches into the gallery. He holds my hand tight, allowing the whispershade to take effect while the guard walks deeper into the room, searching the area with a slight frown and a hand on the pommel of his sword. His iridescent buffers gleam under the spotlight, appearing more like pearls left in the sun.

My heart speeds up as the guard looks past us. If he takes one more step closer, he'll bump into us. Thane's whispershade can hide us from view, but it doesn't prevent touch.

Raising his left hand, Thane gives his wrist a flick. One of the paintings across the room falls off the wall and crashes to the ground.

I'm glad it's not a Devell piece.

"What the shadows?" The guard whirls around, storming across the room to inspect the fallen painting. When he does, Thane tugs on my hand, and we hightail it for the exit.

Our footsteps thunder across the tiles, and the guard shouts, "What the shadows?" so loudly it echoes through the building.

We don't stop running until we reach the end of the footpath leading to the inner city. Coming to a halt between two buildings, Thane takes a sweep of the area while I place a hand on the wall to catch my breath. A stretch of silence passes between us as we look at each other. Then the widest smile I've ever seen spreads across his face before he breaks out in deep laughter.

I bust out laughing myself, despite the burning sensation in my lungs. "Oh my gods," I wheeze. "Did you see that guard's face?"

"I think we scared the shadows out of him." Thane's laughter continues. I've never heard him laugh like this. It's always a grunt or a dark chuckle. But this laugh is brighter, clearer—infectious, even. This is a new side of him, one I very much enjoy.

I press the back of my head to the cool wall. "I shouldn't be having this much fun during a death journey."

Thane shrugs his shoulders. "Better to laugh your way through it."

I swallow hard to clear the dryness in my throat, breathing a little easier now. "Can I be honest with you?"

He nods. "Of course."

"I just... I worry that I won't make it back to Analla. What if that captain doesn't show tomorrow, or even the day after?"

"We'll steal a boat," he says.

I frown and fold my arms.

"Fine. We'll *buy* a boat," he corrects himself.

I sigh. "Being on a speedship will be interesting. I've never been on one before."

"Neither have I."

I push off the wall, wiping my forehead. "Anyway, we should probably get back to the inn before that guard comes looking for us."

Thane gestures in the direction of Irina's inn, allowing me to take the lead.

The bath in our room is perfection. I feel like I can swim in the wide clawfoot tub.

The many scented soaps and the warm water that pumps straight from the heating well are such pleasures. To top it off, the towels are nice and fluffy. I wrap myself in one before putting on the nightgown I got from the wardrobe in Bernwood. Gadonia is way ahead of any other kingdom when it comes to inventions and convenience.

When I walk into the room neither Thane nor I wanted to share, it hits me that there's only one bed. I try not to react as I sit on the edge of the mattress to detangle my hair and then braid it into sections.

As I do, I look at the sofa in the corner of the room, where Thane is making it into a bed.

"I'm curious about something," I say after several minutes tick by.

"Mmm." Thane glances at me.

"Why didn't you push back harder about the rooms? You could've easily told Algar that you were sharing with him, and it would've been final. You know he was joking about Zephra, right?"

"Yeah, I know."

My heart flutters. "So you *wanted* to be in this room with me?"

"I agreed to protect you," he murmurs. "I can't do that if I'm in another room."

"You were in another room in Bernwood," I remind him.

He removes a quilt from the wardrobe. "I put a lock spell around your door."

"You did *what*?"

"While you slept," he adds as he spreads the quilt on the sofa. "No one could approach it or come in, but you could leave whenever you wanted. I'd have felt you leaving, though."

"Thane," I breathe in disbelief.

Maybe Kelrean *did* try to come to my room, after all, but couldn't get close...because of Thane. For all I know, Kelrean assumed I wanted the spell in place so I wouldn't be bothered. It should frustrate me that Thane did that...but it ignites something in me instead.

Thane begins to remove his boots.

I hesitate before saying, "You don't have to sleep there."

"I figured you'd want space."

"This bed is huge. And as long as you don't punch or jab in your sleep, I don't mind sharing."

"I may have a habit of throwing an elbow or two in my sleep."

I pause as I regard him. "I can't tell if you're joking…"

He smiles. "I am."

I laugh. Seriously. I like this side of Thane.

A stretch of silence spreads through the room.

After I'm done with my last braid, I dry my hands off and adjust my nightgown, which seems to be clinging to my curves now. "Well…feel free to climb in." I place my spectacles on a side table, then lift the cream-colored quilt on the bed.

Thane watches every action, eyes blazing, hardly moving.

When I settle in, I flip onto my right side. At first, the room is quiet and still. Thane hardly moves, and I'm practically holding my breath. My pulse quickens as I wait to see if he'll take the invitation.

Then I hear rustling.

Clothes dropping to the floor in gentle wooshes.

The bed dips behind me, and a gust of air flies beneath the quilt as Thane slides into the bed. He doesn't touch me, but I notice the magic-infused bulbs in the room slowly dimming. When I glance over my shoulder, one of his hands is in the air to control them. He only leaves one light on across the room so we're now bathed in darkness.

"You're a bold one, Quinlocke." His voice seems louder in the dark.

"Am I?"

"I took you as a coy woman. I mean, other than when you constantly talk and ask the most annoying questions."

I fight a smile.

I feel him shift closer. His skin is warm, radiating on mine. He smells like smoke and pine, shadows and salt.

"Why do you *really* want me in this bed?"

I gasp when I feel his mouth on the shell of my ear. His warm breath spills down the curve of my neck.

"Unlike you, I'm considerate. You're way too big for that sofa."

He unleashes a throaty laugh. "Lies."

He shifts closer, and I feel his stiff erection press into my backside. I curl my fingers into the pillow beneath my head, trying to bottle my excitement.

"You asked me why I didn't put up more of a fight for my own room, but I noticed you didn't, either. And you know what that tells me?"

I don't answer—*can't* answer. His mouth is now skimming over the slope of my shoulder and causing a delicious stir between my thighs. I hold back a moan and close my eyes, falling victim to that simple act.

"Shall I explain?" he asks, sliding a hand over my hip to find the hem of my nightgown and ease it up.

"Explain," I breathe as he cups my sex.

"It tells me that you want more."

"You don't know that for sure."

The hand that was cupping me slides into my underwear, and I hitch a breath. He skims a finger between my delicate lips. "I do now." His laugh is dark and delicious. "You may think you can resist me, but your body will betray you every time."

Oh, gods.

"And what about you?" I ask, breathless. "What do you want?"

"To be the *only* man who can do this to you for the rest of our time together. Will you give me that?"

He sucks on the bend of my neck while creating small loops around my slick bundle of nerves with his finger. I nod in pleasure, answering his question.

"What else do you want?" I ask.

"To watch you come again. Only this time, I want to witness it while I'm *buried deep inside you.*"

"Is it wise to go *that* deep?" I ask through a breathy moan. It's now I realize I'm rolling my hips and grinding against his hand, desperate for more.

"I didn't mean that in the physical sense."

"Emotionally, then?"

"Precisely."

"Well, you don't have to worry about that," I assure him. "It's impossible for me to fall for an assassin." I can't help but smile.

He pulls his hand out of my underwear and flips me onto my back in a blink. "I'm going to trust your word on that," he murmurs, searching my face. "Shall I?" He tugs my nightgown over my head and then gently starts to remove my underwear.

"Polite of you to ask." I tilt my hips, and he slips them off. When his mouth claims mine, I force him out of his undergarments, then slip from under him so I can be on top. I wrap my arms around the back of his neck, mounting him and catching him by total surprise.

He stares up at me, eyes glazed. One of his hands slides up to my breast, and he squeezes, playing with my nipple, while the other curls around my waist. I rock on top of him, and he expels a ragged breath, eyes roaming my body. For once, he looks powerless, desperate, like he would rather die than be anywhere else but here.

I lean down to clasp his face in my hands and kiss him again, swallowing his groan as I grind my hips. He's unbelievably hard right now.

When I feel like I've worked him up enough, I lower between his legs and settle on my knees. He watches as I lick my palm and then wrap it around his shaft.

"Zaira." Though his voice has a warning tone, his face is soft and vulnerable, as if he wants nothing more in this world.

"Shh."

I pump his length, and he releases a heavy sigh, tipping his head backward. He grows even harder in my palm as a carnal groan unfurls from his chest.

Dropping his head with parted lips, he finds my eyes again, and a look of hunger takes over him.

"Fuck," he rumbles.

I can't help but smile knowing that he's surrendering control to me. Then I lean forward and wrap my mouth around him.

"*Oh, fuck,* Zaira."

I glance up with my mouth closed around him, suckling as I swivel my hand. His mouth forms into a wide *O*, eyes clouding with lust. When I look down again, one of his hands falls to the back of my head. He tugs on my hair, forcing me to look back up at him.

"Don't look away," he pants. "I need to see you."

I keep my eyes trained on him, moaning as I take him deeper into my mouth.

"Shit," he says through partially gritted teeth, throbbing between my lips. "If you keep doing that, I'm gonna—"

Before I know it, I feel the warmth of his invisible hand flip me onto my back.

"Not yet," he murmurs with a crooked smile. "It's your turn." He leans down to kiss me ravenously, grinding hard against me, working both of us up, before breathlessly snatching his mouth away. "Are you sure?" he asks, pressing his forehead to mine.

"Yes." I've never been more certain.

With that confirmation, he hoists my hips so they're at an angle, then grips himself before carefully thrusting into me. My sharp gasp fills the air, followed by his guttural groan. I hold on to him tighter, fingernails piercing into his skin, as he sinks deeper.

I'm quick to realize Thane isn't the kind of guy to rush through it. He takes his time—stroking slowly, sliding his hands up and interlacing our fingers, his flashing eyes holding my gaze with each thrust.

He groans as he drops his face into the crook of my neck.

I moan because he feels so much better than I imagined.

I never want this to end—this night with him. I want him to stay inside me. To keep going. To claim me over and over again if it continuously brings me this much pleasure.

He clutches my hips with his other hand, and that's when I feel something graze my most sensitive area. Surprised, I draw in a breath. He lifts his head up, and a faint smile tugs at the corners of his lips. Then that gentle touch lights me up again. I squeeze his hand, staring into his eyes.

This isn't his invisible hand doing the work. It's something else entirely. It feels *connected* to him. He uses it to stroke relentlessly, sending nothing but waves of pleasure through me.

"What is that?" My words are hardly audible because I'm breathing too hard, too fast, on the cusp of orgasm.

I shudder with pleasure when it happens again.

"Magic," he rasps.

He releases my hands to plant his fists on either side of my head. His thrusts never stop. And neither does the sensation. It feels like someone is simultaneously massaging me while he fucks me. But, by some spell, it's all him, and it drives my body *wild*.

He slams into me, the veins beneath his muscles bulging. He breathes hard, like he's having a hard time controlling himself. Perhaps because he is. So am I.

With every rub, every slide, every stroke, I feel like I'm lifting higher and higher. I feel like we could touch the moon, the stars, and whatever else stands between us and the Crystal Realm. I'm drowning in pure bliss and pleasure, and nothing outside of us matters.

"Come for me, Zaira."

Oh gods.

His voice.

It does something to me. The way he watches me does something to me. Everything about him does something to me. He doesn't stop, not even when I clutch his forearm and throw my head back to cry out.

"Oh, shadows." My hips buck to match the rhythm of his as I fall over the edge.

He groans with deep pleasure. "How beautiful it is to finally feel you come around me."

Slowly, the magical rubbing fades. As it does, he lowers himself so we're chest to chest. Then he crushes his lips to mine. This kiss is tender, passionate, and sweet as he strokes into me slowly. I can't understand how a person so lethal can also be so gentle—so careful and satisfying.

I clench around him. He groans, delighted to feel it, then tears his mouth away so he can pull his hips backward. With a sharp hiss through his teeth, he pulls out of me.

"Oh, fuck." He swiftly pumps himself before coming on my pelvis. "Damn, sweet one." When he's done, he sighs. I miss the feel of him already.

Planting his hands on either side of my head again, he hovers his face above mine, and our eyes connect. A brief moment of silence passes between us as we catch our breaths.

"You keep blowing my mind, mortal," he murmurs in a playful tone.

I sigh happily as his lips drag over mine.

He kisses me once. Twice. Both are ever so sweet.

I want him to take me all over again.

He watches my face, searches it like he always does. It's like I'm a book he's constantly reading—like he's hoping to figure out the plot twist before reaching the last page. But there are no twists. He just saw all of me. There is nothing to hide.

If only it were the same for him.

The skin between his eyebrows wrinkles, and he opens his mouth like he's going to say something but closes it just as quickly. Before I can blink, he's off the bed and heading to the room where the bath is. When he returns, he has a thin towel in his hand. I sit up, and he uses it to wipe me clean.

Once he's done, I put my nightgown on again, then lie back down, staring at the ceiling. Thane does, too, while releasing a heavy sigh.

I look at him. He's already watching me. His face is much more relaxed than it was before, but he still looks like he wants to say something. *Reveal* something. Instead of pestering him about what might be on his mind and ruining the moment, I slide closer and rest my head on his chest.

His whole body stiffens.

This is clearly a new thing for him, but I don't care. It feels necessary right now. I want him close. I inhale his scent as I hug him sideways. Slowly, his body gives into the hug, and he wraps his arm around me. He's warm and comforting...or perhaps I've been so lonely lately that I'm willing to accept any kind of embrace.

I sigh, way more content than I should be. I can't help it, really. It's odd, but I feel *safe* in his arms. Safe...with a damn outlawed shadow assassin. I could blame my feelings on some kind of mysterious spell he's cast, but then I'd be lying to myself. What I'm feeling for him is real—has been for days. I can no longer deny it.

As I drift off to sleep, I think I hear him say, *"Mea trelanak."*

I don't know much Thelasian; however, I studied the basics, and I remember those words very well.

I'm sorry.

Chapter 41

I startle awake when I hear a few thumps and clatters and sit up in bed. Everything appears normal in the room, yet I feel a sense of foreboding come over me...like something bad is going to happen. Perhaps the feeling is warranted. The Shallows aren't too far away, and there are unspeakable horrors on that island that await us.

The sun filters through the gaps in the green curtains, highlighting Thane's empty half of the bed. I run a hand over the spot where he slept, and it's cool to the touch. A lump forms in my throat as a whisper of insecurity flares through me.

Where did he go? Does he regret what we did last night?

I suppose the bigger question is why am *I* not regretting it? Sex with an assassin? I could be hanged for treason if the wrong person were to find out what he is and our connection.

The thumping and clattering happens again in the hallway, along with the sound of someone humming. I climb out of bed and take a peek out the door to see Irina across the hall, cleaning one of the rooms.

I shut the door again. Roosters crow in the distance, but the inn is mostly quiet and calm. I grab my rucksack to find clothes, give myself a quick wash before getting dressed, and then loosen my braids.

The lobby is vacant when I enter. A station in the corner is set up with a teapot along with porcelain mugs and cubes of sugar. The tea calls to me, steam blooming from the pot's spout, but I leave it be and march toward the exit to look for Thane.

The sun drowns me in its bold, warm light when I step outside. The salty air is humid and thick. Fortunately, the occasional breeze helps counteract the heat. With one hand on my hip and the other above my brows to block the beaming rays, I search the busy streets for any sign of my crew. I don't see Thane anywhere, but I can hear Algar's voice. And it doesn't sound like it's coming from the street.

I follow his voice around the side of the inn, which leads to a field of manicured grass and a grove of trees with low-hanging white wisteria. In the distance, I spot Algar slashing a dagger in the air, while Thane stands a few feet away with his arms folded, seemingly unimpressed by Algar's performance.

I feel more relief seeing Thane than I should. I don't know why I ever thought he ran away or bailed on me.

"And then you give it a quick twist like that," I hear Algar say as I approach. "Deep in the right of their gut, just like that, yeah? Twist it hard—left then right—and they're as good as dead. Trust me."

"You have terrible form." Thane's sword is resting on the grass, and he kicks it up with the tip of his boot. His back is to me, so he doesn't notice me coming. Behind Algar is a wooden post several feet taller than both of them. It connects a clothing line to another post on the opposite end of the lawn.

Without warning, Thane swings his blade above Algar's head and cuts through the post. Algar ducks so low he ends up falling on his butt. The post tilts sideways before slamming to the ground. It's a relief there aren't any clothes or sheets hanging on the line.

"A heads-up would've been nice!" Algar shouts. "You could've chopped off my damn head."

Thane inspects his sword. "Perhaps that was the goal."

Hovering nearby, Zephra blows a small spout of fire at Thane. As if he expects it, he throws up a hand and creates an invisible shield to deflect it.

"Nice try, Zephra." Thane eyes her as she chitters like she always does when she's upset. It's almost like she's ranting.

I laugh. One thing's for sure: no matter how much you coddle or feed Zephra, she will never be okay with you harming Algar.

"You training or what?" Rynthea's voice surprises me as she hoofs past with her scythesword.

That's when Thane becomes aware of my presence. He turns a fraction, looking at me from head to toe. I try not to make a fool of myself as I follow Rynthea.

"Have a good rest, sleeping princess?" Algar asks, standing again.

"It was okay," I answer, avoiding Thane's eyes.

"The darkling didn't snore too loudly, did he?" Algar nudges Thane in the ribs.

"No. He was actually really quiet. Slept like a baby, which was a bit strange, considering how destructive he is."

Algar snickers.

"Have any of you seen or heard from Enver?" I inquire.

"Nope." Rynthea sways her blade to create infinity loops. "No sign of him yet."

I shift uneasily. "You think we should find another way to the island?"

"If we don't hear from him within the next few hours, we're leaving," Thane declares. "We can put all our coin together and pay someone to let us borrow their boat."

"It can't just be any kind of boat." Rynthea drops the scythesword on its head, planting it into the ground and leaning on the handle. "There are sea monsters of all kinds out there. And don't even get me started on the zerenias."

My eyes round. "You think those are real?"

"I *know* they are," she says. "My father used to be a fisherman before he opened Kamtaur. Said he saw a man walk the plank and jump straight into the ocean because he took the cotton out of his ears. The zerenias pulled him under, and he was never seen again."

"Horse shit," Algar spits. "There's no way they're real! Sea creatures who eat men and steal their identities just to walk the lands? That's a ridiculous tale! I should know. My father was a terribly underpaid assistant to a sea biologist. He told me all the stories about them weren't true."

"Well, maybe he didn't go far enough," Rynthea says. "You try riding the deep seas without cotton in your ears and tell me how ridiculous it is when they try to eat you."

Algar snorts. Rynthea simply rolls her eyes at him before turning her attention to me. "Do you have that dagger on you?"

"No." I point over my shoulder at the inn. "It's in my rucksack."

"Get it. *Someone* around here has to show you how to use it." She turns to stare Thane down. He must feel her heated gaze because he stops his practice to glare right back at her with a set jaw.

I jog off to get the dagger before they can start tearing into each other like always.

When I return, Rynthea leads the way to the other side of the field, putting some distance between us and the men. Placing her scythesword against a nearby boulder, she reaches for the handle of a dagger on her waist and grips it in hand.

"Show me your best defensive stance," she instructs.

I grip the handle of my dagger and set my feet apart so they're square with my shoulders. Then I bend my knees, sinking into a squat.

Rynthea suppresses a laugh as she watches me lift the dagger overhead. "Have you ever actually fought with a weapon before?"

"Is it that obvious?" I lower the dagger, and my shoulders follow in defeat. "I didn't grow up needing to constantly defend myself like the rest of you. Please don't make fun of me, Rynthea."

She throws up an innocent hand. "I'm not making fun," she says quickly, now bottling a laugh.

I narrow my eyes, trying to fight a smile, too. "But you want to."

"I mean a little—but only because that stance was the saddest thing I've ever seen."

"See!"

"But you should consider yourself lucky that you were able to hold on to your innocence," she adds. "I started training during my third year."

"Your third? *Seriously?*"

"Oh yeah. My father wanted me to know how to protect myself and Torjack, especially when Torjack got his diagnosis." She looks toward the horizon, lost in thought. "My mother wasn't fond of the idea of me holding knives and daggers at such a young age, but I loved it."

"I can imagine." I laugh. "Violence wasn't really a thing in Ember Coast. My parents didn't really know much about sword fighting, either. My father was a doctor and my mother a nurse. They taught me more about resuscitating and healing people than ripping them apart."

"Hmm." Rynthea gives that some thought. "Well, some of us are meant to hurt people while others are meant to mend them." She shrugs. "Plus, had they not taught you those skills, you wouldn't have been able to save my life in that swamp."

She gives me a warm smile.

I return it.

"All right, first we need to adjust your posture and the way you handle the dagger." Rynthea adjusts my arm so that it stays close to my body. Then she uses one of her hooves to push my feet apart and widen my stance—my right foot forward and left back as the anchor. "There are many ways you can use a dagger, but one of my favorites is like this…" She takes a generous step away from me and lunges with the blade. She jabs it forward, her arm protruding from her body quickly yet fiercely. "And if someone is coming at you from the side, you can do this." She flips the hilt backward, so the tip of the blade faces the other way. With a rapid jerk of her hand, she stabs at the air. "Now you try."

I attempt to imitate her demonstration but come a little too close to her arm. She steps out of the way just in time and cocks an eyebrow.

"Sorry." I laugh nervously.

"No worries. Just try again."

I give it another go, making sure not to get too close to her this time as I stab at the air.

"Better," she commends. "You learn quickly."

"Thanks. I've always been a pretty fast learner. It helps to adapt to my surroundings, you know?"

"I know what you mean."

"It was always easier for my sister to adapt." I give the dagger another slash through the air.

"Is she the social type?"

"Very."

Rynthea smiles at me, nodding. "You're doing something selfless for your sister, Zaira." She grabs my forearm and tilts my elbow so it's locked in the proper position. Then she tells me to tighten my grip on the hilt. "I don't know any mortal who would risk their lives doing what you're doing. Most would've sat around whimpering and waiting for the person they love to die."

"*I can't* let her die." I meet her honey-colored eyes. "You still think it's extreme of me? Going to The Shallows and all?"

"Oh, one hundred percent." She laughs. "But I get it. I would do anything for Tor. No matter what we are—mortal, beastial, sorcerer, minotaur—we want the best for our family. Even if it means risking our lives, it's better to take the chance than to do nothing at all."

"Agreed."

"But I have to ask you, Zaira…" She pauses and squints as wisps of sunlight beam down on her. "You're an incredibly smart person. Do you think it's wise to be sleeping with a man like Thane?"

My heart drops. "W-what—"

"I can hear things from very far away. When you're in an inn as quiet as this one"—she gestures behind me—"it's kind of hard to ignore certain sounds."

My face burns, and I drop my eyes, too embarrassed to look at her now. "I…don't know what to say."

"Fortunately for you, I have the ability to shut noise out, too," she says. "As soon as I heard you two start, I tuned it out."

"Well, thank you for that, but that doesn't make this conversation any less awkward," I return with an equally awkward laugh.

"I own an inn. I've heard way worse." She pauses, contemplatively pressing her lips together. "But can I be honest with you?"

"Of course."

"I don't see whatever this is between you and that sorcerer ending well."

I look at Thane, who is practicing with his swords. He has a sword in each hand, swinging them with perfect balance and precision. He performs moves with them that I'm certain not many people in Thelanor could do. The blades catch in the sunlight as he jabs, slices, and swings at the air.

"There's nothing to worry about." I face Rynthea again. "Our emotions aren't involved."

She raises a brow as she picks up her scythesword. "You sure?"

"Yes." My response is firm, but the word hurts my heart as it leaves me, like something is trying to puncture it. "I'm sure."

"Zaira." Thane's voice rises up behind me.

I twist around, worried that he may have overheard me. But I quickly realize that he's not alone.

Standing a few steps away from him is Enver, who says, "Captain Solyen just docked."

Chapter 42

Captain Solyen's personality is not at all what I expected.

Enver talked about him like he was an ordinary man, and though he seems like a common broad-shouldered mortal with a graying beard, golden-brown skin, and a pot belly, he's a *drunk*.

"Look at the lot of you!" he bellows as he meets us on the dock. He walks with his back straight and a silver flask in his right hand. Before he stops in front of us, he takes a swig from the flask, then releases a wet gasp.

Behind him is a massive black ship with silver trimmings. The name *Emellie* is painted on the ship's bow in silver as well. Black-and-ivory sails flap gently in the breeze while several men march along the deck, tossing ropes and washing the deck. One man is in the crow's nest watching us. When I catch his eye, he turns away.

"Captain Solyen, this is the group I was telling you about." Enver gestures to us with a sway of his hand. "They've requested someone to sail them to The Shallows."

Captain Solyen looks at Enver like he's waiting for the punchline. When he doesn't get one, he scans all of us, then a smile spreads across his face. He throws his head back in a laugh—a boisterous, raspy, and slightly annoying laugh. I bet if you listen to him cackle for too long, you'll develop a headache.

Thane sighs while Rynthea huffs, irritated.

"We aren't joking," Rynthea grumbles. "We need a ride to The Shallows *today*."

"And we'll pay you." Thane steps forward with a pouch, holding it by the strings. Captain Solyen's smile fades as he sticks out his hand and accepts the loaded pouch. Tucking his flask beneath his armpit, he opens the pouch and dumps some of the coins into his palm. When he sees all the gold, his eyes grow wide.

"This is a lot of coin you've got here." Solyen looks at us beneath his bushy brows.

"Will it be enough to get us there?" Thane asks.

"Oh—*more than enough*," he assures him, dumping the coins back into the pouch. "But it feels wrong taking money from dead people."

His words make my stomach twist into a thick knot.

"We'll take our chances," Thane tells him.

"You lot are lucky I've got some time on my hands. Next shipment won't be out for another week." Solyen gives each of us a thorough assessment before putting his focus on Enver. "Are they friends of yours?"

"Not all of them," Enver answers. "Just her." He points at me with a smile. I return a half smile but don't miss the way Thane shifts closer to me.

"Well, before you board my sweet *Emellie*, you ought to know that I won't sail you all the way to The Shallows. I'll make a stop and drop a boat for you to row the rest of the way. Unlike you lot, I care about my precious life. Strange things happen the closer you get to that vile island, and I want no part of it."

"Fine." Rynthea shifts on her hooves as she folds her arms.

"'*Fine*,' she says." Solyen chortles to himself. "All right. Get your asses on the ship, since you're so ready to die."

I tuck my thumb under one of the straps of my rucksack and start following everyone to the mouth of the ship—that is until Enver calls my name. He's leaning next to a damp post near the end of the dock. Thane pauses as he eyes me.

"I'll be right there," I assure him.

He nods, giving Enver a bored once-over before turning around again and walking up the gangway.

"Are you absolutely sure about this, Zaira?" Enver asks as I approach him.

"Enver, I don't have a choice."

"You *always* have a choice."

"Oh yeah, you're right," I reply sarcastically. "The better choice here is to let my sister die because I'm a coward."

"Analla wouldn't want you to do this, Zaira, and you know it."

I sigh, shifting my attention to the turquoise waters.

"She would tell you to let it go. To let her handle the consequences," he presses on.

"And she'd also know that I wouldn't listen." I glare at him this time. "I *do* have a choice, Enver, and I've made mine. I'm going."

"How do you know that crew will actually protect you? How do you know they won't leave you hanging as soon as trouble arises?" Enver takes my hand and wraps it in both of his. "You don't know these people, Zaira. You're going to get yourself killed."

"I know them enough."

His eyebrows knit together as he scans me. "I spoke to a visionary last night so I could know more about everyone in your group."

My heart slows in rhythm. "You *what*? Why would you do that?"

"He's a former member of The Divine, Zaira? I can safely assume he's on the run and that they've been searching for him."

I snatch my hand out of his. "Enver, you had no right—"

"I had *every* right," he hisses, thick brows knitting. "You brought danger to my gates! You're lucky I didn't call for Queen Halsenya and report him. The *only* reason I didn't is because I promised you I wouldn't. There has been a bounty on his head for years. You most likely knew this, yet you said *nothing*."

"What does it matter?" I snap. "Like you said, we won't survive The Shallows. We'll all be dead, so there'll be nothing to report to the queen. All your troubles will be gone."

Enver softens now. "Zaira, don't speak like that—"

"I have to go." I give him my back before he can reach for me again and storm up the ramp. The fucking audacity of him.

"What the shadows did he want?" Rynthea asks when I reach her side.

"He just wanted to wish us good luck," I lie, throwing a fake wave at him.

Rynthea makes a noise of disapproval. I'm not sure if she knows I'm lying and possibly heard everything.

When Enver tosses me a wave back, I twist around, close my eyes for a moment, and draw in a deep breath to cool my anger. Then I sit on the nearest bench with Rynthea and send up a prayer of protection to Orvena.

Chapter 43

Once the ship is fueled and crates of food are brought to the cabins, we set sail.

The farther we drift away from Gadonia, it seems to be nothing more than a bright blip in the distance as the sun reflects on buildings trimmed with gold.

"Before you lot get comfortable, you have some rules to follow!" Solyen shouts as he paces back and forth in front of us. "Number one, stay away from the gunwales!"

"The *what*?" Algar asks, gripping a built-in rail.

"The gunwales—the edge of the ship," Solyen explains with a slight roll of his eyes. "This ship is fast, and when I give the wheel a hard steer, I don't send up a warning. One turn can toss you overboard and have you chopped up by the screws." He looks Algar in the eye.

"Yeah, well, you don't have to worry about that." Algar squeezes his eyes shut as he grips the rail tighter, appearing queasy already. Zephra clings to the ankle of his trousers.

"Number two, there will be a point during this journey where you *must* be inside the boat and *must* keep your voices down. I will inform you when that time comes."

"Why?" Rynthea asks.

"Because if you want to make it to The Shallows as quickly as you say, we have to pass through The Void. Ever heard of it?"

"I've heard a bit about it, yeah," she responds.

"Then you'll know The Void is where the worst sea creatures lurk. I don't want them attacking my ship all because a bunch of children can't shut their honey holes."

"Um, what kind of creatures, exactly?" one of Solyen's crew members asks. It's the boy I saw hanging around the crow's nest. He's young—can't be older than his fifteenth or sixteenth year. He seems absolutely petrified as he stares at Solyen's profile.

"Oh, all kinds, boy." Solyen turns his head to eye him. "Sea beasts twice the size of *Emellie* with tongues like snakes. Sharks who eat through metal. Zerenias who sing the sweetest melodies but will bite your bloody dick off once they have you in their clutches."

"Told you," Rynthea mumbles to Algar.

"Not now, Rynthea. Not now." Algar covers his mouth like he's about to be sick.

"Conred, get that one a bucket," Solyen orders, gesturing to Algar. "I don't need him throwing his guts up all over my deck."

Conred runs off, only to return seconds later with a wooden bucket. He pushes it into Algar's chest. Algar wraps his arms around it before stumbling back several feet until his back is pressing against the nearest wall, his shirt a little cockeyed and exposing skin. His back slides down the wall with a squeak of flesh on metal until his butt hits the deck, and he drops his face into the bucket. He looks rough. Zephra hops onto his shoulder again.

"Who knew I was the type to get seasick?" His voice echoes into the hollow of the bucket.

"Don't tell me you've never ridden on a speedship before," Rynthea taunts.

"Never."

"Orvena's sake," she mutters. "Didn't you say your father worked for a sea biologist?"

"He did," Algar mumbles. "But I didn't get to sail with him much, and if I did, we were on regular boats, not ships that go so fast they make you dizzy."

"Rule number three!" Solyen shouts, capturing our attention again. He pauses for a moment, pulls out his flask to unscrew the cap, takes a swig, shrugs, and says, "Actually, there is no rule number three."

"Seriously?" Rynthea mumbles. "This man is going to get us all killed."

"Just make sure you remember rules one and two," Solyen insists before drifting past us. "Carry on. Best that you enjoy your lives now before they come to an end on that island of death." He opens the door to the captain's quarters and disappears inside.

We can't go near the side of the boat, but there are ropes dangling close by, their ends anchored into posts. I walk to one of them and grip it tight, peering over the edge to see the water.

Solyen's magic-powered speedboat is incredibly fast—so fast I can hardly feel the ship rocking or swaying. It seems the *Emellie* is cutting through the sea like a knife through butter.

"Fucking shadows." Algar moans, dropping his face into the bucket again. Zephra gives him two little pats on the head in a *"there, there"* sort of way.

Rynthea removes her rucksack and digs through it until she pulls out a white flower. "Here." She stuffs it into Algar's hand. "Eat a few of those petals."

"What is it?" he croaks.

"Skyflower. I found it in Immalon. It'll curb the nausea."

Algar studies the crumpled flower petals before popping them into his mouth and chewing. Then he sighs and rests his head on the rim of the bucket. With a deep exhale, Rynthea takes the spot beside him.

Thane sits on a bench to sharpen some of his daggers. Our eyes catch, and I give him a smile. A smirk appears before he focuses on his daggers again.

"I take it you love the sea." Someone's voice rises behind me.

I gasp, nearly letting the ropes go as I turn my head to find the culprit.

"Oh no! I'm so sorry!" It's the boy Solyen called Conred. I sway a bit, and he grips the rope to steady it. "Did I startle you?"

"A bit, yeah." I force a laugh.

"I sincerely apologize."

"It's okay."

"May I ask that you stand *behind* the ropes, though?"

"Oh. Uh, yeah. Of course. Sorry." I release the ropes and move back, making sure not to get my feet tangled in the thick lines below.

"It's just that I've seen way too many people trust these things and then we hit a snag in the sea, and they go flying over, ya know?" He releases a nervous laugh.

"Right. That makes sense."

"I'm Conred Joshell." He offers me a hand.

I take it and give it a shake. "Zaira Quinlocke."

I study his features—the deep brown of his skin, the darkness of his coarse hair, and the faded gold streaks in them that can never be replicated. I know exactly where he was born.

"You're from Ember Coast," I say.

"I am!" he exclaims, pleased that I know.

"That's—that's incredible. So am I."

"No way. Do you have any other family around?" he asks.

"Just a sister."

"It's wonderful that you have someone." Conred scratches the top of his head. "I wasn't so lucky."

"I'm sorry to hear that."

"It's not your fault. Besides, after I spent some time in the refugee center in Meriva, I was adopted after just two months. So I'd say that was fortunate."

Ah. That explains why I don't remember his face. I grew to know everyone at the refugee center over the years.

Conred points to the captain's quarters. "Captain Solyen adopted me."

"Oh. That was kind of him."

"Yeah. But other than the fact that he was lonely, I think he just needed a new chief mate. He tells me he wants to pass *Emellie* down to someone one day. He doesn't have children of his own, so…"

"He would leave the ship to you." I nod as it sinks in. "His heir."

"Yep." He takes a step back and looks past me to the others. "The people you're traveling with are an interesting bunch."

"Yeah," I half laugh, half scoff at the comment. "I've heard that quite a lot lately."

He studies each of them with a faint, intrigued smile. "You all seem very close…but distant. I can't quite put my finger on it."

"Yeah, well…" I let the words go. I'm not quite sure how to explain our crew, either. Our relationships are complicated at best and a shit show at the very least. And mine with Thane? Well, our lines have blurred—a lot…

"Anyway, I was just about to go inside for some tea and sweet rolls." Conred points at a door across the deck with a half-moon window. "Would you like some?"

I light up at the mention of food and tea. "I'd love that."

Chapter 44

Emellie's interior smells of wet wood and cinnamon. Beds are built into the hull of the ship, held by metal beams. They are all neatly made with white sheets and gray quilts. A small galley is set up in a corner at the far end, where Conred prepares the tea and rolls.

I sit at one of the two square tables and enjoy the cinnamon scent wafting from a batch of freshly baked cookies on a tray.

"Would you like one?" Conred asks, cocking his head at the cookies on the counter as he prepares the tea. "Beka makes them. He's the quiet one with the nick in his ear. He's a good chef but an even better baker."

Conred approaches the table with a tray of rolls in one hand and a steaming pot of tea in the other.

"That's all right." I reach for a sweet roll. "This roll looks incredible. I'll have to tell Beka I'm a baker, too."

"Are you?"

"Yes—well, I'm more of a baker's apprentice," I explain.

Conred bobs his head as he picks up the teapot and leans over to pour the hot liquid into two tin mugs. As he does, a gold chain falls from his neckline. Attached to it is a pendant shaped like a *C* with a pearl embedded in the center of the letter.

I can't help but gasp when I see the necklace. It looks so similar to mine.

Oh, how I miss my necklace.

Conred catches me looking at the bauble.

"Pearls make me think of home," he comments with a wistful smile, sliding one of the mugs my way.

I lean in to get a closer look. "Me too. Your necklace is really nice."

"My father made jewelry with pearls. He made this for me." Conred fingers his pendant. "He traveled a lot selling his jewelry. It used to make me sad when he wasn't around." He sips his tea, a dejected look clouding his vision. "But sometimes I wonder if he'd still be here if he had been traveling during the attacks. You know?"

"I completely understand."

"But I'm grateful to be with Solyen," he tosses in quickly. "He looks out for me, and it's nice to be out at sea."

"I'm glad he's provided a great life for you." I bite into a sweet roll as three bells on the ceiling give a light jingle. "What are those for?" I ask, pointing up.

"Those just let us know when the waters are getting too choppy," Conred answers. "Light chimes are good, means we're smooth sailing. But if the bells get loud or ring too quickly, it means the waters are getting rough…or that something is attacking the ship."

The door of the cabin swings open, and Thane appears in the frame, dripping in black per usual. He looks from me to Conred, and I assume he doesn't see Conred as much of a threat because he doesn't glower.

"Oh, hello." Conred smiles, looking from Thane to me, then back at Thane again. "Would you like to join us? We're just having some tea."

Thane gives a simple nod, and Conred scurries to the galley to collect another mug.

"I don't believe I caught your name." Conred places the mug down in front of him, pouring hot tea into it.

"Never offered it," Thane mutters, picking up the mug.

"Oh." Conred flushes as he drops down in his chair.

"Don't let his asshole-ish ways get to you."

Conred laughs nervously. After composing himself, he says, "I'm curious why you all want to go to The Shallows so badly. Most people steer clear of that area."

"There's something on the island we need," I inform him.

"What? Like treasure or something?" he asks eagerly.

"That...among other things." I glance at Thane. He's chewing and ignoring us both.

"Well, you all are very brave, I'll give you that. I'm already shaking thinking about how close we have to get to that island. Sort of wishing Solyen left me in Gadonia for this trip." He lets out yet another nervous laugh while staring into his teacup.

"You *should* be scared." Thane licks his fingers before lifting the rim of his mug to his lips and taking a gulp. "You're a child. You don't belong anywhere near The Shallows."

"Well, I'm in my sixteenth year, so I wouldn't say I'm *that* much of a child," Conred objects with a collapsing smile.

Thane sighs. "Why don't you ask Solyen how much longer we have?" His question is more of a demand.

"Uh—sure. I'll do that." Conred gives me an uneasy look as he stands. "Be right back."

When he leaves the cabin, I slap Thane on his upper arm. He doesn't even flinch. "Why are you so mean to everyone? He's being really nice and accommodating to us."

"*Too* nice, if you ask me."

"There is no such thing," I counter.

"In my world, there is."

"Some people are just nice and want company. I wish you'd stop making that out to be a bad trait in people." I fold my arms. "Besides, I feel sorry for him. He seems to be the youngest one on this ship. He probably can't relate much to the rest of the crew."

Thane studies me a moment before polishing off his tea and placing the cup down. Then he digs into the pocket of his leather pants to pull something out.

"I needed him to get out so I could give you something. Hold out your hand."

I shoot him a wary look. "Why?"

With an agitated sigh, he reaches for my wrist and turns my hand over so my palm is facing up. "Close your eyes," he commands, and I do as I'm told—which is a first.

He carefully places something in my palm. The object snakes into my hand until I feel something unusually hot hit my skin.

"Open them."

When I see what it is, all breath escapes me, and tears instantly prickle in my eyes.

"My necklace," I gasp. I whip my gaze up to meet his, stunned. "How did you— I mean, where did this—"

"I took it back."

"What do you mean?" I stammer.

"The day we left Meriva, when you made a stop in the refugee center," he begins. "I went to the pawn shop and spoke to the owner. Told him to give it to me or I'd cut every single one of his fingers off."

"Oh my gods, Thane. Seriously? He'll remember my face. He'll probably think I set him up." I don't want to laugh, but I can't help it. I've clearly been hanging around him for too long if I find threat of dismemberment deeply romantic. Then something dawns on me. "Wait a minute. How did you even know which pawn shop I went to?"

He gives me a knowing look.

"Of course you *followed* me that night." I scoff. "You are quite the stalker."

He shifts in his chair. "I told you, I had to make sure you were serious about going to the temple. After hearing that it was a gift from your mother and seeing you go to the refugee center, I suspected you were an orphan. But then hearing what you said in Frevella's cave about the attacks in your kingdom…" He shook his head in disbelief. "Selling something that important just to hire me proved that you really wanted this journey to happen."

"Oh." I drop my line of vision to the necklace. "I didn't think you were listening when I first told you it was my mother's."

He shakes his head with a lopsided smile. "I wouldn't be any good at what I do if I didn't listen to the important details." He studies the necklace as I finger the gold ribbons. "I'm always listening to what you have to say, Zaira. Your opinions matter more to me now than I want to admit."

I blink my tears away, smiling at him as I curl my fingers around the pendant. "Thank you, Thane."

He nods, then stands as he reaches for the necklace. "I'll help you put it on."

I let him take it as he circles my chair. As he brings the chain down, the pendant lands on my chest. It's still hot, so Analla must be alive. I take that as a small comfort. The familiar feel of it around my neck makes me want to cry. When he clasps it, he walks around me and sits again.

"If you've had it all this time, why did you wait so long to give it back?" I ask.

"Wasn't sure if I wanted you to know that I followed you that night."

"You mean you didn't want me to consider you some kind of stalker before I actually got to know you?" I tease.

He cracks a smile. "Guess you could say that."

He leans in so close that I can feel his breath swim across my skin. I lower my eyes to his lips as he grabs my hip and his fingers dig into my waist.

"Any regrets?" he asks in a low voice.

"About last night?"

"Yeah."

"I don't know yet." I pause. "You?"

His lips press to mine, and he kisses me lightly. "I don't know yet, either."

He kisses me again, drawing me closer and coaxing my lips farther apart. My knees slide between his legs, and I clasp his face in my hands, moaning as his fingers drag up my spine. Before our kiss can deepen, the bells on the ceiling ring loudly. I pull away with a gasp, looking up as they thrash back and forth.

"What the…?" Thane stares up, breathy and confused. Something hard slams into the boat, and we teeter sideways. He catches us, and I cling to him as the mugs fall on the wooden floorboards.

The door of the cabin bursts open, and Rynthea appears with her scythesword in hand, eyes wide with alarm. "Thane, get out here! *Now!*"

"What's happening?" I call as Thane hops up and snatches out one of his swords.

"Something is attacking the ship!" she yells.

Chapter 45

"Stay inside, Zaira." Thane dashes after Rynthea before I can respond. In a flash, he's out of the cabin and on the deck, while Algar shifts past him, stumbling his way inside with Zephra flying close behind him. Something hits the boat again, and I stumble sideways until my shoulder slams into the wall.

"What's out there?" I shriek as Algar grips a ledge.

"A fucking *water dragon*, that's what! Where is their storage? The cupboards! *Something!*" Algar hustles across the room to reach the kitchen and immediately starts searching the cupboards.

Panicked, I ask, "What are you doing?"

He doesn't answer me, just keeps rifling through the cupboards.

I rush to the door and take a few steps out on the deck…and what I see sends a chilling spiral of fear through my body.

Ahead of us, towering above the ship, is indeed a dragon. Its teeth are sharp and pointed, its eyes glowing a vicious blue. Gills bracket either side of its head, and its ridged belly is a pale gray. The rest of it is the color of ice, as if its skin is designed to camouflage with the water. That seems the most terrifying of all.

Not the fangs.

Not its intense eyes.

The *camouflage*.

The thought of such a massive beast swimming close to the shores without a single person knowing...

I shudder.

"Bring out the cannons!" Solyen shouts from a distance. He stands on the other side of the deck with a machete in hand. Like a spider, Thane climbs the ladder to the crow's nest while Rynthea stands guard next to Solyen, gripping the handle of her scythesword and preparing for attack.

When Thane makes it to the crow's nest, he sheathes one of his swords. In the palm of that free hand, he creates a ball of gold light. The dragon notices him and snarls, opening its mouth wider and blowing a blue stream in his direction.

Thane jumps and lands on the deck with a tuck and a roll before the water can reach him. He's damn lucky, too, because the crow's nest now sizzles, as if the liquid is made of acid.

"Zaira, get back inside!" Thane hollers when he catches sight of me.

I run back to the door, but I hear a wild roar and turn to see the dragon launching its head forward, ready to spout another stream of venomous water. When it does, Thane throws up his hands and deflects it with a broad gold shield that sparks from the impact.

The dragon, clearly angry, sinks below the waterline and slams its body into the ship again. Rynthea falls, Thane lurches to the side, and I spot Conred and two other members of Solyen's crew trying to secure the rolling cannons. This is my cue to really get my ass back into the cabin, so I dash inside.

Slamming the door behind me, I spot Algar standing in a storage closet near the galley. Various junk spills out around his feet as his hunched figure digs through it in a frenzy.

I notice a glimpse of pink, presumably the tip of Zephra's wing, poking out from under a pillow on one of the beds. She must be even more terrified than me, considering her size.

"Algar, what the shadows are you doing?" I ask, spying the basket of fish on the counter.

"I learned about those," he says in a hurry, dropping to his knees and searching through the lower half of the cabinets. "Water dragons. My father studied the larger sea creatures—the rare kind—and his favorite were the water dragons. Don't ask me why. He was mental. That's clearly where I get it from."

"Okay?" I say, puzzled, as he digs deeper into the cabinet. He curses under his breath, stands up, and rushes to the next cabinet.

"Water dragons only attack when they feel their nest is being threatened," he goes on. "This dragon is a mother. I can tell by the horns. Male dragons have four, females have two. Trust me, we don't want to go up against an angry daddy dragon. Anyway, in order for this mother to back off *and* to prove to her that we aren't here to tamper with her sea dragon babies, eggs, or whatever, we have to send her a signal of peace."

"Okay." I run my tongue over my lips nervously. "And how do we do that?"

"Yes!" It's like he's struck alvanite. Algar backs out of the cabinet with a bucket of paint in one of his hands. "Fuck yes! I knew they'd have paint around here somewhere."

"Algar, how do we give it the signal?" I ask again, trying to remain calm.

"What's the way to a woman's heart?" he asks, grabbing a paint brush out of the storage closet, too.

Pearls? Gold? Unconditional love?

"Love?"

"No. Food." He rushes to the door with the basket of fish and paint supplies.

Algar hobbles his way outside, and I stand in the frame of the open door, watching as he shouts Thane's name. The dragon bumps the boat again, this time sending dishes flying out of the open cupboards and crashing to the floor. I yelp as I hold on to the rail by the door. Algar says something to Thane, then repeats it to Rynthea and Solyen.

"Are you mad?" Solyen yells.

"Trust me, it will work!" Algar yells back. "Just don't fire the cannons! You'll only piss her off more!"

Solyen isn't pleased. Regardless, he throws up a hand to halt his crew members, who obediently stop loading the cannons. Algar hustles to the center of the deck with the items he's taken from the cupboards.

He removes the lid from the paint can and sloshes the brush into it. Thick silver paint drips from the bristles. He goes to work immediately, stumbling a few times as the boat rocks.

He creates a circle with a hastily drawn wave inside it. It's sloppy work, but Algar apparently deems it acceptable because he stands and mutters to himself while nodding in approval.

The dragon breaches the water again, and her massive head hovers above the ship. Water drips in streams from her chin. Her mouth opens wide, ready to spew more acid-venom.

"Algar, hurry up!" Rynthea shouts.

The dragon's nostrils flare, liquid accumulating in the back of her throat. Thane raises his gold-lit hands, ready to deflect it with another shield, while Rynthea stares up in a defensive stance, scythesword still locked in hand.

"Hey!" Algar calls, waving his hands in the air.

The dragon snarls and brings her head down so that she's eye-to-eye with Algar. Her glowing blue eyes swirl like the tidal pools on Ember Coast, water trickling through her shimmering scales.

"That's right! Right here!" Algar tries to make himself as large as possible. "We don't want to hurt you!" He gestures to the symbol he painted on the deck. "We aren't here to hurt you or your family! This is our signal of peace! We yield to you! All we want is to pass!" He kicks the basket of fish forward.

The dragon finally clamps her mouth shut. She looks from Algar to the painting to the fish and then back to Algar. Her head tips to the right as a low croak sounds in her throat. Blood rushes to my ears as I hold my breath, waiting to see what the water dragon does next.

She blinks at Algar, observing the painting that is smearing around the edges, and the full basket of fish. Then she stretches her mouth open and aims directly for him.

I scream, but he just stands there. That's when I realize she's not going for him. She's aiming for the fish. She takes the entire basket into her mouth, swallows without chewing, then chuffs as she glares at him, expecting more.

Algar puffs out a breath as he approaches her. He drops to his knees before he presses his hands to her muzzle.

I hold my breath.

"Passage...please?" he requests in a trembling voice.

A satisfied rumble sounds in the dragon's throat as she blinks, eyes swiveling to look at everyone on board. Then she pulls her head away with another chuff and backs away from the ship. With one last glimpse at us, she slinks away and disappears beneath the waves.

We all collectively release a breath, standing in disbelief as we stare at the patch of ocean where she descended, waiting to see if she'll return.

After another calm moment, Thane turns to Algar and says, "What just happened? Where did it go?"

"Probably back to her nest," Algar says, panting. "Fuck, that was scary," he wheezes. "Almost pissed on myself."

"Is it coming back?" Thane asks.

"I doubt it. Back in the day, mortals used to share symbols of peace with water dragons when they voyaged," Algar explains. "These symbols helped them get past the water dragons if they encountered them. So she recognized my horribly painted symbol of peace, ate the fish as an offering, *and* she let me place my hands on her." He smiles, seeming proud of that. "They are exceptionally smart, but when it comes to their territory, they attack first and assess later. She thought we were intruding, and that's why she was about to destroy the ship. We had to prove to her that we weren't bringing any trouble."

"So let me get this straight." Solyen steps forward with a hand raised. "Had she not watched you make a fool of yourself, *and* if she hadn't eaten *half of our supply* of fish, my sweet *Emellie* would be sinking to the bottom of the ocean right now?"

"That's correct," he replies. "Better for us to be a little hungry than drowning or getting hit with her venom, right?"

Solyen presses a palm to his head. "Orvena, send love. I need another drink," he grumbles. "Find this man a shirt that doesn't stink like fish and scrub that paint off my deck! We'll be passing The Void soon, and everyone needs to get their asses in the cabin."

"For once, Algar saves the day," Rynthea says when she meets up with him. She claps him on the shoulder and smiles. "Proud of you."

Algar winks at her. "See? A charmer thief comes in handy every once in a while."

Chapter 46

Conred was right. Beka *is* an amazing baker, and an equally great chef, too.

We sit at the tables with the ship crew, eating the remaining fish along with roasted vegetables as the *Emellie* glides through the waters. Since the water dragon, nothing has come up. Thankfully.

Night has fallen, and we're passing through The Void. Captain Solyen has asked us to remain inside and to keep quiet.

I can't imagine what else is out there. What if zerenias start singing? Or giant crabs appear? Or worse, a male water dragon this time?

I want to shake the thoughts off, but it's hard to do considering how loud the wind is howling. I hear faint creaks and groans, but I'm not sure if the sounds are coming from the ship or the creatures outside of it.

After dinner, Rynthea and I take the remaining bunks, while Algar and Thane are given thick cots with fresh quilts to set up beside our beds.

"You should all get some sleep," Conred whispers when he meets at our beds. "Captain Solyen says we're only a few hours out from your stopping point. Remember to keep your voices low for now."

"We will, Conred," I whisper. "Sleep well."

"You too, Zaira." He walks off and climbs into his bed.

The four ship crew members take the top bunks. The crew is nearly asleep by this point, bellies full and minds fuzzy from ale.

"You know what?" Algar whispers from the floor. I look over the edge of the mattress at him. He's lying on his back with his hands tucked behind his head.

"What?" I whisper back.

"I should've become a sea biologist, lived out my father's dream." His voice drops to a low murmur. "I used to hate it because he talked about it nonstop and spent so much time at sea away from us, but now I understand why. The creatures are exhilarating."

"Instead, you became a conman with charmer tricks." Rynthea laughs quietly. "I bet your father is *so* proud."

"He's dead, actually." Algar's eyes fall to Zephra, who is asleep on his chest, purring as she cuddles with her tail. "He and my mother died in a fire. I was there when it happened."

I sit up as Rynthea does, my face falling with concern. Even Thane gives Algar a curious glance before staring at the ceiling once again.

"I'm sorry to hear that, Algar," I whisper.

"It was years ago," he murmurs, brushing it off. "But today reminded me a lot of him."

"I didn't mean to offend you," Rynthea says in a soft voice.

"It's all right, Ryn. Don't stress it." His voice, though riddled with humor, is still sad.

Someone on the other side of the room says, "Shh!"

There's a long silence, filled only by the light snoring of the crew, the soft tinkling of the bells overhead, and the odd groans and creaks of the ship.

Rynthea slides to the end of the bed, giving the top of Algar's head a light ruffle. "No wonder you're such a jester. You joke to bury your feelings."

Algar chuckles under his breath. "No, I've been funny all my life, actually. If I don't laugh through the bullshit, I'll lose my spark, you know?"

"I understand exactly how you feel when it comes to your parents," I say, voice barely a whisper. "I lost my parents during the Ruvain attacks."

"And you know about my parents," Rynthea adds, chin dropping an inch.

Thane sighs. "So we've all had shitty childhoods, then?"

"Seems so. But that's life in Thelanor, isn't it?" Algar says.

We huddle closer together, so our voices blend in with the quiet snores of the crew. "There is no safety here," Algar continues. "No security. So we do what we must to survive. I started stealing and tricking people to keep me fed. Eventually, I started doing it in Junsho and Ruvain."

"And landed your ass in jail," Thane butts in.

Rynthea and I snicker quietly.

"I tried to make an honest living, but that shit was hard." Algar wipes the wrinkles from his forehead. "An honest living doesn't provide as well as an immoral one."

We digest that, sitting in silence for a second.

"Well," Thane says, sighing. "Nothing can be worse than your own father selling you off for a pouch of coins."

Rynthea and Algar stare at Thane, shocked by his sudden confession. He blinks at the tinkling bells on the ceiling with his jaw flexing.

"Is that what happened to you?" Algar whispers, sitting up on his elbows. "Is that why I never saw you again until all those years later?"

Thane nods. Hearing it again out loud is no less painful than when he told me the first time.

"He sold you to The Divine?" Algar prods.

"He sold me to some tradesmen who *then* sold me for twice as much to The Divine." Thane scratches the area of his shirt where his tattoo is. The tattoo that is now branded in exile.

Rynthea points at him. "So *that's* why you're such an asshole. Sorcerer with daddy issues."

I'm surprised to see Thane's mouth twitch as he tries to suppress a laugh.

"Look, can we all just make a promise tonight?" I request, eyeing each of them. "Can we promise that when we reach The Shallows, we'll have one another's backs no matter what? That no matter what happens or what we face, we'll do everything we can to make sure we all get out of that place alive?"

Rynthea gives me a warm smile. "I can't guarantee we'll make it out alive, but I've got your back, Zaira. I promise you that."

"As do I." Algar squeezes my hand. "I have all your backs."

"Same," whispers Rynthea.

We turn our attention to Thane, but he's staring at the wall on the other side of the cabin.

"Thane?" I call in a hushed voice.

Sitting up, he pulls his legs to his chest and rests his arms on his knees. "I've had all your backs thus far. What's stopping me from continuing that in The Shallows?"

I smile as it feels like a weight has fallen off my shoulders. It feels nice to not bicker for once. We're of one accord, all willing to protect one another…sort of like family would.

Thane holds my attention as Rynthea murmurs, "You'd better. I hate admitting this, but you're the most skilled of all of us. And this is coming from someone who has trained for combat her whole life."

"Wow. Is that a compliment from the otherwise hostile minotaur?" Thane smirks.

"All right. Don't milk it, sorcerer." Rynthea slides under her sheets again. "I'm getting some rest. Want to be prepared for whatever that place throws at us."

"Yeah." Algar yawns as he lies back down. "Same."

I climb into my bed again as Thane lounges back on his cot. For a moment, I watch his chest rise and fall as he breathes. It's hard for me *not* to ask more about his childhood.

He once had a brother.

He trained with The Divine.

He has The Shadow Guild's ink on his back.

Now he's here.

What more is there to Thane Valkor's story?

Hopefully, I'll live long enough to find out. Hopefully, we all will.

Because tomorrow we'll arrive at The Shallows.

Chapter 47

The bells on the ceiling jingle, and I sit up in bed.

For a moment, I panic, thinking we're under attack again. But the cabin is still and dark, except for the dim light emanating from a dripping pillar candle in the galley. The creaking and groaning sounds I heard before falling asleep have faded. The bells tinkle on, but the sound is light compared to earlier with the water dragon.

I blow out a breath, squinting at my crew.

Rynthea and Algar are asleep.

I don't need full vision to see that Thane isn't on his cot.

Putting on my spectacles, I swing my legs over the edge of the bed, then walk to the door that leads to the deck, opening it as quietly as possible. I listen for any sounds of danger, fortunate to come across none. The sea is calm, a soothing, dull roar I could listen to all night. The crescent moon hangs in the sky like a beacon, surrounded by infinite twinkling stars.

I step out with caution, looking to the left where Captain Solyen's quarters are.

"We've already passed The Void," a deep voice says.

I nearly jump out of my skin in surprise.

Thane sits near the edge of the boat on a bench facing the moon—his mask, swords, and cowl are nowhere in sight, but he does have a dagger in his hand. Suddenly, he flings the dagger at the nearest wooden beam. It penetrates the wood, lodging right in the center. Bull's-eye. With a flick of his wrist and a flurry of gold, the dagger is freed and returned to Thane's outstretched hand.

"What are you doing out here, Thane?" I ask, folding my arms as a chill wraps around me.

"Couldn't sleep." He scans me up and down, eyes blazing. I'm only wearing a beige tunic that stops mid-thigh and underwear underneath. "Think it's wise to walk around like that on a ship full of men?"

"They're all asleep." I make my way to the bench so I can sit next to him. "Which you should be doing."

"How can I sleep with you in such a state of undress?" he asks, scanning my legs.

I ignore his comment, carrying my gaze around the deck again instead. I don't see any of the ship crew.

"I'm with you now, so I'm safe, right?"

"You're always safe with me, Zaira."

I smile.

We've made it out of The Void unharmed, which is good. The only proof that we passed through is that there are a few tears in the sails.

"I don't sleep much anyway." Thane's voice pulls my attention away from the dead bug.

"I see that."

He tucks the dagger away with a sigh. "When I was in The Divine, they trained us to withstand sleep deprivation, so we'd always be ready to protect the kingdom no matter the hour. I can catch up to three or four hours a night if needed, but not sleeping has been instilled in me." He shrugs. "Old habits truly do die hard."

"Oh." I hug my arms tighter around myself. I want to ask more about his time with The Divine, but I also don't want to push it. He's finally opening up to all of us, but it has to be at his own pace.

The ocean's rumble and whistling wind occupy the silence.

"I want you to be prepared for what we have to do to get the tome...if we make it that far," Thane says. "We have to find the room where it resides. It will most likely be hidden, so I'll need to figure out how to find it. Once I do, it will only take a drop or two of your blood and the tome is mine."

I nod my head.

"Are you worried?" I finally ask. "About The Shallows?"

He tips his chin. "I would be a liar if I said I wasn't."

"Yeah." My teeth sink into my bottom lip. "I'm scared for everyone, you know? I want us all to get what we need and survive that damn place." I scrape a nail over the edge of the bench. "But that's wishful thinking, right?"

"*Highly* wishful." He smirks.

I bite back a smile. "I know I can be a little naive sometimes. Analla always says so."

"I don't know. After spending all this time with you, I'm starting not to see it as naivety," he returns. "You're just optimistic. That trait is hard to come by in Thelanor." He tilts his head both ways to give his neck a crack. "Your home was attacked when you were younger. You lost your parents because of it. Grew up an orphan. Your sister is cursed…and yet you keep this massive amount of hope inside you."

I lower my gaze to study my toes. Hearing him lay my life out like that does make it sound quite depressing.

"Without hope, life in Thelanor is pointless, Thane. I don't like to let those tragic moments define me. I like that I get to control the narrative about who I am. I mean, if you think about it, my emotions are the only thing I truly have authority over. I refuse to waste it on being angry about my past."

Our eyes connect, and his wrinkle around the edges in understanding.

Then he clasps my chin between his thumb and forefinger, keeping hold of my gaze. "It's not just your hope that gets me, Zaira," he murmurs. "It's the goodness in you, too. How can you still have such a good heart *and* good intentions after what you've been through? How can you be so willing to risk your life for something that may not even be there, all to save someone else?"

"I guess that's a part of my optimism," I reply. "I tell myself if I hope hard enough, or pray to Orvena, even, that what I need will come to fruition somehow."

He raises an eyebrow. "But that must come with some form of disappointment."

I shrug. "Sometimes."

He takes the warmth of his fingers away. I instantly miss his touch.

"Anyway"—I throw up my hands to lighten the mood again—"if we don't all make it out alive tomorrow, I want to thank you now."

He looks down. "No need to thank me, Quinlocke."

"No, seriously." I collect his face in my hands. His stubble is coarse beneath my fingers, his scars enhanced by shadows and moonlight. I graze the pad of my thumb over his lips, and he releases a defeated sigh. "You didn't have to come all this way with me. You didn't have to protect me. But you *did*, Thane. I'll owe you for the rest of my life if I survive this."

"What I asked for is enough."

"Yes, but coins are material. They don't represent my feelings. I'll owe you much more than that, especially if we save Analla. You may not believe it, but I think you have a good heart beneath all those weapons, dark clothes, and moody expressions. A good person wouldn't have risked so much just to help another person reach death island." A smile spreads over my face just as it does his.

"That's where you're wrong," he responds. "There is no good left in me. There is no light. It was drowned in darkness years ago. But thanks for believing it's possible for an assassin to have a good heart, I guess."

"I *know* it's possible."

His mouth inches closer to mine. My breathing accelerates as he brings a hand up to cup the back of my head.

"Just promise me something," he whispers on my lips.

"What?"

"Promise me that you won't be too disappointed if none of the stones are there."

"I'll try not to be."

That's a lie. I'll be devastated. But I'll keep hoping.

I clutch a handful of his tunic in one hand as the tip of his nose runs over mine. Then, after removing my spectacles and tucking them into the pocket of my top, he guides my head forward so our lips can touch—gentle at first, then deep and all-consuming.

I moan, exhilarated that I can taste him again. He buries his fingers deep in my hair as his warm tongue parts my lips. I sigh as he kisses me harder, with so much burning passion it seems we'll ignite.

When I rest my back on the bench, he straddles it—straddles me—and kisses the curve of my neck, my collarbone, my chest. This kiss is everything I've been craving since we were interrupted by the dragon. He guides the lower half of his body between my thighs, grinding his erection up and down in a slow, torturous manner against my thin underwear.

"I need to be inside you again," he says in a ragged voice.

"Yes, please."

I let out a small yelp as he picks me up in his arms and carries me across the deck to the nearest washroom. The door creaks when he pushes it open. The space is tight and small, but Thane manages to squeeze us both in and shut the door behind us.

He seats me on the countertop and consumes me again as he pushes the fabric of my tunic up and over my head while his magic tugs at the waistband of my underwear.

Cupping the back of his neck, I reel him in again and press my lips to his. A groan rattles in his throat as his real hand slides up my inner thigh. He skims that same hand up a bit more, grazing my sex. Bringing his mouth to the crook of my neck, he drags the pad of one of his fingers over my sweet bundle of nerves, and a shiver of pleasure runs down my spine.

"Fuck," he growls after hissing through his teeth. "You're always so wet, sweet one."

He dips a finger inside me, followed by another. I writhe on the counter, a needy moan escaping me. I can't stand the teasing anymore. I need him just as badly as he needs me.

I reach for his trousers and untie them, but his invisible hand stops me and pushes me backward so I'm pressed against the wall. Thane's eyes flash, and something warm wraps around my wrists, pulling them to either side of me.

I attempt to free myself but can't budge.

"Thane…"

Lowering to one knee, he pushes my thighs farther apart.

"I just want you to sit there," he murmurs, bringing his face closer to my sex. "Don't move. Just sit there and let me *taste* you."

Oh, gods. He's trying to make me scream from such naughty words.

He runs his tongue over his bottom lip, eyes pinned on mine as he pulls my bottom closer to the edge of the counter. Before I know it, his hot tongue is skimming through me.

"Oh my gods," I gasp. Even though I know it's coming, the feeling is completely unexpected. I've never experienced this before. The sensation is new and intense and…*wonderful*.

My breaths become wild, chaotic, as his tongue circles my bud and sends gratifying vibrations through my body. I squeeze my eyes shut, helpless moans bursting out of me as he burrows deeper.

"Open your eyes, Zaira," he commands between licks. "Look at me."

I peel my eyes open, panting raggedly as he cups my hips and devours me like I'm the sweetest fruit. Every lap of his tongue has the perfect amount of pressure. Every one of his groans makes mine increase in volume.

I feel the restraints around my wrists fade away the longer he watches me. As I gaze down at him, he slides a hand up my tunic and caresses my nipples.

"Thane…" My hips buck as he continues to stroke and suck. "Thane… *please*."

His next groan is deeper. The rolling and kneading of my nipples only elevate the sensations. I've never felt so built up, so overwhelmed with pleasure to the point I'm afraid to let go.

But eventually, I'm left with no choice. Thane's sole focus in this moment is to satisfy me. And it has arrived in full.

I clutch a handful of his thick hair and throw my head back to cry out in pleasure.

But does he stop there? No, he still circles his tongue in gentle swirls that make me twitch. Repeatedly.

"Oh, fuck," I breathe, whimpering.

"Damn, Zaira." He kisses my pelvis. "I swear watching you come for me will never get old."

When he stands, I tug at the strings of his pants, wanting the real thing.

He chuckles. "So greedy."

He's right.

I am greedy.

I'm *insatiable* for this man. I've never felt so drawn to someone, to the point that all I want is for him to take me over and over and over again. This connection we have is both electrifying and terrifying.

Thane pushes his pants down and grips himself. He's already hard as rock. He slowly strokes himself with one hand while the other angles my hips just right. I press my palms down on the counter for balance as he brings his mouth to mine, tasting of my essence.

He gradually kisses me as he slides inside me, filling me inch by every savory inch.

"Oh shit," he curses on my mouth. "So fucking tight."

He begins with slow strokes and fervent kisses. One hand keeps steady on my hip while the other wraps around the back of my neck. His guttural groans fill the confines of the washroom as he swallows my moans.

"It feels so good being lost inside you." He groans into the bend of my neck. "If only I could stay buried deep within you for the rest of my days… Life would truly be marvelous."

"You have no idea how much I want the same thing," I say as his steady strokes evolve into rigid thrusts.

He curses again, sucking on the soft skin of my neck. His thrusts pick up in speed, and his deep moans become twice as loud. The room shines gold from his ignited hands—the same hands holding my face. I circle my legs around his waist to guide him deeper, pleased by the burning light of his clear excitement and enjoyment. I feel him swell inside me, on the brink of release as I inch closer to the edge yet again.

The light brightens the thicker his breathing becomes, to the point it's nearly blinding, but he doesn't stop—not until I feel that familiar heat rise up through my toes and burst through me. I can't help but cry his name as I fall.

In a sudden movement, he snatches his mouth away, jerks back, and pulls out of me. I reach out and fist him until he, too, reaches that precipice with a groan and spills on my thigh.

"Shadows," he rasps, breathless. The glow fades ever so slowly, putting us back in dim, flickering candlelight. "You are so good."

I blush when he gives me a lazy smile. We linger like this for a moment, basking in the bliss of what we've done. Eventually, he snaps out of his trance to pull his trousers up, then finds a hand towel in the bin under the basin to clean me up.

I hop off the counter, smiling up at him as I fix my rumpled tunic and then put my spectacles on. He smiles back, palms one side of my face in his large hand, and kisses me softly.

"I hate that this has to come to an end," I tell him in a soft voice.

He studies the details of my face, his thumb stroking the lobe of my ear. "It'll be for the best, little mortal. You know it."

Sighing, I press my forehead to his chest, but that's when I notice his necklace again. I pick my head back up to lift the scorpion-shaped pendant. It's bumpy and has a thick tail.

"Does this necklace mean something?" I ask.

His eyes darken a notch. "It was a gift for my brother. I gave it to him a few months before he died."

"Oh." I release the pendant. "Why a scorpion? If you don't mind me asking."

He's quiet for a moment as he lifts the pendant to study it himself. "He cried one day because he lost a fight during training. He was beating himself up about how he should've taken a certain punch but didn't want to hurt the other person too badly so he held back. When I gave him this, I told him: 'We can't afford to be doves, Koa. We don't have the privilege of flying high and soaring in peace.'" His throat bobs. "I told him since we weren't raised with grace, we have to be scorpions instead. If we don't strike first—if we don't sting to protect ourselves—we stand to lose everything."

"Wow." I take a moment to let those words marinate. "That's very... profound."

"Not profound enough, obviously." He tucks the pendant away.

We leave the washroom, but before heading to the cabin, Thane walks toward the side of the boat to chuck the hand towel overboard.

"Good idea." I giggle. No one deserves an encounter with a crusty towel.

When Thane sits on the bench, pensively staring at the endless horizon, I join him. I huddle up against him, basking in his warmth. The ocean sound is soothing, almost enough to make me sleepy again.

"I want him dead as much as you do," Thane says after a while. "You know that, right?"

I take my head out of the crook of his arm and look up at his face, which is now bathed in moonlight. "Seferin?" I ask.

He clenches his jaw. "He took everything from me."

Goose bumps dot my flesh when I realize he's about to open up again. This time, they're not from the cold.

"Seferin was one of The Divine's biggest advocates once. Did you know that?"

I shake my head.

"For years, he helped generals and trained some of the soldiers, including me and Koa. We believed in him because he believed in us." Thane scoffs and shakes his head. "He told us that he was going to launch a special unit and recruit some of the strongest guards from The Divine. He promised me and my brother so many good things, said we'd be unstoppable in our magic, and swore he'd *never* separate us. That's all I cared about—never being apart from my brother."

I nod in understanding. "I know that feeling all too well."

"I know you do, sweet one." He plants a gentle kiss on my forehead.

I smile.

"Anyway, Seferin made us swear to keep his plans a secret, and we thought we were in on this wonderful thing. I mean, think about it. This powerful sorcerer wanted to recruit *us* and make us nearly as strong as he was. It sounded like a dream, too good to be true. And you know what they say about things that are too good to be true…" Thane looks out at the dark ocean, shaking his head. "I wanted only the best for myself and Koa. We'd been through so much, so we deserved it."

I don't know where this story is going, but I grab his hand and rub a reassuring thumb over his knuckles.

"We'd leave Meriva and train deep in the forests near Ruvain where no one could hear or see us," he goes on. "We trained so hard and for so long, we were left with no choice but to get better." His jaw ticks as he lowers his gaze to the deck. "Then, one night, Seferin said he needed us to retrieve something from the royal vaults in the Crystal Palace. Neither Koa nor I had been given permission before to patrol *inside* the Crystal Palace. I should've taken that as a sign that something was off. But Seferin gave us the order, so we didn't think twice. We went to the vault and retrieved the Sunderstone Crystal. Alarms immediately went off, and guards came after us. We tried to explain we were there on Seferin's orders, but they didn't listen. They just attacked. I had no choice but to fight back."

Something that looks a lot like shame seizes him.

"I murdered them," he says in a low, pained voice. "And I knew deep down that Seferin knew this would happen because he helped us escape Meriva with the Sunderstone under one condition…"

"That you join The Shadow Guild," I finish.

He nods, and that confirmation makes my heart ache for him and Koa—for their betrayal.

"But I don't understand. Why would he ruin his relationship with the queen and The Divine?" I ask.

"Because he never had good intentions for the kingdom and especially not us, Zaira," he answers through gritted teeth. "He knew from the start we were hopeless fools fueled by dreams and ambition, and he used every ounce of that for his own agenda. All he cares about is power. He wants to dethrone the queen and rule Meriva—he still does."

He pauses, readying himself for the next part. "I knew I had to get Koa and myself out of his clutches. I figured we could start fresh in Yellek or Junsho. A place that allowed refugees. We got *so* close to Yellek, but somehow, the guild found us. They caught us and returned us to the camp. And to teach me a lesson about running, they slit my brother's throat right in front of me."

I stifle a gasp as I cup a hand over my mouth. "No," I whisper, tears burning my eyes.

"Yes. Like I said in Frevella's cave, it's my fault he's dead." Thane's voice thickens as he continues. "If I hadn't tried to run away with him—if I'd just stuck it out there and dealt with the consequences—he'd probably still be alive."

"My gods. I get it now. That's why you want Seferin dead."

He clenches a fist. "That's *exactly* why I want him dead."

"Thane, I'm so sorry that happened." I squeeze his hand tighter, wishing I could soothe the pain I know is in his heart, or take it away. "No one deserves to go through that."

He nods but doesn't bother saying anything. At least, not about Seferin or Koa.

"Let's go back to the cabin." He releases his arm from around me. "You need some sleep."

Heart heavy, I nod in agreement, and we make our way to the door.

Once inside, Thane helps me into bed and even pulls the quilt over my shoulders before getting on his cot and lying down. I want him to join me, but the beds aren't very large, and I'm not sure if he wants Algar and Rynthea to catch us sleeping together like some infatuated couple.

We had our fun, but I must remember we're still on an important quest. And soon this quest will be over.

We'll go our separate ways, and I might not ever see him again.

The reminder of it all saddens me more than I'll ever admit because, truthfully, I'll miss Thane. I wonder if he'll miss me, too.

I turn over in bed and stare at the bottom of the top bunk. Regardless of how I feel, it's completely up to Orvena whether we live to see another day or not.

I can only pray that the goddess keeps us in her arms.

Chapter 48

In the morning, before the sun has even risen, the ship is filled with the smells of breakfast.

Beka has made fried eggs with shrimp and mushrooms, and Conred has squeezed fresh oranges to drink.

The ship crew eats inside while our group takes to the deck to eat our meals. The sun is just rising at this point, the air crisper than the previous day.

After eating, Thane and Rynthea find a corner to train with their weapons. From my seat on the bench, mist sprays on my face and collects on the lenses of my specs. I've unbraided my hair to let the wind blow through my unruly tresses. I run my fingers through it and feel a few kinks. I cannot wait to use one of Analla's hair masks, give it a thorough wash, and then braid it. This journey has not been kind to my hair, but I've kept it pretty clean.

I stand from the bench and walk to one of the ship's posts. I lean my arm against it, steadying myself, as I soak in as much of the sea as I can.

To my left, I spot Algar rise from the bench as well with Zephra on his shoulder and make his way toward me. "You know something, Zaira," he says, eyes on the ocean, too. "I'm going to miss being around you when this is all over."

I smile at his statement. "You know, I'll miss you, too, Algar."

He gives me a lopsided grin.

"Will you miss Thane?" I ask.

He looks from the sea to Thane, who has his back to us as he performs tricks with a dagger. When he rapidly throws the dagger into a post with a spark of gold, Algar sighs and turns away again.

"That's a good question." He pauses, reaching up to give Zephra a piece of shrimp from breakfast. "I'll always care about him, you know? We grew up together and were like brothers for a while. But it's hard for me to connect to this new version of him." He shrugs his free shoulder, lowering his gaze. "I'm not sure I'll miss *this* Thane."

"I honestly don't think he can help who he is now—and I'm not saying that to defend him." *Or because he blew my mind with two incredible orgasms last night...or because he opened up to me about his brother.* "I just don't think he knows how to be anyone or anything else. He was trained to become a *weapon* at such a young age by The Divine." And I can't begin to imagine what he was trained to do if he spent time with The Shadow Guild.

"No. I suppose he can't." Algar sighs.

"Anyway, I hope you don't go back to being a conman again," I tease.

"Oh, but that's all I know, sleeping princess." He gives me a wink.

"That's not true. You know a lot about water dragons. Why don't you become a sea biologist? Fulfill your dad's dream?"

"I'm considering it." He pushes one of his plaits out of his face. "It takes a while for sea biologists to get their feet off the ground when they first start. You need a ship. Tools. Resources. A crew—which you have to pay. There's a lot to it."

"But you seem to be very good at turning nothing into something," I offer. "Plus, once you have all that treasure from The Shallows, you'll be able to buy your own boat and pay people. You could even open your own research laboratory."

"Maybe." He pauses, throat bobbing as he looks at his feet. "Sometimes I think about myself—about how I've spent my life so far—and I know he'd be disappointed in me. He *and* my mother." He hands Zephra another piece of shrimp. "I feel so lost without them."

"Oh, Algar." I reel him in for a hug. He chuckles over my shoulder as Zephra pounces on top of his head. "If it makes you feel any better, you're more than welcome to visit me in Meriva. You'll always have a friend to call on there."

If we live through this.

I pull away, holding on to his upper arms to look him in the eyes.

"You'd really want to keep being friends with a person like me?" His voice is full of surprise.

"Of course. We've all done bad things, Algar. That doesn't make us bad people."

He gives me a wider smile, his teeth catching a wisp of sunlight. "A kind heart like yours is a rarity these days."

I smile wide, but it's just then that I notice the ship has stopped moving.

"Drop the anchors!"

I press a hand to my chest as Captain Solyen's voice booms in the air. "Oh my gods. He *has* got to stop doing that," I grumble.

Thane and Rynthea approach with their rucksacks strapped to their backs.

"This is it," Rynthea announces, looking between me and Algar, her expression serious. "Last chance to back out."

"Never," Algar replies firmly.

"This is it," I repeat in a whisper, my heart rate increasing as I pick up my rucksack from the deck floor and strap it over my shoulder.

We watch as Conred and another crew member grab a set of ropes to lift a boat from a cargo slot on the side of the ship.

"This is as far as we go," Solyen announces as he nears us. He takes a pull from a silver pipe. "Row four miles east and you'll have made it to The Shallows."

He studies us with his dark, intense eyes. His face seems more worn today. He probably hasn't had a drink yet. "Are you lot absolutely sure about this?"

I nod. "We're sure."

"Then Orvena be with you. Go to that boat there." He points to the small boat the crew is prepping. "My boys will lower you down."

Once we're settled into the rowboat, Solyen approaches again. "As agreed, I'll wait here until sunset. But if you're not back by the time the sun reaches the horizon, I'll have no choice but to leave you behind." He inclines a bushy eyebrow. "This part of the sea is not one I wish to be in when it gets dark. It's worse than The Void. You row your way back, and when you're close enough, you sound *this* horn." He accepts a copper horn from one of the crew members. "Once we hear it, we'll know you're on the way and will bring you back up when you reach us." He hands the horn to Algar, who slips it into his bag.

"Listen, before we take off, do you think you can watch my Zephra?" Algar grabs Zephra and offers her to Solyen. She clearly doesn't like the action because she scurries back to his shoulder, glaring at Solyen like he's the enemy. "No, Zephra, you'll be all right. Listen to me." He grabs her again and cups her body in his hands, forcing her to look into his eyes. "I can't have you on that island with me, all right? It's too dangerous for you. I want you to wait here, where it's safe."

She chitters. I swear it's like she's arguing with him.

Algar only smiles at her before kissing the top of her head softly and offering her to Solyen. This time, she doesn't put up a fight. She drops into Solyen's oversize palm, but not without staring sadly at Algar and making a whimpering noise.

A wave of sadness washes over me for them. I can only imagine what she's thinking. She probably won't ever see him again. She probably won't see *any* of us again.

"I love you, Zeph," Algar says in a soothing voice.

She lets out a soft squeak.

"Just feed her fruit and nuts for now, if you have any," Algar says, blinking quickly to clear the tears in his eyes. "No honey or sweets, or she'll rip through your ship like it's made of paper."

Solyen blinks at Zephra, like he's trying to figure out how something so small could possibly cause that much damage.

Algar gives the captain a nod, and Solyen yells, "Right! Let 'em down, boys!"

The crew works the cranks, and the boat teeters left. Slowly, we're lowered down toward the water. Before we get too far, I peer up at Conred, who is clinging to the thick ropes with both hands as he eyes me.

"Good luck," he mouths.

"Thanks," I mouth back.

Rynthea grabs one of the oars as soon as the boat hits the water. She hands the other to Thane, who helps her steady the boat. "Let's start rowing."

"Unnecessary." Thane places his glowing hand over the water, and the boat's hull shifts under the influence of whatever magic he's using. We coast forward toward what resembles land in the distance, sailing fast enough that a gentle, balmy breeze buffets us.

The ride is eerily quiet. None of us say much. It feels like we're riding to our doom…yet somehow, I still have hope.

Looking over my shoulder, I spot the *Emellie*, only now she's a speck—one that grows smaller and smaller the closer we get to the island.

We still can go back. I can tell Thane to stop, turn the boat around, return us to the ship—that this is a foolish plan. A part of me longs to do that—the weaker, less confident, risk-averse side of me. But the stronger half is louder. That half believes I can do this. She's alert and ready, willing to risk everything for her sister.

We're only a short stretch away. The dangers and horror aren't just in The Shallows. They're everywhere in Thelanor, and yet we survived.

We made it *here*.

What makes this island so different?

All I have to do is get one of the stones, save Analla, and return to my life of peace and comfort. It seems simple enough…as long as I force myself to believe anything is possible.

I take off my specs and wipe the sea spray off of the lenses using my tunic. Sitting up straight, I slide them back on and squint at something on the horizon.

It's small, only a dark disruption poking up from the sea, but I know exactly what it is—*The Shallows*.

Chapter 49

As we draw near, the indistinct bump on the horizon becomes a mass of dark treetops and mountains with sharp points. The sharp points look like black volcanoes as swirls of smoke hover at the tips.

A sudden fog envelops us, as if the treacherous island is welcoming us to the slaughter.

I keep my breath steady as Thane decreases the speed of the boat and shifts the hull slightly to the left.

Quiet.

That's all I can think as we sail along. Not even the ocean makes much noise. The water becomes murkier, but I still spot glowing fish with pointed teeth scuttling by. Ironically, they're avoiding the bold light emanating from Thane's hand.

As we close in, the scent of sulfur permeates the air. There is another smell, too—rot. Dead bodies, possibly. I cringe at the thought.

Thane pulls his hand back into the boat when the shore comes into view through the haze. We drift to the shoreline and hit land with a bump. Hesitantly, we look around before climbing out and lugging the boat onto the sand. As I scan farther down the beach, I realize our boat isn't the only one beached. There are countless others, all haphazardly lining the shore—paint chipped, wood broken, their owners now ghosts.

A graveyard of boats. The sight of them fills me with dread and doubt.

How many people have come here to do the exact same thing we're about to do? How many had arrived overflowing with ambition and dreams? How many assumed they would be lucky enough to survive?

"Try not to focus on that," Rynthea says, tipping her head toward the boats, as if she's read my mind.

I clear my throat and turn with her to focus on the looming jungle ahead. The treetops aren't green. They're black, like their leaves have been permanently charred. Beneath our feet, sand intertwines with thick black veins of hardened lava, as if this island is flesh and blood.

"From what I remember on the map, the Temple of Elphar is directly in the center of The Shallows," Thane announces, throwing up a glowing compass. It hovers in front of him, revealing the location we're in, as well as the location of the temple. The temple is a blinking gold dot that is *very* far away. So much land to cover.

"And the treasure?" Rynthea inquires.

"Most likely buried somewhere near or inside the temple. I'll be able to detect it better when we get closer." Digging into his pocket, Thane pulls out Frevella's Kelvanite Sphere. "Drusako," he whispers, rubbing it with his fingers four times. The sphere comes to life, bursting with green light. As I move in closer, I see that the light forms an arrow. It's pointing ahead…toward the jungle.

Of course it is.

"Let's go," Thane commands, already marching forward.

Rynthea and I look at each other at the same time. She shakes her head but follows his lead. I stay close to Algar, my fingers wrapped around the dagger sheathed at my hip.

When we reach the edge of the jungle, Thane lifts a hand, and a bolt of gold bursts forth. It cuts through a thick cluster of vines and damp leaves, leaving behind a dark, gaping hole. The others disappear into the new trail. I can't help but give the ocean one last look, knowing this may be the last time I see it.

I draw in a breath and follow them into darkness.

"Algar, I need you to hold this." Thane hands him the sphere.

Algar frowns. "Why *me*?"

"Because I need both of my hands. One for my sword and the other for magic in case anything comes up."

"Oh. Right. Suppose that makes sense." Algar holds on tight to the sphere while looking ahead. "Well, it's telling us to keep going straight."

"We have to make this quick," Rynthea murmurs, surveilling the dark gaps of the jungle. "Remember, Frevella told you the sphere will only last us an hour."

"How long will it take to reach the temple?" I ask.

"About an hour...if we're lucky." Thane sends up four orbs of light to surround us. He moves with caution, his sword raised in front of him, mask up, eyes vigilant.

The light spreads throughout the jungle, revealing unknown creatures hidden in thick black trunks and others lingering in the dark crowns of the trees. Many have thin fur, oversize eyes, and long fingers. They watch us pass, motionless, like they know we're fools.

We carry on for who knows how many miles, walking at least twenty minutes without any trouble. But then the Kelvanite Sphere blinks red, and Algar comes to a halt.

When it flashes green again, Algar says, "The arrow switched directions." He looks to our right. "Safest way is that way." He points in the same direction as the arrow.

We follow him, passing by a slimy black creek and a wall made of hardened lava. The heat becomes unbearable the deeper we venture into the jungle. Eventually, the ground is splintered with thin cracks, and between them there are streams of fiery orange lava.

The soles of my feet begin to heat, but I keep my balance, making sure to stay on firm ground and avoid the lava altogether—until I slam into Rynthea's solid back.

"Why have we stopped?" I ask, shifting to her side.

Ahead of us, the ground is completely lava. There is a path of elevated stepping stones that leads to the other side of the jungle. Each platform has a distance of at least two or three feet between them. A person would *definitely* have to jump between each stone to get to the other side. With expanses that wide, we'll be lucky to make each jump. Plus, the platforms are big enough for only one person to stand on. One slip, and you're as good as dead.

And as if the lava isn't menacing enough, there are creatures, too. Made of dark-brown scales, they have multiple eyes and claws sharp enough to cut through rock. Their bellies are stuck to the pillar walls. To our good fortune, their eyes are closed—hopefully asleep.

"Algar, you'll have to teleport Zaira and Rynthea to the other side,"

Thane says in a low voice, sheathing his sword. "I'll cross on foot…"

Algar draws in a breath as he swings his gaze to me. I take his hand. In the blink of an eye, we're on the other side of the towering path.

Algar returns to retrieve Rynthea. But before they can teleport back together, she holds up a hand to stop him. They exchange words, and Algar nods reluctantly. Then he teleports back to my side, alone.

"What'd she say?" I ask.

"She wants me to save my strength, since teleporting requires a lot of my energy. She's going to cross herself."

I swallow the lump in my throat, watching as Thane hops from steady land to the first platform. He leaps across three more as Rynthea jumps onto the first. My heart races as Thane lands on the second to last platform and some of the stone crumbles.

"Careful," I whisper, chewing my thumbnail.

He stands upright again, causing more stone to fall. It's diminishing in size, and knowing Rynthea has to occupy the same platform and then jump to one more stone to reach safer ground spikes my anxiety.

"Try to land as softly as you can on this one," Thane says over his shoulder.

Rynthea, three platforms back, nods as she clenches her fists and braces herself for the next jump.

Thane finishes off strong. He bounds from the disintegrating platform, reaches the final stone, then launches himself toward the ground in front of us, landing in a crouch.

"All good?" Algar asks, throwing a hand down to help him stand.

Thane grabs his hand and rises to his feet. "All good."

We turn our attention to Rynthea, who is sizing up the jump to the crumbling platform. It's nearly half the width of the one she's currently on, so she'll have less space to land. With her size, that's terrifying.

"Come on, Rynthea," I whisper. "You got this."

She takes a steadying breath, then runs forward, leaping in the air and landing on the platform. More of it breaks off, chunks falling into the lava below with a hiss. She throws her hands out to balance herself.

Her nostrils flare as she studies the last block in front of her. She hops, making it to the final stone, but the last jump to reach safer ground is the biggest of all. Rynthea takes a step back, clenches her fists again, and charges forward. She soars through the air, and my mouth goes dry.

My nerves seize every part of me…because I know that despite her efforts, she isn't going to make it.

When she lands, one of her hooves stumbles backward, and she slips from the edge.

I gasp. "No!"

"Shit." Thane sprints toward Rynthea, both hands outstretched and swirling in gold. He catches her before she hits the lava and grunts as he hauls her back up. He reaches down to help Rynthea up, and when she's on her two hooves, her eyes are misty.

She draws in a shaky breath, closing her eyes for a split second before opening them again. The haze of tears is now gone. She turns to Thane and takes hold of his shoulders, giving him a thankful nod. He nods his head in return—a mutual understanding.

"Rynthea, are you okay?" I ask as she marches around me with her hands on her hips and her head thrown back, most likely still digesting the fact that she was almost melted alive.

"I'm fine. It's all right." She drops her head and reaches for her scythesword, gripping it tight in her hands. "Let's keep moving."

An inkling of relief takes hold of me, but as Algar follows her, I swear I see something slink away behind a tree ahead.

"Right. It's guiding us this way." Algar points blindly as he looks at the sphere. He advances, peering around warily with the sphere cupped in one of his hands.

But a stiff breeze drifts by, stopping me in my tracks and causing the hairs on my arms and neck to stand on end. Rynthea raises her scythesword, like she, too, felt the sudden change in atmosphere.

Someone is watching us…or some*thing*.

Just then, a sharp hiss fills the air, and Rynthea swings around just in time to cut through a massive snake.

No, not just a snake. It is an enormous serpent with sharp, jagged scales protruding all over its body like a deadly suit of armor. Its bloodred eyes are split with vertical pupils that look right at us.

"Behind you, Thane!" Rynthea shouts.

Chapter 50

The moss-green serpent coils and strikes at Thane, but he ducks in time and plunges his sword through its center. Three more emerge from the forest, and all the breath escapes me as they coil rapidly around the trees, spiraling toward the canopy.

At first, I can see them.

And then they disappear, as if they have become part of the bark.

"They can change color to camouflage." Thane growls as he stands before me with his sword. "They're probably going to a higher vantage for a better strike."

"Backs together," Rynthea orders.

The four of us press our backs together, scanning our surroundings. Leaves rustle and branches snap. To my right, I can see bones scattered around the base of the trees. I grip the hilt of my dagger tighter, heart pounding, really wishing I knew how to better protect myself. This dagger stands no chance against snakes this size.

"Rynthea, to your left," Thane calls.

Rynthea grunts as she gives the handle of her scythesword a twist and slices through a wide-mouthed serpent diving out of a tree.

"Oh shit," Algar whispers behind me.

"Duck, Zaira!" Rynthea hollers, spinning around. I drop and roll just as the tip of her blade pierces through the head of another serpent. Her scythesword catches in its chin, and she yanks it upward, splitting its head in half.

A short distance away, another hiss breaks the air. Only this hiss sounds *deeper*, louder. Like it comes from a creature twice the size of the serpents.

I don't want to look. But I can't help myself.

As Thane and Rynthea cut through one more serpent, I spot something with six glowing yellow eyes staring at me from a dark gap in the jungle.

"What. The fuck. Is *that*?" Algar's face loses all color as he backs away.

The creature stalks toward us. Its foot is as big as an elephant's, with claws as sharp as the dagger I carry. Its body is a muddy brown except for its scaly chest, which is a putrid yellow. Its massive head has the nostrils of a snake with rows of teeth three times bigger and sharper than a shark's.

Slimy drool drips from the corners of its mouth as it steps out of the shadows and hisses.

Oh shit.

It's one of those creatures that was sleeping on the wall near the platform steps. All six of its thin-slitted eyes blink at me and Algar as we back away with our hands raised defensively.

I've never tasted true fear before. Not until this very moment. It's an acidic, sharp taste—one that coats my tongue and accumulates so much it could clog my throat.

"Uh, friends?" Algar calls in warning.

The creature's claws pierce into moist dirt, passing over thick roots and bones as it clicks its teeth.

"Shit," I hear Thane mutter. I don't dare look back.

I assume all the serpents are gone now because both he and Rynthea run past us, putting themselves between us and the monster with their weapons up and defenses raised.

Rynthea eyes Thane. "I'll take the flank. You take the head."

He nods.

But before either of them can charge forward, two more of those creatures appear behind the first one.

"Shit," Rynthea curses. "Never mind."

"Forget how it's done. Let's just fucking kill them." Thane sprints toward the first creature, and the others screech loudly, rising on their hind legs and opening their mouths wider. One storms for Rynthea while another stomps toward me.

Algar grabs my arm and teleports us out of the way before the creature comes too close. We stand several feet behind the creatures now, watching Rynthea catch one of Thane's swords when he tosses it to her. She climbs onto the back of one of the creatures and stabs it through the head with a heavy grunt. The creature collapses in an instant.

In a swift motion, Thane slides beneath the belly of the other beast, vanishing for a split second before reappearing. As he comes back out, yellow liquid and guts spill from beneath the monster before it falls.

The last one turns to search for me and Algar, charging in our direction again with an angry cry. Thane throws up his hands with a grunt, and the creature veers to the left, slamming into a tree trunk. It shakes off the blow, blinks, then opens its mouth to hiss louder at us.

And just like the serpent…it disappears.

"You've got to be fucking kidding me," Algar says under his breath. "That thing camouflages, too?"

Panicking, I sweep my gaze around the area.

Thane scans our surroundings while Rynthea holds on tight to her scythesword. I do the same with my dagger.

The jungle grows still as we wait.

Listen.

Then I feel it.

Hot air blows down my back, and that same acidic fear I tasted before floods my mouth again. Goose bumps spread over every inch of my skin as the heat of its breath grows hotter.

"B-behind me," I stammer.

I don't dare turn around, and I damn sure don't move. Not until the animal hisses and Algar yells my name.

Before the creature can eat me alive, something yanks me off my feet. Thane uses his magic to push me away, and I land on my stomach as the creature reveals itself exactly where I was just standing. Thane launches forward with his hands illuminated in gold and shadows.

Rynthea roars as she slings her scythesword and hooks it through the creature's jaw. When she yanks back and frees her weapon, the creature shrieks in pain. Its jaw has disconnected from its head, now dangling like loose skin. Thane climbs atop it and stabs it through the neck in a flurry of gold.

The creature buckles as Algar grips my waist from behind and hauls me to my feet.

"All good?" he asks, panting.

"Yeah." With shaky hands, I dust dirt off my top and trousers.

Rynthea and Thane are finishing off the creature. After one final stab through the head from Thane, it falls.

Silence sweeps through the jungle again.

We pause, holding our breaths, waiting to see if anything else comes. Fortunately, the jungle remains still. No other creatures appear...but that doesn't mean we're any safer.

I shuffle to join Thane and Rynthea, a bit rattled.

"You okay?" Thane asks, stroking my jaw with his fingertips.

"Yeah, I'm fine," I answer, though my hands are still shaking.

He studies me thoroughly, cupping one half of my face. When he accepts that I'm all right, he sighs and drops his hands. "Okay. Come on. Can't waste any more time here."

Algar pulls the sphere from his pocket as he blows out a relieved breath. "To the right, it says."

Even though my legs feel like liquid, I follow him and the others. I have a feeling those serpents and six-eyed creatures were only the start of our problems.

There's more out there. I can *feel* it.

Hopefully, we make it to the temple before anything else notices we're around.

Chapter 51

Farther along, the air thickens and the temperature increases, producing a tiring humidity. The fabric of my tunic sticks to my back as a wave of thirst strikes me.

We trudge through the sand, half expecting something to pop out of it and grab us, but the Kelvanite Sphere keeps us from encountering any other danger. We follow Algar's lead as he clings to the sphere. My boots sink with each step, and there are times I have to really yank my leg up so my foot comes out.

Algar hobbles a few more yards before stopping.

"Orvena bless," I breathe, pressing my hands on my knees and drawing in a few deep breaths.

Algar studies the orb when Rynthea and I join him. We pull out our canteens to take a few swigs of water. As I swipe my hand over the back of my mouth, Thane meets up with us, and we all release a sigh as we stare at our next grueling challenge ahead.

The trees no longer stand upright but tilt forward like blown candles. I spot another cluster of trees at the very bottom of a deep, wide crater that only several large explosions could have made.

We're at the rim of the bowl. I now understand how the island has gotten its name—from the shallow pit in the middle of it.

It's here where the Temple of Elphar lies silent—ominous.

It's where we need to be.

"There." Thane points at the broken tips of a tan stone building swallowed up by trees in the distance. "That's the Temple of Elphar."

I feel my heartbeat pick up speed. We're *so* close. I can't believe this. Are we really going to make it? Orvena must be listening to my prayers.

Something red flashes in the corner of my eye, and I look at the sphere in Algar's hand. The arrow is pointing to the left, in warning.

"What's this thing doing?" Algar gives the sphere a shake. "Maybe its time has run out."

Thane takes the sphere from him before facing the area it's pointing to. "It's giving us a warning." Thane takes another step and squints his eyes. "There are stairs that way, but we shouldn't take them." The sphere flashes green again, and Thane faces the crater. "It's pointing ahead. We have to go straight down."

"Well, let's go." Rynthea hikes her rucksack higher on her shoulders and starts the march forward, entering the crater. This time, Thane hands the sphere to me.

"You good holding on to it?"

"Sure." I cradle it in my hands, following him down the steep hill.

"Careful," Thane calls to me over his shoulder. "Watch your footing."

"Okay." I walk slowly, digging the heels of my boots into the dirt with each step to keep myself grounded. I hold the sphere close to my chest, my pulse thrumming, hope swelling in my chest. The hill levels out the farther down we go, but then I make the foolish mistake of looking up to see how close we are to the temple and my foot slips. I let out a sharp gasp and fall on one knee before completely rolling downhill.

"Zaira!" Thane shouts. I try to stop myself by digging my fingers into the dirt, but with every roll, my efforts to stop myself become more useless. I'm falling too hard, too fast. My head hits the ground several times. I hear a loud *crack* and squeeze my eyes shut. Then a hot, familiar grip wraps around the upper half of my body and brings me to an abrupt stop.

Groaning, I lie on the ground for a second, staring up at the hazy, milk-gray sky. I wait for the pain to flood my body…but nothing comes. That crack must have been a broken bone, right?

Seconds later, Thane and Rynthea are hovering above me.

"Are you okay?" Rynthea reaches for my hand with concern etched on her face.

"I... Yeah. I think so." She lugs me up, and I stumble a bit. Thane presses his hand to the small of my back to keep me steady.

"Zaira?" Algar pants as he runs to meet up with us. "Thank Orvena Thane stopped your fall in time."

"I'm okay, everyone. Really."

"Does anything feel broken?" Thane asks, gently touching a knot on my forehead. I wince from the pressure.

"I don't think so." I give my arms a shake. My ribs don't hurt. My legs seem stable. Nothing feels broken.

"You're bleeding." Rynthea takes off her rucksack and digs through it. She pulls out a clean white cloth and wipes my cheek with it. It stings, but I swallow the pain. Sighing, Rynthea hands the cloth to me. I wipe my cheek again, but that's when I see it.

My heart drops to my stomach.

The sphere, now at my feet, isn't glowing anymore.

A big crack snakes through it. Panicked, I bend down to pick it up.

"No." I rub it four times and give the command *drusako* like Frevella instructed. We should still have some time left. "No, come on. Please," I plead. "We're so close!"

I look up at Thane, who is staring at the sphere, jaw locked.

"Gods damn it." Rynthea huffs as Algar throws his hands to the top of his head with a panicked look in his eyes.

"I—I'm so sorry!" I cry. "This is all my fault."

"No, it's not." Thane closes his eyes for a split second, exhaling before opening them again. "It's mine. I handed you the sphere. I should've held on to it."

"But I *fell* with it. I heard it crack." I swallow to clear the emotion building up in my throat. We're too damn close to the temple for me to cry now.

"It's fine," Rynthea assures us, holding her hands up and eyeing each of us, as if she's taming children. "The temple shouldn't be too far away. We can get there, take what we need, and go back the way we came to reach the shore. We'll be fine. Let's not lose hope now."

"We won't know which way to go or what's coming for us," I say, voice wavering.

"I'll hear and smell anything before it attacks." Rynthea straightens her back, but her words don't fill me with much hope. We don't know what's ahead or which parts of the jungle to avoid. Rynthea scoffs. "We've made it for *days* across half of Thelanor without a magical sphere. What's a few more steps?" She gestures to the bottom of the valley. "And we can see the temple. It can't be that far away now. We can do this."

No one speaks, but we don't have to in order to read one another's minds. Without the sphere to guide us, there is an even slimmer chance of making it through the rest of this jungle alive.

Thane clears his throat. "The minotaur is right." Rynthea rolls her eyes at him, but he continues. "We have to press on. We'll keep our ears up and our weapons close. We'll take it slow. There's still plenty of time to get what we need and make it back to the ship."

Not if we're attacked again, I think.

Thane takes the sphere from me and tucks it into his pocket.

"We press on," he repeats, looking into my eyes. "For Analla."

Hearing him say my sister's name brings a surge in me. The doubt is still there, but for a fleeting second, I allow my fear to distract me from my ultimate goal. *Saving Analla.*

"Okay?" Thane places a compassionate hand on my upper arm.

Lips quivering, I nod.

When his attention lands on Algar, Algar sighs and bobs his head.

"We can do this." Rynthea smiles with glistening eyes. "As long as we have each other's backs and fight like warriors, we'll make it to that damn temple. It's all right, Zaira. Don't beat yourself up over this."

I smile as she gives my shoulder a firm squeeze. When she starts walking, I join at her side, swallowing my anxieties.

"I need a distraction," I grumble.

"Of what kind?" asks Rynthea.

"I don't know. Just talk about something—*anything* so I'm not thinking mean things about myself."

"Okay…uh…" She pauses, eyes bouncing around the jungle. "Did you know Torjack is the last male minotaur in Thelanor?"

I blink rapidly, surprised. "Are you serious?"

"Yes. From what I've heard, there are three other female minotaurs in Thelanor. But Torjack is the last male. If he dies before he has a child, there won't be any more to continue the lineage."

"Wow." I step over a steaming puddle. "So you *really* need to keep him healthy and alive, then."

"I do. I can't let it end with us," she says. "If he mates with one of the other females, we'll carry on. When I get some treasure, we can build our own sanctuary for minotaurs. Torjack can have a shit ton of kids, and I'll have my own—hybrids of some kind, since there aren't any more males—and we'll grow in numbers again. We can teach the young how to fight and protect themselves like I was taught, so they can grow up and know how to defend themselves. No more horns being stolen. No more being used. No more living in fear. Instead, people will learn to respect us."

"That would be great for the minotaurs."

"It would. I dream about it often." She releases a rare, happy sigh. "A place where we'll be safe. A place of our own. A haven. I can imagine it being like Immalon. Closed off from the rest of the world. A place of peace and happiness."

I smile, watching her eyes drift, seemingly lost in thought.

"The first thing I'll buy is a place of my own." Algar squeezes in between me and Rynthea. "I'll have one of those little built-in bath basins for Zephra to swim in. She'll have all of her favorite meals and snacks. She'll live the life."

I laugh. "And what about *your* life?"

"I'll pay off a few debts I owe. Who knows? As long as my Zephra's happy, I'm happy. All I need is a roof over my head and food in my belly. Nothing else matters...but having a shit ton of coin does help."

One of Thane's orbs levitates past my head, highlighting the steam wafting up from the floor of the jungle. Why is it so hot in this area, anyway? All the volcanoes are outside the crater, yet it feels like we're walking right over one.

"I just want one of those stones," I say after some time.

Rynthea veers left. "And soon you'll have one."

We hike, lost in our own thoughts for a while, until Rynthea breaks the silence. "Look." She points ahead and, through a thin gap in the trees, is the temple.

Half of it is in ruins, heaps of tan stone crumbled on the ground, and the roof in even worse shape. As we move closer, I spot a dark, hollow arch that must lead to the inside of the temple.

This landmark should be a gloomy, depressing sight. But there is a stream of light shining on it, making it a beacon in the dark, as if even the skies know it's a special place.

Without another word, Rynthea jogs toward the temple. Algar limps after her. I can't help but stand still a moment, soaking in the accomplishment of making it here and bracing myself for what's to come.

I'll get the stone.

I'll free Analla.

I'll go back to my old, peaceful life.

Drink tea. Read books. Bake. Rest.

The mere thought of it brings me so much peace of mind.

Thane walks up alongside me, and the heat of his body sends warm currents through me. "Things change once we're in there," he murmurs in my ear.

I turn to look him in the eye. "*Everything* changes."

He tugs his mask down, revealing his sculpted, rosy lips. He studies my features like he always does, but there's something off about his demeanor. His shoulders seem more tense. Isn't he at least a little relieved that we've made it this far? And his eyes look…worried.

He's been like this all morning—a bit distant and quiet. I assumed he was mentally preparing himself for The Shallows…but now, I'm not so sure.

"There's something I should tell you before we go in," he murmurs. "I told you about Azidel's tome and what it can do. It's very powerful, and that's why I—"

A deep growl rumbles in the distance. Thane immediately stops talking, eyes swooping to the jungle as he brings his mask back up.

The growl gets louder. Closer.

I can feel the bass of it rattling in my chest.

Something is stalking us…and it sounds *massive*.

Rynthea and Algar are still a few yards away from the temple when a mass of black appears before them. The creature wastes no time swiping Rynthea with a giant claw, sending her body crashing into a tree trunk.

I scream her name when she flops to the ground, motionless, while the creature prowls toward Algar with a snarl, ready to strike.

Chapter 52

This is the creature we're meant to be looking out for.
Not the serpents.
Not the six-eyed beasts.
This one.
This giant thing made of all black, with sharp claws and blazing red eyes. Wisps of black shadows waft off its body in place of fur.
A wolf.
It must be a wolf…only it's three times the size of a regular one, with teeth as long and sharp as swords.

"Shadowhound," Thane breathes in disbelief. He throws up a hand and hauls Algar out of the way before the shadowhound can swipe at him, too. Algar grunts as he tumbles to the ground. As his body goes down, his head hits a rock. He lies motionless.

The shadowhound snarls again, lowering its haunches and glaring at Thane.

"Oh my gods," I whisper.

"Hide, Zaira. *Now*." Thane sinks into a defensive stance, bracing himself for the creature's attack. I sprint toward Rynthea, who groans as I approach.

"Oh my goodness. Rynthea? Are you okay?" I drop to my knees, inspecting the damage. Her hand is pressed to her waist, where she is unsuccessfully trying to stem the bleeding from three deep gashes.

My blood runs cold.

She could bleed to death if I don't find a way to stop the flow.

I glance over my shoulder. Thane is now in a standoff with the shadowhound, walking slowly in a semicircle with his swords locked in hand. Algar remains unconscious on the ground. But that's okay. Hopefully, he's only playing dead, which is better than actually being dead.

"Okay, let me see…" I set down my rucksack and fish through it until I find an old chemise. It's too small to wrap around Rynthea's entire midsection, so I fold it in half and press it to her wounds. She hisses through her teeth. I can't help thinking that her wounds appear eerily similar to the scars on King Draedor's face.

"I have a healing elixir in here, too," I say, digging through the rucksack again. "Don't judge me, but I stole it from Immalon."

"You steal?" Rynthea sputters through gritted teeth. I can tell she wants to smile but is in too much pain. Her eyes are starting to glaze over.

"Not usually. Here." I pop the cork and bring the elixir to her lips. "It's high strength, so it should work faster."

Her face scrunches as she gulps it down. "Ugh. That's fucking disgusting."

A growl splits the air. From the corner of my eye, I can see the shadowhound pounce forward. I turn to see Thane throw up a hand and force the beast back with a mighty whorl of gold. The shadowhound flies backward but lands on all fours.

It lowers its stance, flaring its nostrils, assessing Thane again before going in for another attack. This time, it has anticipated Thane's magical blow and lunges to the right. When it circles back around, it slams the top of its head into Thane's back.

Thane grunts as he falls. The beast attempts a bite at him, but Thane flips onto his back and shoots it in the muzzle with a stream of gold. It whimpers and backs off, giving him just enough time to roll away and jump to his feet.

However, while he fights one shadowhound, another shows up. It notices Algar, yellow teeth bared, sensing an easy meal.

"Algar!" I yell.

Another shadowhound appears a short distance away from me and Rynthea. It growls low, red eyes flaring, whispers of gray smoke surrounding its head. One pounce forward and we'll be lunch.

"My scythesword." Rynthea's words are strained as she points behind me. I dive for her weapon.

The shadowhound snarls and launches itself toward us as I toss Rynthea her scythesword.

An agonized yelp splits the air as Rynthea roars, swinging her scythesword at the beast. She hits it directly in the chest, and the shadowhound goes down. Grunting, she kicks it off her blade with a hoof. It lands beside her like a lump of meat, its teeth mere inches from her thigh. The short tip of her scythesword is drowned in black blood.

"Get. Algar," she croaks.

Right. *Algar.* The shadowhound is right above him now.

"Hey!" I scream, scrambling to my feet. "Get away from him!"

This beast lifts its head, and its snout quivers as it reveals glistening teeth and magenta gums. I let it lock its sights on me.

What now, Zaira?

Thane can't help me. He's still fighting off his own shadowhound, and Rynthea can hardly move.

I panic as the creature stalks toward me. I frantically search my surroundings, looking for anything to help me fend off the shadowhound. There's a cave off to the left, just big enough for me to squeeze into. I dart for it, and the shadowhound belts out a vicious bark as its paws pound into the ground. I feel it closing in on me, the heat from its savage pants warming my back. I duck into the cave just as the creature speeds headlong into it with its teeth bared. I hear a hard *snap* as its fangs break off on the entrance.

Catching my breath, I slide backward and burrow deeper in the cave. Holy Crystal. I can't believe I made it.

The growls echo, and the shadowhound sticks a paw inside, swiping left and right. I move back as far as I can, pressing my back against the rocky wall. This is a shallow cave, though. It could still reach me.

The shadowhound keeps clawing inside with vicious snarls. While it does, I grab my dagger. There's hardly any light, so I can't see exactly where to strike, but I go for it anyway.

Raising my arm, I yell as I slice downward. The dagger penetrates its flesh, and the shadowhound yelps like a wounded puppy. I snatch the dagger back out, and it jerks its paw away.

Breathing rapidly, heart hammering, I wait to see if it'll run off. The paw drifts away from the cave, and I catch it limping off. Even though it's leaving, I don't dare move.

I close my eyes for a fleeting second to pull myself together and collect my breath. My lungs burn, and my heart feels like it's about to burst out of my chest. My hands shake, and my veins pump with more adrenaline than I've felt before.

I'm safe for now.

Suddenly, something pierces through my skin, and white-hot pain floods my thigh. My eyes fly open, and I unleash a high-pitched scream. The shadowhound's other paw has silently made its way back into the cave and has impaled my upper thigh—and the claw is stuck.

I wail as it tries to yank its paw backward, taking me with it.

I've really pissed this thing off.

I lift the dagger again, fighting through the agonizing pain, and give its other paw several stabs. The shadowhound yelps and rips its claw out. It hurts more coming out than going in.

"Fuck!" I wail. "Oh gods. Orvena, help me." Hands shaking, I study my leg as best as I can in the dim light. Blood gushes from a massive gash, running onto the gravel. "Oh goodness. Okay. Okay, breathe, Z. Think."

Hands trembling, I remove my rucksack and pull out a pair of pants, ripping them into three sections with my dagger. I tuck one piece of the fabric under my thigh to soak up the pool of blood forming. I bite down on another piece, readying myself for what's about to come next—the tourniquet.

My muffled scream bounces off the walls of the cave as I give another piece of fabric a yank above my wound, tying it as tightly as possible. With tears swelling in my eyes, I look down at my leg. The tourniquet is useless. My blood is soaking right through the fabric.

"Damn it," I whimper. I rifle through my bag again and pull out the last bottle of healing elixir I took from Immalon. I pop the cork and chug it down. It tastes like shit and burns like acid.

"Zaira!" I hear Thane call.

My breathing has turned ragged. Blood is soaking the whole tourniquet.

A shadow appears at the mouth of the cave.

Gods. Please don't let it be that hound again.

"Zaira." Thane's voice echoes in the cave, and I nearly cry with relief.

Oh, thank Orvena. "I'm...I'm in here!"

He hurries inside, crouching low.

"Gods, what happened to you?" He goes to touch my leg but pulls back, seeming unsure how to proceed.

"One of those shadowhounds got me with its claw."

He tosses up an orb of gold light to illuminate the cave. I belt out a scream when I see a corpse to the left of him, resting against one of the walls.

"That corpse will have a friend if I don't get you out of here," he says, eyeing my thigh.

"It's bleeding a lot," I tell him. "But I drank a healing elixir, so it should stop soon. Where's Rynthea and Algar?"

"Whatever you gave Rynthea worked. She just killed two more of the hounds…but not easily. They struck her again. Fortunately, it wasn't as bad as the first strike."

"And Algar?"

"He's fine. Still a little out of it, but fine. We need to get you out of here."

When Thane throws my arm over his shoulders and hauls me up against him, I bite back a pained cry. He crouches forward, assisting me out of the cave while keeping me close to his body.

Near the temple, I catch Rynthea sitting next to Algar. In the center of the field are five dead shadowhounds. One is so badly mutilated, I can't tell which part is the head and which is the tail.

"How did you know what those were?" I ask as Thane guides us toward our friends.

"It's one of Xaimur's creations," he answers. "Read about it during academics when I was with The Divine. Most people think they're myths. I'm sure you've heard the stories about how Xaimur created wicked creatures to combat Orvena's virtue?"

"Yeah, I have."

"Well, The Shallows wasn't always a bad place, according to the books. This place was called Noreven once before. It was a paradise, and Orvena spent a lot of time here among the mortals. This is where Azidel resided."

"Okay," I reply with a groan. To keep him talking and to distract myself from the pain shooting in my thigh, I ask, "But what does that have to do with Xaimur?"

"Xaimur wasn't pleased to know she was empowering the mortals. After all, how could he corrupt them if they were magical?" We dodge a puddle of wolf guts. "So he used his own magic to try and destroy the island, hence this massive crater we're in. But Orvena took Azidel and hid him in a blessed temple. *That* temple." He tips his head at Elphar's temple, which is a short distance ahead. "Elphar was the son of Azidel, and he possessed magic, too. He traveled often and brought back a lot of food, goods, and treasure as a way to thank Orvena for protecting them. But I assume it all became too much. Xaimur kept throwing his creatures at Azidel in hopes of stealing his power. He killed off many mortals while this happened, so Azidel decided to send Elphar away from Noreven for good. No one truly knows what happened between Orvena and Azidel afterward, but what we do know is nothing created by Xaimur can enter that temple."

"And you studied all of this?" I ask, side-eyeing him.

Thane places me on the ground next to Algar, who is resting his head on a large stone with his eyes closed. His skin looks ashen and devoid of its usual color.

"Yes." Thane takes the wrap off of my thigh. "It's healing. Good."

I look down with him, watching the skin slowly stitch back together.

Rynthea lifts her head. Her chest is covered in blood, but her first wounds are slowly healing.

"Rynthea. Are you okay?" I ask.

"Stupid hound nicked me again, but I'll be all right." A grunt slips out of her as she wipes some of the blood off her buffers.

I put my focus on Algar. "Algar?"

He doesn't budge.

Worry niggles at me. *"Algar?"* I try again.

Rynthea's eyebrows pull together as she slides closer to him. "Hey. Algar?" She shakes him by the shoulder, causing his head to loll to the side.

"What happened to him?" I move closer, ignoring the lingering pain in my thigh.

"I don't know. He was just fine," Rynthea replies in a panicky voice.

Thane drops to one knee and gives Algar a thorough once-over. Then he pulls him forward by his shirt to reveal the back of his neck. I gasp, and Rynthea and I both lean backward when we see the slimy, bloated gray thing attached to his skin.

"Shit. It's a leech." Thane lifts a hand above Algar's neck, and the leech's skin sizzles before it falls off and curls into a crisp on the jungle floor. I back away as Thane uses his magic to flick it away from us.

"I've seen leeches," Rynthea says, head shaking. "Never that size or that color."

"Welcome to The Shallows," Thane mutters. "Help me lay him all the way down."

Rynthea helps place Algar flat on his back. His lips are now turning blue, and more of the color is draining from his face.

"It must've been venomous." Thane opens Algar's mouth to reveal yellow foam accumulating on the perimeter of his tongue.

"No." My chest tightens. "How do we get it out of him?"

Panic begins to set in as we realize the severity of his situation.

Thane sighs, dropping his head. "I can draw it out…"

"Okay, so do it!" Rynthea demands, perched on her knees now.

"It's not that simple," Thane retorts. "He's on the brink of death. To bring him back, that'll require me to tap into full black magic."

"Aren't you already using that?" Rynthea questions with a frown. "With all the shadows that come off of you when you fight. Seems pretty black to me!"

"That's not full black magic," he counters. "You need a *source* to do that. What you've seen me using is gray magic, which means I use little parts of black and merge it with the white, which is safer. That's what we were taught in The Shadow Guild."

"Wait a minute. The *what*?" Rynthea counters.

Thane eyes her. "That's beside the point right now. We need to focus on Algar."

I can tell it takes everything in her not to blow up on him. But he's right. Algar is more important right now than whatever fucked-up-ness happened in Thane's past.

"What happens if you use it?" I ask him.

"My thoughts become corrupted," he answers in a lower voice. "I can lose control. Once the black magic sucks away all my energy, I'm forced to find energy elsewhere. Normally from another sorcerer…or a mortal, which is why I said you need a source to continuously use black magic." He pauses, eyes falling to Algar again. "As my own control slips away, it makes it easier for someone more powerful to control me, too."

I frown. "Like who?"

"You know who."

I pause, blinking. I know exactly who.

"Well, Algar needs us," I assert. "We can't let him die. You'll have to use it, just this once."

"I agree," says Rynthea. "You're strong. I'm sure you can control it."

Thane looks down at Algar, his brows furrowing and his hands curling into fists. He shakes his head left and right, as if battling with his own thoughts. Then, with a sigh, he closes his eyes and exhales.

"You and Rynthea need to move back," he instructs.

We do as we're told, shifting farther away from the men. He sets his hands above Algar's chest, and instead of his eyes sparking their usual gold, they darken. The bright gold transitions to black, and inky veins crawl along the whites of his eyes.

The amber in his palms melts away to be replaced with tendrils of black. This isn't like the shadows he gives off when fighting or defending. This is a thick, inky smoke—one that could suffocate a person if he wanted it to.

Thane's lips are moving, but he's speaking too low for me to understand. It has to be a sorcerer's chant of some kind. The more his lips move, more smoke appears, curling around his hands and snaking up his forearms. As he repeats the incantation, droplets are being drawn out of Algar's chest.

They accumulate into one yellowish ball no bigger than a cherry. Thane finally stops chanting and shifts the venom a great distance away from us. It splashes abruptly on the ground. Thane finally drops his hands with a weary grunt. The shadows disappear, almost as if his body has absorbed them.

"Thane?" I call softly.

He flicks his gaze my way with a ticking jaw, and my breath hitches. His eyes are still black, and there is something cold about his stare. Something truly menacing.

It terrifies me.

Rynthea leans forward and glares at Thane, blocking me with an arm across my chest, her other hand on the dagger at her waist.

"Snap out of it, *sorcerer*," Rynthea warns.

Thane closes his eyes, breathing in through his nostrils. When he exhales and opens his eyes again, they're back to normal. Mostly.

"A-are you okay?" I ask warily.

"Fine," he mumbles, looking away.

Algar sucks in a sharp breath and springs up, immediately drawing one of his daggers and babbling incoherently.

"Settle down." Rynthea goes to him, forcing his arm down. She can't help but laugh.

"What the shadows just happened?" he wheezes.

"Thane just saved your life," Rynthea informs him.

"Did he? I knew he still cared about me." Algar looks for his friend, but Thane is already wandering away.

I press my hands to a nearby stone to stand but can't pull my eyes away from Thane. His hands are shaking as he stares at them, lines of concern etched into his forehead.

Yes, Thane saved Algar's life. He barely hesitated to do so, despite the repercussions he could've faced from using black magic.

But was it the right thing to do? Did we push him too far?

As I stare at him, recalling that cold, wicked look in his eyes, I wonder just how much it has cost him to save our friend.

Chapter 53

We sit for several minutes to reorient ourselves, but howls start up in the distance. More shadowhounds are on the way.

"We need to get inside before more of those things sniff us out." Thane has pulled himself together enough to focus, now leading the way toward the temple as I put on my rucksack and tighten the straps. My thigh is still aching and sore, but I can tell it's healing.

We trail Thane to the entrance. As we approach the towering building, I have to wrap my mind around the fact that we've made it. This is a place that many people only *dream* about—but I'm here.

Up close, the temple is coated with a thin layer of red dirt and wrapped in thorny, dark-green vines. About twenty crumbling steps pave the way up to an arched entrance. Sculptures of doves line the stone rails.

We take the stairs by twos, stopping short of the entryway when Thane throws up a hand.

"There are runes," he murmurs, studying the arch. "I heard there would be."

I look with him, taking notice of the symbols carved into the stone bordering the top of the entrance. "What does it say?" I ask.

"Abundance is obtained only by wisdom and blood," Thane answers, reading the runes aloud.

"What is *that* supposed to mean?" Rynthea rubs her chest as she stares up, too. Blood is leaking through the gaps of her waistcoat where she was struck the second time.

"It means you can only enter with a blood offering." Thane reaches up to touch the rune, and it sparks a silvery white. He draws in a sharp breath. "It senses my magic." After he says that, the tunnel flashes in the same white light as the runes before melting into darkness again.

He steps backward, seeming perplexed.

"I think I know how we can get in. We'll have to do it with a bit of a twist, but it could work." Thane whips out a dagger and passes it to Rynthea by the handle. "Carve the third symbol into my palm."

Rynthea's eyebrows pull together as she looks from the dagger to the symbols above. "Okay?" She takes the dagger, still confused. "And then what?"

"The third symbol means wisdom," he explains, pointing up. "This temple seeks wisdom and blood in those who want in. It doesn't explain how. If we all carve that third symbol into our palms and brand ourselves with wisdom, we might get access."

"Oh, gods," Algar says, eyes rolling. "*More* blood?"

"Yes," Thane says. "And hopefully it'll be the last bit of blood drawn from us on this island."

Rynthea frowns at the runes. "What if we get trapped inside? Or we do something wrong, and this temple kills us as soon as we enter?"

"I'll go in first," Thane says, glancing at the entrance. "If I die or something happens to me, then you'll know. But the treasure you're looking for is most likely in there because I don't sense it out here."

Rynthea continues to frown, but her shoulders soften as she looks from me to Algar and then at Thane again. "Fine," she mumbles.

Thane's eyes dart my way. "You okay with having your hand cut?"

"If that's what gets us in, yes."

The hounds howl again, and the leaves on the trees rustle, a whisper that trouble is on the way.

Thane sticks his hand out, palm up, as he looks Rynthea in the eyes. "Do it."

Sighing, she straightens her back and places the tip of the dagger on his skin. She gives the rune a quick glance before dragging the blade across his flesh.

I refrain from wincing as blood accumulates on the surface of his hand. Thane doesn't react, of course. He simply stares at his hand while Rynthea looks between his palm and the third rune.

"There." Rynthea drops his hand and steps back.

Thane inspects it before nodding. "Good enough." He faces the entrance again. The howls are closing in.

"Let's hurry this up, please," Algar pleads with a nervous peek over his shoulder.

Thane presses his bloody palm to the temple, and the runes flicker like a faint heartbeat. Squaring his shoulders, he drops his hand and takes a step inside.

A knot forms in my throat as I wait to see what kind of threat will come for him. Surely *something* will happen if he's wrong about carving the rune into our hands. What if he walks in and something chops him into pieces? Or a thousand arrows fly out of the walls all at once and pierce him from head to toe?

My heart drums faster as he carries himself deeper into the tunnel. When he disappears in the darkness, I wait with bated breath.

One second.

Two seconds.

Three seconds.

Four seconds.

Five seconds later, rapid footsteps pound on the floor, and Thane materializes again. "It worked," he breathes. To my surprise, I can tell he's smiling behind his mask.

"Oh, thank Orvena," I sigh. "Rynthea, do you want me to do yours?"

"Sure."

She flips the dagger and offers it to me by the handle. I give the rune a good look before pressing the tip into her palm and cutting two straight lines downward and a single curve between them. Her nostrils flare, but she pushes through, keeping her other hand pressed to her chest.

When I'm done with hers, I turn to Algar, who slaps a hand over his eyes while holding out a palm.

"Just get it over with," he groans.

I fight a smile as I start on his hand, too. "We're so close," I remind him. "It's almost over."

"Yeah." He winces as I dig the blade a little deeper to pierce through the skin. He hisses at the sting. "Wait until people hear the stories. They'll never believe any of this."

Despite the howls growing louder, I crack a grin and finish up his hand.

"Okay, you two go on in. See if you can find any treasure," Thane instructs.

"Be careful," I call after them as they press their bloodied hands to the outer wall of the temple. When they're inside, darkness cocooning them, I face Thane and offer him my hand.

"You won't feel a thing," he assures me, wrapping his long fingers around my wrist. The warmth of his hand intensifies and sparks gold beneath mine. Then he sticks the dagger into my palm to begin the symbol. He's right. I can't feel him cutting me.

"You know a lot of sorcery." I watch as he works on the first line.

"I wouldn't have been able to save your precious mortal life so many times if I hadn't gotten the hang of it."

I laugh. "I guess that's true."

Sighing, I peer up at the temple. Milky light shines from a gap in the treetops and bathes half of my face. I take a moment to soak it in. For all I know, this could be the last time I see any kind of natural light.

"Ready?" I ask, leveling gazes with Thane.

He nods, but there's a slight reluctance. Maybe, secretly, like me, he doesn't want our time together to end. Maybe he knows that once I have one of the prosperity stones and we're back in Gadonia, we'll drift apart.

Forever.

I reel him in for a tight hug. He freezes for a split second before wrapping me in his arms. "What's this for?" he asks over my shoulder.

"For staying true to your word." I lean back and hold his waist with my good hand. "You protected me. I wasn't so sure in the beginning, but… it was worth it."

His eyes fall as he lowers his head. "I told you I don't like to fail."

"You did." I place a kiss on his cheek. "Thank you again—not just for this, but for helping me save my sister's life."

He doesn't smile behind his mask. If anything, his eyes seem to sadden. "Zaira, I need to tell you something. I tried to tell you before, but—"

He's cut off by a howl close by…too close.

"Whatever you want to say might have to wait. We need to get inside." I press my hand to the temple like the others did.

Thane trails behind me as I stumble through the dark tunnel. I don't stop until I make it to an expansive room where streaks of light from the broken roof shine down on the ruins and rubble below.

Tunnels run in all directions like wheels on a spoke. Some have been blocked by collapsed stone, but the other passages lead to tunnels leaking with thin strips of light. A statue of Orvena is in the center of the temple, along with towering, jagged crystal pillars. Vines wrap around Orvena, starting at her feet and climbing to her head. One of the statue's arms is broken, but in her still-intact hand is a sword. She's been sculpted to wear robes and strappy sandals, and on her back is a pair of large wings.

I've never seen a statue of our goddess with wings. Is this her true form?

Water leaks from the gaps in the ceiling, splashing on fractured marble floors and accumulating into various puddles. It smells stale. More vines crawl up the walls, while some hang from the roof. There's an altar in the room with a throne made of marble that's crumbled to ruins. The steep steps leading to the throne are probably the only thing in this temple that aren't damaged.

Regardless, something about this temple carries a majestic grace. It seems to be filled with life and energy, despite how badly damaged it is. It feels like a beacon of hope in the midst of chaos—a feeling only Orvena could create. Xaimur tried to tear her creations down, and he failed.

I notice Rynthea and Algar standing near an old fountain.

"I'm not seeing any treasure." Rynthea frowns as her eyes swivel to Thane.

Thane walks past me and throws up several orbs of light, one for each walkable tunnel. The orbs float through, highlighting the walls until their light fades. Only one orb returns. The rest, I assume, are lost in darkness.

"That way," Thane says as the orb melts into his palm again. He doesn't wait for us to catch up as he advances. Water drips on my shoulder as I follow his lead, ducking and weaving cobwebs.

This particular tunnel leads to a tower where the roof is completely gone and left in shambles. What's stored inside, however, is enough to fill me with joy and relief.

The room is packed with wooden trunks filled to the brim with gold coins, goblets, crystals, and pearls.

"Holy Orvena," Algar says in awe.

"Wow. The sorcerer wasn't lying," Rynthea murmurs.

Without another word, she and Algar dash ahead, ripping their rucksacks off their backs and dropping to their knees in front of one of the trunks to shovel treasure into them.

I smile as I watch them fill their rucksacks, then laugh when Algar says, "We should just take one of the trunks with us, right? No way we're leaving so much of this behind!"

"It'd only slow us down," Rynthea tells him. "Fill your bag with as much as you can." She looks at me. "Zaira, should I fill yours? I'll carry it for you if it gets too heavy."

"Uh, sure. Yeah." I can do with some coin myself once Analla and I are stable.

I remove my rucksack and hand it over to her. Once she takes it, I search for Thane. He's standing near the mouth of the room with expressionless eyes, observing Rynthea and Algar as they laugh and send praises to Orvena.

When his eyes turn up to meet mine, he says, "Come with me."

He ducks out before I can ask where we're going. When I make it back to the main area, I see him walking toward another tunnel across the way that's already lit with one of his orbs.

"Wait—Thane." I walk as quickly as I can, but my thigh is still a little tender. He pauses, waiting for me to catch up. Then he presses on, and for some reason, my heart is beating twice as fast. Not from running or hurrying, but because his mood has changed entirely.

He's nervous. Thane doesn't get nervous.

Thane follows his orb of light around another corner. When it stops, it hovers in front of a solid wall. He comes to a halt and faces it, running the pads of his fingers along a vertical crack. His fingers light up as he presses down, and then the wall splits open.

The walls groan as they part, revealing a room that is much smaller than the one where the treasure is stored. Against the wall are two wooden chairs, and on one of them sits a *corpse* with tattered beige robes hanging off its bones.

Chapter 54

"We'll need this." Thane breaks off one of the corpse's fingers.

"Are the stones here?" I ask as he steps a few paces to the right.

His eyes narrow as he scans the space, thinking. "Right here," he murmurs, making his way to the middle of the room.

I stand completely still, hardly able to breathe as he uses the finger to press a barely visible indent in the stone floor. As he does, the floor glows gold, and the bone splinters into hundreds of shards and begins to levitate.

I stare at them in awe.

Thane takes a leap back as a small section in the floor opens up and an ivory pedestal elevates from it. Floating above it is a brown, leather-bound book, worn around the edges with foreign gold runes etched into the front and back cover. A green, shimmering aura surrounds it like a cushion, highlighting its weathered pages.

Thane blows out a satisfied breath. I've never seen his eyes glitter like that—the same way Rynthea's and Algar's did over the treasure.

"Is that Azidel's tome?" I ask, inching closer.

Thane's head lifts to look at me. The bright amber in his irises seems to glow. "It is."

My heart thunders in my chest as I look him up and down. He's smiling underneath his mask—not at me, but at the book.

A flood of emotions begins to bud in the pit of my stomach.

I hate that one comes so close to fear. I want to get the tome for him, but there are so many unknowns. What if it all goes wrong? What if the reason no one could get the book before is because they died trying?

My fear heightens when he pulls out a dagger from his vest and holds it at his side. I suck in a breath, scuffling backward.

"I'm not going to hurt you, Zaira. Remember?" He trains his eyes on mine. "I never would."

I swallow hard and nod, pleased by the warmth in his voice. "Okay."

Thane drops his mask so I can see his whole face, doing so in a way to show he means no harm. It's a handsome face. One I enjoyed kissing only this morning. I relax.

Finally, he looks back at the tome, turning his dagger over in his hand, awe still in his eyes.

"I'll always hate that Seferin ruined my life," he says, shaking his head. "I looked for many ways to return his ill favor—to ruin him, too. The Sunderstone he had us steal contains some of the strongest, blackest magic. When I found out he was planning to use it to overthrow the kingdom and kill the queen, that felt like the perfect opportunity. All that gloating he did—boasting to the guild, building the Grim. Giving them all that false hope. Without the stone, he'd accomplish none of it."

He runs his fingers over his blade, as if testing its edge. "I used the knowledge of his plans to my advantage. I was going to ruin the very thing he was after, so one night, I took my blades and killed the general. Then I killed the other superiors. And then I killed thirty-seven of the assassins they'd trained and recruited. Right after that, I ran away again and took the Sunderstone with me."

"Thane," I breathe, heart pounding and aching for him at the same time. Now I understand completely why Maliek and The Shadow Guild were coming after him so hard. "Why didn't you tell me all of this before? I—I don't even know what to say right now."

"There isn't much you can say," he replies.

"So…if he's looking for you, why were you in Meriva that day? At the Tilted Crystal? So many people are a part of the Grim there."

"Because I was visiting Koa's grave." He lowers his dagger to his thigh. "And I wanted to see Helena."

"Oh."

"I also wanted to get a lead on Seferin because I want to kill him. I've been in hiding for the past year. I was tired of hiding. I wanted him to know that I was looking for him. I knew he'd catch wind of my appearance."

"But you'll die if he catches you."

"I didn't care… I was ready to leave this world so long as it meant taking him out with me…but then I walked into that tavern and met *you*."

His eyes meet mine, and warmth floods through my chest.

"With you," he continues, "I saw how much hurt he's caused beyond me. With you, it all became clear. I knew exactly what to do in order to end his worthless life. The plan came so suddenly. I couldn't let it slip through my fingers."

My hearts sinks, and a wave of sadness rinses through me. With that comment, he makes me feel like I'm simply a means to an end. Nothing more. It's disheartening. Once he kills Seferin, what comes next? I know I shouldn't wonder this, as we're not supposed to get too invested in each other, but what will I become to him when it's all said and done?

My mind circles back to Analla. She's why I'm in this temple, and I'm not leaving until I get what I came for. I can't let my emotions get in the way when I'm this close.

I lift my chin and take a deep breath. If I make the tome his, he'll be able to help me get the prosperity stones and maybe even kill Seferin. Both are massive wins…but this doesn't make his confession hurt any less.

This thing between us is not supposed to be deep, I remind myself.

But it feels like it.

"Well, we should get this over with, then." I gesture to the tome. "You need my blood, right?"

He nods. "Just a drop or two will do. Hopefully, it works."

"Okay." I start to walk his way but pause when his eyes spark and his shoulders tense.

"Zaira, look out!" he shouts as he runs toward me.

Out of thin air, someone grabs me from behind and wrangles me into their arms. The sharp, cold edge of a blade presses to my throat. When I see the glowing blue hands, I know exactly who it is we're dealing with.

Maliek.

He's back.

Chapter 55

"You're supposed to be dead," Thane snarls as he swiftly draws one of his swords.

"Look at me," Maliek shoots back. "I *am* dead." The blue light fades from his hands, bringing emphasis to his gray, pallid skin. It was pale before, but not *this* pale.

Shuffling footsteps gather around us. My heart sinks in my chest as a handful of assassins surrounds us with their weapons drawn and eyes pinned on Thane.

"Let me guess." Thane levels his sword at Maliek. I grunt as Maliek lugs me backward. "Seferin used the blackest magic he could conjure to bring you back to life. Tell me, how many lives has he stolen in order to restore your body?"

Maliek doesn't answer. Instead, he presses the blade deeper into my throat. It stings as he holds it close, and I fight a whimper. One yank of his arm and I'll be dead.

Just like Koa.

Thane doesn't want to show it, but I'm certain I see his eyes flare as he focuses on the knife at my throat. "Let her go."

"Now why would I do that?" Maliek wraps his arm tighter around my chest. "She's your noble one, no?"

Thane lifts the sword as the other assassins close in.

"It's amazing how far you're willing to go for your selfish needs, Valkor." Maliek chuckles darkly. "We barely had a problem crossing the island because you and your strange little crew did most of the work for us. And the hounds? Thank you for taking care of those for us as well. There were only two around the temple when we arrived, and despite losing four men, they were quite easy to take down, considering how distracted they were by the mess you made."

Thane clenches his jaw.

"Now," Maliek rasps, holding on to me tighter. "I want *two* things. The Sunderstone *and* Azidel's tome."

"You'll get neither," Thane bites back.

I drop my hand, slowly reaching for the dagger sheathed at my waist. Thane watches the action, then gives a discreet nod.

"Has he told you yet, pretty little mortal?" Maliek yanks me sideways, and I pull my hand from the dagger as he twists me around, forcing me to face him. His eyes are just as cold and blue as they were, and there's a massive scar on his forehead that wasn't there before. Black veins resembling spider legs crawl from his throat to his chin. He definitely *looks* dead. "Did he tell you why you're *really* in this temple?"

"I know why I'm here," I seethe.

"Do you now?" Maliek flashes a wicked grin, taking a childish peek over me at Thane. "Because during our hunt for him, we heard you were looking for the prosperity stones."

"Maliek, I will *kill* you!" Thane barks.

"Did he tell you that all the prosperity stones are gone? That they were used *centuries* ago to save previous lives? He's known all along."

Everything inside me becomes hollow. "What?" I whisper.

I look at Thane, tears forming in my eyes. He gives Maliek a blank look, and Maliek laughs as he studies the shock written on my face.

"Oh, come on now, Valkor. Tell her the truth for once."

My body goes more numb with each second Thane avoids my eyes. I don't trust Maliek, but I can't help remembering the words Thane said to me before.

Promise me that you won't be too disappointed if none of the stones are there.

Those were his words exactly.

Did he really know all along? Could he have been lying this whole time just to get me here for his own selfish reasons?

"Zaira, just listen to me…" Thane puts his hands out, pleading with me.

This time, I look away, my bottom lip trembling.

Maliek laughs at Thane's supplication.

"Did he tell you he knew this information before your ridiculous quest even began?"

I want to look at Thane to confirm this is true, but my body won't let me. I'm too afraid the disappointment will sink in, the heartache. The pain. The *anger*.

He knew. All this time, he knew.

He never intended to help me. He used me.

You wear your heart on your sleeve, Quinlocke, and that'll get you killed one day.

"You're lying," I whisper, directing my anger at Maliek.

"Oh, believe me, I tell no lies." Maliek is gloating now. "He got you to trust him, all so you could win him that beautiful tome there…and you fell for his bullshit."

This time, when I look at Thane, he's angry. His eyes are lit a bright gold, and his teeth are bared. The other assassins inch closer, but he doesn't bother giving them attention. He's only looking at Maliek.

But I want him to look at me.

I *need* him to look at me.

I manage to maneuver myself out of Maliek's grasp, and one of the assassins rushes my way. Maliek holds up a hand to stop him. "No, no. Let's see how this plays out," he says with humor in his tone.

I run to Thane and take his face in my hands. His eyes are sad—no. Defeated. I've never seen Thane Valkor defeated. A rawness accumulates in my throat as I hold back my tears.

"Tell me he's lying, Thane!" I beg, holding his face tighter.

He's quiet for a few seconds, which increases my dread. Then he says, "We still have time to figure it out, Zaira. That tome is powerful. I'm sure there is a spell in it that I can use to break your sister's curse—"

My hands fall as I stare at him, feeling a heaviness settle on my chest now.

"See?" Maliek bellows. "He's *using* you, little mortal. Just like he uses everyone! He lies and manipulates because that is what he's best at! All he needed was someone desperate enough to come here. He gave you false hope! Listen to him! He's still trying."

I look from Maliek's shit-eating grin to Thane's now-unreadable gaze.

Confusion shakes me to my core as I take another step back. My brain is telling me one thing, yet my heart screams another. I want to believe Thane can find a spell in the tome, but what if he's wrong? What if there's nothing he can do?

I'll have no stones. No spells. Nothing. Analla will be dead based on yet another possibility—only this time it'll hurt twice as much because I trusted him.

My breathing quickens, and eventually I wheeze as my tears fall.

I can't lose my sister.

I can't.

Thane rushes to me and tries holding me by my shoulders, but I shake my head and back away.

"No," I say through labored breaths. "Please—don't touch me."

He gives me a baffled stare as I do my best to control my breath and fight off the panic swirling inside me. Gods, how could I be so stupid?

"Zaira, I'm sorry," he pleads. "I told you this shouldn't have gotten as deep as it did between us—"

"But it did, and you *lied* to me, Thane! For days, you've been lying to me! I've sacrificed so much just to come to this island! You got what you wanted, but now my sister is going to die. Don't you understand that?"

His head shakes quickly. "I won't let that happen, Zaira. We have the tome—I can figure something out. I can still help you save her."

Maliek chuckles behind me, and I want to slap him, but I'm too pissed at the man in front of me. The man I had so much faith in. The man I thought could change.

Thane comes closer, taking my hand in his. "You can still trust me. I can help you."

I keep my gaze on him a few seconds longer, doing my best to fight the anguish. Then I close my eyes and breathe as evenly as possible. As hurt and devastated as I am, I can't let this end here. Not like this. I have to find another way to save Analla, and if I can't, I at least have to get back to her.

I still have time. I can figure something else out with or without Thane.

But first I need to make it off this damn island.

I snatch the dagger from my waist and move past Thane. Sliding the edge of the blade across my uncut palm, I fight a wince as I march to the pedestal and raise my hand above it.

I'm the so-called brave and noble mortal they need.

Okay.

So be it.

Let's see if it's true.

Blood drips down rapidly, coating the leather cover and dripping over the edge of the pedestal.

To my surprise, the book drops to the pedestal with a loud *smack*, and the glittering green aura dissolves. I pick it up. It's heavier than it looks. My blood is smeared on the cover and the edges of some of the pages.

"Get him," Maliek orders. "But keep him alive. We still need the Sunderstone."

The assassins charge at Thane, gripping him by the upper arms. Oddly, he doesn't fight them off this time. He just stares at me with a lost look in his damp eyes.

I don't know what he's thinking.

I wish I didn't care.

I turn toward Maliek.

"Hand it here." Maliek sticks out his hand while using the other to point a sword at me.

"Only if you talk to Seferin," I demand, holding the book back.

Maliek's head tilts. "What about?"

"My sister. Tell him that he has to break her curse—that he *has* to set her free and never bother us again."

He sneers, looking me over. "Is that all?"

"Yes. I'll travel back with you, and you can tell him that I willingly gave you the tome. Because *you* work for *him*, right? You follow his every order, and he trusts your intel?"

Maliek's smirk slips.

"He'll have the tome, and he'll be even more powerful," I go on.

"Zaira, no," Thane pleads. One of the assassins forces him to his knees, slamming him down so hard something cracks. He groans in pain.

"I just want her back," I whisper in a broken voice.

"Fine." Maliek sticks his hand out farther. "I'll tell Seferin you cooperated."

I stare into Maliek's eyes for a moment, then look at Thane. His head is hung low, lashes fanning across his cheekbones.

He looks...broken.

"Thank you for telling me the truth," I say loudly, peering up at Maliek again. I rush in to hug him tight, and he freezes, unsure of what to do with the gesture.

Then he roars in agony as I plunge my dagger through his cold, dead heart.

Chapter 56

"Get up, Thane!" I yell as I snatch the dagger out of Maliek's chest. Maliek's sword clatters to the ground, and dark-red—nearly black—blood drips out of his mouth. I didn't think he'd physically react, seeing as he's already dead. Clearly, he's not dead enough.

Maliek throws a weak punch at me, and I duck just in time. Grappling for me, he misses and stumbles forward, landing on his face. Blood spills from under him, and the room fills with grunts and clashing swords.

I look over to where Thane is lying on his back, struggling to fend off one of the assassins' swords with his own blade. The gleaming edge is mere inches from his face, ready to slice through his flesh. He manages to shove the assassin off of him and hop to his feet before it can reach him.

One of the assassins grabs me, and I yell as another tries taking the tome. A blast of gold knocks one of them away. The one holding me loses his footing, slams down on his back, and cracks his skull when Thane gives his wrist a hard twist.

"Go, Zaira! Take the others and get out of here!" Thane shouts as more assassins rush him.

Thane goes for his swords and resumes the fight while I run for the tunnel with the tome tucked under my armpit. I pant wildly, stumbling through the ruined hall and jumping over thick piles of vines to reach the room full of treasure.

I hate to leave him alone, but I need to keep the tome out of The Shadow Guild's clutches.

A wave of relief rolls through me as I near the treasure room. Rynthea and Algar have their rucksacks fully stuffed with treasure and are now trying to tuck more into their pockets.

"Hey, you two," I call.

They turn to look at me at the same time as I step through the doorway.

"We need to get out of here," I demand. "Right now."

"What's going on?" Algar asks.

"Maliek," I say, and that name is enough for both of them to frown. "He and his assassins just attacked us."

"Wait—*what? Maliek?*" Rynthea says in shock. "I thought Thane killed him!"

"He *did* kill him…and I just killed him again…"

Algar scratches the back of his head, completely puzzled.

"I'm not understanding. If he was dead when Thane killed him, how did he manage to come here and attack again?" Rynthea snaps.

"An evil sorcerer brought him back to life somehow— Look, It's a long story, but to sum it up, they're after Thane because of this." I hold Azidel's tome in the air.

Rynthea and Algar stare at it, their faces warped with confusion.

"What is that?" Rynthea asks.

"I'll explain more later, but right now we *really* need to get out of here."

"What about the stones?" she asks.

"Thane lied." My chest tightens just thinking about it again. "The stones were taken a long time ago…and he knew."

"Motherfucker," Rynthea spits.

"Where is Thane?" Algar asks, peering past my shoulder in search of his friend.

"Who cares about that liar?" Rynthea growls, snatching up her scythesword. "He'll catch up with us if he makes it out alive. Let's go. Now."

Rynthea tosses me my loaded rucksack while Algar tries to pick up a few more coins on our way out. As we retrace our steps and sprint through the dark tunnels, Thane's words repeat in my head.

That tome is powerful. I'm sure there is a spell in it that I can use to break your sister's curse…

I can only hope that's true.

Chapter 57

To my revelation, the creatures were much more intent on keeping us away from the temple than they are on preventing our escape from the island. Their efforts aren't nearly as intense as we make our way to shore, which suits me just fine.

There are no shadowhounds waiting to attack, though we do notice the corpses of the ones we battled twitching. Rynthea says they're likely coming to life again—that abominations like that don't simply die. We don't stick around long enough to find out, but we do hear their howls when we finally make it to the rim of the bowl.

Oddly, they aren't my biggest concern.

What we really have to worry about are that there are no shadow assassins following us.

Fortunately, we're able to avoid the reptilian creatures while wading through the forest. We do stumble past a few massive wasps near their nests, but Rynthea angrily cuts through them, leaving yellowish-green goop all over the place.

No one seems to be tailing us as we reach the platform path over the lava. Algar teleports me to the safer side, then returns and teleports Rynthea. She's too weak to make the jumps safely.

Teleporting two of us clearly takes a toll on Algar, because once he releases Rynthea, he leans over with his hands on his knees and sucks in gulps of air. It takes him a few minutes to collect himself, and once he's stable enough, we take off again.

The closer we get to the beach where we left our rowboat, the more hopeful I become that we're really going to make it off this dreaded island. Relief buzzes through me, making me a little light-headed—or maybe it's just the physical and emotional exhaustion finally catching up.

We've done the impossible and survived against all odds, and believe me, the odds have been substantial. We battled terrible creatures and defied death.

I step over a log across the path, shaking my head in disbelief. No, we haven't just defied death. We told it to fuck right off. Algar actually died, and Rynthea came close to it, but here we are, still alive and breathing.

We wouldn't be if it weren't for Thane, though, and that notion pains me.

A heavy feeling settles in my stomach at the thought that we left Thane behind to fend for himself. I look over my shoulder while reminding myself that he knows what to do. He's handled and protected himself for years. Still, that doesn't make me any less worried about him.

It seems ridiculous to worry this much. He's broken my heart. I shouldn't care…but I do. And I don't want him to die.

"I smell the sea," Rynthea says after sniffing the air. "We're getting close." She picks up her pace.

I take a deep breath and roll my shoulders back as the path widens, and it doesn't take long to catch glimpses of the beach through the gaps of bushes ahead.

I look back once more for Thane as we trudge across the dark sands. Algar drops his rucksack, and Rynthea marches toward the boat and drops her bag inside it.

Leaves rustle close by, and I startle, thinking it's one of the assassins from The Shadow Guild—until I see a familiar outline break through the edge of the forest.

Relief springs to my chest just as quickly as the reminder of his betrayal. I fight to hold back tears once again and turn away from him as he approaches so he won't see them fall.

Rynthea, however, has no problem expressing her feelings. "You bastard," she snarls as she points a stern finger at him. "I knew you couldn't be trusted!"

Thane clings to silence.

I cut my gaze to Algar. He can't even look him in the eye.

"You're lucky I don't feed you to one of the monsters on this fucking island!" Rynthea rages on. "Tell us everything. Now, sorcerer."

"I…" Thane trails off, but that single word alone is full of pain. His silence seems even louder as the ocean roars around us.

"He was once a part of The Shadow Guild, he stole a crystal, and now Seferin wants it back," I provide when the silence has gone on for too long. "That's not all he's been hiding, though."

"What do you mean?" Algar asks, limping toward me.

I hold the tome in the air again. "This is the Tome of Azidel," I explain. "Azidel was the first and most powerful sorcerer of Thelanor. In order to retrieve it, the blood of a brave and noble mortal had to be offered. Thane knew all of this. He just needed a person who was desperate enough to come to The Shallows." I grit my teeth to fight a new wave of tears. "He dragged me here to get this so he can be the next most powerful sorcerer in Thelanor. He did all of this for revenge."

"Wait a minute." Algar holds up his hands, frowning at Thane. "You brought us all here and lied to Zaira about the stones so you could get a fucking *book*?"

I finally look at Thane, just as he turns his head and clenches his jaw, refusing to answer.

"I knew you were hiding something." Rynthea clenches her fist as she steps closer to him. I can tell she wants to pummel him into the ground.

"I can't believe this." Algar scoffs, not in pure disbelief, but in a way that he should've known all along and is upset that he didn't piece it together. "You jeopardized Zaira's life! Are you shitting me? Now her sister will die because you were greedy for power. How can you be so selfish?" He comes chest to chest with Thane, pointing a finger at him. "And all this time, I thought the old you was still in there somewhere. I thought you could still be redeemed. I should've known better."

"I don't understand why you're so angry!" Thane finally snaps. "You have your treasure! You got what you came for!"

"Yes, but at what cost?" Algar shoots back. "I did this for the treasure, yes, but also because I thought we were doing a good thing here! Breaking a curse, helping Zaira? That felt necessary. Yes, I wanted to change my life with all this coin and crystal, but I just— *Fuck*, Thane! I just thought for once, everything would work out and I could have a *family* again. That, if we survived all of this, there would be people I could call on when I didn't want to spend my nights alone."

The tears sting my eyes as Algar limps backward.

"But that was never going to happen…was it?" Algar's voice softens so much an ache develops deep in my chest. With tears in his eyes and a disappointed shake of his head, he gives Thane his back. "I'm fucking done. I tried being there, but you're too fucked in the head to bother."

When Algar approaches the rowboat, Rynthea storms past me, reels her elbow back, and punches Thane square in the face.

He grunts as he lands flat on his back on the hard sand. Blood leaks from his nose and mouth as Rynthea stands over him and grimaces with flaring nostrils.

"I've been looking for a reason to do that since the day we met." She looks Thane up and down, still seething. "Get in the boat, Zaira. You don't need him anymore."

I *don't* need him anymore…

But there was a point when he was all I needed in order to survive. I counted on him. Relied on him. I saw the best parts of him. I *gave* myself to him, all because I had the stupid idea that he could change—that he could be a better person and get rid of his dark life if he saw just a sliver of light.

But it was all a lie.

He used my vulnerability like a cloth and expected it to wipe away all the mess he's created. He knew during *every single second* of our journey that the stones weren't there. All the opportunities he had to tell me, and he didn't bother sparing me the heartache once.

Yes, maybe I'm the fool for believing that the stones could still be around after so long, but I would rather he crush my hope with the truth than lie and use me every step of the way.

Analla is going to die, and I just risked my life over and over again, all to wind up back where I started. It's an awful feeling, sitting with this.

He may as well have taken a dagger and stabbed me in the chest. Perhaps that would've been less painful.

With a grunt, Thane gets up and brushes the sand off of his clothes. I step closer to him with a trembling bottom lip, looking deep into his eyes. I want him to take it all back. To apologize. To *say* he regrets it. I want him to say everything he feels all so I can tell him that I will *never, ever* forgive him for this. I want him to understand my hurt so he can hurt, too.

"I'm really sorry, Zaira," he whispers. His eyes are wet. His voice defeated.

Hearing those words come out of his mouth reminds me of the same ones he uttered in Gadonia.

Mea trelanak.

So that's what he meant.

Sorry for lying to you.

Sorry for wasting your time.

Sorry for breaking your heart before you even realized it.

I shove the tome into his chest so hard he grunts again. That doesn't stop him from wrapping his arms around it. He cradles it, as if this book is more important than anything else in his life.

Perhaps it is.

We all board our rowboat after pushing it into the water. Algar offers to help row, but his overuse of magic has left him weak. Thane is also drained after bringing Algar back to life and fighting off the assassins.

Rynthea gives me a little wink as she hands me the second oar. "We can handle it from here."

I force a smile her way, dropping the flat blade into the water.

Chapter 58

We arrive at the *Emellie* just before sunset, and Algar gives his horn a blow to alert the crew.

Captain Solyen and the crew are shocked to see that we've made it out alive, and when we board, they bombard us with questions.

After we settle their curiosity by answering a few of their questions, the ship sets sail.

The ship ride is...*quiet*, to say the least. Despite Algar and Rynthea having treasure and bright futures ahead, their spirits are far from joyous.

As night falls, it's time to tuck away in the cabins. I stare at the bedding on the floor where Thane slept only last night. He opted to stay on the deck for the night. He probably won't even sleep.

I roll over, waiting for Rynthea and Algar to fall asleep before crying quietly into my pillow.

Once we make it to the docks of Gadonia, Rynthea, Algar, and I decide to return to Irina's inn, but not without Thane calling for me to wait.

I ignore him, pressing on, but he catches up with me.

"Zaira, will you please let me explain myself?" he asks, stepping in front of me and cutting me off mid-stride. "I studied the tome all night, and—"

"Did you find a spell to break Analla's curse?" I demand, finally looking at him.

"Not yet, but if I can combine two of the spells, I might be able to—"

"Might?" I repeat, cutting him off. "Might isn't good enough, Thane. I need you to be certain."

"I know this can work. I just need time to go over the spells and to find the right materials."

Rynthea steps between us to get in Thane's face. "She doesn't want your help. Take your book of spells and fuck off."

Thane's jaw locks as they glower at each other. Rynthea doesn't dare back down. After a few seconds, he turns his gaze to me, then shakes his head and walks away.

Rynthea proceeds to Irina's inn once Thane is a good distance away. I follow her lead, but I can't help looking over my shoulder to see him walking with his head down. It hurts my heart to see him this way, but I don't have it in me to forgive him right now.

After we've freshened up at the inn, we decide to head to a tavern in the heart of the city where the music is lively and the Gadonians are cheerful.

"What are you going to do now?" Algar asks as he sits on the stool next to me.

It's strange to see how people can just live normal, exciting lives after everything I've gone through. Truthfully, I don't think I'm ever going to be the same. The excited, bright-eyed Zaira has been washed away, now replaced by a sad, empty version with a broken heart.

Zephra sits on Algar's shoulder, ogling me as he awaits my response. He was so happy to be reunited with her on the ship, and she squealed with delight when she saw her charmer again.

"I'm going to ask Captain Solyen if he'll sail me to Meriva," I tell him.

"And what about your sister?" he asks warily.

I avoid his eyes by putting my focus on the barrels of ale behind the bar counter instead. "There's one more thing I can do to make things right for her."

There's a brief moment of silence.

"Zaira." Algar leans forward. I cave and give him my attention. "You don't plan on doing something reckless, do you? Wasn't venturing to The Shallows enough?"

"No, I don't plan on doing anything reckless," I lie. "Maybe I'll tell the queen that Seferin has my sister. I have so much information I've learned about The Shadow Guild now. Maybe they'll be more inclined to help me if I give them intel..."

"The guild will *kill* you, Zaira. And your sister." Algar looks at me a bit more closely. "I need you *not* to get yourself killed after all we've been through."

"Well, I don't know what else to do, Algar," I snap, and my voice is loud enough for Rynthea to place her fresh pint of ale down next to me.

"What's going on?" she asks as I drop my face in my hands.

"Zaira's planning on doing something *really* unwise," Algar informs her. I look up, and his eyes are still glued to me. "Listen to me, Zaira. It might be time to cut your losses. Even if you do tell the queen what you know, that palace has ears. They'll run right to the Grim and inform them. Seferin will find out, and he'll kill your sister before the curse can. Then he'll come for you. Is that what you want?"

"No," I mutter, frustrated.

"He's right." Rynthea places a gentle hand on my shoulder. "You did everything you could, Zaira. You truly went above and beyond. I don't see any other way for your sister to get out of this alive. I'm so sorry."

An ache takes over my whole body. I stare at Rynthea until my vision blurs and then look at a hazy version of Algar and Zephra. When my tears fall and a sob racks my body, they wrap their arms around me and hold me close.

Neither of them says a word.

They simply allow me the time to cry.

To process my denial.

To understand what I'm about to lose.

But neither of them knows my tears are just a coverup.

Chapter 59

It's well after midnight by the time Captain Solyen's crew files up the gangway to the ship. On board, they mill around, laughing and getting ready to sail.

Rynthea and Algar are still fast asleep at Irina's inn. I could tell they were worried about me. While they ate their stew and drank ale at the tavern, I sat on the porch, drowning in my thoughts. And when it was time for them to go back to Irina's, I told them I was going to hang outside and watch the sunrise over the harbor.

I hate lying to them—it makes me no better than Thane. But my lies are to protect them, not use them. That makes a difference in my mind.

As I turn my plan over in my mind for the hundredth time, Enver stops by with a gentle hello. He apologizes for doubting me, then offers tea and my favorite honey loaf. This is the first time I've turned the sweet bread down. I'm not in the mood to talk to him, and, picking up on that, he gives me a hug around the shoulders and leaves.

When I spot Captain Solyen stumbling his way toward his ship, I collect my belongings and jog toward the port.

"Here." I stand on the deck of the *Emellie*, stuffing a handful of coins in his palm. "I need to get to Meriva *now*."

He examines me closely, eyebrows drawn together, trying to understand the urgency.

"Please," I add softly.

"What about the other three?"

"The Shallows was a lot for them. They aren't strong enough to travel yet." And they're going to be furious when they find out I've left without them. Guilt makes my stomach churn. The ship ride to Meriva will take nearly fourteen hours. If I want to make it there in time, I have to leave immediately. "Maybe you can give them passage in a few days?"

"Yeah. All right." Solyen hollers for his crew to prepare to sail.

As I walk on board toward the cabin, I notice a dark silhouette in the distance. Sitting on the beach, close to the ocean, is Thane. That stupid tome is in his lap, and he's looking my way. I can't make out his facial expression, but I do see his eyes spark that familiar gold as he closes the tome and stands up.

I enter the cabin, settling into one of the chairs at the table and mentally going over my plan again.

As the boat starts to move, an abrupt flurry of gold appears a few steps away from me. I gasp when I see Thane with his nostrils mildly flared. He strides right up to me with a frown.

"What do you think you're doing, Zaira?" he asks in a gravelly voice.

"What does it look like? I'm going back to Meriva Empire."

"In the middle of the night?"

"Yes. I need to get back so I can bargain with Seferin to save my sister," I inform him, folding my arms.

"He'll kill you," he counters in an irritated, matter-of-fact tone.

"Not if I trade my life for Analla's. My blood freed the tome. Maybe he can use that."

"He'll kill her and then squeeze every ounce of life out of you," he seethes with a frown. "Going directly to him is reckless and foolish, and you know it. Otherwise, you'd have done so from the beginning."

"Exactly," I respond, and he looks me all over, confused. "Which is why there's more to my new plan…but I can't do it without your magic."

His eyes narrow a bit. "Why didn't you just come to me first, then?" he asks. "I told you I'd help."

I work hard to swallow. "Because I needed to know you were one hundred percent willing to come aboard for me—that for once you weren't just thinking about yourself. If you hadn't, I still would've tried anyway, and yes, it may have resulted in failure, but at least I'd go out knowing I did everything I could for Analla."

He seems to contemplate all of this as he studies my face. Then his shoulders soften. "I said I'd help you save her, Zaira. I know you don't want to believe it after everything, but I meant that. I'm right here. Put me to work."

My traitorous heart flutters. I was expecting a bit more resistance from him, but there's a look in his eyes. One of certainty along with a whisper of desperation.

Though I feel myself softening for him, I shake my head. "This doesn't change anything between us," I add, pointing a stern finger at him. "I want nothing more than to be angry with you and to never speak to you again, but that would be selfish on my part—especially when I know you have something we can use." I point at the tome still tucked under his arm. "Is there a spell in there that allows you to hear me if we're in different locations?"

"There is a mindflare spell," he returns, "but I don't need the tome for that. It's a common spell. I just need a lock of your hair or a drop of blood to make it work."

"And what about a spell to enhance the properties of an elixir?"

At that, he narrows his eyes. "I'm sure there's something in the tome I can work with. Why?" His head cocks a bit. "What are you planning, Zaira?"

I gesture to the chair beside me. "Sit and I'll explain."

He does, and as I go over everything I have in mind, his eyes widen more and more. This plan is dangerous, with a *very* slim chance of survival.

But if we do it right—if we go in prepared—even he knows that it just might work.

Chapter 60

As I walk off the gangway in Meriva, I notice the streets of the Commons are exactly the same as any other night. A few people walk by themselves along the cobblestone roads, merchants are closing shop, and the familiar scent of the salty canal stings my nose as I pass it.

The cold gets to me, so I dig through my rucksack for a long-sleeve sweater. It hardly helps, but I figure I should embrace the chill because it makes me feel something. It reminds me that I'm still here, still capable of rectifying things.

Someone falls into step beside me, matching my pace.

I look to my left at Thane, who nods at me before disappearing completely with an enhanced whispershade. It's best if no one in the kingdom sees him. I don't want Seferin to have any kind of warning or heads-up about Thane being around.

I slow my pace as I near a familiar alley and walk through it. It's darker here, with stacked multi-level homes overlooking the street. It isn't exactly in the Scraps, but it's close.

At the end of the alley is an open door with soft wafts of pink smoke billowing out and licking the ground. I step into the sorceress's apothecary and spot a woman behind the counter wearing a gray scarf on her head. A beady-eyed white owl is perched on her shoulder, watching me as the woman does.

"Welcome back," the sorceress greets in a raspy voice.

I give her a nod of recognition.

I've been here several times with Analla, most times for healing elixirs, medicines, and the sort. Her shop is filled with all sorts of crystals and trinkets. Animal and beast furs line one of the walls, and above are floating pink orbs. The scent of sulfur is barely masked by a strong floral fragrance.

Behind her is a shelf with several vials filled with liquids of various colors.

Approaching the counter, I dig into my satchel and request one of the vials. She raises a curious eyebrow at me before turning to retrieve one containing dark-purple liquid.

"Big plans, yes?" she asks, sliding the glass vial across the counter.

I place the coins in her hands. "Yes." I scoop up the small bottle and study the swirling concoction inside.

She picks up the coins and slips them into a pouch tied at her waist.

"Thank you."

"Use it wisely, little mortal," she calls as I twist around to leave. I glance over my shoulder to catch her smirking while stroking a finger along her owl's chest.

Thane brushes past me as I leave the sorceress's shop. Our eyes meet as I tuck the vial in my satchel. I wait for him to gather all the supplies he needs, and then we're on our way toward the Scraps.

My nose is numb by the time we reach the downtrodden area of the kingdom. Several people linger, but hardly any of them bother looking my way. Fortunately, no skrellins appear, either. I'd once been so afraid to walk through here, but nothing can scare me more than The Shallows. Nothing but losing my sister to this dreaded curse, anyway.

A line of trees and bushes marks the end of the Scraps, and I push through them, stepping over thick roots and stumbling into cobwebs.

When I finally stop in the forest, out of plain view, Thane loses the whispershade, and I hand him the vial. He gets straight to work, lowering to one knee and placing that, along with the other objects he acquired, on the ground. With his hand hovering above the vial, he murmurs a chant twice until the elixir glows in the dark.

He picks up the vial and hands it back to me. "It'll wear off within half an hour once it's activated, so don't use it until we've made it to the keep."

I nod, clutching the vial.

We take the familiar hour-long hike, and by this point my eyelids are growing heavy and my body is riddled with exhaustion, but I refuse to stop until I see The Shadow Nest.

As I approach, I hear rapid string music playing and people chatting. The area is alive, just as it is every night. I can't help thinking how only a corrupt sorcerer like Seferin would make a home on a piece of land that was once called Hollow Acre.

Legends say a dark sorcerer performed a ritual here centuries ago in an attempt to become a god. The ritual backfired and ripped a hole between the Crystal and Shadow Realms, killing everyone who lived on the land. A warning was etched into a pillar of stone a short distance away from The Shadow Nest: *whosoever claims this land shall fall within a fortnight.*

Since then, no kingdom has dared claim the land, because they believe whoever does will be cursed to fall next. Not even the savage leaders of Ruvain are foolish enough to try it.

But Seferin...well, it doesn't surprise me that he, a power-hungry man who thinks he can defy the odds, has planted his roots here.

A lot of bad shit happens on this land—unspeakable things, according to my sister. People are often found hanging from tree branches when she's on for the night. No one ever knows how those people wind up there, as none of them are visitors of The Shadow Nest.

Just random dead bodies.

Seeing this building again while standing on land that hums with darkness makes me think about Thane and his brother, Koa. I bet this was where Seferin took them on those late nights, and even the night when he helped them escape the Crystal Palace after stealing the Sunderstone from the vault.

My chest tightens as I think about Thane, who has gone ahead of me with his whispershade. *Orvena, please let this work.*

Two masked guards on patrol marching along a paved bridge connected to the building catch my periphery. They have no weapons because as sorcerers, their hands *are* the weapons.

I see a flash of gold light near them, and after several pained grunts, Thane appears where the guards were. He raises a thumb, confirming he's taken them out and that this side of the grounds is clear.

Good. Now to get inside.

I dash across the field and press my back against the building.

I try the kitchen door again, but it's locked.

"Damn it," I mutter.

I circle the building a bit more and come across a small window a few feet above ground level that I'm certain leads to the dungeons—or at least will get me close to them.

I throw back an elbow to break the glass, then pause as I look around to make sure no one heard. Thane must still be keeping the area clear. When I don't see anyone, I kick the rest of the glass out with my foot and slip inside.

I hurry toward Analla's cell, and my heart drops when I see her. She lies on her side, barely breathing. Her hair is mostly gray now, her skin dry, and her lips split.

"Analla," I whisper.

She doesn't move.

My heart starts to beat faster. "Analla," I try again, eyes burning with the urge to cry.

A faint moan slips out of her as she rustles a bit.

I let go a sigh of relief. She isn't dead yet. Thank the goddess.

She stirs sluggishly, and when her tired eyes catch me, they widen with surprise.

"Zaira." Her voice is coarse, faint.

I grab the bars, watching as she uses all her strength to sit up. She crawls toward me with great effort. When she collapses, I gasp, but she's up again. When she finally makes it to the bars, I reach for her hand. She's ice-cold.

"What are you doing here?" she asks in a dry whisper.

"I came to save you," I say, a sorrowful laugh bubbling out of me.

She doesn't smile. I don't think she has the energy to.

She's so thin now, her face hollow, dark circles surrounding her eyes. Purplish bruises the shape of fingerprints encircle her neck. I cringe at the sight of them, hating the thought that she may have been abused and tortured down here. Fortunately, her eyes still have a bit of warmth. The same beautiful brown.

I glance at the liphanet crystal in the corner, the one containing the wretched curse Seferin placed on her. I stare at it for so long, my bottom lip begins to quiver.

"I tried to get a prosperity stone, but they were long gone." My voice breaks as I look down at our hands. Hers lies limp in mine. Tears start to fall as I feel the weight of her hand in mine while remembering everything that happened at the temple. "I thought it would work out. I was a hopeful fool."

"Hey. No." She swallows hard. "Don't you cry." She whimpers a bit as she reaches through the bars with both hands to clasp my face. "I should've just quit my job like you said, right?" She laughs, but it's dry, humorless. Her lips tremble as she drops her hands, losing strength. "It isn't your job to save me. It's just my time to go."

"I *can't* lose you, too." I cling to her arm. "I'll have no one."

"That won't matter when you have a bright spirit like yours. Many people will flock to you." She gives me a weak smile. "You're the kindest, smartest little sister ever. Even during the times when you're a pain in my ass."

I hiccup a laugh, pressing my forehead to the bars as she does. We're quiet a moment, minus my sniffling.

When the plan settles back in like an anchor, I swipe my tears away. "Like I said, I can't lose you. I promised I'd get you out of this, and I never break a promise."

Her brows knit together as I stand and back away.

"What are you talking about?" she rasps. "There's nothing you can do anymore, Z. This is it."

"No." I look at one end of the dungeon. I think I can find the red door again and sneak inside that way. I dig in my satchel and take out the vial Thane worked his magic on. Removing the cork, I chug the liquid inside. It's disgusting and thick as it goes down.

When I look at Analla, she's confused for a split second. "What did you just take?" she asks. Then her eyes widen with terror. "No. What did you just do?" she croaks.

"I have a plan to get you out, but not enough time to explain. You'll just have to trust me."

"What plan?" she counters, eyes glistening. "Please don't do anything rash! I need you, too!"

"Just trust me," I insist.

"Zaira, listen to me, *please*," she begs, using the last bit of strength she has to reach through the bars for my pant leg. I refuse to hear her.

Pulling away, I run to the end of the dungeon as she rasps my name again. I find the stairs, and my pulse skitters as I take them up by twos.

I move quickly because if I don't, the fear will kick in and I'll lose faith in myself.

I'm doing this.

We're doing this.

I grab the handle to the red door and push it open. It groans on the hinges, and I brace myself as I enter the hallway. Sultry music snakes through the air, but this area is clear. After my heart settles, I sneak through the hallway and make my way toward the music.

The atmosphere grows heavy, and a strange sensation wraps around me as I proceed. It's almost like someone is controlling the energy in the room, pushing me further away from consciousness. I squeeze my eyes shut and open them again, clinging to focus.

The first room I pass is dim, flickering with weak candlelight, and clouded with smoke. Nightmaidens wearing black or red silk masks dance over half-naked men lying flat on richly colored rugs. Their movements graze the men, setting off their arousal. It's slow, deliberate— seductive.

All of them seem to be in a trance…or under a spell.

I saunter past the next room, where two naked acrobats dangle from the ceiling while a cluster of people sitting on the floor snort kopa. Their eyes are dilated, and ridiculous smiles spread across their faces as they look at one another.

I notice a spiral staircase ahead and scurry up. On the landing, two guards stand before tall double doors at the end of the corridor, and when they notice me, they grimace and solidify their stance.

"You're not supposed to be up here," one of them bellows. "Get back where you belong."

"I need to speak to Seferin," I demand. "I have something he wants."

The guards glance at each other and scoff. "Fuck off, *mortal*."

I snatch the dagger Thane gave me and point it at them. "Tell him I need to see him. Now!" My voice is steady and firm, but my hands are shaking.

The guard on the right sneers.

The one on the left raises a stern brow. "I suggest you leave, or we'll slit your pretty little throat right here, right now."

I should be frightened by that threat, but after enduring The Shallows, it's going to take a lot more than a couple of sorcerer guards to scare me. "I'm not going anywhere until I speak to him. I know he's in there, and I'm sure he'll want to hear what I have to say."

As my words echo against the stone walls, one of the doors behind the guards clanks and peels open.

A man steps out. I know exactly who he is as soon as our eyes meet.

Black suit. Red tie. Warm ivory skin. Sleek black hair. Dark, beady eyes.

Seferin.

Chapter 61

There's no denying that Seferin is a handsome man. I can see why he appealed to Analla so much, especially since she flocks to powerful men with dark features.

Seferin has a strong jaw, full light-pink lips, and slightly pointed ears. He appears young, yet everything about his demeanor is practiced and calm, as if he's roamed Thelanor for many, *many* years. His youth likely has something to do with his practice of black magic.

There's nothing but pure evil in his eyes, though. How Analla hadn't seen such malevolence at first sight confuses me. This man is a walking xerven.

"Well, hello." Seferin's sharp-toothed smile makes my skin crawl. "Zaira, correct?"

I try not to react to him knowing my name and lift the dagger higher. "I know you have my sister in your dungeon, and I want her out."

One of the guards rushes for me, but I swing the dagger and slash at his face, performing one of the moves Rynthea taught me. Blood wells and trickles down his cheek. "You bitch!" he roars, grabbing hold of my upper arm and yanking me toward him. "I'll enjoy killing you, you little shit," he spits in my face.

"No, no. Let her go." Seferin's voice is much too relaxed, considering

I've just attacked one of his people.

I pull myself away from the guard, throwing him a grimace before focusing on Seferin again and pointing the dagger at him.

Seferin takes a step forward and tilts his head, studying my weapon. "A gift?"

"What?" I snap, mildly confused.

"That's a dagger from The Divine, no?" He lifts a hand, and the dagger flies out of mine to land in his. He catches it by the blade's edge, hands curling around the metal as he inspects the hilt. There's no blood on him, despite how sharp the dagger is.

"Ah." Seferin chuckles to himself. "Yes. I can sense his magic. This belonged to *Thane Valkor*."

My heart drums a faster rhythm at Thane's name. He senses his magic? Does that mean he knows Thane is nearby? Or does he only sense it on the weapon because it was his?

"You two," Seferin calls, not taking his eyes off of me. "Leave."

The guards carry themselves through the corridor without hesitation. Seferin finally turns his eyes away so he can go to the double doors. He opens one of them wider.

"Come in." He gestures inside the room. "Let's have a chat about your darling sister…and the thing you have that I need."

My throat dries. I swallow to moisten it.

Pulse pounding in my ears, I trudge forward and move past him to enter the room. As soon as I'm inside, though, all the air leaves my lungs because standing near the window with deeply furrowed brows is Maliek.

His arms are folded, mask up, and blue eyes narrowed. If looks could kill, I'd surely be dead—just like he's supposed to be.

Fuck.

His presence throws off the plan. I hadn't factored him in. How the shadows is he even here right now?

I run a hand across my forehead, feeling heat bloom at the center to activate Thane's mindflare spell. *We have a problem, Thane. Maliek is here.*

The con to this spell is he can hear me, but I can't hear him.

"Please have a seat." Seferin walks past me to sit in a large leather chair behind the only desk in the room. His walk is more of a slow stride, as if he has all the time in the world.

I can't bring myself to move. I just stare at Maliek, waiting to see if he'll dash across the room and stab me, just as I stabbed him in the temple. How did Seferin get his body all the way here from The Shallows so quickly? How is Maliek even still standing?

"Don't worry. He won't harm you," Seferin informs me.

"How is he here?" I'm glad my voice doesn't waver.

"You'd be surprised what my magic can do." Seferin gestures to one of the chairs on the opposite side of his desk.

I glance at Maliek again before moving with caution and sitting. The study doors swing open again, and two nightmaidens in masks stroll inside. One sashays to Maliek, while another slinks her way to Seferin like a feline.

"We need more." The girl drops to her knees next to Seferin's chair with dilated pupils. She looks like one of Xaimur's xerven, too.

"Not now. *Leave.*" Seferin waves her off.

She pouts before shooting a glare at me, like I'm the reason she's being denied her fix.

When she rises and meets with the other girl, they wrap themselves around Maliek like seductive serpents. He doesn't react, nor does he uncross his arms. He's too busy glaring at me.

"The Maliek you killed on that island is, in fact, dead," Seferin says. I turn my gaze to the sorcerer behind the desk. He's leaning back in his chair, scanning me with intense, dark eyes. "But it's a good thing I kept a vial of his blood and created a new one. Losing a fighter as skilled as he is would be such a waste. And to a mortal, no less."

I tip my chin.

Seferin's lips quirk up to create a smirk. "You intrigue me, Zaira Quinlocke."

I work twice as hard to swallow the bitter taste on my tongue. "Do I?"

"Absolutely. I don't know many mortals who'd risk their lives to acquire a stone in The Shallows that they aren't even sure is there."

"It was better than doing nothing."

"And how did you feel when you found out they'd already been taken? When you realized Valkor withheld the truth from you all along?"

Stupid. Pathetic. Angry. *Heartbroken.*

I clench a fist in my lap. "Don't change the subject. I want you to let Analla go."

"If she weren't a thieving whore, she wouldn't be in this situation."

It takes everything in me not to snap back. He's trying to get under my skin. I can tell by the way his smirk widens, how he looks at me expectantly, waiting for a reaction.

I refuse to give him one.

"I studied everything there is to know about you once I found out you were traveling with Valkor." Seferin rises from his chair and glides around the desk, pressing the pads of his fingers together. "Such a simple girl with a tragic past. You only want good things for yourself and your sister. A refugee child. *An orphan.* You bake bread and treats for a living, for the gods' sakes. You shouldn't be mixed up in the chaos he's created. But he came close to getting what he wanted in the end, right? Azidel's tome?"

I press my lips together, refusing to answer.

"Don't worry. I *know* he was going after it. And I think I know why you're here." He stops behind me, smelling like wine and metal. Strange, considering he has no metal on him. Then I realize it's a particular metal. Copper. *The scent of blood.* I gulp. "But just so I don't get ahead of myself, tell me why you've come all this way, *Zaira*."

"I can give you the tome," I say, keeping my voice firm. "In exchange, you set my sister free."

"Where is the tome now?"

"I hid it, but if you free her, I can lead you to it."

"Hmm." Seferin steps sideways.

I glance at him.

He's staring at the bookcase behind his desk, filled to the brim with leather-bound books. In an instant, he steps away from me and teleports to the other side of the room before I can blink.

"You know, for a while, I couldn't figure out what Valkor was thinking by traveling to The Shallows. Then it hit me that he was going for the tome. I figured surely he wouldn't succeed in acquiring it. Any sorcerer in their right mind would never consider the risk worth it, and I didn't think there was a mortal's blood worthy enough to secure Azidel's tome. Even if there were, that mortal had to be one hundred percent willing to offer their blood to obtain it. Do you know what that means, Zaira?"

I shift in my chair. "No."

"It means a mortal cannot be forced into the Temple of Elphar to retrieve it for a sorcerer. The mortal must willingly enter, and they must trust the sorcerer who presents it to them. If it were the case of any person being able to get it, the tome would've been taken a long time ago. But no." Seferin waves a finger in the air with a sly smile. "This person has to be there because their whole heart *desires* to be. This person has to have more hope in their heart than fear, and even less hatred. The tome sought the blood of a mortal who cares for others much more than they care for themselves, just as Azidel's wife had."

I frown, confused.

Sensing my confusion, Seferin continues.

"Azidel's wife was a selfless woman, if you didn't know. She risked her life in order to spare Azidel's so he could have enough time to secure the tome in the temple before Xaimur could come for him. He succeeded because of her sacrifice. And all this time, you were the perfect match to her." Seferin provides a wicked chuckle. "If there is one thing about Valkor, he has *always* been the perfect student. Always the one to understand the most complex situations and remember the tiniest of details. Great at getting people to trust him, too. After all, we let him roam freely among us, just to have him turn around and slaughter nearly half of our guild."

Seferin appears next to me again.

"Well, I don't care about Thane or the tome. You can have it," I tell him. "Just please let my sister go. I'm willing to do anything for her."

I avoid his eyes as he pushes some of my hair back in a gentler way than I expected. Then he runs his cool knuckles over my cheek.

I turn away.

Not yet.

Seferin scans me with his devious eyes, a hint of curiosity burning in his vision. "I should take back what I said. You're no simple mortal at all," he murmurs near my ear. "You are *exactly* what I need to elevate my status in Thelanor even more. You are what I like to call *the perfect source*. Your sister should never have been the one I kept in my dungeon."

He snaps his fingers. "The cell is unlocked. Bring Analla to me," he orders.

Maliek brushes the seductive girls off and rushes them out of the room as he goes.

Seferin places a hand on my shoulder and gives it a possessive squeeze. Now that I know her cell is unlocked, I don't brush him off. I straighten in my chair as he gives me a thorough observation. A chill slides down my spine at the sight of his faint smile that hardly reaches his cold, emotionless eyes.

Something about this situation amuses him far too much.

All the while, I'm counting how many seconds he keeps his hand on me.

It's been seven seconds now.

I sense he's about to pull away, so I grab his hand and hold it in mine, softening my gaze. "Thank you for this," I say, clinging to him. "For showing her a little mercy."

Eight. Nine. Ten. Eleven—

He says nothing in response, just stares down at me with all-consuming eyes. Then he snatches his hand away.

Does he know I'm bluffing? That I don't actually have the tome?

Eleven seconds. That's how long he touched me.

With the mindflare, I send another thought to Thane. *Now.*

Several minutes later, Analla appears with Maliek gripping her by the hair. In her hand is the liphanet crystal.

"Analla!" I push out of my chair and dash her way, but Seferin rushes in front of me, holding me back with a solid hand.

"Before you reunite, I need you to take the crystal, Zaira, and bind your soul to it."

I stare at the crystal briefly before eyeing him.

"Take it." His smile fades, and his nostrils flare. "If you want your sister to live, you'll take it. But you must know that once you have it in your hands, you will become my source. You won't die, I'll be sure of it, but you will become weaker over time as I draw from you. You will become the mortal who strengthens my magic. You will fuel the land I reign in. After all," he sneers, "the braver the heart, the stronger the magic."

"But can't you get that kind of strength from the tome?"

"I could…but why bother when you're right here?"

I look from him, to Analla, to the crystal.

"You'll let her go?" I ask.

He gives me a subtle nod.

"Zaira, don't." Analla steps away with the crystal and holds it close to her chest. "I won't let you do this."

"Analla, I'm doing it for you." I move around him to grab her arm and give it a gentle squeeze. "You heard him. I won't die." I swallow, peering at Seferin. "Will I still get to see her, at least?"

"No." His answer is firm. Final. He narrows his eyes.

I'm stalling. I think he can sense it.

Maliek pushes Analla forward, and she trips over herself. Her knees slam to the marble floor, but that doesn't stop her from raising her shaking arms in the air with the crystal in her hands.

"I'll end it here," she declares. "It'll end right now with me. I won't let you have my sister!"

My heart drops once again. She's going to smash it and probably destroy the parts of her soul inside it. She could die if it breaks.

Seferin sighs and rolls his eyes, clearly bored and growing impatient. He bobs his head at Maliek, who marches toward her and grips her throat.

"No!" I yell.

She groans as he elevates her by the throat and chokes her.

"Stop!" I scream. "What are you doing?!"

"Take the crystal," Seferin growls, side-eyeing me. "Take it and your sister will be restored. She'll live the rest of her mortal years in peace, however long that lasts."

"Okay, I'll take it! Just stop choking her!"

Analla still clings to the crystal, struggling to shake her head behind Maliek's grip as a vein bulges out on her forehead. Maliek only squeezes tighter, though, curling his fingers, ready to close them in a fist and end her life.

He'll do it, too. I know he will. Seferin isn't bluffing. Whether Analla is dead or alive, he's going to make me take that damn crystal.

Anxious, I rub my forehead hard to get the mindflare going. *Now!*

I snatch the crystal from her hands before Maliek can choke the life out of her. Analla lets out a broken cry. The crystal is hot in my hands, pointy and light in weight.

Maliek lets Analla fall to a heap on the floor. As if the curse is fading as it transitions to me, Analla's hair goes from brittle gray to voluminous brown. Her cheeks plump just a bit, too, and the dark rings around her eyes disappear.

With a sinister smile forming, Seferin does a gesture with his hand and directs the tips of his fingers at me.

I immediately think it's too late for the other half of my plan to work.

I expect something to happen from Seferin—for some kind of pain to seize me, or for my body to weaken…but nothing comes.

Seferin frowns. "What the f—"

His eyes flicker up instantly, as if he knows that whatever is wrong with him has something to do with me. I take that moment to swing the tip of the crystal upward and slam it into the side of his face. He howls, stumbling backward and clutching his bleeding face as I scream, "Analla, run!"

Analla shoves away from Maliek and bolts toward the door, but Maliek throws up a hand and wraps an invisible grip around her, hauling her backward.

"You *bitch*!" Seferin snarls, lurching toward me and clutching the collar of my shirt. He grips hard and yanks me toward him, causing some of the threads in the neckline to snap. There's a deep gash in his cheek, running from beneath his sharp cheekbone to the dip beside his left nostril.

"What?" I breathe. "Men like you have made a bad habit of touching women without permission. You placed your hands on me multiple times—you still are, in fact—and because of that, your magic has been muted."

"What?" he hisses, grimacing.

I dig into my pocket, retrieving the empty vial I bought from the sorceress and dangling it in the air by my fingertips. "Muting elixir," I inform him. "Only more enhanced, thanks to the tome. I'm certain you've heard of it."

And fuck me, I didn't truly think this would work.

Maliek slams Analla to the floor, stealing my attention. He uses that same invisible grip to keep her pinned down, then draws a dagger and reels his arm back, ready to launch it at me.

Seferin pulls away from me to throw up a hand and shouts, "Don't!"

Maliek freezes.

"We need her," Seferin says.

I don't need any of this shit. I just need my sister.

My eyes dart to the door as I wipe nervous sweat from my forehead and signal the mindflare again. *It's now or never, Thane!*

Seferin notices where my eyes have gone and says, "Don't be foolish, Zaira." His voice is eerily calm. "You'll never succeed. Muting elixirs fade after time, and your weak attempt prior did nothing but draw a little blood."

Maliek lowers his arm and sheathes his dagger, like it's all over.

Come on, where are you? I wonder as Maliek takes a step toward me.

Finally, something hits the door hard, and it flies open. A body stumbles in backward and slams down on a glass table in the center of the room.

It's one of the guards from the corridor. A deep slit is in his throat, and blood oozes from his mouth while his lifeless eyes stare at the ceiling.

Analla screams as two sharp bolts of gold zip above her, one slamming into Maliek while another blasts harder into Seferin. Maliek flips backward, tumbling on a wooden chair and breaking it, while Seferin crashes into the bookshelf behind his desk with a deep groan.

Grunting, Maliek pushes himself back up and draws his sword as he eyes his attacker.

I place my attention on the attacker, too, relieved to see warm brown skin under a mask and hood, and eyes sparking a familiar gold.

Thane.

My heart races twice as fast as he briefly carries his gaze to me, offers an assuring nod, and then charges for Maliek.

As he does, I sprint toward my sister.

Chapter 62

Maliek yells at the top of his lungs, and metal clashes as furious, strained grunts swell in the room.

"Come on, we have to go!" I grab Analla's arm and help her to her feet.

Thane growls as Maliek soars across the room, slamming into the wall farthest from the desk and then landing on the floor.

Seferin is still on the floor, struggling to get up. I'm surprised that bolt didn't kill him. I suppose it'll take more than that.

Eyes glowing gold, Thane strides toward Seferin, the man he really came for, but Maliek doesn't stay down. He growls as he shoots back up and pounces on Thane, tackling him.

Maliek presses down hard on his sword, trying to cut him with the edge, but Thane uses his to block it. "Go!" he says in a strained voice.

With a hard grunt, he shoves Maliek off.

"Who the shadows is he?" Analla asks, bewildered.

"Long story," I murmur.

I glance over my shoulder as I lead Analla to the window. Thane and Maliek are fighting again.

I look at Seferin, but my heart drops as I watch him crawl toward a hidden door between one of the bookshelves. Panic rolls through me in a frigid wave as I look at Thane again, wanting to get his attention, but he's too preoccupied with Maliek.

We have to get out of here before he calls for more help.

A few more guards enter the room just as Thane slashes Maliek across the face, then lights him up with a powerful burst of gold.

"Zaira! Go out the window!" Thane shouts as he launches a shimmering shield to block the swift bolts of magic from the guards—bolts aimed right at Analla and me.

As Thane resists another strike, Analla and I climb out the window, work our way down a trellis, and run away as fast as we can.

I can't believe my plan worked.

And now Thane is risking everything so my sister and I can escape.

Don't get me wrong, I'm still *extremely* upset with him for what happened at the temple, but I've never been happier to have him at my side than now.

In Gadonia, I spotted him lingering by the shore close to Irina's inn. I kept replaying what he said about the tome in my head over and over again.

I'm sure there is a spell in it that I can use to break your sister's curse...

I kept wondering how I could trust him again after what he did. Then I figured the only way I could gather even an inkling of faith in him again was if he joined me while sailing to Meriva without me having to say a single word.

If he saw me board the ship alone, I hoped he would know for certain that I was about to face Seferin on my own, and he'd show up to make sure that never happened.

Because if he did that, then I'd know he actually cares and wants to help me.

Actions will always speak much louder than words.

After poring over the tome on the ship all night, he was able to find a spell to increase the effect of the muting elixir, but it required a few items from the sorceress's shop. Items he grabbed himself.

A sorcerer as powerful as Seferin wouldn't go down with a simple muting elixir. We needed something stronger. I knew if Seferin still had full access to his magic, Thane wouldn't be able to take him down, and I wouldn't be able to save my sister.

While Thane went around the keep taking out as many guards as possible, I stalled Seferin to have enough time to mute him. The only issue was that I couldn't quite do that to him until Seferin freed Analla from that cell, seeing as his magic controlled the locks.

After he released her, I could mute Seferin. Thane could kill him, like he wanted, and I would have my sister back.

It seemed like a good plan—until I realized Maliek was around. He was an obstacle I didn't account for, but Thane has defeated him many times. With some of the spells from Azidel's tome, I hoped it would be easier.

I was ninety-nine percent certain the plan wouldn't work and that I'd risk my life, Analla's, and Thane's for nothing…but like Thane said before, I have way too much optimism. He couldn't stand it at one point, yet this was one of those rare moments when we needed it most.

And because I held on to hope, a miracle has happened…

But we aren't safe just yet.

Chapter 63

Escaping with my sister is both terrifying and exhilarating. Knowing that she is within an arm's reach, racing to safety, brings me more peace than it should in this dire moment.

I suppose all the dangers we faced before this make this mad dash feel lukewarm in comparison. Even with the tree branches scraping my face, the brambles scratching my arms, leaves catching in my hair, spiderwebs sticking to my skin—it is nothing to me now.

"This way!" I yell, making a sharp right through a clearing. I'm not sure how long we've been running—maybe ten or fifteen minutes—before I finally spot the trail of lanterns marking the way to Meriva in the distance. Almost there.

"Wait!" Analla wheezes, stopping to press a palm to one of the tree trunks.

"Analla, we can't stop. We have to get off of this cursed land now."

"I—I know. I'm just— My body is still weak, Zaira."

She looks up at me with misty brown eyes, dragging in breath after breath. I swallow hard, taking a sweep of our surroundings as I rush to her.

"Can you walk at least?" I ask, tossing one of her arms over my shoulder. She bobs her head. "Yeah."

"Good. Cause we can't stay here. Seferin probably has people looking for us right now."

"Fucking shadows," she curses.

Fucking shadows is right. If we don't make it away from The Shadow Nest and closer to Meriva, we both are going to die, if not by Seferin's hand, then by one of his henchmen's.

Fortunately, Analla is able to keep going. We don't take the lit trail. It's too obvious, and it's best for us to stay hidden in the depths of the forest. I keep a close eye out, taking a route through the woods parallel to the lit path, holding on to her tightly as we weave between thick tree trunks. Owls hoot, and the slightest noises cause her to gasp, but I keep going. No looking back. It will only slow us down.

We press on as the minutes tick by. I know we're closer to Meriva when a loud gong reverberates through my bones—the clock striking the next hour. The trail of lanterns ends, and as we break through the trees, houses and other dwellings come into view.

"We're almost there," I say. "We just need to reach the port."

Analla finally pulls her arm from my shoulder, and I take her hand. She clings to it, and we walk along slick cobblestones with alert eyes. As we get deeper in the city, we pass the Tilted Crystal. I spot Bolivar through the glass standing behind the counter, cleaning a mug with a rag. He's speaking to a patron on a stool across from him who is making animated gestures with their hands. He doesn't notice us go by, but Crumb does. I feel so much guilt shooing the dog away, but we must go undetected.

Next, we pass The Flour Tower, and that's when I feel a tightness in my chest as we drift past the dark stone building. I imagine the scent of hot bread, steeped tea, sweet cakes, and the sunlight on my skin as it pours through the stained-glass window.

My eyes water, but not nearly as much as when I pass the refugee center. For a split second, I stop and stare at the massive wooden double doors, wanting so badly to go inside and hug every single child. To hug the director and bid her farewell, because that's what this is. Farewell. I risked *everything* to save Analla, and now a powerful Grim sorcerer and The Shadow Guild will make it their mission to hunt us down.

I peer up at the tall roof. The one Thane jumped off of the second day we met.

I blink rapidly and take in a deep breath. He's made standing here with my sister possible. My plan wouldn't have worked without him. No doubt, more guards heard the fighting and swarmed the place.

What if they've killed him? What if he can't beat his way out of the battle this time?

Orvena, please let him survive.

"Z?" Analla calls, tugging on my hand. "You okay?"

I turn my gaze to hers but can hardly see her through my tears. Sniffling, I wipe them away with the back of my arm. "Yeah. I'm okay. I just…" I close my eyes, and the ache in my chest intensifies, carrying over to my heart now.

"Aw, sis," she whispers, wrapping her arms around me. "I'm so sorry I got you into this mess."

"It's fine. I'm okay." I tip my chin, spotting Solyen's ship ahead, the sails billowing in the wind. "Come on. We should go."

Solyen's speedship is docked in the same location. The gangway is still lowered, so I take Analla's hand and hurry on board. Conred is sitting on one of the benches, whittling away at a piece of wood.

"Zaira, there you are!" he says, placing his carving knife and hunk of wood down.

"Hi, Conred. Solyen on board? We need to leave now. Like *right now*."

"Solyen went to one of the taverns." Conred swings his eyes to Analla, eyebrows stitching as he gives her a rapid scan. "Who's this?"

"My sister, Analla. When will Solyen be back?" I ask.

"I'm not sure."

"Gods, no. He said he'd be here when I returned. He knew we had to leave right away."

"Yeah, well, you know how he gets when he needs a drink." Conred shrugs as if it's no big deal.

"Which tavern?" I demand, and the intensity in my tone causes Conred to frown.

"Zaira, are you okay?"

"*Which tavern*, Conred?"

His throat bobs as he swallows. "I'm not sure. Is everything all right?"

"No, everything is not all right. We need to get out of here as soon as possible or…"

Wait.

What if, in turn, Thane was right behind us? Perhaps we can spare a minute or two just to see.

I search the docks for his familiar form, a spark of gold—anything that may prove he's nearby. But there's nothing. My heart squeezes so tight I think I might collapse.

I wanted him to help me, but I don't want him to die.

I don't care how angry I am. I'll be devastated if he's dead.

"There you are, little girl!" Solyen's voice booms. *Thank Orvena.* "We were just fixing to leave you! You said two hours max! Started to itch for a drink!" He has a mug in his hand, and as he nears us, some of the ale sloshes over the rim. "Conred, there're two barrels of ale at the bottom of the gangway. Roll 'em on board, will ya?"

I shift from foot to foot. As badly as I want to hold out for Thane, I can't risk it. And he most likely won't want me to. "Solyen, we need to go now," I plead, expecting Seferin's men to storm the dock at any minute.

"Yeah, yeah. I hear ya. Who is this?" His eyes are fixed on Analla.

"My sister, Analla."

Solyen looks between us, like he wants to ask something but doesn't have the patience to hear the answer. "Right." He lumbers past me, sipping his ale. "Where to now?"

"Junsho, please."

"That'll be more coin, understand?"

"Yeah, sure. Let's just leave quickly, please." I grip the rough railing of the ship to keep from fidgeting. As much as we need to get away before Seferin finds us, a part of me is holding out hope that the only man with the ability to tie me in knots is still alive and will come sauntering up that gangway.

There's still nothing in the distance. I sigh as Solyen starts yelling orders at his crew.

"Should he be steering a ship if he's drunk?" asks Analla.

"Trust me, he's always drunk," I say. "I'd be more concerned if he were sober and trying to steer." I turn and lean against the railing, spotting Conred halfway up the gangway with the second barrel.

After a stretch of silence, Analla says, "Oh, no." She tugs at the sleeve of my top as her eyes grow wide. "I—I think they found us, Z."

My breath catches as I spin to see a dark silhouette jogging up the gangway. For a split second, I think she's right—that it's an assassin from The Shadow Guild.

But then his hands swirl with gold, eyes flaring, as he propels Conred and the barrel up the gangway and onto the ship with a gust of magic. Conred topples over the barrel of ale, tumbling onto the deck of the ship and cursing loudly at Thane.

I'm surprised I remain steady enough not to collapse with relief.

Holy Crystal. He made it. Thane is back. He survived.

"What in Xaimur's hells is—" Solyen can't even finish what he's about to say because a throwing star slams into a wooden beam right above his head.

Thane throws a massive whorl of gold at a cluster of sorcerers in dark hoods and buffers on the dock who are sprinting toward the ship, then creates a thick wall of fire. It stretches to the sky, and the sorcerers leap back, glaring at the fire with illuminated eyes.

But one of them in the middle stands their ground with their fists clenched. Wafts of purple surround their hands and brew in their eyes. They're slighter in build than the other six of the guild.

"Hey!" someone shouts. I turn my head to the sound, and two Meriva guards are storming toward the chaos, swords already drawn. The person with purple essence turns their head slowly, and that's when I see a thick, silky braid lying over their shoulder. It's a woman. She throws up a hand, blasting the guards and disintegrating them to ash.

Literal ash. Just like that. With hardly any effort.

I don't have much time to consider the fact that so many of The Shadow Guild are standing on the other side of Thane's mounting fire, especially when he shouts, "I can't hold them off for much longer! Move this fucking ship!"

I swear Solyen sobers up in that very moment, dropping his ale and running for the helm. The boat lurches in an instant, and Analla crashes into me as we're both thrown toward the center cabin. My back hits the door as she hisses, "Shit," and yanks my arm. She hauls me to the side, just before a barrel of ale rolls in our direction and slams into the cabin door.

"Crystal's sake," I breathe, watching the wood splinter and the liquid drench the deck, spilling in different directions. I hear Thane grunt and notice his arms shaking as he holds up both hands, trying to keep the fire in place. From here, I can see a streak of lavender cutting through the middle of his flames and the woman stepping right through them with a sword in hand.

Thane roars louder, keeping his stance. The fire wraps around her, but she fights against it with a shield of lavender. Then, when we are far enough away that the attackers are no more than specks, Thane drops his arms and slams his palms down on the ship's railing. He breathes raggedly, head hanging low, sucking in much-needed air.

Numb, I stand in the middle of the deck as Meriva grows more and more distant, the tips of the Crystal Palace gleaming in the moonlight. The Shadow Guild appears to be nothing but ants as they scatter, likely returning to Seferin's keep. They know not to linger in Meriva for too long, especially after killing two guards.

Once we are a safe distance away from the kingdom, Thane finally lowers his defenses and turns around to meet my eyes.

I stare at him.

He stares at me.

And because I'm so overcome with relief and elation and my blood is humming with adrenaline, I hurry across the deck and throw my arms around his neck.

He catches me and holds on tight, releasing a satisfied sigh over my shoulder before saying, "I'm here. I've got you."

Chapter 64

The ship bobs and dips as I help Analla into the cabin and lead her to a bed that Conred has prepared for her. He's also offered her a bar of soap and one of his tunics so she can wash and change out of the filthy nightmaiden's dress she wore in Seferin's dungeon. Conred is taller, so of course the shirt is too big, the hem stopping just below her knees and the neckline sagging to reveal her collarbone. It's better than nothing.

"Here you go." I return to Analla after scooping fresh water from a barrel into a tin cup and offering it to her. "Drink this. You need to hydrate."

She takes the cup, guzzling it down so quickly, water dribbles from the corners of her mouth and down her chin. I get her a refill, and she drinks it much slower this time. Once done, she places the empty cup down and releases a satisfied gasp.

"The guy that saved us," she says, meeting my eyes. "Who is he?"

My heartbeat stutters at the mere thought of Thane. "Just…a friend."

"Friends don't hug like you two did," she counters, eyeing me suspiciously.

"He helped me during my journey, when I was looking for the prosperity stones." I wave a flippant hand, as if it's no big deal.

But it is, in fact, a big deal.

Major, really, considering he's sitting right outside of the cabin. "Like I said, it's a long story. I'll tell you all about it when you're a bit more healed."

Analla scans me with slightly narrowed eyes like she always does when she's reading me. "You love him."

It isn't a question. It's a matter-of-fact statement that causes my heart to bang a notch quicker.

"W-what?" I sputter.

She only smiles, lying on her side and placing her head on the pillow.

"I—I don't think it's that…" It can't be that, can it? Love an assassin? A *shadow* assassin? No…

"Please. With the way he looks at you and the way you looked when you saw him…" She huffs a laugh. "I know love when I see it, sis."

I stand still a moment, unsure what to say to that.

"Gods, I hate feeling so weak," she mutters as I slide a quilt over her. I'm grateful for the change of topic. I sit on the end of the bed, and she reaches for my hand.

"Will you be okay until we get to Junsho?" I ask, giving her my hand. "I can get you something to eat."

"No, no." She blinks slower, snuggling deeper into her pillow. "I think I just need to sleep for now."

"Okay." I squeeze her hand.

"Thank you, Zaira," she murmurs, her eyes watering. "For everything. I don't know what I would do without you. I love you so much."

Warmth wraps around me as I smile at my sister, and it really hits me that she's back. That I saved her from Seferin—now uncursed—and she's on her way to restoration. There are things we'll have to deal with later, like The Shadow Guild and Seferin's wrath, but we're safe for now.

Together.

That's all I wanted.

"I love you, too," I tell her, lowering so I can hug her.

"Forever?" she asks in my hair. I pull back a bit, and her eyelids flutter closed, already succumbing to sleep.

"And always," I whisper.

She releases a long, satisfied breath, and I watch her a moment as the muscles in her face slowly relax and she slips into a soft slumber. I stand and drop a kiss on her cheek before looking at the cabin door. My mind instantly circles back to Thane.

I step outside and onto the deck again, spotting him sitting on one of the backless benches, nursing a wound on his thigh. He's removed his mask and buffers and is wearing only a black tunic with the sleeves rolled up to his elbows, black trousers, and boots.

Ocean mist sprays on my skin, and my hair blows in the breeze as I start his way. He raises his chin, gaze meeting mine when he sees me coming.

"Zaira—" He starts to stand up as I near him, but I stop him by placing a hand to his shoulder and easing him back down.

"Don't," I murmur. "You're hurt."

"It's nothing I haven't felt before," he says, peering up at me with soft eyes.

I study all his other injuries. The gash on his bicep. The cut on his ear that is now caked in blood. The red mark on his cheek that will surely turn into a bruise. The crimson splotch on the white of his left eye.

He watches me as I inspect him, and when our eyes connect again, he cups one side of my face and says, "I'm so sorry for hurting you, Zaira."

"Yeah." I cling to his hand with my own, lowering my gaze to block the wave of sadness threatening me. "It did hurt. A lot." He spreads his legs apart, and I stand between them, caressing his face, too, stroking the old scar that runs over his full lips. "I thought you were dead," I say in a trembling voice. "I didn't want you to die."

"I would have for you," he says. "Seferin wouldn't have let you live—at least, not in peace. If he was going to take a life, I was going to make sure it was mine. That's the least I could've done to make things right."

I gently run my fingers over the top of his injured ear. "How would it have made things right if you were *gone*?" I ask, gripping his face in both of my hands now, wanting to shake some sense into him. "I would have lived with that guilt forever."

"Wouldn't have mattered." He places a hand on my hip. "Your life would be better without me, Zaira, and we both know it."

"Don't say that."

"It's true."

My vision blurs and my mouth quivers as emotion clogs my throat.

"But since I'm here now," he continues, "since I get the chance to see your beautiful face again, to breathe the air you breathe, and to feel your soft skin on mine, I plan to spend however long it takes proving I'm worthy of your trust."

He brings himself to a stand with a mild grunt, now towering over me. I drop my arms as both of his hands cradle my face and crane my neck just enough to find his amber eyes.

"And hopefully one day, you'll forgive me," he rasps, his warm breath skating over my lips, taunting, teasing, sending sparks of heat through my veins. "All I know is that I can't continue my days without you. The time we've spent together, however brief, has altered something inside me, Zaira. I didn't believe there was anything else good in this world. I didn't think there was any good left in *me*. But then I met you—this bright fucking light," he says through a breathy laugh. "*My sun*, shining that radiant light on the darkest parts of my heart and soul."

"Thane," I whisper, still biting back my tears. My knees feel weaker, my body softer, all because I'm in his arms. All from his voice and the power of his words.

"If you give me another chance," he goes on, "if you allow me into your life again, I'll make this right. Okay? I'll do better—I'll become better *for you*."

Tears accumulate at the rims of my eyes, casting him in a half blur.

This is one of those moments when I want to curse my tender heart for softening so easily, for believing in the power of trust. My forgiving heart that's now beating like a drum, faster and faster in his wake. The heart that—

That *loves* him.

You love him...

Analla was right. No matter how much I try denying it, or rejecting him, or pretending he means nothing to me, it's inevitable because rebuffing what my heart desires is impossible. His absence made me ache like never before, and thinking about a life without him felt flat, dull, and bland.

My mind goes back to the night we met in the Tilted Crystal—the instant connection I felt at the mere sight of him. The urge to fly closer to him as if he were the flame and I the moth. A danger, yes, but also a magnet. There were many others in that tavern I could've asked to help me, but I chose *him*.

The carriage ride in Bernwood, when my heart felt like it'd come alive for the first time as he kissed me.

And in Gadonia, when it leaped to life all over again while we kissed in the art gallery and blistered afterward while tangled between soft sheets and quilts, wanting nothing else but each other.

His laugh, and the rare moments when he showed me his vulnerable side and I showed him mine.

The way his gaze softened and my guard lowered the longer we were together...

And now this, standing chest to chest, wanting nothing more than to kiss him a thousand times and scream, *yes*. This is real, raw, and deep passion I feel for this man. My soul aches for his. *Yearns* for every single part of him.

How can I walk away from him again when he creates such beautiful chaos inside me? How can I run from the man who holds my raw heart in his hands and is so desperate to mend it?

We all make mistakes.

I know this, and yet I was so hard on him. I didn't even give him the chance to properly apologize, even though I knew he so badly wanted to.

I want to believe he had good intentions about not telling me about the stones. He just went about it the wrong way.

And how can I blame him? After all he's been through and all the darkness he's faced—all that he's lost—how can I fault him for something that may have been instinct?

"Swear you'll never lie to me again," I demand, gripping a handful of his tunic. "Swear you'll never betray me again, Thane. If your goal is to win back my trust, I need to hear you say it right now."

"I'll never lie to you again, Zaira." My heart flutters as he brings a hand beneath my chin and tips my head back a bit more. "And I would rather suffer a miserable death than ever even *think* about breaking your heart again."

Flutters burst in my stomach and heat flares in my chest with his every word. And when he brings his mouth down, kissing me ever so softly at first, I sigh.

But when he breathes the words, "Please forgive me, *my sun*," on my lips, I melt.

His sun. *His* light.

I close my eyes, and hot tears trail down my cheeks as I meet his kiss with urgency, my arms lacing around the back of his neck and our bodies fusing. The ocean roars around us, and despite the *Emellie* gently rocking, we hold steady. His hands roam the curves of my body as he slides them down my waist and then digs the pads of them into my hips, groaning as our tongues collide.

The ship gives a harder rock, and Thane stumbles just a bit, the backs of his legs bumping into the bench and forcing him to sit. Even so, our lips barely part ways.

I come down with him, planting my knees on either side of his outer thighs, loving the taste of him, the feel of his large, warm hands, the way my heart blossoms and feels reenergized simply by having him this close.

But as much as I want this to go deeper, and for us to find the nearest empty room, I slow down and, with all the willpower in me, break the kiss, grab the hands that are cupping my ass to stop him, and say, "Fine. I'll give you another chance. But we're taking it slow this time."

"Yeah." He swallows and nods, lips swollen and damp. "I'll give you all the time you need—the rest of my life if you allow it, sweet one."

Smiling, I place one more kiss on his lips, believing every word he says is the truth.

Epilogue

"There. All done." I finish wrapping Thane's wrist with a clean strip of linen before giving it a soft pat. "I'll see if Conred has anything we can use to speed up your healing."

We've been sailing for close to an hour. While on the deck, we talked a bit more about what comes next when we dock in Junsho. We're inside the cabin, settled on the edge of one of the beds close to Analla's.

Analla is still fast asleep.

The ship crew is at the table, playing cards.

Knowing The Shadow Guild is after us has me a bit uneasy, but also knowing Thane is by our side and he has Azidel's tome eases some of those worries. He's assured me there are places we can hide and spells we can use that'll make it hard for Seferin to ever find us.

I'm hopeful about it. He was in hiding for over a year before showing up in Meriva again.

Before I can get too far away, Thane catches my hand and reels me toward him. I wind up between his thighs and can't help shaking my head and smiling as he reaches up to clasp my face in his hands.

"Kiss me one last time before you go," he murmurs, already bringing my face down so our lips can meet.

He kisses me softly, tenderly, and the strongest, most delightful buzz courses through my bones. Shadows. Do I really want to go through with taking it slow? Climbing him like a tree seems much more ideal.

I break the kiss and replace my lips with my index finger, pressing it to his mouth. "I think you're trying to unravel me."

He smirks behind my finger. "Is it working?"

I huff a laugh as he lowers his gaze. For some reason, he frowns as he sweeps the backs of his fingers across my chest. "Where's your necklace?"

I instantly look down. My stomach hollows as I rub my chest. "Oh my gods."

"What?" he asks, now a bit more concerned.

My eyes drift to the cabin door, as if my necklace will just appear there. "I—I don't know where it is. It must've fallen off while we were escaping or..."

As I snap my gaze back to Thane's worried and partially confused eyes, it hits me like a ton of alvanite.

No...it didn't fall. It was *snatched* off of me.

I remember feeling a popping sensation when Seferin grabbed me by the collar of my shirt. I thought it was just threads breaking loose, but that was my chain snapping.

He took my necklace. Oh gods. I didn't even notice.

Panicking, I start to run for the door so I can search for it on the deck, but before I can go anywhere, dizziness strikes me, and the interior of the cabin feels as if it's expanding and then contracting.

"Zaira," Thane calls with more urgency. "Are you okay?"

The ship crew quiets as they look at me.

"Is there something you need, Zaira?" Conred asks.

The oddest sensation comes over me before I can answer him or Thane. Something putrid and cold seeps through my skin, and an icy chill slithers through my veins. The edges of my vision tunnel, and black shadows swirl inward. Everything is so black. I can't see.

Several of the crew members gasp while one of them curses loudly.

"What's happening to her?" I hear Conred call out.

Their voices are drowned out by the sound of my roaring pulse and panicked breathing.

Then a familiar, sinister voice enters my mind.

Mind and marrow. Soul and dreams.
I'll take from you to restore my means.

The chant is repeated.

Again.

And again.

And again.

The blackness in my vision clears, and I feel my knees weaken. Thane catches me before I can collapse on the floor, and he holds me close.

"What just happened?" he asks as our eyes connect. "What did you see?"

"I didn't see anything. It was all black," I answer as the crew steps in closer, surrounding us. "I heard someone."

Thane leads me back to the bed so I can sit. "Do you know where your necklace is, Zaira?" There's a unique tone to his question, like he has an idea of what the answer might be but needs to be certain it's not true.

"Seferin," I croak, shivering. Why am I so cold now? "I heard Seferin's voice. I—I think he has it."

Thane lowers to a squat in front of me with panic swimming in his eyes. "Fuck."

"What?" I reach for his hand. "What does this mean?"

He gives my hand a weak squeeze. "It means…" He swallows hard. "It means you—"

I widen my eyes, waiting for him to tell me. When he turns to Analla and shakes his head, it dawns on me—what he's struggling to say.

"It means I'm the one who's cursed now," I whisper.

Acknowledgments

Two years ago, after completing my first ever romantasy trilogy, I told myself I'd *never* write another one again.

Fantasies are hard work, and though I love a good challenge, I'd never felt myself so creatively drained afterward. I thought my brain was broken for months and didn't think I'd get through that phase.

But miraculously, I did.

And as inspiration slowly settled in, ideas for *Mayhem and the Mortal* started taking shape. The way the words so effortlessly flowed from my fingertips was magical. I remember getting teary-eyed because I was doing it. I was making it work! Writing it made me remember why I love the art of storytelling so much.

I wouldn't have gone through with finalizing it, though, had it not been for the encouragement I received from a few people in my life.

I have to thank my husband, Juan, most of all. He's my rock and the *only* reason I was able to complete this book and meet my deadlines. Thank you for being such an incredible partner and a wonderful dad to our kids. I love you so much.

To my boys—the three wonderful reasons I push through every day—I love you, my babies. I wake up every morning so grateful that I was chosen to be your mother.

So much of my gratitude also goes to my incredible agent, Georgana Grinstead, who I adore so much, and to the president of The Seymour Agency, Nicole Resciniti. You two were there from day one—way before I even wrote the first word—and you saw me all the way through 'til the end. Thank you for your continued support and the love you give. For providing for my family when I was in crunch mode. For your constant check-ins and pep talks. I feel so fortunate and blessed to have you.

This book wouldn't even be in any readers' hands had it not been for the boss who took me under her wing at Entangled. Liz Pelletier, thank you for taking a chance on my work, for embracing my voice, and for giving my novel the care it deserved. I'll never forget your reaction when you reached Thane's first fight scene in Redclaw. It warmed my heart and made me so eager to get more chapters to you. Thank you for believing in me.

Justine Bylo. Words don't feel like enough when it comes to the many thanks I have to give you. Thank you for your patience through the editing process. Your kindness. Your warmth. Your understanding. Thank you for embracing my vision for the story, and for making *Mayhem and the Mortal* the best possible version it could be. We did it! I'm so proud of us!

To the entire Entangled Team—from marketing, to cover designs, to publicity—you're all incredible!

Thank you to my alpha and beta readers, my ARC team, and my behind-the-scenes team who are always keeping me afloat. Y'all are the best. I'm blessed to have you!

And as always, I must thank every reader who picked up *Mayhem and the Mortal* and gave it a chance. There are so many books in the world, yet you took a chance on mine. I'm humbled and grateful. Truly.

She's a barmaid who doesn't believe in fairy tales.

He's a prince cursed to live one.

Perfect for readers who love the wit of *The Princess Bride*, the adventure of classic fantasy quests, and romances that balance danger with delicious banter.